D0661095

The Strange Case of
DR JEKYLL AND MR HYDE

THE MERRY MEN
and Other Stories

The Strange Case of
DR JEKYLL AND
MR HYDE
THE MERRY MEN
and Other Stories

—————— ◆ ——————

Robert Louis Stevenson

WORDSWORTH CLASSICS

This edition published 1993
by Wordsworth Editions Limited
Cumberland House, Crib Street, Ware,
Hertfordshire SG12 9ET

ISBN 1-57335-367-1

*Printed and bound in Great Britain
by Mackays of Chatham plc, Chatham, Kent
Typeset in the Uk by Antony Gray*

INTRODUCTION

The Strange Case of Dr Jekyll and Mr Hyde was written for money. In 1886, Robert Louis Stevenson was living with his wife and stepson in Skerryvore, a house in Bournemouth given to Stevenson on his marriage six years earlier. Although Stevenson had made a name for himself with his essays for *The Cornhill Magazine* and other journals, the household finances were in poor shape. *Treasure Island* (1883) had been a great success, but its juvenile market limited monetary returns.

Stevenson himself was unwell and largely housebound. Then one night, he dreamt large parts of *Dr Jekyll* and is said to have been reproachful when woken in the middle of a particularly exciting passage. He wrote the story in three days and, as was his habit, he gave it to his wife, whose critical judgement he valued highly. Fanny Stevenson was an austere though fair critic – 'chary of praise, and prodigal of counsel' in Stevenson's words – and she pointed out that the story had been written as a simple thriller when it would be much more effective recast as an allegory.

Though angry at first, Stevenson saw the justice of her remarks, and burnt the entire manuscript so that he would not be tempted to lift passages from it when he rewrote the story. Rewrite it he did over the next three days, and the book was published later that year, being well received particularly by *The Times*. Stevenson was not freed from financial anxiety until his father's death the following year, but he had at last found a huge adult audience. *Dr Jekyll* is a thriller, but an allegorical thriller as Fanny suggested. It is a study of the duality of man's nature, and it reflects Stevenson's fascination with the subject, which stems, perhaps, from the Scottish Calvinistic tradition in which he was raised. Hogg's *Confessions of a Justified Sinner* (1824) is a fascinating study of the duality of nature inherent in Calvinism and was a familiar book to Stevenson.

Dr Jekyll also reflects a post-Darwinian awareness of the animality of man, and the struggle between man's nature and nurture. To a lesser extent, this theme is also present in two other stories in this selection, 'Markheim', a macabre tale of murder and conscience, and

'Olalla', a strange mystery story set in Spain.

These last two stories, together with the remaining ones, were published in 1887 under the title of *The Merry Men*. They had been written over the previous eight years, and are of varying quality. The title story has real merit, but 'Will o' the Mill' and 'The Treasure of Franchard' reveal themselves as early works, written before Stevenson had mastered the short-story form. Finally, there is 'Thrawn Janet', which is a masterpiece. There is a feeling of stark terror in it that is matched only by that other Celtic master of the supernatural, Sheridan Le Fanu.

Robert Louis Stevenson, the son of a well-known harbour and lighthouse engineer, was born in 1850 and educated at Edinburgh Academy and Edinburgh University. Although he was admitted as a barrister, he never practised and he determined to make his living as a writer. He started writing for The Cornhill Magazine *in 1876. In 1878 his account of a canoe trip in France and Belgium,* An Inland Voyage, *was published, followed by* Travels with a Donkey *in 1879. In 1880 he married Fanny Osborne in America, and wrote* Treasure Island *(1883) for her son Lloyd;* Dr Jekyll *and* Kidnapped *were published in 1886. When, in the following year, his father died, Stevenson's inheritance was substantial enough for the family to escape abroad, away from the cold and damp weather that had so aggravated the lung condition from which Stevenson had suffered since childhood. Eventually the family settled in Samoa where Stevenson died in 1894.*

FURTHER READING

J. Calder: *Robert Louis Stevenson* 1980
D. Daiches: *Robert Louis Stevenson* 1946
D. Daiches: *Stevenson and the Art of Fiction* 1951
M. Lascelles: *The Story-Teller Retrieves the Past* 1980
P. Maixner (ed.): *Robert Louis Stevenson: The Critical Heritage* 1981

CONTENTS

THE STRANGE CASE OF
DR JEKYLL AND MR HYDE

THE MERRY MEN AND OTHER STORIES

THE MERRY MEN

WILL O' THE MILL

The Strange Case of
DR JEKYLL AND MR HYDE

Story of the Door

MR UTTERSON the lawyer was a man of a rugged countenance, that was never lighted by a smile; cold, scanty and embarrassed in discourse; backward in sentiment; lean, long, dusty, dreary, and yet somehow lovable. At friendly meetings, and when the wine was to his taste, something eminently human beaconed from his eye; something indeed which never found its way into his talk, but which spoke not only in these silent symbols of the after-dinner face, but more often and loudly in the acts of his life. He was austere with himself; drank gin when he was alone, to mortify a taste for vintages; and though he enjoyed the theatre, had not crossed the doors of one for twenty years. But he had an approved tolerance for others; sometimes wondering, almost with envy, at the high pressure of spirits involved in their misdeeds; and in any extremity inclined to help rather than to reprove. 'I incline to Cain's heresy,' he used to say quaintly: 'I let my brother go to the devil in his own way.' In this character it was frequently his fortune to be the last reputable acquaintance and the last good influence in the lives of down-going men. And to such as these, so long as they came about his chambers, he never marked a shade of change in his demeanour.

No doubt the feat was easy to Mr Utterson; for he was undemonstrative at the best, and even his friendships seemed to be founded in a similar catholicity of good-nature. It is the mark of a modest man to accept his friendly circle ready made from the hands of opportunity; and that was the lawyer's way. His friends were those of his own blood, or those whom he had known the longest; his affections, like ivy, were the growth of time, they implied no aptness in the object. Hence, no doubt, the bond that united him to Mr Richard Enfield, his distant kinsman, the well-known man about town. It was a nut to crack for many, what these two could see in each other, or what subject they could find in common. It was reported by those who encountered them in their Sunday walks, that they said nothing, looked singularly dull, and would hail with obvious relief the appearance of a friend. For all that, the two men put the greatest store by these excursions, counted them the chief jewel of each week, and not only set aside occasions of pleasure, but even resisted the calls of business, that they might enjoy them uninterrupted.

It chanced on one of these rambles that their way led them down a by-street in a busy quarter of London. The street was small and what is called quiet, but it drove a thriving trade on the week-days. The inhabitants were all doing well, it seemed, and all emulously hoping to do better still, and laying out the surplus of their gains in coquetry; so that the shop fronts stood along that thoroughfare with an air of invitation, like rows of smiling saleswomen. Even on Sunday, when it veiled its more florid charms and lay comparatively empty of passage, the street shone out in contrast to its dingy neighbourhood, like a fire in a forest; and with its freshly painted shutters, well-polished brasses, and general cleanliness and gaiety of note, instantly caught and pleased the eye of the passenger.

Two doors from one corner, on the left hand going east, the line was broken by the entry of a court; and just at that point, a certain sinister block of building thrust forward its gable on the street. It was two storeys high; showed no window, nothing but a door on the lower storey and a blind forehead of discoloured wall on the upper; and bore in every feature the marks of prolonged and sordid negligence. The door, which was equipped with neither bell nor knocker, was blistered and distained. Tramps slouched into the recess and struck matches on the panels; children kept shop upon the steps; the schoolboy had tried his knife on the mouldings; and for close on a generation no one had appeared to drive away these random visitors or to repair their ravages.

Mr Enfield and the lawyer were on the other side of the by-street; but when they came abreast of the entry, the former lifted up his cane and pointed.

'Did you ever remark that door?' he asked; and when his companion had replied in the affirmative, 'It is connected in my mind,' added he, 'with a very odd story.'

'Indeed!' said Mr Utterson, with a slight change of voice, 'and what was that?'

'Well, it was this way,' returned Mr Enfield: 'I was coming home from some place at the end of the world, about three o'clock of a black winter morning, and my way lay through a part of town where there was literally nothing to be seen but lamps. Street after street, and all the folks asleep – street after street, all lighted up as if for a procession, and all as empty as a church – till at last I got into that state of mind when a man listens and listens and begins to long for the sight of a policeman. All at once, I saw two figures: one a little man who was stumping along eastward at a good walk, and the other a girl of maybe eight or ten who was running as hard as she was able down a cross-street. Well, sir, the two ran into one another naturally enough at the corner; and then came the horrible part of the thing; for the man trampled calmly over the child's body and left her screaming on the ground. It sounds nothing to hear, but it was hellish to see. It wasn't like a man; it was like some damned Juggernaut. I gave a view halloa, took to my heels, collared my gentleman, and brought him back to where there was already quite a group about the screaming child. He was perfectly cool and made no resistance, but gave me one look, so ugly that it brought out the sweat on me like running. The people who had turned out were the girl's own family; and pretty soon the doctor, for whom she had been sent, put in his appearance. Well, the child was not much the worse, more frightened, according to the Sawbones; and there you might have supposed would be an end to it. But there was one curious circumstance. I had taken a loathing to my gentleman at first sight. So had the child's family, which was only natural. But the doctor's case was what struck me. He was the usual cut-and-dry apothecary, of no particular age and colour, with a strong Edinburgh accent, and about as emotional as a bagpipe. Well, sir, he was like the rest of us: every time he looked at my prisoner, I saw that Sawbones turned sick and white with the desire to kill him. I knew what was in his mind, just as he knew what was in mine; and killing being out of the question, we did the next best. We told the man we could and would make such a scandal out of this, as should make his name stink from one end of London to the other. If he had any friends or any credit, we undertook that he should lose them. And all the time, as we were pitching it in red hot, we were keeping the women off him as best we could, for they were as wild as harpies. I never saw a circle of such hateful faces; and there was the man in the middle, with a kind of black sneering coolness – frightened too, I could see that – but carrying it off, sir, really like Satan. 'If you choose to make capital out of this accident,' said he, 'I am naturally helpless. No gentleman but wishes to avoid a scene,' says he. 'Name your figure.' Well, we screwed him up to a hundred pounds for the child's family; he would have clearly liked to stick out; but there was something about the lot of us that meant mischief, and at last he struck. The next thing was to get the money; and where do you think he carried us but to that place with the door? – whipped out a key, went in, and presently came back with the matter of ten pounds in gold and a cheque for the balance on Coutts's, drawn payable to bearer, and signed with a name that I can't mention, though it's one of the points of my story, but it was a name at least very well known and often printed. The figure was stiff: but the signature was good for more than that, if it was only genuine. I took the liberty of pointing out to my gentleman that the whole business looked apocryphal; and that a man does not, in real life, walk into a cellar door at four in the morning and come out of it with another man's cheque for close upon a hundred pounds. But he was quite easy and sneering. 'Set your mind at rest,' says he; 'I will stay with you till the banks open, and cash the cheque myself.' So we all set off, the doctor, and the child's father, and our friend and myself, and passed the rest of the night in my chambers; and next day, when we had breakfasted, went in a body to the bank. I gave in the cheque myself, and said I had every reason to believe it was a forgery. Not a bit of it. The cheque was genuine.'

'Tut-tut!' said Mr Utterson.

'I see you feel as I do,' said Mr Enfield. 'Yes, it's a bad story. For my man was a fellow that nobody could have to do with, a really damnable man; and the person that drew the cheque is the very pink of the proprieties, celebrated too, and (what makes it worse) one of your fellows who do what they call good. Blackmail, I suppose; an honest man paying through the nose for some of the capers of his youth. Blackmail House is what I call that place with the door, in consequence. Though even that, you know, is far from explaining all,' he added; and with the words fell into a vein of musing.

From this he was recalled by Mr Utterson asking rather suddenly: 'And you don't know if the drawer of the cheque lives there?'

'A likely place, isn't it?' returned Mr Enfield. 'But I happen to have noticed his address; he lives in some square or other.'

'And you never asked about – the place with the door?' said Mr Utterson.

'No, sir: I had a delicacy,' was the reply. 'I feel very strongly about putting questions; it partakes too much of the style of the day of judgment. You start a question, and it's like starting a stone. You sit quietly on the top of a hill; and away the stone goes, starting others; and presently some bland old bird (the last you would have thought of) is knocked on the head in his own back garden, and the family have to change their name. No, sir, I make it a rule of mine: the more it looks like Queer Street, the less I ask.'

'A very good rule, too,' said the lawyer.

'But I have studied the place for myself,' continued Mr Enfield. 'It seems scarcely a house. There is no other door, and nobody goes in or out of that one, but, once in a great while, the gentleman of my adventure. There are three windows looking on the court on the first floor; none below; the windows are always shut, but they're clean. And then there is a chimney, which is generally smoking; so somebody must live there. And yet it's not so sure; for the buildings are so packed together about that court, that it's hard to say where one ends and another begins.'

The pair walked on again for a while in silence; and then – 'Enfield,' said Mr Utterson, 'that's a good rule of yours.'

'Yes, I think it is,' returned Enfield.

'But for all that,' continued the lawyer, 'there's one point I want to ask: I want to ask the name of that man who walked over the child.'

'Well,' said Mr Enfield, 'I can't see what harm it would do. It was a man of the name of Hyde.'

'Hm,' said Mr Utterson. 'What sort of a man is he to see?'

'He is not easy to describe. There is something wrong with his appearance; something displeasing, something downright detestable. I never saw a man I so disliked, and yet I scarce know why. He must be deformed somewhere; he gives a strong feeling of deformity, although I couldn't specify the point. He's an extraordinary-looking man, and yet I really can name nothing out of the way. No, sir; I can make no hand of it; I can't describe him. And it's not want of memory; for I declare I can see him this moment.'

Mr Utterson again walked some way in silence, and obviously under a weight of consideration. 'You are sure he used a key?' he inquired at last.

'My dear sir . . . ' began Enfield, surprised out of himself.

'Yes, I know,' said Utterson; 'I know it must seem strange. The fact is, if I do not ask you the name of the other party, it is because I know it already. You see, Richard, your tale has gone home. If you have been inexact in any point, you had better correct it.'

'I think you might have warned me,' returned the other, with a touch of sullenness. 'But I have been pedantically exact, as you call it. The fellow had a key; and, what's more, he has it still. I saw him use it, not a week ago.'

Mr Utterson sighed deeply, but said never a word; and the young man presently resumed. 'Here is another lesson to say nothing,' said he. 'I am ashamed of my long tongue. Let us make a bargain never to refer to this again.'

'With all my heart,' said the lawyer. 'I shake hands on that, Richard.'

Search for Mr Hyde

THAT EVENING Mr Utterson came home to his bachelor house in sombre spirits, and sat down to dinner without relish. It was his custom of a Sunday, when this meal was over, to sit close by the fire, a volume of some dry divinity on his reading-desk, until the clock of the neighbouring church rang out the hour of twelve, when he would go soberly and gratefully to bed. On this night, however, as soon as the cloth was taken away, he took up a candle and went into his business room. There he opened his safe, took from the most private part of it a document endorsed on the envelope as Dr Jekyll's Will, and sat down with a clouded brow to study its contents. The will was holograph; for Mr Utterson, though he took charge of it now that it was made, had refused to lend the least assistance in the making of it; it provided not only that, in case of the decease of Henry Jekyll, M.D., D.C.L., LL.D., F.R.S., &c., all his possessions were to pass into the hands of his 'friend and benefactor Edward Hyde'; but that in case of Dr Jekyll's 'disappearance or unexplained absence for any period exceeding three calendar months,' the said Edward Hyde should step into the said Henry Jekyll's shoes without further delay, and free from any burthen or obligation, beyond the payment of a few small sums to the members of the doctor's household. This document had long been the lawyer's eyesore. It offended him both as a lawyer and as a lover of the sane and customary sides of life, to whom the fanciful was the immodest. And hitherto it was his ignorance of Mr Hyde that had swelled his indignation; now, by a sudden turn, it was his knowledge. It was already bad enough when the name was but a name of which he could learn no more. It was worse when it began to be clothed upon with detestable attributes; and out of the shifting, insubstantial mists that had so long baffled his eye, there leaped up the sudden, definite presentment of a fiend.

'I thought it was madness,' he said, as he replaced the obnoxious paper in the safe; 'and now I begin to fear it is disgrace.'

With that he blew out his candle, put on a great-coat, and set forth in the direction of Cavendish Square, that citadel of medicine, where his friend, the great Dr Lanyon, had his house and received his crowding patients. 'If any one knows, it will be Lanyon,' he had thought.

The solemn butler knew and welcomed him; he was subjected to no stage of delay, but ushered direct from the door to the dining-room, where Dr Lanyon sat alone over his wine. This was a hearty, healthy, dapper, red-faced gentleman, with a shock of hair prematurely white, and a boisterous and decided manner. At sight of Mr Utterson, he sprang up from his chair and welcomed him with both hands. The geniality, as was the way of the man, was somewhat theatrical to the eye; but it reposed on genuine feeling. For these two were old friends, old mates both at school and college, both thorough respecters of themselves and of each other, and, what does not always follow, men who thoroughly enjoyed each other's company.

After a little rambling talk, the lawyer led up to the subject which so disagreeably preoccupied his mind.

'I suppose, Lanyon,' he said, 'you and I must be the two oldest friends that Henry Jekyll has?'

'I wish the friends were younger,' chuckled Dr Lanyon. 'But I suppose we are. And what of that? I see little of him now.'

'Indeed!' said Utterson. 'I thought you had a bond of common interest.'

'We had,' was his reply. 'But it is more than ten years since Henry Jekyll became too fanciful for me. He began to go wrong, wrong in mind; and though, of course, I continue to take an interest in him for old sake's sake as they say, I see and I have seen devilish little of the man. Such unscientific balderdash,' added the doctor, flushing suddenly purple, 'would have estranged Damon and Pythias.'

This little spirt of temper was somewhat of a relief to Mr Utterson. 'They have only differed on some point of science,' he thought; and being a man of no scientific passions (except in the matter of conveyancing), he even added: 'It is nothing worse than that!' He gave his friend a few seconds to recover his composure, and then approached the question he had come to put.

'Did you ever come across a *protégé* of his – one Hyde?' he asked.

'Hyde?' repeated Lanyon. 'No. Never heard of him. Since my time.'

That was the amount of information that the lawyer carried back with him to the great, dark bed on which he tossed to and fro until the small hours of the morning began to grow large. It was a night of little ease to his toiling mind, toiling in mere darkness and besieged by questions.

Six o'clock struck on the bells of the church that was so conveniently near to Mr Utterson's dwelling, and still he was digging at the problem. Hitherto it had touched him on the intellectual side alone; but now his imagination also was engaged, or rather enslaved; and as he lay and tossed in the gross darkness of the night and the curtained room, Mr Enfield's tale went by before his mind in a scroll of lighted pictures. He would be aware of the great field of lamps of a nocturnal city; then of the figure of a man walking swiftly; then of a child running from the doctor's; and then these met, and that human Juggernaut trod the child down and passed on regardless of her screams. Or else he would see a room in a rich house, where his friend lay asleep, dreaming and smiling at his dreams; and then the door of that room would be opened, the curtains of the bed plucked apart, the sleeper recalled, and, lo! there would stand by his side a figure to whom power was given, and even at that dead hour he must rise and do its bidding. The figure in these two phases haunted the lawyer all night; and if at any time he dozed over, it was but to see it glide more stealthily through sleeping houses, or move the more swiftly, and still the more swiftly, even to dizziness, through wider labyrinths of lamp-lighted city, and at every street corner crush a child and leave her screaming. And still the figure had no face by which he might know it; even in his dreams it had no face, or one that baffled him and melted before his eyes; and thus it was that there sprang up and grew apace in the lawyer's mind a singularly strong, almost an inordinate, curiosity to behold the features of the real Mr Hyde. If he could but once set eyes on him, he thought the mystery would lighten and perhaps roll altogether away, as was the habit of mysterious things when well examined. He might see a reason for his friend's strange preference or bondage (call it which you please), and even for the startling clauses of the will. And at least it would be a face worth seeing: the face of a man who was without bowels of mercy: a face which had but to show itself to raise up, in the mind of the unimpressionable Enfield, a spirit of enduring hatred.

From that time forward, Mr Utterson began to haunt the door in the by-street of shops. In the morning before office hours, at noon when business was plenty and time scarce, at night under the face of the fogged city moon, by all lights and at all hours of solitude or concourse, the lawyer was to be found on his chosen post.

'If he be Mr Hyde,' he had thought, 'I shall be Mr Seek.'

And at last his patience was rewarded. It was a fine dry night; frost in the air; the streets as clean as a ball-room floor; the lamps, unshaken by any wind, drawing a regular pattern of light and shadow. By ten o'clock, when the shops were closed, the by-street was very solitary, and, in spite of the low growl of London from all round, very silent. Small sounds carried far; domestic sounds out of the houses were clearly audible on either side of the roadway; and the rumour of the approach of any passenger preceded him by a long time. Mr Utterson had been some minutes at his post when he was aware of an odd light footstep drawing near. In the course of his nightly patrols he had long grown accustomed to the quaint effect with which the footfalls of a single person, while he is still a great way off, suddenly spring out distinct from the vast hum and clatter of the city. Yet his attention had never before been so sharply and decisively arrested; and it was with a strong, superstitious prevision of success that he withdrew into the entry of the court.

The steps drew swiftly nearer, and swelled out suddenly louder as they turned the end of the street. The lawyer, looking forth from the entry, could soon see what manner of man he had to deal with. He was small, and very plainly dressed; and the look of him, even at that distance, went somehow strongly against the watcher's inclination. But he made straight for the door, crossing the roadway to save time; and as he came, he drew a key from his pocket, like one approaching home.

Mr Utterson stepped out and touched him on the shoulder as he passed. 'Mr Hyde, I think?'

Mr Hyde shrank back with a hissing intake of the breath. But his fear was only momentary; and though he did not look the lawyer in the face, he answered coolly enough: 'That is my name. What do you want?'

'I see you are going in,' returned the lawyer. 'I am an old friend of Dr Jekyll's – Mr Utterson, of Gaunt Street – you must have heard my name; and meeting you so conveniently, I thought you might admit me.'

'You will not find Dr Jekyll; he is from home,' replied Mr Hyde, blowing in the key. And then suddenly, but still without looking up, 'How did you know me?' he asked.

'On your side,' said Mr Utterson, 'will you do me a favour?'

'With pleasure,' replied the other. 'What shall it be?'

'Will you let me see your face?' asked the lawyer.

Mr Hyde appeared to hesitate; and then, as if upon some sudden reflection, fronted about with an air of defiance; and the pair stared at each other pretty fixedly for a few seconds. 'Now I shall know you again,' said Mr Utterson. 'It may be useful.'

'Yes,' returned Mr Hyde, 'it is as well we have met; and *à propos*, you should have my address.' And he gave a number of a street in Soho.

'Good God!' thought Mr Utterson, 'can he too have been thinking of the will?' But he kept his feelings to himself, and only grunted in acknowledgment of the address.

'And now,' said the other, 'how did you know me?'

'By description,' was the reply.

'Whose description?'

'We have common friends,' said Mr Utterson.

'Common friends!' echoed Mr Hyde, a little hoarsely. 'Who are they?'

'Jekyll, for instance,' said the lawyer.

'He never told you,' cried Mr Hyde, with a flush of anger. 'I did not think you would have lied.'

'Come,' said Mr Utterson, 'that is not fitting language.'

The other snarled aloud into a savage laugh; and the next moment, with extraordinary quickness, he had unlocked the door and disappeared into the house.

The lawyer stood awhile when Mr Hyde had left him, the picture of disquietude. Then he began slowly to mount the street, pausing every step or two, and putting his hand to his brow like a man in mental perplexity. The problem he was thus debating as he walked was one of a class that is rarely solved. Mr Hyde was pale and dwarfish; he gave an impression of deformity without any namable malformation, he had a displeasing smile, he had borne himself to the lawyer with a sort of murderous mixture of timidity and boldness, and he spoke with a husky, whispering and somewhat broken voice, all these were points against him; but not all of these together could explain the hitherto unknown disgust, loathing and fear with which Mr Utterson regarded him. 'There must be something else,' said the perplexed gentleman. 'There *is* something more, if I could find a name for it. God bless me, the man seems hardly human! Something troglodytic, shall we say? or can it be the old story of Dr Fell? or is it the mere radiance of a foul soul that thus transpires through, and transfigures, its clay continent? The last, I think; for, O my poor old Harry Jekyll, if ever I read Satan's signature upon a face, it is on that of your new friend!'

Round the corner from the by-street there was a square of ancient, handsome houses, now for the most part decayed from their high estate, and let in flats and chambers to all sorts and conditions of men: map-engravers, architects, shady lawyers, and the agents of obscure enterprises. One house, however, second from the corner, was still occupied entire; and at the door of this, which wore a great air of wealth and comfort, though it was now plunged in darkness except for the fan-light, Mr Utterson stopped and knocked. A well-dressed, elderly servant opened the door.

'Is Dr Jekyll at home, Poole?' asked the lawyer.

'I will see, Mr Utterson,' said Poole, admitting the visitor, as he spoke, into a large, low-roofed, comfortable hall, paved with flags, warmed (after the fashion of a country house) by a bright, open fire, and furnished with costly cabinets of oak. 'Will you wait here by the fire, sir? or shall I give you a light in the dining-room?'

'Here, thank you,' said the lawyer; and he drew near and leaned on the tall fender. This hall, in which he was now left alone, was a pet fancy of his friend the doctor's; and Utterson himself was wont to speak of it as the pleasantest room in London. But tonight there was a shudder in his blood; the face of Hyde sat heavy on his memory; he felt (what was rare with him) a nausea and distaste of life; and in the gloom of his spirits, he seemed to read a menace in the flickering of the firelight on the polished cabinets and the uneasy starting of the shadow on the roof. He was ashamed of his relief when Poole presently returned to announce that Dr Jekyll was gone out.

'I saw Mr Hyde go in by the old dissecting-room door, Poole,' he said. 'Is that right, when Dr Jekyll is from home?'

'Quite right, Mr Utterson, sir,' replied the servant. 'Mr Hyde has a key.'

'Your master seems to repose a great deal of trust in that young man, Poole,' resumed the other, musingly.

'Yes, sir, he do indeed,' said Poole. 'We have all orders to obey him.'

'I do not think I ever met Mr Hyde?' asked Utterson.

'O dear no, sir. He never *dines* here,' replied the butler 'Indeed, we see very little of him on this side of the house; he mostly comes and goes by the laboratory.'

'Well, good-night, Poole.'

'Good-night, Mr Utterson.'

And the lawyer set out homeward with a very heavy heart. 'Poor Harry Jekyll,' he thought, 'my mind misgives me he is in deep waters! He was wild when he was young; a long while ago, to be sure; but in the law of God there is no statute of limitations. Ah, it must be that; the ghost of some old sin, the cancer of some concealed disgrace; punishment coming, *pede claudo*, years after memory has forgotten and self-love condoned the fault.' And the lawyer, scared by the thought, brooded awhile on his own past, groping in all the corners of memory, lest by chance some Jack-in-the-Box of an old iniquity should leap to light there. His past was fairly blameless; few men could read the rolls of their life with less apprehension; yet he was humbled to the dust by the many ill things he had done, and raised up again into a sober and fearful gratitude by the many that he had come so near to doing, yet avoided. And then by a return on his former subject, he conceived a spark of hope. 'This Master Hyde, if he were studied,' thought he, 'must have secrets of his own: black secrets, by the look of him; secrets compared to which poor Jekyll's worst would be like sunshine. Things cannot continue as they are. It turns me cold to think of this creature stealing like a thief to Harry's bedside; poor Harry, what a wakening! And the danger of it! for if this Hyde suspect the existence of the will, he may grow impatient to inherit. Ay I must put my shoulder to the wheel – if Jekyll will but let me,' he added, 'if Jekyll will only let me.' For once more he saw before his mind's eye, as clear as a transparency, the strange clauses of the will.

Dr Jekyll was quite at Ease

A FORTNIGHT LATER, by excellent good fortune, the doctor gave one of his pleasant dinners to some five or six old cronies, all intelligent reputable men, and all judges of good wine; and Mr Utterson so contrived that he remained behind after the others had departed. This was no new arrangement, but a thing that had befallen many scores of

times. Where Utterson was liked, he was liked well. Hosts loved to
detain the dry lawyer, when the light-hearted and the loose-tongued
had already their foot on the threshold; they liked to sit awhile in his
unobtrusive company, practising for solitude, sobering their minds in
the man's rich silence, after the expense and strain of gaiety. To this
rule Dr Jekyll was no exception; and as he now sat on the opposite side
of the fire – a large, well-made, smooth-faced man of fifty, with
something of a slyish cast perhaps, but every mark of capacity and
kindness – you could see by his looks that he cherished for Mr
Utterson a sincere and warm affection.

'I have been wanting to speak to you, Jekyll,' began the latter. 'You
know that will of yours?'

A close observer might have gathered that the topic was distasteful;
but the doctor carried it off gaily. 'My poor Utterson,' said he, 'you are
unfortunate in such a client. I never saw a man so distressed as you
were by my will; unless it were that hide-bound pedant, Lanyon, at
what he called my scientific heresies. O, I know he's a good fellow –
you needn't frown – an excellent fellow, and I always mean to see more
of him; but a hide-bound pedant for all that; an ignorant, blatant
pedant. I was never more disappointed in any man than Lanyon.'

'You know I never approved of it,' pursued Utterson, ruthlessly
disregarding the fresh topic.

'My will? Yes, certainly, I know that,' said the doctor, a trifle sharply.
'You have told me so.'

'Well, I tell you so again,' continued the lawyer. 'I have been
learning something of young Hyde.'

The large handsome face of Dr Jekyll grew pale to the very lips, and
there came a blackness about his eyes. 'I do not care to hear more,' said
he. 'This is a matter I thought we had agreed to drop.'

'What I heard was abominable,' said Utterson.

'It can make no change. You do not understand my position,'
returned the doctor, with a certain incoherency of manner. 'I am
painfully situated, Utterson; my position is a very strange – a very
strange one. It is one of those affairs that cannot be mended by talking.'

'Jekyll,' said Utterson, 'you know me: I am a man to be trusted. Make
a clean breast of this in confidence; and I make no doubt I can get you
out of it.'

'My good Utterson,' said the doctor, 'this is very good of you, this is
downright good of you, and I cannot find words to thank you in. I
believe you fully; I would trust you before any man alive, ay, before
myself, if I could make the choice; but indeed it isn't what you fancy; it
is not so bad as that; and just to put your good heart at rest, I will tell

you one thing: the moment I choose, I can be rid of Mr Hyde. I give you my hand upon that; and I thank you again and again; and I will just add one little word, Utterson, that I'm sure you'll take in good part: this is a private matter, and I beg of you to let it sleep.'

Utterson reflected a little, looking in the fire.

'I have no doubt you are perfectly right,' he said at last, getting to his feet.

'Well, but since we have touched upon this business, and for the last time, I hope,' continued the doctor, 'there is one point I should like you to understand. I have really a very great interest in poor Hyde. I know you have seen him; he told me so; and I fear he was rude. But I do sincerely take a great, a very great interest in that young man; and if I am taken away, Utterson, I wish you to promise me that you will bear with him and get his rights for him. I think you would, if you knew all; and it would be a weight off my mind if you would promise.'

'I can't pretend that I shall ever like him,' said the lawyer.

'I don't ask that,' pleaded Jekyll, laying his hand upon the other's arm; 'I only ask for justice; I only ask you to help him for my sake, when I am no longer here.'

Utterson heaved an irrepressible sigh. 'Well,' said he, 'I promise.'

The Carew Murder Case

NEARLY A YEAR LATER, in the month of October, 18—, London was startled by a crime of singular ferocity, and rendered all the more notable by the high position of the victim. The details were few and startling. A maid-servant living alone in a house not far from the river had gone upstairs to bed about eleven. Although a fog rolled over the city in the small hours, the early part of the night was cloudless, and the lane, which the maid's window overlooked, was brilliantly lit by the full moon. It seems she was romantically given; for she sat down upon her box, which stood immediately under the window, and fell into a dream of musing. Never (she used to say, with streaming tears, when she narrated that experience), never had she felt more at peace with all men or thought more kindly of the world. And as she so sat she became aware of an aged and beautiful gentleman with white hair drawing near along the lane; and advancing to meet him, another and very small gentleman, to whom at first she paid less attention. When they had come within speech (which was just under the maid's eyes) the older man bowed and accosted the other with a very pretty manner of politeness. It did not seem as if the subject of his address were of great importance; indeed, from his pointing, it sometimes appeared as if he were only inquiring his way; but the moon shone on his face as he spoke, and the girl was pleased to watch it, it seemed to breathe such an innocent and old-world kindness of disposition, yet with something high too, as of a well-founded self-content. Presently her eye wandered to the other, and she was surprised to recognise in him a certain Mr Hyde, who had once visited her master, and for whom she had conceived a dislike. He had in his hand a heavy cane, with which he was trifling; but he answered never a word, and seemed to listen with an ill-contained impatience. And then all of a sudden he broke out in a great flame of anger, stamping with his foot, brandishing the cane, and carrying on (as the maid described it) like a madman. The old gentleman took a step back, with the air of one very much surprised and a trifle hurt; and at that Mr Hyde broke out of all bounds, and clubbed him to the earth. And next moment, with ape-like fury, he was trampling his victim under foot, and hailing down a storm of blows, under which the bones were audibly shattered and the body jumped upon the roadway. At the horror of these sights and sounds the maid fainted.

It was two o'clock when she came to herself and called for the police. The murderer was gone long ago; but there lay his victim in the middle of the lane, incredibly mangled. The stick with which the deed had been done, although it was of some rare and very tough and heavy wood, had broken in the middle under the stress of this insensate cruelty; and one splintered half had rolled in the neighbouring gutter – the other, without doubt, had been carried away by the murderer. A purse and a gold watch were found upon the victim; but no cards or papers, except a sealed and stamped envelope, which he had been probably carrying to the post, and which bore the name and address of Mr Utterson.

This was brought to the lawyer the next morning, before he was out of bed; and he had no sooner seen it, and been told the circumstances, than he shot out a solemn lip. 'I shall say nothing till I have seen the body,' said he; 'this may be very serious. Have the kindness to wait while I dress.' And with the same grave countenance he hurried through his breakfast and drove to the police station, whither the body had been carried. As soon as he came into the cell, he nodded.

'Yes,' said he, 'I recognise him. I am sorry to say that this is Sir Danvers Carew.'

'Good God, sir!' exclaimed the officer, 'is it possible?' And the next moment his eye lighted up with professional ambition. 'This will make a deal of noise,' he said. 'And perhaps you can help us to the man.' And he briefly narrated what the maid had seen, and showed the broken stick.

Mr Utterson had already quailed at the name of Hyde; but when the stick was laid before him, he could doubt no longer: broken and battered as it was, he recognised it for one that he had himself presented many years before to Henry Jekyll.

'Is this Mr Hyde a person of small stature?' he inquired.

'Particularly small and particularly wicked-looking, is what the maid calls him,' said the officer.

Mr Utterson reflected; and then, raising his head, 'If you will come with me in my cab,' he said, 'I think I can take you to his house.'

It was by this time about nine in the morning, and the first fog of the season. A great chocolate-coloured pall lowered over heaven, but the wind was continually charging and routing these embattled vapours; so that as the cab crawled from street to street, Mr Utterson beheld a marvellous number of degrees and hues of twilight; for here it would be dark like the back-end of evening; and there would be a glow of a rich, lurid brown, like the light of some strange conflagration; and here, for a moment, the fog would be quite broken up, and a haggard shaft of daylight would glance in between the swirling wreaths. The dismal quarter of Soho seen under these changing glimpses, with its muddy ways, and slatternly passengers, and its lamps, which had never been extinguished or had been kindled afresh to combat this mournful reinvasion of darkness, seemed, in the lawyer's eyes, like a district of some city in a nightmare. The thoughts of his mind, besides, were of the gloomiest dye; and when he glanced at the companion of his drive, he was conscious of some touch of that terror of the law and the law's officers which may at times assail the most honest.

As the cab drew up before the address indicated, the fog lifted a little and showed him a dingy street, a gin palace, a low French eating-house, a shop for the retail of penny numbers and two-penny salads, many ragged children huddled in the doorways, and many women of many different nationalities passing out, key in hand, to have a morning glass; and the next moment the fog settled down again upon that part, as brown as umber, and cut him off from his blackguardly surroundings. This was the home of Henry Jekyll's favourite; of a man who was heir to a quarter of a million sterling.

An ivory-faced and silvery-haired old woman opened the door. She had an evil face, smoothed by hypocrisy; but her manners were excellent. Yes, she said, this was Mr Hyde's, but he was not at home; he had been in that night very late, but had gone away again in less than an hour: there was nothing strange in that; his habits were very irregular, and he was often absent; for instance, it was nearly two months since she had seen him till yesterday.

'Very well then, we wish to see his rooms,' said the lawyer; and when the woman began to declare it was impossible, 'I had better tell you who this person is,' he added. 'This is Inspector Newcomen, of Scotland Yard.'

A flash of odious joy appeared upon the woman's face. 'Ah!' said she, 'he is in trouble! What has he done?'

Mr Utterson and the inspector exchanged glances. 'He don't seem a very popular character,' observed the latter. 'And now, my good woman, just let me and this gentleman have a look about us.'

In the whole extent of the house, which but for the old woman remained otherwise empty, Mr Hyde had only used a couple of rooms; but these were furnished with luxury and good taste. A closet was filled with wine; the plate was of silver, the napery elegant; a good picture hung upon the walls, a gift (as Utterson supposed) from Henry Jekyll, who was much of a connoisseur; and the carpets were of many plies and agreeable in colour. At this moment, however, the rooms bore every mark of having been recently and hurriedly ransacked; clothes lay about the floor, with their pockets inside out; lockfast drawers stood open; and on the hearth there lay a pile of gray ashes, as though many papers had been burned. From these embers the inspector disinterred the butt end of a green cheque book which had resisted the action of the fire; the other half of the stick was found behind the door; and as this clinched his suspicions, the officer declared himself delighted. A visit to the bank, where several thousand pounds were found to be lying to the murderer's credit, completed his gratification.

'You may depend upon it, sir,' he told Mr Utterson: 'I have him in my hand. He must have lost his head, or he never would have left the stick, or, above all, burned the cheque book. Why, money's life to the man. We have nothing to do but wait for him at the bank, and get out the handbills.'

This last, however, was not so easy of accomplishment; for Mr Hyde had numbered few familiars – even the master of the servant-maid had only seen him twice; his family could nowhere be traced; he had never been photographed; and the few who could describe him differed widely, as common observers will. Only on one point were they agreed; and that was the haunting sense of unexpressed deformity with which the fugitive impressed his beholders.

Incident of the Letter

IT WAS LATE in the afternoon when Mr Utterson found his way to Dr Jekyll's door, where he was at once admitted by Poole, and carried down by the kitchen offices and across a yard which had once been a garden, to the building which was indifferently known as the laboratory or the dissecting-rooms. The doctor had bought the house from the heirs of a celebrated surgeon; and his own tastes being rather chemical than anatomical, had changed the destination of the block at the bottom of the garden. It was the first time that the lawyer had been received in that part of his friend's quarters; and he eyed the dingy windowless structure with curiosity, and gazed round with a distasteful sense of strangeness as he crossed the theatre, once crowded with eager students and now lying gaunt and silent, the tables laden with chemical apparatus, the floor strewn with crates and littered with packing straw, and the light falling dimly through the foggy cupola. At the further end, a flight of stairs mounted to a door covered with red baize; and through this Mr Utterson was at last received into the doctor's cabinet. It was a large room, fitted round with glass presses, furnished, among other things, with a cheval-glass and a business table, and looking out upon the court by three dusty windows barred with iron. The fire burned in the grate; a lamp was set lighted on the chimney-shelf, for even in the houses the fog began to lie thickly; and there, close up to the warmth, sat Dr Jekyll, looking deadly sick. He did not rise to meet his visitor, but held out a cold hand, and bade him welcome in a changed voice.

'And now,' said Mr Utterson, as soon as Poole had left them, 'you have heard the news?'

The doctor shuddered. 'They were crying it in the square,' he said. 'I heard them in my dining-room.'

'One word,' said the lawyer. 'Carew was my client, but so are you; and I want to know what I am doing. You have not been mad enough to hide this fellow?'

'Utterson, I swear to God,' cried the doctor, 'I swear to God I will never set eyes on him again. I bind my honour to you that I am done with him in this world. It is all at an end. And indeed he does not want my help; you do not know him as I do; he is safe, he is quite safe; mark my words, he will never more be heard of.'

The lawyer listened gloomily; he did not like his friend's feverish manner. 'You seem pretty sure of him,' said he; 'and for your sake, I hope you may be right. If it came to a trial, your name might appear.'

'I am quite sure of him,' replied Jekyll; 'I have grounds for certainty that I cannot share with any one. But there is one thing on which you may advise me. I have – I have received a letter; and I am at a loss whether I should show it to the police. I should like to leave it in your hands, Utterson; you would judge wisely, I am sure; I have so great a trust in you.'

'You fear, I suppose, that it might lead to his detection?' asked the lawyer.

'No,' said the other. 'I cannot say that I care what becomes of Hyde; I am quite done with him. I was thinking of my own character, which this hateful business has rather exposed.'

Utterson ruminated awhile; he was surprised at his friend's selfishness, and yet relieved by it. 'Well,' said he, at last, 'let me see the letter.'

The letter was written in an odd, upright hand, and signed 'Edward Hyde'; and it signified, briefly enough, that the writer's benefactor, Dr Jekyll, whom he had long so unworthily repaid for a thousand generosities, need labour under no alarm for his safety, as he had means of escape on which he placed a sure dependence. The lawyer liked this letter well enough: it put a better colour on the intimacy than he had looked for; and he blamed himself for some of his past suspicions.

'Have you the envelope?' he asked.

'I burned it,' replied Jekyll, 'before I thought what I was about. But it bore no postmark. The note was handed in.'

'Shall I keep this and sleep upon it?' asked Utterson.

'I wish you to judge for me entirely,' was the reply. 'I have lost confidence in myself.'

'Well, I shall consider,' returned the lawyer. 'And now one word more: it was Hyde who dictated the terms in your will about that disappearance?'

The doctor seemed seized with a qualm of faintness; he shut his mouth tight and nodded.

'I knew it,' said Utterson. 'He meant to murder you. You have had a fine escape.'

'I have had what is far more to the purpose,' returned the doctor solemnly: 'I have had a lesson – O God, Utterson, what a lesson I have had!' And he covered his face for a moment with his hands.

On his way out, the lawyer stopped and had a word or two with Poole. 'By the by,' said he, 'there was a letter handed in today: what was the messenger like?' But Poole was positive nothing had come except by post; 'and only circulars by that,' he added.

This news sent off the visitor with his fears renewed. Plainly the letter had come by the laboratory door; possibly, indeed, it had been written in the cabinet; and, if that were so, it must be differently judged, and handled with the more caution. The news-boys, as he went, were crying themselves hoarse along the footways: 'Special edition. Shocking murder of an M.P.' That was the funeral oration of one friend and client; and he could not help a certain apprehension lest the good name of another should be sucked down in the eddy of the scandal. It was, at least, a ticklish decision that he had to make; and, self-reliant as he was by habit, he began to cherish a longing for advice. It was not to be had directly; but perhaps, he thought, it might be fished for.

Presently after, he sat on one side of his own hearth, with Mr Guest, his head clerk, upon the other, and midway between, at a nicely calculated distance from the fire, a bottle of a particular old wine that had long dwelt unsunned in the foundations of his house. The fog still slept on the wing above the drowned city, where the lamps glimmered like carbuncles; and through the muffle and smother of these fallen clouds, the procession of the town's life was still rolling in through the great arteries with a sound as of a mighty wind. But the room was gay with firelight. In the bottle the acids were long ago resolved; the imperial dye had softened with time, as the colour grows richer in stained windows; and the glow of hot autumn afternoons on hillside vineyards was ready to be set free and to disperse the fogs of London. Insensibly the lawyer melted. There was no man from whom he kept fewer secrets than Mr Guest; and he was not always sure that he kept as many as he meant. Guest had often been on business to the doctor's: he knew Poole; he could scarce have failed to hear of Mr Hyde's familiarity about the house; he might draw conclusions: was it not as well, then, that he should see a letter which put that mystery to rights? and, above all, since Guest, being a great student and critic of handwriting, would consider the step natural and obliging? The clerk, besides, was a man of counsel; he would scarce read so strange a document without dropping a remark; and by that remark Mr Utterson might shape his future course.

'This is a sad business about Sir Danvers,' he said.

'Yes, sir, indeed. It has elicited a great deal of public feeling,' returned Guest. 'The man, of course, was mad.'

'I should like to hear your views on that,' replied Utterson. 'I have a document here in his handwriting; it is between ourselves, for I scarce know what to do about it; it is an ugly business at the best. But there it is; quite in your way: a murderer's autograph.'

Guest's eyes brightened, and he sat down at once and studied it with passion. 'No, sir,' he said; 'not mad; but it is an odd hand.'

'And by all accounts a very odd writer,' added the lawyer.

Just then the servant entered with a note.

'Is that from Dr Jekyll, sir?' inquired the clerk. 'I thought I knew the writing. Anything private, Mr Utterson?'

'Only an invitation to dinner. Why? do you want to see it?'

'One moment. I thank you, sir'; and the clerk laid the two sheets of paper alongside and sedulously compared their contents. 'Thank you, sir,' he said at last, returning both; 'it's a very interesting autograph.'

There was a pause, during which Mr Utterson struggled with himself. 'Why did you compare them, Guest?' he inquired suddenly.

'Well, sir,' returned the clerk, 'there's a rather singular resemblance; the two hands are in many points identical; only differently sloped.'

'Rather quaint,' said Utterson.

'It is, as you say, rather quaint,' returned Guest.

'I wouldn't speak of this note, you know,' said the master.

'No, sir,' said the clerk. 'I understand.'

But no sooner was Mr Utterson alone that night than he locked the note into his safe, where it reposed from that time forward. 'What!' he thought. 'Henry Jekyll forge for a murderer!' And his blood ran cold in his veins.

Remarkable Incident of Dr Lanyon

TIME RAN ON; thousands of pounds were offered in reward, for the death of Sir Danvers was resented as a public injury; but Mr Hyde had disappeared out of the ken of the police as though he had never existed. Much of his past was unearthed, indeed, and all disreputable: tales came out of the man's cruelty, at once so callous and violent, of his vile life, of his strange associates, of the hatred that seemed to have surrounded his career; but of his present whereabouts, not a whisper. From the time he had left the house in Soho on the morning of the murder, he was simply blotted out; and gradually, as time drew on, Mr Utterson began to recover from the hotness of his alarm, and to grow more at quiet with himself. The death of Sir Danvers was, to his way of thinking, more than paid for by the disappearance of Mr Hyde. Now that that evil influence had been withdrawn, a new life began for Dr Jekyll. He came out of his seclusion, renewed relations with his friends, became once more their familiar guest and entertainer; and whilst he had always been known for charities, he was now no less distinguished for religion. He was busy, he was much in the open air, he did good; his face seemed to open and brighten, as if with an inward consciousness of service; and for more than two months the doctor was at peace.

On the 8th of January Utterson had dined at the doctor's with a small party; Lanyon had been there; and the face of the host had looked from one to the other as in the old days when the trio were inseparable friends. On the 12th, and again on the 14th, the door was shut against the lawyer. 'The doctor was confined to the house,' Poole said, 'and saw no one.' On the 15th he tried again, and was again refused; and having now been used for the last two months to see his friend almost daily, he found this return of solitude to weigh upon his spirits. The fifth night he had in Guest to dine with him; and the sixth he betook himself to Dr Lanyon's.

There at least he was not denied admittance; but when he came in, he was shocked at the change which had taken place in the doctor's appearance. He had his death-warrant written legibly upon his face. The rosy man had grown pale; his flesh had fallen away; he was visibly balder and older; and yet it was not so much these tokens of a swift physical decay that arrested the lawyer's notice, as a look in the eye and quality of manner that seemed to testify to some deep-seated terror of the mind. It was unlikely that the doctor should fear death; and yet that was what Utterson was tempted to suspect. 'Yes,' he thought; 'he is a doctor, he must know his own state and that his days are counted; and the knowledge is more than he can bear.' And yet when Utterson remarked on his ill looks, it was with an air of great firmness that Lanyon declared himself a doomed man.

'I have had a shock,' he said, 'and I shall never recover. It is a question of weeks. Well, life has been pleasant; I liked it; yes, sir, I used to like it. I sometimes think if we knew all, we should be more glad to get away.'

'Jekyll is ill, too,' observed Utterson. 'Have you seen him?'

But Lanyon's face changed, and he held up a trembling hand. 'I wish to see or hear no more of Dr Jekyll,' he said, in a loud, unsteady voice. 'I am quite done with that person; and I beg that you will spare me any allusion to one whom I regard as dead.'

'Tut, tut!' said Mr Utterson; and then, after a considerable pause, 'Can't I do anything?' he inquired. 'We are three very old friends, Lanyon; we shall not live to make others.'

'Nothing can be done,' returned Lanyon; 'ask himself.'

'He will not see me,' said the lawyer.

'I am not surprised at that,' was the reply. 'Some day, Utterson, after I am dead, you may perhaps come to learn the right and wrong of this. I cannot tell you. And in the meantime, if you can sit and talk with me of other things, for God's sake, stay and do so; but if you cannot keep clear of this accursed topic, then, in God's name, go, for I cannot bear it.'

As soon as he got home, Utterson sat down and wrote to Jekyll, complaining of his exclusion from the house, and asking the cause of this unhappy break with Lanyon; and the next day brought him a long answer, often very pathetically worded, and sometimes darkly mysterious in drift. The quarrel with Lanyon was incurable. 'I do not blame our old friend,' Jekyll wrote, 'but I share his view that we must never meet. I mean from henceforth to lead a life of extreme seclusion; you must not be surprised, nor must you doubt my friendship, if my door is often shut even to you. You must suffer me to go my own dark way. I have brought on myself a punishment and a danger that I cannot name. If I am the chief of sinners, I am the chief of sufferers also. I could not think that this earth contained a place for sufferings and terrors so unmanning; and you can do but one thing, Utterson, to lighten this destiny, and that is to respect my silence.' Utterson was amazed; the dark influence of Hyde had been withdrawn, the doctor had returned to his old tasks and amities; a week ago, the prospect had smiled with every promise of a cheerful and an honoured age; and now in a moment, friendship and peace of mind and the whole tenor of his life were wrecked. So great and unprepared a change pointed to madness; but in view of Lanyon's manner and words, there must lie for it some deeper ground.

A week afterwards Dr Lanyon took to his bed, and in something less than a fortnight he was dead. The night after the funeral, at which he had been sadly affected, Utterson locked the door of his business room, and sitting there by the light of a melancholy candle, drew out and set before him an envelope addressed by the hand and sealed with the seal of his dead friend. 'PRIVATE: for the hands of J. G. Utterson ALONE, and in case of his predecease *to be destroyed unread*,' so it was emphatically superscribed; and the lawyer dreaded to behold the contents. 'I have buried one friend today,' he thought: 'what if this should cost me another?' And then he condemned the fear as a disloyalty, and broke the seal. Within there was another enclosure, likewise sealed, and marked upon the cover as 'not to be opened till the death or disappearance of Dr Henry Jekyll.' Utterson could not trust his eyes. Yes, it was disappearance; here again, as in the mad will, which he had long ago restored to its author, here again were the idea of a disappearance and the name of Henry Jekyll bracketed. But in the will, that idea had sprung from the sinister suggestion of the man Hyde; it was set there with a purpose all too plain and horrible. Written by the hand of Lanyon, what should it mean? A great curiosity came to the trustee, to disregard the prohibition and dive at once to the bottom of these mysteries; but professional honour and faith to his dead friend were stringent obligations; and the packet slept in the inmost corner of his private safe.

It is one thing to mortify curiosity, another to conquer it; and it may be doubted if, from that day forth, Utterson desired the society of his surviving friend with the same eagerness. He thought of him kindly; but his thoughts were disquieted and fearful. He went to call indeed; but he was perhaps relieved to be denied admittance; perhaps, in his heart, he preferred to speak with Poole upon the doorstep, and surrounded by the air and sounds of the open city, rather than to be admitted into that house of voluntary bondage, and to sit and speak with its inscrutable recluse. Poole had, indeed, no very pleasant news to communicate. The doctor, it appeared, now more than ever confined himself to the cabinet over the laboratory, where he would sometimes even sleep: he was out of spirits, he had grown very silent, he did not read; it seemed as if he had something on his mind. Utterson became so used to the unvarying character of these reports, that he fell off little by little in the frequency of his visits.

Incident at the Window

IT CHANCED ON SUNDAY, when Mr Utterson was on his usual walk with Mr Enfield, that their way lay once again through the by-street; and that when they came in front of the door, both stopped to gaze on it.

'Well,' said Enfield, 'that story's at an end, at least. We shall never see more of Mr Hyde.'

'I hope not,' said Utterson. 'Did I ever tell you that I once saw him, and shared your feeling of repulsion?'

'It was impossible to do the one without the other,' returned Enfield. 'And, by the way, what an ass you must have thought me, not to know that this was a back way to Dr Jekyll's! It was partly your own fault that I found it out even when I did.'

'So you found it out, did you?' said Utterson. 'But if that be so, we may step into the court and take a look at the windows. To tell you the truth, I am uneasy about poor Jekyll; and even outside, I feel as if the presence of a friend might do him good.'

The court was very cool and a little damp, and full of premature twilight, although the sky, high up overhead, was still bright with sunset. The middle one of the three windows was half-way open; and sitting close beside it, taking the air with an infinite sadness of mien, like some disconsolate prisoner, Utterson saw Dr Jekyll.

'What! Jekyll!' he cried. 'I trust you are better.'

'I am very low, Utterson,' replied the doctor drearily; 'very low. It will not last long, thank God.'

'You stay too much indoors,' said the lawyer. 'You should be out, whipping up the circulation, like Mr Enfield and me. (This is my cousin – Mr Enfield – Dr Jekyll.) Come, now; get your hat, and take a quick turn with us.'

'You are very good,' sighed the other. 'I should like to very much; but no, no, no; it is quite impossible; I dare not. But indeed, Utterson, I am very glad to see you; this is really a great pleasure. I would ask you and Mr Enfield up, but the place is really not fit.'

'Why then,' said the lawyer, good-naturedly, 'the best thing we can do is to stay down here, and speak with you from where we are.'

'That is just what I was about to venture to propose,' returned the doctor, with a smile. But the words were hardly uttered, before the smile was struck out of his face and succeeded by an expression of such abject terror and despair, as froze the very blood of the two gentlemen below. They saw it but for a glimpse, for the window was instantly thrust down; but that glimpse had been sufficient, and they turned and left the court without a word. In silence, too, they traversed the by-street; and it was not until they had come into a neighbouring thoroughfare, where even upon a Sunday there were still some stirrings of life, that Mr Utterson at last turned and looked at his companion. They were both pale; and there was an answering horror in their eyes.

'God forgive us! God forgive us!' said Mr Utterson.

But Mr Enfield only nodded his head very seriously, and walked on once more in silence.

The Last Night

MR UTTERSON was sitting by his fireside one evening after dinner, when he was surprised to receive a visit from Poole.

'Bless me, Poole, what brings you here?' he cried; and then, taking a second look at him, 'What ails you?' he added; 'is the doctor ill?'

'Mr Utterson,' said the man, 'there is something wrong.'

'Take a seat, and here is a glass of wine for you,' said the lawyer. 'Now, take your time, and tell me plainly what you want.'

'You know the doctor's ways, sir,' replied Poole, 'and how he shuts himself up. Well, he's shut up again in the cabinet; and I don't like it, sir – I wish I may die if I like it. Mr Utterson, sir, I'm afraid.'

'Now, my good man,' said the lawyer, 'be explicit. What are you afraid of?'

'I've been afraid for about a week,' returned Poole, doggedly disregarding the question; 'and I can bear it no more.'

The man's appearance amply bore out his words; his manner was altered for the worse; and except for the moment when he had first announced his terror, he had not once looked the lawyer in the face. Even now, he sat with the glass of wine untasted on his knee, and his eyes directed to a corner of the floor. 'I can bear it no more,' he repeated.

'Come,' said the lawyer, 'I see you have some good reason, Poole; I see there is something seriously amiss. Try to tell me what it is.'

'I think there's been foul play,' said Poole, hoarsely.

'Foul play!' cried the lawyer, a good deal frightened, and rather inclined to be irritated in consequence. 'What foul play? What does the man mean?'

'I daren't say, sir,' was the answer; 'but will you come along with me and see for yourself?'

Mr Utterson's only answer was to rise and get his hat and great-coat; but he observed with wonder the greatness of the relief that appeared upon the butler's face, and perhaps with no less, that the wine was still untasted when he set it down to follow.

It was a wild, cold, seasonable night of March, with a pale moon, lying on her back as though the wind had tilted her, and a flying wrack of the most diaphanous and lawny texture. The wind made talking difficult, and flecked the blood into the face. It seemed to have swept the streets unusually bare of passengers, besides; for Mr Utterson thought he had never seen that part of London so deserted. He could have wished it otherwise; never in his life had he been conscious of so sharp a wish to see and touch his fellow-creatures; for, struggle as he might, there was borne in upon his mind a crushing anticipation of calamity. The square, when they got there, was all full of wind and dust, and the thin trees in the garden were lashing themselves along the railing. Poole, who had kept all the way a pace or two ahead, now pulled up in the middle of the pavement, and in spite of the biting weather, took off his hat and mopped his brow with a red pocket-handkerchief. But for all the hurry of his coming, these were not the dews of exertion that he wiped away, but the moisture of some strangling anguish; for his face was white, and his voice, when he spoke, harsh and broken.

'Well, sir,' he said, 'here we are, and God grant there be nothing wrong.'

'Amen, Poole,' said the lawyer.

Thereupon the servant knocked in a very guarded manner; the door was opened on the chain; and a voice asked from within, 'Is that you, Poole?'

'It's all right,' said Poole. 'Open the door.'

The hall, when they entered it, was brightly lighted up; the fire was built high; and about the hearth the whole of the servants, men and women, stood huddled together like a flock of sheep. At the sight of Mr Utterson, the housemaid broke into hysterical whimpering; and the cook, crying out, 'Bless God! it's Mr Utterson,' ran forward as if to take him in her arms.

'What, what? Are you all here?' said the lawyer, peevishly. 'Very irregular, very unseemly: your master would be far from pleased.'

'They're all afraid,' said Poole.

Blank silence followed, no one protesting; only the maid lifted up her voice, and now wept loudly.

'Hold your tongue!' Poole said to her, with a ferocity of accent that testified to his own jangled nerves; and indeed when the girl had so suddenly raised the note of her lamentation, they had all started and turned towards the inner door with faces of dreadful expectation. 'And now,' continued the butler, addressing the knife-boy, 'reach me a candle, and we'll get this through hands at once.' And then he begged Mr Utterson to follow him, and led the way to the back garden.

'Now, sir,' said he, 'you come as gently as you can. I want you to hear, and I don't want you to be heard. And see here, sir, if by any chance he was to ask you in, don't go.'

Mr Utterson's nerves, at this unlooked-for termination, gave a jerk that nearly threw him from his balance; but he re-collected his courage, and followed the butler into the laboratory building and through the surgical theatre, with its lumber of crates and bottles, to the foot of the stair. Here Poole motioned him to stand on one side and listen; while he himself, setting down the candle and making a great and obvious call on his resolution, mounted the steps, and knocked with a somewhat uncertain hand on the red baize of the cabinet door.

'Mr Utterson, sir, asking to see you,' he called; and even as he did so, once more violently signed to the lawyer to give ear.

A voice answered from within: 'Tell him I cannot see any one,' it said, complainingly.

'Thank you, sir,' said Poole, with a note of something like triumph in his voice; and taking up his candle, he led Mr Utterson back across the yard and into the great kitchen, where the fire was out and the beetles were leaping on the floor.

'Sir,' he said, looking Mr Utterson in the eyes, 'was that my master's voice?'

'It seems much changed,' replied the lawyer, very pale, but giving look for look.

'Changed? Well, yes, I think so,' said the butler. 'Have I been twenty years in this man's house, to be deceived about his voice? No, sir; master's made away with; he was made away with eight days ago, when we heard him cry out upon the name of God; and *who's* in there instead of him, and *why* it stays there, is a thing that cries to Heaven, Mr Utterson!'

'This is a very strange tale, Poole; this is rather a wild tale, my man,' said Mr Utterson, biting his finger. 'Suppose it were as you suppose, supposing Dr Jekyll to have been – well, murdered, what could induce the murderer to stay? That won't hold water; it doesn't commend itself to reason.'

'Well, Mr Utterson, you are a hard man to satisfy, but I'll do it yet,' said Poole. 'All this last week (you must know), him, or it, or whatever it is that lives in that cabinet, has been crying night and day for some sort of medicine and cannot get it to his mind. It was sometimes his way – the master's, that is – to write his orders on a sheet of paper and throw it on the stair. We've had nothing else this week back; nothing but papers, and a closed door, and the very meals left there to be smuggled in when nobody was looking. Well, sir, every day, ay, and twice and thrice in the same day, there have been orders and complaints, and I have been sent flying to all the wholesale chemists in town. Every time I brought the stuff back, there would be another paper telling me to return it, because it was not pure, and another order to a different firm. This drug is wanted bitter bad, sir, whatever for.'

'Have you any of these papers?' asked Mr Utterson.

Poole felt in his pocket and handed out a crumpled note, which the lawyer, bending nearer to the candle, carefully examined. Its contents ran thus: 'Dr Jekyll presents his compliments to Messrs. Maw. He assures them that their last sample is impure and quite useless for his present purpose. In the year 18—, Dr J. purchased a somewhat large quantity from Messrs. M. He now begs them to search with the most sedulous care, and should any of the same quality be left, to forward it to him at once. Expense is no consideration. The importance of this to Dr J. can hardly be exaggerated.' So far the letter had run composedly enough; but here, with a sudden splutter of the pen, the writer's emotion had broken loose. 'For God's sake,' he had added, 'find me some of the old.'

'This is a strange note,' said Mr Utterson; and then sharply, 'How do you come to have it open?'

'The man at Maw's was main angry, sir, and he threw it back to me like so much dirt,' returned Poole.

'This is unquestionably the doctor's hand, do you know?' resumed the lawyer.

'I thought it looked like it,' said the servant, rather sulkily; and then, with another voice, 'But what matters hand of write?' he said. 'I've seen him!'

'Seen him?' repeated Mr Utterson. 'Well?'

'That's it!' said Poole. 'It was this way. I came suddenly into the theatre from the garden. It seems he had slipped out to look for this drug, or whatever it is; for the cabinet door was open, and there he was at the far end of the room, digging among the crates. He looked up when I came in, gave a kind of cry, and whipped upstairs into the cabinet. It was but for one minute that I saw him, but the hair stood upon my head like quills. Sir, if that was my master, why had he a mask upon his face? If it was my master, why did he cry out like a rat and run from me? I have served him long enough. And then . . . ' the man paused, and passed his hand over his face.

'These are all very strange circumstances,' said Mr Utterson, 'but I think I begin to see daylight. Your master, Poole, is plainly seized with one of those maladies that both torture and deform the sufferer; hence, for aught I know, the alteration of his voice; hence the mask and his avoidance of his friends; hence his eagerness to find this drug, by means of which the poor soul retains some hope of ultimate recovery – God grant that he be not deceived! There is my explanation; it is sad enough, Poole, ay, and appalling to consider; but it is plain and natural, hangs well together, and delivers us from all exorbitant alarms.'

'Sir,' said the butler, turning to a sort of mottled pallor, 'that thing was not my master, and there's the truth. My master' – here he looked round him, and began to whisper – 'is a tall fine build of a man, and this was more of a dwarf.' Utterson attempted to protest. 'O, sir,' cried Poole, 'do you think I do not know my master after twenty years? do you think I do not know where his head comes to in the cabinet door, where I saw him every morning of my life? No, sir, that thing in the mask was never Dr Jekyll – God knows what it was, but it was never Dr Jekyll; and it is the belief of my heart that there was murder done.'

'Poole,' replied the lawyer, 'if you say that, it will become my duty to make certain. Much as I desire to spare your master's feelings, much as I am puzzled about this note, which seems to prove him to be still alive, I shall consider it my duty to break in that door.'

'Ah, Mr Utterson, that's talking!' cried the butler.

'And now comes the second question,' resumed Utterson: 'Who is going to do it?'

'Why, you and me, sir,' was the undaunted reply.

'That is very well said,' returned the lawyer; 'and whatever comes of it, I shall make it my business to see you are no loser.'

'There is an axe in the theatre,' continued Poole; 'and you might take the kitchen poker for yourself.'

The lawyer took that rude but weighty instrument into his hand, and balanced it. 'Do you know, Poole,' he said, looking up, 'that you and I are about to place ourselves in a position of some peril?'

'You may say so, sir, indeed,' returned the butler.

'It is well, then, that we should be frank,' said the other. 'We both think more than we have said; let us make a clean breast. This masked figure that you saw, did you recognise it?'

'Well, sir, it went so quick, and the creature was so doubled up, that I could hardly swear to that,' was the answer. 'But if you mean, was it Mr Hyde? – why, yes, I think it was! You see, it was much of the same bigness; and it had the same quick light way with it; and then who else could have got in by the laboratory door? You have not forgot, sir, that at the time of the murder he had still the key with him? But that's not all. I don't know, Mr Utterson, if ever you met this Mr Hyde?'

'Yes,' said the lawyer, 'I once spoke with him.'

'Then you must know, as well as the rest of us, that there was something queer about that gentleman – something that gave a man a turn – I don't know rightly how to say it, sir, beyond this: that you felt it in your marrow – kind of cold and thin.'

'I own I felt something of what you describe,' said Mr Utterson.

'Quite so, sir,' returned Poole. 'Well, when that masked thing like a monkey jumped from among the chemicals and whipped into the cabinet, it went down my spine like ice. O, I know it's not evidence, Mr Utterson; I'm book-learned enough for that; but a man has his feelings; and I give you my bible-word it was Mr Hyde!'

'Ay, ay,' said the lawyer. 'My fears incline to the same point. Evil, I fear, founded – evil was sure to come – of that connection. Ay, truly, I believe you; I believe poor Harry is killed; and I believe his murderer (for what purpose, God alone can tell) is still lurking in his victim's room. Well, let our name be vengeance. Call Bradshaw.'

The footman came at the summons, very white and nervous.

'Pull yourself together, Bradshaw,' said the lawyer. 'This suspense, I know, is telling upon all of you; but it is now our intention to make an end of it. Poole, here, and I are going to force our way into the cabinet. If all is well, my shoulders are broad enough to bear the blame.

Meanwhile, lest anything should really be amiss, or any malefactor seek to escape by the back, you and the boy must go round the corner with a pair of good sticks, and take your post at the laboratory door. We give you ten minutes to get to your stations.'

As Bradshaw left, the lawyer looked at his watch. 'And now, Poole, let us get to ours,' he said; and taking the poker under his arm, he led the way into the yard. The scud had banked over the moon, and it was now quite dark. The wind, which only broke in puffs and draughts into that deep well of building, tossed the light of the candle to and fro about their steps, until they came into the shelter of the theatre, where they sat down silently to wait. London hummed solemnly all around; but nearer at hand, the stillness was only broken by the sound of a footfall moving to and fro along the cabinet floor.

'So it will walk all day, sir,' whispered Poole; 'ay, and the better part of the night. Only when a new sample comes from the chemist, there's a bit of a break. Ah, it's an ill conscience that's such an enemy to rest! Ah, sir, there's blood foully shed in every step of it! But hark again, a little closer – put your heart in your ears, Mr Utterson, and tell me, is that the doctor's foot?'

The steps fell lightly and oddly, with a certain swing, for all they went so slowly; it was different indeed from the heavy creaking tread of Henry Jekyll. Utterson sighed. 'Is there never anything else?' he asked.

Poole nodded. 'Once,' he said. 'Once I heard it weeping!'

'Weeping? how that?' said the lawyer, conscious of a sudden chill of horror.

'Weeping like a woman or a lost soul,' said the butler. 'I came away with that upon my heart, that I could have wept too.'

But now the ten minutes drew to an end. Poole disinterred the axe from under a stack of packing straw; the candle was set upon the nearest table to light them to the attack; and they drew near with bated breath to where that patient foot was still going up and down, up and down in the quiet of the night.

'Jekyll,' cried Utterson, with a loud voice, 'I demand to see you.' He paused a moment, but there came no reply. 'I give you fair warning, our suspicions are aroused, and I must and shall see you,' he resumed; 'if not by fair means, then by foul – if not of your consent, then by brute force!'

'Utterson,' said the voice, 'for God's sake, have mercy!'

'Ah, that's not Jekyll's voice – it's Hyde's!' cried Utterson. 'Down with the door, Poole!'

Poole swung the axe over his shoulder; the blow shook the building, and the red baize door leaped against the lock and hinges. A dismal screech, as of mere animal terror, rang from the cabinet. Up went the axe again, and again the panels crashed and the frame bounded; four times the blow fell; but the wood was tough and the fittings were of excellent workmanship; and it was not until the fifth that the lock burst in sunder, and the wreck of the door fell inwards on the carpet.

The besiegers, appalled by their own riot and the stillness that had succeeded, stood back a little and peered in. There lay the cabinet before their eyes in the quiet lamplight, a good fire glowing and chattering on the hearth, the kettle singing its thin strain, a drawer or two open, papers neatly set forth on the business table, and nearer the fire, the things laid out for tea; the quietest room, you would have said, and, but for the glazed presses full of chemicals, the most commonplace that night in London.

Right in the midst there lay the body of a man sorely contorted and still twitching. They drew near on tiptoe, turned it on its back, and beheld the face of Edward Hyde. He was dressed in clothes far too large for him, clothes of the doctor's bigness; the cords of his face still moved with a semblance of life, but life was quite gone; and by the crushed phial in the hand and the strong smell of kernels that hung upon the air, Utterson knew that he was looking on the body of a self-destroyer.

'We have come too late,' he said sternly, 'whether to save or punish. Hyde is gone to his account; and it only remains for us to find the body of your master.'

The far greater proportion of the building was occupied by the theatre, which filled almost the whole ground storey, and was lighted from above, and by the cabinet, which formed an upper storey at one end and looked upon the court. A corridor joined the theatre to the door on the by-street; and with this, the cabinet communicated separately by a second flight of stairs. There were besides a few dark closets and a spacious cellar. All these they now thoroughly examined. Each closet needed but a glance, for all were empty, and all, by the dust that fell from their doors, had stood long unopened. The cellar, indeed, was filled with crazy lumber, mostly dating from the times of the surgeon who was Jekyll's predecessor; but even as they opened the door, they were advertised of the uselessness of further search by the fall of a perfect mat of cobweb which had for years sealed up the entrance. Nowhere was there any trace of Henry Jekyll, dead or alive.

Poole stamped on the flags of the corridor. 'He must be buried here,' he said, hearkening to the sound.

'Or he may have fled,' said Utterson, and he turned to examine the door in the by-street. It was locked; and lying near by on the flags, they found the key, already stained with rust.

'This does not look like use,' observed the lawyer.

'Use!' echoed Poole. 'Do you not see, sir, it is broken? much as if a man had stamped on it.'

'Ah,' continued Utterson, 'and the fractures, too, are rusty.' The two men looked at each other with a scare. 'This is beyond me, Poole,' said the lawyer. 'Let us go back to the cabinet.'

They mounted the stair in silence, and still, with an occasional awestruck glance at the dead body, proceeded more thoroughly to examine the contents of the cabinet. At one table there were traces of chemical work, various measured heaps of some white salt being laid on glass saucers, as though for an experiment in which the unhappy man had been prevented.

'That is the same drug that I was always bringing him,' said Poole; and even as he spoke, the kettle with a startling noise boiled over.

This brought them to the fireside, where the easy chair was drawn cosily up, and the tea things stood ready to the sitter's elbow, the very sugar in the cup. There were several books on a shelf; one lay beside the tea things open, and Utterson was amazed to find it a copy of a pious work for which Jekyll had several times expressed a great esteem, annotated, in his own hand, with startling blasphemies.

Next, in the course of their review of the chamber, the searchers came to the cheval-glass, into whose depth they looked with an involuntary horror. But it was so turned as to show them nothing but the rosy glow playing on the roof, the fire sparkling in a hundred repetitions along the glazed front of the presses, and their own pale and fearful countenances stooping to look in.

'This glass has seen some strange things, sir,' whispered Poole.

'And surely none stranger than itself,' echoed the lawyer, in the same tone. 'For what did Jekyll' – he caught himself up at the word with a start, and then conquering the weakness – 'what could Jekyll want with it?' he said.

'You may say that!' said Poole.

Next they turned to the business table. On the desk, among the neat array of papers, a large envelope was uppermost, and bore, in the doctor's hand, the name of Mr Utterson. The lawyer unsealed it, and several enclosures fell to the floor. The first was a will, drawn in the same eccentric terms as the one which he had returned six months before, to serve as a testament in case of death and as a deed of gift in case of disappearance; but in place of the name of Edward Hyde, the lawyer, with indescribable amazement, read the name of Gabriel John Utterson. He looked at Poole, and then back at the papers, and last of all at the dead malefactor stretched upon the carpet.

'My head goes round,' he said. 'He has been all these days in possession; he had no cause to like me; he must have raged to see himself displaced; and he has not destroyed this document.'

He caught the next paper; it was a brief note in the doctor's hand, and dated at the top. 'O Poole!' the lawyer cried, 'he was alive and here this day. He cannot have been disposed of in so short a space; he must be still alive, he must have fled! And then, why fled? and how? and in that case can we venture to declare this suicide? O, we must be careful. I foresee that we may yet involve your master in some dire catastrophe.'

'Why don't you read it, sir?' asked Poole.

'Because I fear,' replied the lawyer, solemnly. 'God grant I have no cause for it!' And with that he brought the paper to his eye, and read as follows:

> My dear Utterson, – When this shall fall into your hands I shall have disappeared under what circumstances I have not the penetration to foresee; but my instincts and all the circumstances of my nameless situation tell me that the end is sure and must be early. Go then and first read the narrative which Lanyon warned me he was to place in your hands; and if you care to hear more, turn to the confession of
>
> Your unworthy and unhappy friend,
>
> HENRY JEKYLL.

'There was a third enclosure?' asked Utterson.

'Here, sir,' said Poole, and gave into his hands a considerable packet sealed in several places.

The lawyer put it in his pocket. 'I would say nothing of this paper. If your master has fled or is dead, we may at least save his credit. It is now ten; I must go home and read these documents in quiet; but I shall be back before midnight, when we shall send for the police.'

They went out, locking the door of the theatre behind them; and Utterson, once more leaving the servants gathered about the fire in the hall, trudged back to his office to read the two narratives in which this mystery was now to be explained.

Dr Lanyon's Narrative

ON THE NINTH OF JANUARY, now four days ago, I received by the evening delivery a registered envelope, addressed in the hand of my colleague and old school-companion, Henry Jekyll. I was a good deal surprised by this; for we were by no means in the habit of correspondence; I had seen the man, dined with him, indeed, the night before; and I could imagine nothing in our intercourse that should justify the formality of registration. The contents increased my wonder; for this is how the letter ran:

10th December 18—

DEAR LANYON, – You are one of my oldest friends; and although we may have differed at times on scientific questions, I cannot remember, at least on my side, any break in our affection. There was never a day when, if you had said to me, 'Jekyll, my life, my honour, my reason, depend upon you,' I would not have sacrificed my fortune or my left hand to help you. Lanyon, my life, my honour, my reason, are all at your mercy; if you fail me tonight, I am lost. You might suppose, after this preface, that I am going to ask you for something dishonourable to grant. Judge for yourself.

I want you to postpone all other engagements for tonight – ay even if you were summoned to the bedside of an emperor; to take a cab, unless your carriage should be actually at the door; and, with this letter in your hand for consultation, to drive straight to my house. Poole, my butler, has his orders; you will find him waiting your arrival with a locksmith. The door of my cabinet is then to be forced; and you are to go in alone; to open the glazed press (letter E) on the left hand, breaking the lock if it be shut; and to draw out, *with all its contents as they stand*, the fourth drawer from the top or (which is the same thing) the third from the bottom. In my extreme distress of mind, I have a morbid fear of misdirecting you; but even if I am in error, you may know the right drawer by its contents: some powders, a phial, and a paper book. This drawer I beg of you to carry back with you to Cavendish Square exactly as it stands.

That is the first part of the service: now for the second. You should be back, if you set out at once on the receipt of this, long before midnight; but I will leave you that amount of margin, not only in the fear of one of those obstacles that can neither be prevented nor foreseen, but because an hour when your servants are in bed is to be preferred for what will then remain to do. At midnight then, I have to ask you to be alone in your consulting-room, to admit with your own hand into the house a man who will present himself in my name, and to place in his hands the drawer that you will have brought with you from my cabinet. Then you will have played your part, and earned my gratitude completely. Five minutes afterwards, if you insist upon an explanation, you will have understood that these arrangements are of capital importance; and that by the neglect of one of them, fantastic as they must appear, you might have charged your conscience with my death or the shipwreck of my reason.

Confident as I am that you will not trifle with this appeal, my heart sinks and my hand trembles at the bare thought of such a possibility. Think of me at this hour, in a strange place, labouring under a blackness of distress that no fancy can exaggerate, and yet well aware that, if you will but punctually serve me, my troubles will roll away like a story that is told. Serve me, my dear Lanyon, and save

Your friend,
H. J.

P.S. – I had already sealed this up when a fresh terror struck upon my soul. It is possible that the post office may fail me, and this letter not come into your hands until tomorrow morning. In that case, dear Lanyon, do my errand when it shall be most convenient for you in the course of the day; and once more expect my messenger at midnight. It may then already be too late; and if that night passes without event, you will know that you have seen the last of Henry Jekyll.

Upon the reading of this letter, I made sure my colleague was insane; but till that was proved beyond the possibility of doubt, I felt bound to do as he requested. The less I understood of this farrago, the less I was in a position to judge of its importance; and an appeal so worded could not be set aside without a grave responsibility. I rose accordingly from table, got into a hansom, and drove straight to Jekyll's house. The butler was awaiting my arrival; he had received by the same post as mine a registered letter of instruction, and had sent at once for a locksmith and a carpenter. The tradesmen came while we were yet speaking; and we moved in a body to old Dr Denman's surgical theatre, from which (as you are doubtless aware) Jekyll's private cabinet is most conveniently entered. The door was very strong, the lock excellent; the carpenter avowed he would have great trouble, and have to do much damage, if force were to be used; and the locksmith was near despair. But this last was a handy fellow, and after two hours' work, the door stood open. The press marked E was unlocked; and I took out the drawer, had it filled up with straw and tied in a sheet, and returned with it to Cavendish Square.

Here I proceeded to examine its contents. The powders were neatly enough made up, but not with the nicety of the dispensing chemist; so that it was plain they were of Jekyll's private manufacture; and when I opened one of the wrappers, I found what seemed to me a simple crystalline salt of a white colour. The phial, to which I next turned my attention, might have been about half full of a blood-red liquor, which was highly pungent to the sense of smell, and seemed to me to contain phosphorus and some volatile ether. At the other ingredients I could make no guess. The book was an ordinary version book, and contained little but a series of dates. These covered a period of many years; but I observed that the entries ceased nearly a year ago, and quite abruptly. Here and there a brief remark was appended to a date, usually no more than a single word: 'double' occurring perhaps six times in a total of several hundred entries; and once very early in the list, and followed by several marks of exclamation, 'total failure!!!' All this, though it whetted my curiosity, told me little that was definite. Here were a phial of some tincture, a paper of some salt, and the record of a series of experiments that had led (like too many of Jekyll's investigations) to no end of practical usefulness. How could the presence of these articles in my house affect either the honour, the sanity, or the life of my flighty colleague? If his messenger could go to one place, why could he not go to another? And even granting some impediment, why was this gentleman to be received by me in secret? The more I reflected, the more convinced I grew that I was dealing with a case of cerebral disease; and though I dismissed my servants to bed, I loaded an old revolver, that I might be found in some posture of self-defence.

Twelve o'clock had scarce rung out over London, ere the knocker sounded very gently on the door. I went myself at the summons, and found a small man crouching against the pillars of the portico.

'Are you come from Dr Jekyll?' I asked.

He told me 'yes' by a constrained gesture; and when I had bidden him enter, he did not obey me without a searching backward glance into the darkness of the square. There was a policeman not far off, advancing with his bull's-eye open; and at the sight, I thought my visitor started and made greater haste.

These particulars struck me, I confess, disagreeably; and as I followed him into the bright light of the consulting-room, I kept my hand ready on my weapon. Here, at last, I had a chance of clearly seeing him. I had never set eyes on him before, so much was certain. He was small, as I have said; I was struck besides with the shocking expression of his face, with his remarkable combination of great muscular activity and great apparent debility of constitution, and – last but not least – with the odd, subjective disturbance caused by his neighbourhood. This bore some resemblance to incipient rigor, and was accompanied by a marked sinking of the pulse. At the time, I set it down to some idiosyncratic, personal distaste, and merely wondered at the acuteness of the symptoms; but I have since had reason to believe the cause to lie much deeper in the nature of man, and to turn on some nobler hinge than the principle of hatred.

This person (who had thus, from the first moment of his entrance, struck in me what I can only describe as a disgustful curiosity) was dressed in a fashion that would have made an ordinary person laughable; his clothes, that is to say, although they were of rich and sober fabric, were enormously too large for him in every measurement – the trousers hanging on his legs and rolled up to keep them from the ground, the waist of the coat below his haunches, and the collar sprawling wide upon his shoulders. Strange to relate, this ludicrous accoutrement was far from moving me to laughter. Rather, as there was something abnormal and misbegotten in the very essence of the creature that now faced me – something seizing, surprising and revolting – this fresh disparity seemed but to fit in with and to reinforce it; so that to my interest in the man's nature and character there was added a curiosity as to his origin, his life, his fortune and status in the world.

These observations, though they have taken so great a space to be set down in, were yet the work of a few seconds. My visitor was, indeed, on fire with sombre excitement.

'Have you got it?' he cried. 'Have you got it?' And so lively was his impatience that he even laid his hand upon my arm and sought to shake me.

I put him back, conscious at his touch of a certain icy pang along my blood. 'Come, sir,' said I. 'You forget that I have not yet the pleasure of your acquaintance. Be seated, if you please.' And I showed him an example, and sat down myself in my customary seat and with as fair an imitation of my ordinary manner to a patient as the lateness of the hour, the nature of my pre-occupations, and the horror I had of my visitor would suffer me to muster.

'I beg your pardon, Dr Lanyon,' he replied, civilly enough, 'What you say is very well founded; and my impatience has shown its heels to my politeness. I come here at the instance of your colleague, Dr Henry Jekyll, on a piece of business of some moment; and I understood . . . ' he paused and put his hand to his throat, and I could see, in spite of his collected manner, that he was wrestling against the approaches of the hysteria – 'I understood, a drawer . . . '

But here I took pity on my visitor's suspense, and some perhaps on my own growing curiosity.

'There it is, sir,' said I, pointing to the drawer, where it lay on the floor behind a table, and still covered with the sheet.

He sprang to it, and then paused, and laid his hand upon his heart; I could hear his teeth grate with the convulsive action of his jaws; and his face was so ghastly to see that I grew alarmed both for his life and reason.

'Compose yourself,' said I.

He turned a dreadful smile to me, and, as if with the decision of despair, plucked away the sheet. At sight of the contents, he uttered one loud sob of such immense relief that I sat petrified. And the next moment, in a voice that was already fairly well under control, 'Have you a graduated glass?' he asked.

I rose from my place with something of an effort, and gave him what he asked.

He thanked me with a smiling nod, measured out a few minims of the red tincture and added one of the powders. The mixture, which was at first of a reddish hue, began, in proportion as the crystals melted, to brighten in colour, to effervesce audibly, and to throw off small fumes of vapour. Suddenly, and at the same moment, the ebullition ceased, and the compound changed to a dark purple, which faded again more slowly to a watery green. My visitor, who had watched these metamorphoses with a keen eye, smiled, set down the glass upon the table, and then turned and looked upon me with an air of scrutiny.

'And now,' said he, 'to settle what remains. Will you be wise? will you be guided? will you suffer me to take this glass in my hand, and to go forth from your house without further parley? or has the greed of curiosity too much command of you? Think before you answer, for it shall be done as you decide. As you decide, you shall be left as you were before, and neither richer nor wiser, unless the sense of service rendered to a man in mortal distress may be counted as a kind of riches of the soul. Or, if you shall so prefer to choose, a new province of knowledge and new avenues to fame and power shall be laid open to you, here, in this room, upon the instant; and your sight shall be blasted by a prodigy to stagger the unbelief of Satan.'

'Sir,' said I, affecting a coolness that I was far from truly possessing, 'you speak enigmas, and you will perhaps not wonder that I hear you with no very strong impression of belief. But I have gone too far in the way of inexplicable services to pause before I see the end.'

'It is well,' replied my visitor. 'Lanyon, you remember your vows: what follows is under the seal of our profession. And now, you who have so long been bound to the most narrow and material views, you who have denied the virtue of transcendental medicine, you who have derided your superiors – behold!'

He put the glass to his lips, and drank at one gulp. A cry followed; he reeled, staggered, clutched at the table and held on, staring with injected eyes, gasping with open mouth; and as I looked, there came, I thought, a change – he seemed to swell – his face became suddenly black, and the features seemed to melt and alter – and the next moment I had sprung to my feet and leaped back against the wall, my arm raised to shield me from that prodigy, my mind submerged in terror.

'O God!' I screamed, and 'O God!' again and again; for there before my eyes – pale and shaken, and half fainting, and groping before him with his hands, like a man restored from death – there stood Henry Jekyll!

What he told me in the next hour I cannot bring my mind to set on paper. I saw what I saw, I heard what I heard, and my soul sickened at it; and yet, now when that sight has faded from my eyes I ask myself if I believe it, and I cannot answer. My life is shaken to its roots; sleep has left me; the deadliest terror sits by me at all hours of the day and night; I feel that my days are numbered, and that I must die; and yet I shall die incredulous. As for the moral turpitude that man unveiled to me, even with tears of penitence, I cannot, even in memory, dwell on it without a start of horror. I will say but one thing, Utterson, and that (if you can bring your mind to credit it) will be more than enough. The creature who crept into my house that night was, on Jekyll's own confession, known by the name of Hyde and hunted for in every corner of the land as the murderer of Carew.

HASTIE LANYON.

Henry Jekyll's Full Statement of the Case

I WAS BORN in the year 18— to a large fortune, endowed besides with excellent parts, inclined by nature to industry, fond of the respect of the wise and good among my fellow-men, and thus, as might have been supposed, with every guarantee of an honourable and distinguished future. And indeed, the worst of my faults was a certain impatient gaiety of disposition, such as has made the happiness of many, but such as I found it hard to reconcile with my imperious desire to carry my head high, and wear a more than commonly grave countenance before the public. Hence it came about that I concealed my pleasures; and that when I reached years of reflection, and began to look round me, and take stock of my progress and position in the world, I stood already committed to a profound duplicity of life. Many a man would have even blazoned such irregularities as I was guilty of; but from the high views that I had set before me, I regarded and hid them with an almost morbid sense of shame. It was thus rather the exacting nature of my aspirations, than any particular degradation in my faults, that made me what I was, and, with even a deeper trench than in the majority of men, severed in me those provinces of good and ill which divide and compound man's dual nature. In this case, I was driven to reflect deeply and inveterately on that hard law of life which lies at the root of religion, and is one of the most plentiful springs of distress. Though so profound a double-dealer, I was in no sense a hypocrite; both sides of me were in dead earnest; I was no more myself when I laid aside restraint and plunged in shame, than when I laboured, in the eye of day, at the furtherance of knowledge or the relief of sorrow and suffering. And it chanced that the direction of my scientific studies, which led wholly towards the mystic and the transcendental, reacted and shed a strong light on this consciousness of the perennial war among my members. With every day, and from both sides of my intelligence, the moral and the intellectual, I thus drew steadily nearer to that truth by whose partial discovery I have been doomed to such a dreadful shipwreck: that man is not truly one, but truly two. I say two, because the state of my own knowledge does not pass beyond that point. Others will follow, others will outstrip me on the same lines; and I hazard the guess that man will be ultimately known for a mere polity of multifarious, incongruous, and independent denizens. I, for my part, from the nature of my life, advanced infallibly in one direction, and in one direction only. It was on the moral side, and in my own person, that I learned to recognise the thorough and primitive duality of man; I saw that, of the two natures that contended in the field of my consciousness, even if I could rightly be said to be either, it was only because I was radically both; and from an early date, even before the course of my scientific discoveries had begun to suggest the most naked possibility of such a miracle, I had learned to dwell with pleasure, as a beloved daydream, on the thought of the separation of these elements. If each, I told myself, could but be housed in separate identities, life would be relieved of all that was unbearable; the unjust might go his way, delivered from the aspirations and remorse of his more upright twin; and the just could walk steadfastly and securely on his upward path, doing the good things in which he found his pleasure, and no longer exposed to disgrace and penitence by the hands of this extraneous evil. It was the curse of mankind that these incongruous faggots were thus bound together – that in the agonised womb of consciousness these polar twins should be continuously struggling. How, then, were they dissociated?

I was so far in my reflections, when, as I have said, a side light began to shine upon the subject from the laboratory table. I began to perceive more deeply than it has ever yet been stated, the trembling immateriality, the mist-like transience, of this seemingly so solid body in which we walk attired. Certain agents I found to have the power to shake and to pluck back that fleshly vestment, even as a wind might toss the curtains of a pavilion. For two good reasons, I will not enter deeply into this scientific branch of my confession. First, because I have been made to learn that the doom and burthen of our life is bound for ever on man's shoulders; and when the attempt is made to cast it off, it but returns upon us with more unfamiliar and more awful pressure. Second, because, as my narrative will make, alas I too evident, my discoveries were incomplete. Enough, then, that I not only recognised my natural body for the mere aura and effulgence of certain of the powers that made up my spirit, but managed to compound a drug by which these powers should be dethroned from their supremacy, and a second form and countenance substituted, none the less natural to me because they were the expression, and bore the stamp, of lower elements in my soul.

I hesitated long before I put this theory to the test of practice. I knew well that I risked death; for any drug that so potently controlled and shook the very fortress of identity, might by the least scruple of an overdose or at the least inopportunity in the moment of exhibition, utterly blot out that immaterial tabernacle which I looked to it to change. But the temptation of a discovery so singular and profound at last overcame the suggestions of alarm. I had long since prepared my tincture; I purchased at once, from a firm of wholesale chemists, a large quantity of a particular salt, which I knew, from my experiments, to be the last ingredient required; and, late one accursed night, I compounded the elements, watched them boil and smoke together in the glass, and when the ebullition had subsided, with a strong glow of courage, drank off the potion.

The most racking pangs succeeded: a grinding in the bones, deadly nausea, and a horror of the spirit that cannot be exceeded at the hour of birth or death. Then these agonies began swiftly to subside, and I came to myself as if out of a great sickness. There was something strange in my sensations, something indescribably new, and, from its very novelty, incredibly sweet. I felt younger, lighter, happier in body; within I was conscious of a heady recklessness, a current of disordered sensual images running like a mill race in my fancy, a solution of the bonds of obligation, an unknown but not an innocent freedom of the soul. I knew myself, at the first breath of this new life, to be more wicked, tenfold more wicked, sold a slave to my original evil; and the thought, in that moment, braced and delighted me like wine. I stretched out my hands, exulting in the freshness of these sensations; and in the act, I was suddenly aware that I had lost in stature.

There was no mirror, at that date, in my room; that which stands beside me as I write was brought there later on, and for the very purpose of those transformations. The night, however, was far gone into the morning – the morning, black as it was, was nearly ripe for the conception of the day – the inmates of my house were locked in the most rigorous hours of slumber; and I determined, flushed as I was with hope and triumph, to venture in my new shape as far as to my bedroom. I crossed the yard, wherein the constellations looked down upon me, I could have thought, with wonder, the first creature of that sort that their unsleeping vigilance had yet disclosed to them; I stole through the corridors, a stranger in my own house; and coming to my room, I saw for the first time the appearance of Edward Hyde.

I must here speak by theory alone, saying not that which I know, but that which I suppose to be most probable. The evil side of my nature, to which I had now transferred the stamping efficacy, was less robust and less developed than the good which I had just deposed. Again, in the course of my life, which had been, after all, nine-tenths a life of effort, virtue and control, it had been much less exercised and much less exhausted. And hence, as I think, it came about that Edward Hyde was so much smaller, slighter, and younger than Henry Jekyll. Even as good shone upon the countenance of the one, evil was written broadly and plainly on the face of the other. Evil besides (which I must still believe to be the lethal side of man) had left on that body an imprint of deformity and decay. And yet when I looked upon that ugly idol in the glass, I was conscious of no repugnance, rather of a leap of welcome. This, too, was myself. It seemed natural and human. In my eyes it bore a livelier image of the spirit, it seemed more express and single, than the imperfect and divided countenance I had been hitherto accustomed to call mine. And in so far I was doubtless right. I have observed that when I wore the semblance of Edward Hyde, none could come near to me at first without a visible misgiving of the flesh. This, as I take it, was because all human beings, as we meet them, are commingled out of good and evil: and Edward Hyde, alone, in the ranks of mankind, was pure evil.

I lingered but a moment at the mirror: the second and conclusive experiment had yet to be attempted; it yet remained to be seen if I had lost my identity beyond redemption and must flee before daylight from a house that was no longer mine: and hurrying back to my cabinet, I once more prepared and drank the cup, once more suffered the pangs of dissolution, and came to myself once more with the character, the stature, and the face of Henry Jekyll.

That night I had come to the fatal cross-roads. Had I approached my discovery in a more noble spirit, had I risked the experiment while under the empire of generous or pious aspirations, all must have been otherwise, and from these agonies of death and birth I had come forth an angel instead of a fiend. The drug had no discriminating action; it was neither diabolical nor divine; it but shook the doors of the prison-house of my disposition; and, like the captives of Philippi, that which stood within ran forth. At that time my virtue slumbered; my evil, kept awake by ambition, was alert and swift to seize the occasion; and the thing that was projected was Edward Hyde. Hence, although I had now two characters as well as two appearances, one was wholly evil, and the other was still the old Henry Jekyll, that incongruous compound of whose reformation and improvement I had already learned to despair. The movement was thus wholly toward the worse.

Even at that time, I had not yet conquered my aversion to the dryness of a life of study. I would still be merrily disposed at times; and as my pleasures were (to say the least) undignified, and I was not only well known and highly considered, but growing towards the elderly man, this incoherency of my life was daily growing more unwelcome. It was on this side that my new power tempted me until I fell in slavery. I had but to drink the cup, to doff at once the body of the noted professor, and to assume, like a thick cloak, that of Edward Hyde. I smiled at the notion; it seemed to me at the time to be humorous; and I made my preparations with the most studious care. I took and furnished that house in Soho to which Hyde was tracked by the police; and engaged as housekeeper a creature whom I well knew to be silent and unscrupulous. On the other side, I announced to my servants that a Mr Hyde (whom I described) was to have full liberty and power about my house in the square; and, to parry mishaps, I even called and made myself a familiar object in my second character. I next drew up that will to which you so much objected; so that if anything befell me in the person of Dr Jekyll, I could enter on that of Edward Hyde without pecuniary loss. And thus fortified, as I supposed, on every side I began to profit by the strange immunities of my position.

Men have before hired bravos to transact their crimes, while their own person and reputation sat under shelter. I was the first that ever did so for his pleasures. I was the first that could thus plod in the public eye with a load of genial respectability, and in a moment, like a schoolboy, strip off these lendings and spring headlong into the sea of liberty. But for me, in my impenetrable mantle, the safety was complete. Think of it – I did not even exist! Let me but escape into my laboratory door, give me but a second or two to mix and swallow the draught that I had always standing ready, and, whatever he had done, Edward Hyde would pass away like the stain of breath upon a mirror; and there in his stead, quietly at home, trimming the midnight lamp in his study, a man who could afford to laugh at suspicion, would be Henry Jekyll.

The pleasures which I made haste to seek in my disguise were, as I have said, undignified; I would scarce use a harder term. But in the hands of Edward Hyde they soon began to turn towards the monstrous. When I would come back from these excursions, I was often plunged into a kind of wonder at my vicarious depravity. This familiar that I called out of my own soul, and sent forth alone to do his good pleasure, was a being inherently malign and villainous; his every act and thought centred on self; drinking pleasure with bestial avidity from any degree of torture to another; relentless like a man of stone. Henry Jekyll stood at times aghast before the acts of Edward Hyde; but the situation was apart from ordinary laws, and insidiously relaxed the grasp of conscience. It was Hyde, after all, and Hyde alone, that was guilty. Jekyll was no worse; he woke again to his good qualities seemingly unimpaired; he would even make haste, where it was possible, to undo the evil done by Hyde. And thus his conscience slumbered.

Into the details of the infamy at which I thus connived (for even now I can scarce grant that I committed it) I have no design of entering. I mean but to point out the warnings and the successive steps with which my chastisement approached. I met with one accident which, as it brought on no consequence, I shall no more than mention. An act of cruelty to a child aroused against me the anger of a passer-by, whom I recognised the other day in the person of your kinsman; the doctor and the child's family joined him; there were moments when I feared for my life; and at last, in order to pacify their too just resentment, Edward Hyde had to bring them to the door, and pay them in a cheque drawn in the name of Henry Jekyll. But this danger was easily eliminated from the future by opening an account at another bank in the name of Edward Hyde himself; and when, by sloping my own hand backwards, I had supplied my double with a signature, I thought I sat beyond the reach of fate.

Some two months before the murder of Sir Danvers, I had been out for one of my adventures, had returned at a late hour, and woke the next day in bed with somewhat odd sensations. It was in vain I looked about me; in vain I saw the decent furniture and tall proportions of my room in the square; in vain that I recognised the pattern of the bed curtains and the design of the mahogany frame; something still kept insisting that I was not where I was, that I had not wakened where I seemed to be, but in the little room in Soho where I was accustomed to sleep in the body of Edward Hyde. I smiled to myself, and, in my psychological way, began lazily to inquire into the elements of this illusion, occasionally, even as I did so, dropping back into a comfortable morning doze. I was still so engaged when, in one of my more wakeful moments, my eye fell upon my hand. Now, the hand of Henry Jekyll (as you have often remarked) was professional in shape and size; it was large, firm, white and comely. But the hand which I now saw, clearly enough in the yellow light of a mid-London morning, lying half shut on the bed-clothes, was lean, corded, knuckly, of a dusky pallor, and thickly shaded with a swart growth of hair. It was the hand of Edward Hyde.

I must have stared upon it for near half a minute, sunk as I was in the mere stupidity of wonder, before terror woke up in my breast as sudden and startling as the crash of cymbals; and bounding from my bed, I rushed to the mirror. At the sight that met my eyes, my blood was changed into something exquisitely thin and icy. Yes, I had gone to bed Henry Jekyll, I had awakened Edward Hyde. How was this to be explained? I asked myself; and then, with another bound of terror – how was it to be remedied? It was well on in the morning; the servants were up; all my drugs were in the cabinet – a long journey, down two pair of stairs, through the back passage, across the open court and through the anatomical theatre, from where I was then standing horror-struck. It might indeed be possible to cover my face; but of what use was that, when I was unable to conceal the alteration in my stature? And then, with an overpowering sweetness of relief, it came back upon my mind that the servants were already used to the coming and going of my second self. I had soon dressed, as well as I was able, in clothes of my own size; had soon passed through the house, where Bradshaw stared and drew back at seeing Mr Hyde at such an hour and in such a strange array; and ten minutes later, Dr Jekyll had returned to his own shape, and was sitting down, with a darkened brow, to make a feint of breakfasting.

Small indeed was my appetite This inexplicable incident, this reversal of my previous experience, seemed, like the Babylonian finger on the wall, to be spelling out the letters of my judgment; and I began to reflect more seriously than ever before on the issues and possibilities of my double existence. That part of me which I had the power of projecting had lately been much exercised and nourished; it had seemed to me of late as though the body of Edward Hyde had grown in stature, as though (when I wore that form) I were conscious of a more generous tide of blood; and I began to spy a danger that, if this were much prolonged, the balance of my nature might be permanently overthrown, the power of voluntary change be forfeited, and the character of Edward Hyde become irrevocably mine. The power of the drug had not been always equally displayed. Once, very early in my career, it had totally failed me; since then I had been obliged on more than one occasion to double, and once, with infinite risk of death, to treble the amount; and these rare uncertainties had cast hitherto the sole shadow on my contentment. Now, however, and in the light of that morning's accident, I was led to remark that whereas, in the beginning, the difficulty had been to throw off the body of Jekyll, it had of late gradually but decidedly transferred itself to the other side. All things therefore seemed to point to this: that I was slowly losing hold of my original and better self, and becoming slowly incorporated with my second and worse.

Between these two I now felt I had to choose. My two natures had memory in common, but all other faculties were most unequally shared between them. Jekyll (who was composite), now with the most sensitive apprehensions, now with a greedy gusto, projected and shared in the pleasures and adventures of Hyde; but Hyde was indifferent to Jekyll, or but remembered him as the mountain bandit remembers the cavern in which he conceals himself from pursuit. Jekyll had more than a father's interest; Hyde had more than a son's indifference. To cast in my lot with Jekyll was to die to those appetites which I had long secretly indulged and had of late begun to pamper. To cast it in with Hyde was to die to a thousand interests and aspirations, and to become, at a blow and for ever, despised and friendless. The bargain might appear unequal; but there was still another consideration in the scales; for while Jekyll would suffer smartingly in the fires of abstinence, Hyde would be not even conscious of all that he had lost. Strange as my circumstances were, the terms of this debate are as old and common-place as man; much the same inducements and alarms cast the die for any tempted and trembling sinner; and it fell out with me, as it falls with so vast a majority of my fellows, that I chose the better part, and was found wanting in the strength to keep to it.

Yes, I preferred the elderly and discontented doctor, surrounded by friends, and cherishing honest hopes; and bade a resolute farewell to the liberty, the comparative youth, the light step, leaping pulses and secret pleasures, that I had enjoyed in the disguise of Hyde. I made this choice perhaps with some unconscious reservation, for I neither gave up the house in Soho, nor destroyed the clothes of Edward Hyde, which still lay ready in my cabinet. For two months, however, I was true to my determination; for two months I led a life of such severity as I had never before attained to, and enjoyed the compensations of an approving conscience. But time began at last to obliterate the freshness of my alarm; the praises of conscience began to grow into a thing of course; I began to be tortured with throes and longings, as of Hyde struggling after freedom; and at last, in an hour of moral weakness, I once again compounded and swallowed the transforming draught.

I do not suppose that when a drunkard reasons with himself upon his vice, he is once out of five hundred times affected by the dangers that he runs through his brutish physical insensibility; neither had I, long as I had considered my position, made enough allowance for the complete moral insensibility and insensate readiness to evil which were the leading characters of Edward Hyde. Yet it was by these that I was punished. My devil had been long caged, he came out roaring. I was conscious, even when I took the draught, of a more unbridled, a more furious propensity to ill. It must have been this, I suppose, that stirred in my soul that tempest of impatience with which I listened to the civilities of my unhappy victim; I declare at least, before God, no man morally sane could have been guilty of that crime upon so pitiful a provocation; and that I struck in no more reasonable spirit than that in which a sick child may break a plaything. But I had voluntarily stripped myself of all those balancing instincts by which even the worst of us continues to walk with some degree of steadiness among temptations; and in my case, to be tempted, however slightly, was to fall.

Instantly the spirit of hell awoke in me and raged. With a transport of glee, I mauled the unresisting body, tasting delight from every blow; and it was not till weariness had begun to succeed that I was suddenly, in the top fit of my delirium, struck through the heart by a cold thrill of terror. A mist dispersed; I saw my life to be forfeit; and fled from the scene of these excesses, at once glorying and trembling, my lust of evil gratified and stimulated, my love of life screwed to the topmost peg. I ran to the house in Soho, and (to make assurance doubly sure) destroyed my papers; thence I set out through the lamplit streets, in the same divided ecstasy of mind, gloating on my crime, light-headedly devising others in the future, and yet still hastening and still harkening in my wake for the steps of the avenger. Hyde had a song upon his lips as he compounded the draught, and as he drank it pledged the dead man. The pangs of transformation had not done tearing him, before Henry Jekyll, with streaming tears of gratitude and remorse, had fallen upon his knees and lifted his clasped hands to God. The veil of self-indulgence was rent from head to foot, I saw my life as a whole: I followed it up from the days of childhood, when I had walked with my father's hand, and through the self-denying toils of my professional life, to arrive again and again, with the same sense of unreality, at the damned horrors of the evening. I could have screamed aloud; I sought with tears and prayers to smother down the crowd of hideous images and sounds with which my memory swarmed against me; and still, between the petitions, the ugly face of my iniquity stared into my soul. As the acuteness of this remorse began to die away, it was succeeded by a sense of joy. The problem of my conduct was solved. Hyde was thenceforth impossible; whether I would or not, I was now confined to the better part of my existence; and, oh, how I rejoiced to think it! with what willing humility I embraced anew the restrictions of natural life! with what sincere renunciation I locked the door by which I had so often gone and come, and ground the key under my heel!

The next day came the news that the murder had been over-looked, that the guilt of Hyde was patent to the world, and that the victim was a man high in public estimation. It was not only a crime, it had been a tragic folly. I think I was glad to know it; I think I was glad to have my better impulses thus buttressed and guarded by the terrors of the scaffold. Jekyll was now my city of refuge; let but Hyde peep out an instant, and the hands of all men would be raised to take and slay him.

I resolved in my future conduct to redeem the past; and I can say with honesty that my resolve was fruitful of some good. You know yourself how earnestly in the last months of last year I laboured to relieve suffering; you know that much was done for others, and that the days passed quietly, almost happily for myself. Nor can I truly say that I wearied of this beneficent and innocent life; I think instead that I daily enjoyed it more completely; but I was still cursed with my duality of purpose; and as the first edge of my penitence wore off, the lower side of me, so long indulged, so recently chained down, began to growl for licence. Not that I dreamed of resuscitating Hyde; the bare idea of that would startle me to frenzy: no, it was in my own person that I was once more tempted to trifle with my conscience; and it was as an ordinary secret sinner that I at last fell before the assaults of temptation.

There comes an end to all things; the most capacious measure is filled at last; and this brief condescension to my evil finally destroyed the balance of my soul. And yet I was not alarmed; the fall seemed natural, like a return to the old days before I had made my discovery. It was a fine, clear January day, wet under foot where the frost had melted, but cloudless overhead; and the Regent's Park was full of winter chirrupings and sweet with spring odours. I sat in the sun on a bench; the animal within me licking the chops of memory; the spiritual side a little drowsed, promising subsequent penitence, but not yet moved to begin. After all, I reflected, I was like my neighbours; and then I smiled, comparing myself with other men, comparing my active goodwill with the lazy cruelty of their neglect. And at the very moment of that vainglorious thought, a qualm came over me, a horrid nausea and the most deadly shuddering. These passed away, and left me faint; and then as in its turn the faintness subsided, I began to be aware of a change in the temper of my thoughts, a greater boldness. a contempt of danger, a solution of the bonds of obligation I looked down; my clothes hung formlessly on my shrunken limbs; the hand that lay on my knee was corded and hairy. I was once more Edward Hyde. A moment before I had been safe of all men's respect, wealthy, beloved – the cloth laying for me in the dining-room at home; and now I was the common quarry of mankind, hunted, houseless, a known murderer, thrall to the gallows.

My reason wavered, but it did not fail me utterly. I have more than once observed that, in my second character, my faculties seemed sharpened to a point and my spirits more tensely elastic; thus it came about that, where Jekyll perhaps might have succumbed, Hyde rose to the importance of the moment. My drugs were in one of the presses of my cabinet: how was I to reach them? That was the problem that (crushing my temples in my hands) I set myself to solve. The laboratory door I had closed. If I sought to enter by the house, my own servants would consign me to the gallows. I saw I must employ another hand, and thought of Lanyon. How was he to be reached? how persuaded? Supposing that I escaped capture in the streets, how was I to make my way into his presence? and how should I, an unknown and displeasing visitor, prevail on the famous physician to rifle the study of his colleague, Dr Jekyll? Then I remembered that of my original character, one part remained to me: I could write my own hand; and once I had conceived that kindling spark, the way that I must follow became lighted up from end to end.

Thereupon, I arranged my clothes as best I could, and summoning a passing hansom, drove to an hotel in Portland Street, the name of which I chanced to remember. At my appearance (which was indeed comical enough, however tragic a fate these garments covered) the driver could not conceal his mirth. I gnashed my teeth upon him with a gust of devilish fury; and the smile withered from his face – happily for him – yet more happily for myself, for in another instant I had certainly dragged him from his perch. At the inn, as I entered, I looked about me with so black a countenance as made the attendants tremble; not a look did they exchange in my presence; but obsequiously took my orders, led me to a private room, and brought me wherewithal to write. Hyde in danger of his life was a creature new to me: shaken with inordinate anger, strung to the pitch of murder, lusting to inflict pain. Yet the creature was astute; mastered his fury with a great effort of the will; composed his two important letters, one to Lanyon and one to Poole, and, that he might receive actual evidence of their being posted, sent them out with directions that they should be registered.

Thenceforward, he sat all day over the fire in the private room, gnawing his nails; there he dined, sitting alone with his fears, the waiter visibly quailing before his eye; and thence, when the night was fully come, he set forth in the corner of a closed cab, and was driven to and fro about the streets of the city. He, I say – I cannot say, I. That child of Hell had nothing human; nothing lived in him but fear and hatred. And when at last, thinking the driver had begun to grow suspicious, he discharged the cab and ventured on foot, attired in his misfitting clothes, an object marked out for observation, into the midst of the nocturnal passengers, these two base passions raged within him like a tempest. He walked fast, hunted by his fears, chattering to himself, skulking through the less frequented thoroughfares, counting the minutes that still divided him from midnight. Once a woman spoke to him, offering, I think, a box of lights. He smote her in the face, and she fled.

When I came to myself at Lanyon's, the horror of my old friend perhaps affected me somewhat: I do not know; it was at least but a drop in the sea to the abhorrence with which I looked back upon these hours. A change had come over me. It was no longer the fear of the gallows, it was the horror of being Hyde that racked me. I received Lanyon's condemnation partly in a dream; it was partly in a dream that I came home to my own house and got into bed. I slept after the prostration of the day, with a stringent and profound slumber which not even the nightmares that wrung me could avail to break. I awoke in the morning shaken, weakened, but refreshed. I still hated and feared the thought of the brute that slept within me, and I had not of course forgotten the appalling dangers of the day before; but I was once more at home, in my own house and close to my drugs; and gratitude for my escape shone so strong in my soul that it almost rivalled the brightness of hope.

I was stepping leisurely across the court after breakfast, drinking the chill of the air with pleasure, when I was seized again with those indescribable sensations that heralded the change; and I had but the time to gain the shelter of my cabinet, before I was once again raging and freezing with the passions of Hyde. It took on this occasion a double dose to recall me to myself; and, alas! six hours after, as I sat looking sadly in the fire, the pangs returned, and the drug had to be re-administered. In short, from that day forth it seemed only by a great effort as of gymnastics, and only under the immediate stimulation of the drug, that I was able to wear the countenance of Jekyll. At all hours of the day and night I would be taken with the premonitory shudder; above all, if I slept, or even dozed for a moment in my chair, it was always as Hyde that I awakened. Under the strain of this continually impending doom and by the sleeplessness to which I now condemned myself, ay, even beyond what I had thought possible to man, I became, in my own person, a creature eaten up and emptied by fever, languidly weak both in body and mind, and solely occupied by one thought: the horror of my other self. But when I slept, or when the virtue of the medicine wore off, I would leap almost without transition (for the pangs of transformation grew daily less marked) into the possession of a fancy brimming with images of terror, a soul boiling with causeless hatreds, and a body that seemed not strong enough to contain the raging energies of life. The powers of Hyde seemed to have grown with the sickliness of Jekyll. And certainly the hate that now divided them was equal on each side. With Jekyll, it was a thing of vital instinct. He had now seen the full deformity of that creature that shared with him some of the phenomena of consciousness, and was co-heir with him to death: and beyond these links of community, which in themselves made the most poignant part of his distress, he thought of Hyde, for all his energy of life, as of something not only hellish but inorganic. This was the shocking thing; that the slime of the pit seemed to utter cries and voices; that the amorphous dust gesticulated and sinned; that what was dead, and had no shape, should usurp the offices of life. And this again, that that insurgent horror was knit to him closer than a wife, closer than an eye; lay caged in his flesh, where he heard it mutter and felt it struggle to be born; and at every hour of weakness, and in the confidence of slumber, prevailed against him, and deposed him out of life. The hatred of Hyde for Jekyll was of a different order. His terror of the gallows drove him continually to commit temporary suicide, and return to his subordinate station of a part instead of a person; but he loathed the necessity, he loathed the despondency into which Jekyll was now fallen, and he resented the dislike with which he was himself regarded. Hence the apelike tricks that he would play me, scrawling in my own hand blasphemies on the pages of my books, burning the letters and destroying the portrait of my father; and indeed, had it not been for his fear of death, he would long ago have ruined himself in order to involve me in the ruin. But his love of life is wonderful; I go further; I, who sicken and freeze at the mere thought of him, when I recall the abjection and passion of this attachment, and when I know how he fears my power to cut him off by suicide, I find it in my heart to pity him.

It is useless, and the time awfully fails me, to prolong this description; no one has ever suffered such torments, let that suffice; and yet even to these, habit brought – no, not alleviation – but a certain callousness of soul, a certain acquiescence of despair; and my punishment might have gone on for years, but for the last calamity which has now fallen, and which has finally severed me from my own face and nature. My provision of the salt, which had never been renewed since the date of the first experiment, began to run low. I sent out for a fresh supply, and mixed the draught; the ebullition followed, and the first change of colour, not the second; I drank it, and it was without efficiency. You will learn from Poole how I have had London ransacked; it was in vain; and I am now persuaded that my first supply was impure, and that it was that unknown impurity which lent efficacy to the draught.

About a week has passed, and I am now finishing this statement under the influence of the last of the old powders. This, then, is the last time, short of a miracle, that Henry Jekyll can think his own thoughts or see his own face (now how sadly altered!) in the glass. Nor must I delay too long to bring my writing to an end; for if my narrative has hitherto escaped destruction, it has been by a combination of great prudence and great good luck. Should the throes of change take me in the act of writing it, Hyde will tear it in pieces; but if some time shall have elapsed after I have laid it by, his wonderful selfishness and circumscription to the moment will probably save it once again from the action of his apelike spite. And indeed the doom that is closing on us both has already changed and crushed him. Half an hour from now, when I shall again and for ever reindue that hated personality, I know how I shall sit shuddering and weeping in my chair, or continue, with the most strained and fear-struck ecstasy of listening, to pace up and down this room (my last earthly refuge) and give ear to every sound of menace. Will Hyde die upon the scaffold? or will he find the courage to release himself at the last moment? God knows; I am careless; this is my true hour of death, and what is to follow concerns another than myself. Here, then, as I lay down the pen, and proceed to seal up my confession, I bring the life of that unhappy Henry Jekyll to an end.

THE MERRY MEN
and Other Stories

THE MERRY MEN

CHAPTER I

Eilean Aros

IT WAS A BEAUTIFUL MORNING in the late July when I set forth on
foot for the last time for Aros. A boat had put me ashore the night
before at Grisapol; I had such breakfast as the little inn afforded, and,
leaving all my baggage till I had an occasion to come round for it by
sea, struck right across the promontory with a cheerful heart.

I was far from being a native of these parts, springing, as I did, from
an unmixed lowland stock. But an uncle of mine, Gordon Darnaway,
after a poor, rough youth, and some years at sea, had married a young
wife in the islands; Mary Maclean she was called, the last of her family;
and when she died in giving birth to a daughter, Aros, the sea-girt farm,
had remained in his possession. It brought him in nothing but the
means of life, as I was well aware; but he was a man whom ill-fortune
had pursued; he feared, cumbered as he was with the young child, to
make a fresh adventure upon life; and remained in Aros, biting his nails
at destiny. Years passed over his head in that isolation, and brought
neither help nor contentment. Meantime our family was dying out in
the lowlands; there is little luck for any of that race; and perhaps my
father was the luckiest of all, for not only was he one of the last to die,
but he left a son to his name and a little money to support it. I was a
student of Edinburgh University, living well enough at my own
charges, but without kith or kin; when some news of me found its way
to Uncle Gordon on the Ross of Grisapol; and he, as he was a man who
held blood thicker than water, wrote to me the day he heard of my
existence, and taught me to count Aros as my home. Thus it was that I
came to spend my vacations in that part of the country, so far from all
society and comfort, between the codfish and the moorcocks; and thus
it was that now, when I had done with my classes, I was returning
thither with so light a heart that July day.

The Ross, as we call it, is a promontory neither wide nor high, but as
rough as God made it to this day; the deep sea on either hand of it, full
of rugged isles and reefs most perilous to seamen – all overlooked from
the eastward by some very high cliffs and the great peak of Ben Kyaw.
The Mountain of the Mist, they say the words signify in the Gaelic
tongue; and it is well named. For that hill-top, which is more than

three thousand feet in height, catches all the clouds that come blowing from the seaward; and, indeed, I used often to think that it must make them for itself; since when all heaven was clear to the sea level, there would ever be a streamer on Ben Kyaw. It brought water, too, and was mossy* to the top in consequence. I have seen us sitting in broad sunshine on the Ross, and the rain falling black like crape upon the mountain. But the wetness of it made it often appear more beautiful to my eyes; for when the sun struck upon the hill sides, there were many wet rocks and watercourses that shone like jewels even as far as Aros, fifteen miles away.

The road that I followed was a cattle-track. It twisted so as nearly to double the length of my journey; it went over rough boulders so that a man had to leap from one to another, and through soft bottoms where the moss came nearly to the knee. There was no cultivation anywhere, and not one house in the ten miles from Grisapol to Aros. Houses of course there were – three at least; but they lay so far on the one side or the other that no stranger could have found them from the track. A large part of the Ross is covered with big granite rocks, some of them larger than a two-roomed house, one beside another, with fern and deep heather in between them where the vipers breed. Anyway the wind was, it was always sea air, as salt as on a ship; the gulls were as free as moorfowl over all the Ross; and whenever the way rose a little, your eye would kindle with the brightness of the sea. From the very midst of the land, on a day of wind and a high spring, I have heard the Roost roaring like a battle where it runs by Aros, and the great and fearful voices of the breakers that we call the Merry Men.

Aros itself – Aros Jay, I have heard the natives call it, and they say it means *The House of God* – Aros itself was not properly a piece of the Ross, nor was it quite an islet. It formed the south-west corner of the land, fitted close to it, and was in one place only separated from the coast by a little gut of the sea not forty feet across the narrowest. When the tide was full, this was clear and still, like a pool on a land river; only there was a difference in the weeds and fishes, and the water itself was green instead of brown; but when the tide went out, in the bottom of the ebb, there was a day or two in every month when you could pass dryshod from Aros to the mainland. There was some good pasture, where my uncle fed the sheep he lived on; perhaps the feed was better because the ground rose higher on the islet than the main level of the Ross, but this I am not skilled enough to settle. The house was a good one for that country, two storeys high. It looked westward over a bay,

* Boggy

with a pier hard by for a boat, and from the door you could watch the vapours blowing on Ben Kyaw.

On all this part of the coast, and especially near Aros, these great granite rocks that I have spoken of go down together in troops into the sea, like cattle on a summer's day. There they stand, for all the world like their neighbours ashore; only the salt water sobbing between them instead of the quiet earth, and clots of sea-pink blooming on their sides instead of heather; and the great sea conger to wreathe about the base of them instead of the poisonous viper of the land. On calm days you can go wandering between them in a boat for hours, echoes following you about the labyrinth; but when the sea is up, Heaven help the man that hears that cauldron boiling.

Off the south-west end of Aros these blocks are very many, and much greater in size. Indeed, they must grow monstrously bigger out to sea, for there must be ten sea miles of open water sown with them as thick as a country place with houses, some standing thirty feet above the tides, some covered, but all perilous to ships; so that on a clear, westerly blowing day I have counted from the top of Aros, the great rollers breaking white and heavy over as many as six-and-forty buried reefs. But it is nearer in shore that the danger is worst; for the tide, here running like a mill race, makes a long belt of broken water – a *Roost* we call it – at the tail of the land. I have often been out there in a dead calm at the slack of the tide; and a strange place it is, with the sea swirling and combing up and boiling like the cauldrons of a linn, and now and again a little dancing mutter of sound as though the *Roost* were talking to itself. But when the tide begins to run again, and above all in heavy weather, there is no man could take a boat within half a mile of it, nor a ship afloat that could either steer or live in such a place. You can hear the roaring of it six miles away. At the seaward end there comes the strongest of the bubble; and it's here that these big breakers dance together – the dance of death, it may be called – that have got the name, in these parts, of the Merry Men. I have heard it said that they run fifty feet high; but that must be the green water only, for the spray runs twice as high as that. Whether they got the name from their movements, which are swift and antic, or from the shouting they make about the turn of the tide, so that all Aros shakes with it, is more than I can tell.

The truth is, that in a south-westerly wind, that part of our archipelago is no better than a trap. If a ship got through the reefs, and weathered the Merry Men, it would be to come ashore on the south coast of Aros, in Sandag Bay, where so many dismal things befell our family, as I propose to tell. The thought of all these dangers, in the place I knew so long, makes me particularly welcome the works now going forward to set lights upon the headlands and buoys along the channels of our iron-bound, inhospitable islands.

The country people had many a story about Aros, as I used to hear from my uncle's man, Rorie, an old servant of the Macleans, who had transferred his services without afterthought on the occasion of the marriage. There was some tale of an unlucky creature, a sea-kelpie, that dwelt and did business in some fearful manner of his own among the boiling breakers of the Roost. A mermaid had once met a piper on Sandag beach, and there sang to him a long, bright midsummer's night, so that in the morning he was found stricken crazy, and from thenceforward, till the day he died, said only one form of words; what they were in the original Gaelic I cannot tell, but they were thus translated: 'Ah, the sweet singing out of the sea.' Seals that haunted on that coast have been known to speak to man in his own tongue, presaging great disasters. It was here that a certain saint first landed on his voyage out of Ireland to convert the Hebrideans. And, indeed, I think he had some claim to be called saint; for, with the boats of that past age, to make so rough a passage, and land on such a ticklish coast, was surely not far short of the miraculous. It was to him, or to some of his monkish underlings who had a cell there, that the islet owes its holy and beautiful name, the House of God.

Among these old wives' stories there was one which I was inclined to hear with more credulity. As I was told, in that tempest which scattered the ships of the Invincible Armada over all the north and west of Scotland, one great vessel came ashore on Aros, and before the eyes of some solitary people on a hill-top, went down in a moment with all hands, her colours flying even as she sank. There was some likelihood in this tale; for another of that fleet lay sunk on the north side, twenty miles from Grisapol. It was told, I thought, with more detail and gravity than its companion stories, and there was one particularity which went far to convince me of its truth: the name, that is, of the ship was still remembered, and sounded, in my ears, Spanishly. The *Espirito Santo* they called it, a great ship of many decks of guns, laden with treasure and grandees of Spain, and fierce soldadoes, that now lay fathoms deep to all eternity, done with her wars and voyages, in Sandag Bay, upon the west of Aros. No more salvos of ordnance for that tall ship, the 'Holy Spirit,' no more fair winds or happy ventures; only to rot there deep in the sea-tangle and hear the shoutings of the Merry Men as the tide ran high about the island. It was a strange thought to me first and last, and only grew stranger as I learned the more of Spain, from which she had set sail with so proud a company, and King Philip, the wealthy king, that sent her on that voyage.

And now I must tell you, as I walked from Grisapol that day, the *Espirito Santo* was very much in my reflections. I had been favourably remarked by our then Principal in Edinburgh College, that famous writer, Dr Robertson, and by him had been set to work on some papers of an ancient date to rearrange and sift of what was worthless; and in one of these, to my great wonder, I found a note of this very ship, the *Espirito Santo*, with her captain's name, and how she carried a great part of the Spaniard's treasure, and had been lost upon the Ross of Grisapol; but in what particular spot, the wild tribes of that place and period would give no information to the king's inquiries. Putting one thing with another, and taking our island tradition together with this note of old King Jamie's perquisitions after wealth, it had come strongly on my mind that the spot for which he sought in vain could be no other than the small bay of Sandag on my uncle's land; and being a fellow of a mechanical turn, I had ever since been plotting how to weigh that good ship up again with all her ingots, ounces, and doubloons, and bring back our house of Darnaway to its long-forgotten dignity and wealth.

This was a design of which I soon had reason to repent. My mind was sharply turned on different reflections; and since I became the witness of a strange judgment of God's, the thought of dead men's treasures had been intolerable to my conscience. But even at that time I must acquit myself of sordid greed; for if I desired riches, it was not for their own sake, but for the sake of a person who was dear to my heart – my uncle's daughter, Mary Ellen. She had been educated well, and had been a time to school upon the mainland; which, poor girl, she would have been happier without. For Aros was no place for her, with old Rorie the servant, and her father, who was one of the unhappiest men in Scotland, plainly bred up in a country place among Cameronians, long a skipper sailing out of the Clyde about the islands, and now, with infinite discontent, managing his sheep and a little 'long-shore fishing for the necessary bread. If it was sometimes weariful to me, who was there but a month or two, you may fancy what it was to her who dwelt in that same desert all the year round, with the sheep and flying sea-gulls, and the Merry Men singing and dancing in the Roost!

CHAPTER II

What the Wreck had brought to Aros

IT WAS HALF-FLOOD when I got the length of Aros; and there was nothing for it but to stand on the far shore and whistle for Rorie with the boat. I had no need to repeat the signal. At the first sound, Mary was at the door flying a handkerchief by way of answer, and the old long-legged serving-man was shambling down the gravel to the pier. For all his hurry, it took him a long while to pull across the bay; and I observed him several times to pause, go into the stern, and look over curiously into the wake. As he came nearer, he seemed to me aged and haggard, and I thought he avoided my eye. The coble had been repaired, with two new thwarts and several patches of some rare and beautiful foreign wood, the name of it unknown to me.

'Why, Rorie,' said I, as we began the return voyage, 'this is fine wood. How came you by that?'

'It will be hard to chessel,' Rorie opined reluctantly; and just then, dropping the oars, he made another of those dives into the stern which I had remarked as he came across to fetch me, and, leaning his hand on my shoulder, stared with an awful look into the waters of the bay.

'What is wrong?' I asked, a good deal startled.

'It will be a great feesh,' said the old man, returning to his oars; and nothing more could I get out of him, but strange glances and an ominous nodding of the head. In spite of myself, I was infected with a measure of uneasiness; I turned also, and studied the wake. The water was still and transparent, but, out here in the middle of the bay, exceeding deep. For some time I could see naught; but at last it did seem to me as if something dark – a great fish, or perhaps only a shadow – followed studiously in the track of the moving coble. And then I remembered one of Rorie's superstitions: how in a ferry in Morven, in some great, exterminating feud among the clans, a fish, the like of it unknown in all our waters, followed for some years the passage of the ferry-boat, until no man dared to make the crossing.

'He will be waiting for the right man,' said Rorie.

Mary met me on the beach, and led me up the brae and into the house of Aros. Outside and inside there were many changes. The garden was fenced with the same wood that I had noted in the boat; there were chairs in the kitchen covered with strange brocade; curtains of brocade hung from the window; a clock stood silent on the dresser: a lamp of brass was swinging from the roof; the table was set for dinner with the finest of linen and silver; and all these new riches were displayed in the plain old kitchen that I knew so well, with the high-backed settle, and the stools, and the closet bed for Rorie; with the wide chimney the sun shone into, and the clear-smouldering peats; with the pipes on the mantelshelf and the three-cornered spittoons, filled with sea-shells instead of sand, on the floor; with the bare stone walls and bare wooden floor, and the three patchwork rugs that were of yore its sole adornment – poor man's patchwork, the like of it unknown in cities, woven with homespun, and Sunday black, and sea-cloth polished on the bench of rowing. The room, like the house, had been a sort of wonder in that countryside, it was so neat and habitable; and to see it now, shamed by these incongruous additions, filled me with indignation and a kind of anger. In view of the errand I had come upon to Aros, the feeling was baseless and unjust; but it burned high, at the first moment, in my heart.

'Mary, girl,' said I, 'this is the place I had learned to call my home, and I do not know it.'

'It is my home by nature, not by the learning,' she replied; 'the place I was born and the place I'm like to die in; and I neither like these changes, nor the way they came, nor that which came with them. I would have liked better, under God's pleasure, they had gone down into the sea, and the Merry Men were dancing on them now.'

Mary was always serious; it was perhaps the only trait that she shared with her father; but the tone with which she uttered these words was even graver than of custom.

'Ay,' said I, 'I feared it came by wreck, and that's by death; yet when my father died, I took his goods without remorse.'

'Your father died a clean strae death, as the folk say,' said Mary.

'True,' I returned; 'and a wreck is like a judgment. What was she called?'

'They ca'd her the *Christ-Anna*,' said a voice behind me; and, turning round, I saw my uncle standing in the doorway.

He was a sour, small, bilious man, with a long face and very dark eyes; fifty-six years old, sound and active in body, and with an air somewhat between that of a shepherd and that of a man following the sea. He never laughed, that I heard; read long at the Bible; prayed much, like the Cameronians he had been brought up among; and indeed, in many ways, used to remind me of one of the hill-preachers in the killing times before the Revolution. But he never got much comfort, nor even, as I used to think, much guidance, by his piety. He had his black fits when he was afraid of hell; but he had led a rough life, to which he would look back with envy, and was still a rough, cold, gloomy man.

As he came in at the door out of the sunlight, with his bonnet on his head, and a pipe hanging in his button-hole, he seemed, like Rorie, to have grown older and paler, the lines were deeplier ploughed upon his face, and the whites of his eyes were yellow, like old stained ivory, or the bones of the dead.

'Ay,' he repeated, dwelling upon the first part of the word, 'the *Christ-Anna*. It's an awfu' name.'

I made him my salutations, and complimented him upon his look of health; for I feared he had perhaps been ill.

'I'm in the body,' he replied, ungraciously enough; 'aye in the body and the sins of the body, like yoursel'. Denner,' he said abruptly to Mary, and then ran on to me: 'They're grand braws, thir that we hae gotten, are they no? Yon's a bonny knock,* but it'll no gang; and the napery's by ordnar. Bonny, bairnly braws; it's for the like o' them folk sells the peace of God that passeth understanding; it's for the like o' them, an' maybe no even sae muckle worth, folk daunton God to His face and burn in muckle hell; and it's for that reason the Scripture ca's them, as I read the passage, the accursed thing. Mary, ye girzie,' he interrupted himself to cry with some asperity, 'what for hae ye no put out the twa candlesticks?'

'Why should we need them at high noon?' she asked.

But my uncle was not to be turned from his idea. 'We'll bruik† them while we may,' he said; and so two massive candlesticks of wrought silver were added to the table equipage, already so unsuited to that rough sea-side farm.

'She cam' ashore Februar' 10, about ten at nicht,' he went on to me. 'There was nae wind, and a sair run o' sea; and she was in the sook o' the Roost, as I jaloose. We had seen her a' day, Rorie and me, beating to the wind. She wasnae a handy craft, I'm thinking, that *Christ-Anna*; for she would neither steer nor stey wi' them. A sair day they had of it; their hands was never aff the sheets, and it perishin' cauld – ower cauld to snaw; and aye they would get a bit nip o' wind, and awa' again, to pit the emp'y hope into them. Eh, man! but they had a sair day for the last o't! He would have had a prood, prood heart hat won ashore upon the back o' that.'

'And were all lost?' I cried. 'God help them!'

'Wheesht!' he said sternly. 'Nane shall pray for the deid on my hearth-stane.'

* Clock. † Enjoy.

I disclaimed a Popish sense for my ejaculation; and he seemed to accept my disclaimer with unusual facility, and ran on once more upon what had evidently become a favourite subject.

'We fand her in Sandag Bay, Rorie an' me, and a' thae braws in the inside of her. There's a kittle bit, ye see, about Sandag; whiles the sook rins strong for the Merry Men; an' whiles again, when the tide's makin' hard an' ye can hear the Roost blawin' at the far-end of Aros, there comes a back-spang of current straucht into Sandag Bay. Weel, there's the thing that got the grip on the *Christ-Anna*. She but to have come in ram-stam an' stern forrit; for the bows of her are aften under, and the back-side of her is clear at hie-water o' neaps. But, man! the dunt that she cam' doon wi' when she struck! Lord save us a'! but it's an unco life to be a sailor – a cauld, wanchancy life. Mony's the gliff I got mysel' in the great deep; and why the Lord should hae made yon unco water is mair than ever I could win to understand. He made the vales and the pastures, the bonny green yaird, the halesome, canty land –

> And now they shout and sing to Thee,
> For Thou hast made them glad,

as the Psalms say in the metrical version. No that I would preen my faith to that clink neither; but it's bonny, and easier to mind. 'Who go to sea in ships,' they hae't again –

> And in
> Great waters trading be,
> Within the deep these men God's works
> And His great wonders see.

Weel, it's easy sayin' sae. Maybe Dauvit wasnae very weel acquant wi' the sea. But, troth, if it wasnae prentit in the Bible, I wad whiles be temp'it to think it wasnae the Lord, but the muckle, black deil that made the sea. There's naething good comes oot o't but the fish; an' the spentacle o' God riding on the tempest, to be shüre, whilk would be what Dauvit was likely ettling at. But, man, they were sair wonders that God showed to the *Christ-Anna* – wonders, do I ca' them? Judgments, rather: judgments in the mirk nicht among the draygons o' the deep. And their souls – to think o' that – their souls, man, maybe no prepared! The sea – a muckle yett to hell!'

I observed, as my uncle spoke, that his voice was unnaturally moved and his manner unwontedly demonstrative. He leaned forward at these last words, for example, and touched me on the knee with his spread

fingers, looking up into my face with a certain pallor, and I could see
that his eyes shone with a deep-seated fire, and that the lines about his
mouth were drawn and tremulous.

Even the entrance of Rorie, and the beginning of our meal, did not
detach him from his train of thought beyond a moment. He conde-
scended, indeed, to ask me some questions as to my success at college,
but I thought it was with half his mind; and even in his extempore
grace, which was, as usual, long and wandering, I could find the trace of
his preoccupation, praying, as he did, that God would 'remember in
mercy fower puir, feckless, fiddling, sinful creatures here by their lee-
lane beside the great and dowie waters.'

Soon there came an interchange of speeches between him and Rorie.

'Was it there?' asked my uncle.

'Ou, ay!' said Rorie.

I observed that they both spoke in a manner of aside, and with some
show of embarrassment, and that Mary herself appeared to colour, and
looked down on her plate. Partly to show my knowledge, and so relieve
the party from an awkward strain, partly because I was curious, I
pursued the subject.

'You mean the fish?' I asked.

'Whatten fish?' cried my uncle. 'Fish, quo' he! Fish! Your een are fu'
o' fatness, man; your heid dozened wi' carnal leir. Fish! it's a bogle!'

He spoke with great vehemence, as though angry; and perhaps I was
not very willing to be put down so shortly, for young men are
disputatious. At least I remember I retorted hotly, crying out upon
childish superstitions.

'And ye come frae the College!' sneered Uncle Gordon. 'Gude kens
what they learn folk there; it's no muckle service onyway. Do ye think,
man, that there's naething in a' yon saut wilderness o' a world oot wast
there, wi' the sea grasses growin', an' the sea beasts fechtin', an' the sun
glintin' down into it, day by day? Na; the sea's like the land, but
fearsomer. If there's folk ashore, there's folk in the sea – deid they may
be, but they're folk whatever; and as for deils, there's nane that's like the
sea deils. There's no sae muckle harm in the land deils, when a's said
and done. Lang syne, when I was a callant in the south country, I mind
there was an auld, bald bogle in the Peewie Moss. I got a glisk o' him
mysel' sittin' on his hunkers in a hag, as gray's a tombstane. An', troth,
he was a fearsome-like taed. But he steered naebody. Nae doobt, if ane
that was a reprobate, ane the Lord hated, had gane by there wi' his sin
still upon his stamach, nae doobt the creature would hae lowped upo'
the likes o' him. But there's deils in the deep sea would yoke on a
communicant! Eh, sirs, if ye had gane doon wi' the puir lads in the

Christ-Anna, ye would ken by now the mercy o' the seas. If ye had sailed it for as lang as me, ye would hate the thocht of it as I do. If ye had but used the een God gave ye, ye would hae learned the wickedness o' that fause, saut, cauld, bullering creature, and of a' that's in it by the Lord's permission: labsters an' partans, an' sic like, howking in the deid; muckle, gutsy, blawing whales; an' fish – the hale clan o' them – cauld-wamed, blind-eed uncanny ferlies. O, sirs,' he cried, 'the horror – the horror o' the sea!'

We were all somewhat staggered by this outburst; and the speaker himself, after that last hoarse apostrophe, appeared to sink gloomily into his own thoughts. But Rorie, who was greedy of superstitious lore, recalled him to the subject by a question.

'You will not ever have seen a teevil of the sea?' he asked.

'No clearly,' replied the other. 'I misdoobt if a mere man could see ane clearly and conteenue in the body. I hae sailed wi' a lad – they ca'd him Sandy Gabart; he saw ane, shüre eneuch, an' shüre eneuch it was the end of him. We were seeven days oot frae the Clyde, – a sair wark we had had – gaun north wi' seeds an' braws an' things for the Macleod. We had got in ower near under the Cutchull'ns, an' had just gane about by Soa, an' were off on a lang tack, we thocht would maybe hauld as far's Copnahow. I mind the nicht weel; a mune smoored wi' mist; a fine gaun breeze upon the water, but no steedy; an' – what nane o' us likit to hear – anither wund gurlin' owerheid, amang thae fearsome, auld stane craigs o' the Cutchull'ns. Weel, Sandy was forrit wi' the jib sheet; we couldnae see him for the mains'l, that had just begude to draw, when a' at ance he gied a skirl. I luffed for my life, for I thocht we were ower near Soa; but na, it wasnae that, it was puir Sandy Gabart's deid skreigh, or near hand, for he was deid in half an hour. A't he could tell was that a sea deil, or sea bogle, or sea spenster, or sic-like, had clum up by the bowsprit, an' gi'en him ae cauld, uncanny look. An', or the life was oot o' Sandy's body, we kent weel what the thing betokened, and why the wund gurled in the taps o' the Cutchull'ns; for doon it cam' – a wund do I ca' it! it was the wund o' the Lord's anger – an' a' that nicht we foucht like men dementit, and the niest that we kenned we were ashore in Loch Uskevagh, an' the cocks were crawing in Benbecula.'

'It will have been a merman,' Rorie said.

'A merman!' screamed my uncle with immeasurable scorn. 'Auld wives' clavers! There's nae sic things as mermen.'

'But what was the creature like?' I asked.

'What like was it? Gude forbid that we suld ken what like it was! It had a kind of a heid upon it – man could say nae mair.'

Then Rorie, smarting under the affront, told several tales of mermen, mermaids, and sea-horses that had come ashore upon the islands and attacked the crews of boats upon the sea; and my uncle, in spite of his incredulity, listened with uneasy interest.

'Aweel, aweel,' he said, 'it may be sae; I may be wrang; but I find nae word o' mermen in the Scriptures.'

'And you will find nae word of Aros Roost, maybe,' objected Rorie, and his argument appeared to carry weight.

When dinner was over, my uncle carried me forth with him to a bank behind the house. It was a very hot and quiet afternoon; scarce a ripple anywhere upon the sea, nor any voice but the familiar voice of sheep and gulls; and perhaps in consequence of this repose in nature, my kinsman showed himself more rational and tranquil than before. He spoke evenly and almost cheerfully of my career, with every now and then a reference to the lost ship or the treasures it had brought to Aros. For my part, I listened to him in a sort of trance, gazing with all my heart on that remembered scene, and drinking gladly the sea-air and the smoke of peats that had been lit by Mary.

Perhaps an hour had passed when my uncle, who had all the while been covertly gazing on the surface of the little bay, rose to his feet and bade me follow his example. Now I should say that the great run of tide at the south-west end of Aros exercises a perturbing influence round all the coast. In Sandag Bay, to the south, a strong current runs at certain periods of the flood and ebb respectively; but in this northern bay – Aros Bay, as it is called – where the house stands and on which my uncle was now gazing, the only sign of disturbance is towards the end of the ebb, and even then it is too slight to be remarkable. When there is any swell, nothing can be seen at all; but when it is calm, as it often is, there appear certain strange, undecipherable marks – sea-runes, as we may name them – on the glassy surface of the bay. The like is common in a thousand places on the coast; and many a boy must have amused himself as I did, seeking to read in them some reference to himself or those he loved. It was to these marks that my uncle now directed my attention, struggling, as he did so, with an evident reluctance.

'Do ye see yon scart upo' the water?' he inquired; 'yon ane wast the gray stane? Ay? Weel, it'll no be like a letter, wull it?'

'Certainly it is,' I replied. 'I have often remarked it. It is like a C.'

He heaved a sigh as if heavily disappointed with my answer, and then added below his breath: 'Ay, for the *Christ-Anna*.'

'I used to suppose, sir, it was for myself,' said I; 'for my name is Charles.'

'And so ye saw't afore?' he ran on, not heeding my remark. 'Weel,

weel, but that's unco strange. Maybe, it's been there waitin', as a man wad say, through a' the weary ages. Man, but that's awfu'.' And then, breaking off: 'Ye'll no see anither, will ye?' he asked.

'Yes,' said I. 'I see another very plainly, near the Ross side, where the road comes down – an M.'

'An M,' he repeated, very low; and then, again after another pause: 'An' what wad ye make o' that?' he inquired.

'I had always thought it to mean Mary, sir,' I answered, growing somewhat red, convinced as I was in my own mind that I was on the threshold of a decisive explanation.

But we were each following his own train of thought to the exclusion of the other's. My uncle once more paid no attention to my words; only hung his head and held his peace; and I might have been led to fancy that he had not heard me, if his next speech had not contained a kind of echo from my own.

'I would say naething o' thae clavers to Mary,' he observed, and began to walk forward.

There is a belt of turf along the side of Aros Bay where walking is easy; and it was along this that I silently followed my silent kinsman. I was perhaps a little disappointed at having lost so good an opportunity to declare my love; but I was at the same time far more deeply exercised at the change that had befallen my uncle. He was never an ordinary, never, in the strict sense, an amiable, man; but there was nothing in even the worst that I had known of him before, to prepare me for so strange a transformation. It was impossible to close the eyes against one fact; that he had, as the saying goes, something on his mind; and as I mentally ran over the different words which might be represented by the letter M – misery, mercy, marriage, money, and the like – I was arrested with a sort of start by the word murder. I was still considering the ugly sound and fatal meaning of the word, when the direction of our walk brought us to a point from which a view was to be had to either side, back towards Aros Bay and homestead, and forward on the ocean, dotted to the north with isles, and lying to the southward blue and open to the sky. There my guide came to a halt, and stood staring for awhile on that expanse. Then he turned to me and laid a hand on my arm.

'Ye think there's naething there?' he said, pointing with his pipe; and then cried out aloud, with a kind of exultation: 'I'll tell ye, man! The deid are down there – thick like rattons!'

He turned at once, and, without another word, we retraced our steps to the house of Aros.

I was eager to be alone with Mary; yet it was not till after supper, and then but for a short while, that I could have a word with her. I lost no time beating about the bush, but spoke out plainly what was on my mind.

'Mary,' I said, 'I have not come to Aros without a hope. If that should prove well founded, we may all leave and go somewhere else, secure of daily bread and comfort; secure, perhaps, of something far beyond that, which it would seem extravagant in me to promise. But there's a hope that lies nearer to my heart than money.' And at that I paused. 'You can guess fine what that is, Mary,' I said. She looked away from me in silence, and that was small encouragement, but I was not to be put off. 'All my days I have thought the world of you,' I continued; 'the time goes on and I think always the more of you; I could not think to be happy or hearty in my life without you: you are the apple of my eye.' Still she looked away, and said never a word; but I thought I saw that her hands shook. 'Mary,' I cried in fear, 'do ye no like me?'

'O, Charlie man,' she said, 'is this a time to speak of it? Let me be, a while; let me be the way I am; it'll not be you that loses by the waiting!'

I made out by her voice that she was nearly weeping, and this put me out of any thought but to compose her. 'Mary Ellen,' I said, 'say no more: I did not come to trouble you: your way shall be mine, and your time too; and you have told me all I wanted. Only just this one thing more: what ails you?'

She owned it was her father, but would enter into no particulars, only shook her head, and said he was not well and not like himself, and it was a great pity. She knew nothing of the wreck. 'I havenae been near it,' said she. 'What for would I go near it, Charlie lad? The poor souls are gone to their account long syne; and I would just have wished they had ta'en their gear with them – poor souls!'

This was scarcely any great encouragement for me to tell her of the *Espirito Santo*; yet I did so, and at the very first word she cried out in surprise. 'There was a man at Grisapol,' she said, 'in the month of May – a little, yellow, black-avised body, they tell me, with gold rings upon his fingers, and a beard; and he was speiring high and low for that same ship.'

It was towards the end of April that I had been given these papers to sort out by Dr Robertson: and it came suddenly back upon my mind that they were thus prepared for a Spanish historian, or a man calling himself such, who had come with high recommendations to the Principal, on a mission of inquiry as to the dispersion of the great Armada. Putting one thing with another, I fancied that the visitor 'with the gold rings upon his fingers' might be the same with Dr Robertson's historian from Madrid. If that were so, he would be more likely after treasure for himself than information for a learned society. I made up my mind, I should lose no time over my undertaking; and if the ship lay sunk in Sandag Bay, as perhaps both he and I supposed, it should not be for the advantage of this ringed adventurer, but for Mary and myself, and for the good, old, honest, kindly family of the Darnaways.

CHAPTER III

Land and Sea in Sandag Bay

I WAS EARLY AFOOT next morning; and as soon as I had a bite to eat, set forth upon a tour of exploration. Something in my heart distinctly told me that I should find the ship of the Armada; and although I did not give way entirely to such hopeful thoughts, I was still very light in spirits and walked upon air. Aros is a very rough islet, its surface strewn with great rocks and shaggy with fern and heather, and my way lay almost north and south across the highest knoll, and though the whole distance was inside of two miles, it took more time and exertion than four upon a level road. Upon the summit I paused. Although not very high – not three hundred feet, as I think – it yet out-tops all the neighbouring lowlands of the Ross, and commands a great view of sea and islands. The sun, which had been up some time, was already hot upon my neck; the air was listless and thundery, although purely clear; away over the north-west, where the isles lie thickliest congregated, some half a dozen small and ragged clouds hung together in a covey; and the head of Ben Kyaw wore, not merely a few streamers, but a solid hood of vapour. There was a threat in the weather. The sea, it is true, was smooth like glass: even the Roost was but a seam on that wide mirror, and the Merry Men no more than caps of foam; but to my eye and ear, so long familiar with these places, the sea also seemed to lie uneasily; a sound of it, like a long sigh, mounted to me where I stood; and, quiet as it was, the Roost itself appeared to be revolving mischief. For I ought to say that all we dwellers in these parts attributed, if not prescience, at least a quality of warning, to that strange and dangerous creature of the tides.

I hurried on, then, with the greater speed, and had soon descended the slope of Aros to the part that we call Sandag Bay. It is a pretty large piece of water compared with the size of the isle; well sheltered from all but the prevailing wind; sandy and shoal and bounded by low sand-hills to the west, but to the eastward lying several fathoms deep along a ledge of rocks. It is upon that side that, at a certain time each flood, the current mentioned by my uncle sets so strong into the bay; a little later, when the Roost begins to work higher, an undertow runs still more strongly in the reverse direction; and it is the action of this last, as I suppose, that has scoured that part so deep. Nothing is to be seen out of Sandag Bay but one small segment of the horizon and, in heavy weather, the breakers flying high over a deep sea reef.

From half-way down the hill, I had perceived the wreck of February last, a brig of considerable tonnage, lying, with her back broken, high and dry on the east corner of the sands; and I was making directly towards it, and already almost on the margin of the turf, when my eyes were suddenly arrested by a spot, cleared of fern and heather, and marked by one of those long, low, and almost human-looking mounds that we see so commonly in graveyards. I stopped like a man shot. Nothing had been said to me of any dead man or interment on the island; Rorie, Mary, and my uncle had all equally held their peace; of her at least, I was certain that she must be ignorant; and yet here, before my eyes, was proof indubitable of the fact. Here was a grave; and I had to ask myself, with a chill, what manner of man lay there in his last sleep, awaiting the signal of the Lord in that solitary, sea-beat resting-place? My mind supplied no answer but what I feared to entertain. Shipwrecked, at least, he must have been; perhaps, like the old Armada mariners, from some far and rich land oversea; or perhaps one of my own race, perishing within eyesight of the smoke of home. I stood awhile uncovered by his side, and I could have desired that it had lain in our religion to put up some prayer for that unhappy stranger, or, in the old classic way, outwardly to honour his misfortune. I knew, although his bones lay there, a part of Aros, till the trumpet sounded, his imperishable soul was forth and far away, among the raptures of the everlasting Sabbath or the pangs of hell; and yet my mind misgave me even with a fear, that perhaps he was near me where I stood, guarding his sepulchre, and lingering on the scene of his unhappy fate.

Certainly it was with a spirit somewhat overshadowed that I turned away from the grave to the hardly less melancholy spectacle of the wreck. Her stem was above the first arc of the flood; she was broken in two a little abaft the foremast – though indeed she had none, both masts having broken short in her disaster; and as the pitch of the beach was very sharp and sudden, and the bows lay many feet below the stern, the fracture gaped widely open, and you could see right through her poor hull upon the farther side. Her name was much defaced, and I could not make out clearly whether she was called *Christiania*, after the Norwegian city, or *Christiana*, after the good woman, Christian's wife, in that old book the *Pilgrim's Progress*. By her build she was a foreign ship, but I was not certain of her nationality. She had been painted green, but the colour was faded and weathered, and the paint peeling off in strips. The wreck of the mainmast lay alongside, half buried in sand. She was a forlorn sight, indeed, and I could not look without emotion at the bits of rope that still hung about her, so often handled of yore by shouting seamen; or the little scuttle where they had passed up and down to their affairs; or that poor noseless angel of a figure-head that had dipped into so many running billows.

I do not know whether it came most from the ship or from the grave, but I fell into some melancholy scruples, as I stood there, leaning with one hand against the battered timbers. The homelessness of men and even of inanimate vessels, cast away upon strange shores, came strongly in upon my mind. To make a profit of such pitiful misadventures seemed an unmanly and a sordid act; and I began to think of my then quest as of something sacrilegious in its nature. But when I remembered Mary, I took heart again. My uncle would never consent to an imprudent marriage, nor would she, as I was persuaded, wed without his full approval. It behoved me, then, to be up and doing for my wife; and I thought with a laugh how long it was since that great sea-castle, the *Espirito Santo*, had left her bones in Sandag Bay, and how weak it would be to consider rights so long extinguished and misfortunes so long forgotten in the process of time.

I had my theory of where to seek for her remains. The set of the current and the soundings both pointed to the east side of the bay under the ledge of rocks. If she had been lost in Sandag Bay, and if, after these centuries, any portion of her held together, it was there that I should find it. The water deepens, as I have said, with great rapidity, and even close alongside the rocks several fathoms may be found. As I walked upon the edge I could see far and wide over the sandy bottom of the bay; the sun shone clear and green and steady in the deeps; the bay seemed rather like a great transparent crystal, as one sees them in a lapidary's shop; there was naught to show that it was water but an internal trembling, a hovering within of sun-glints and netted shadows, and now and then a faint lap and a dying bubble round the edge. The shadows of the rocks lay out for some distance at their feet, so that my own shadow, moving, pausing, and stooping on the top of that, reached sometimes half across the bay. It was above all in this belt of shadows that I hunted for the *Espirito Santo*, since it was there the undertow ran strongest, whether in or out. Cool as the whole water seemed this broiling day, it looked, in that part, yet cooler, and had a mysterious invitation for the eyes. Peer as I pleased, however, I could see nothing but a few fishes or a bush of sea-tangle, and here and there a lump of rock that had fallen from above and now lay separate on the sandy floor. Twice did I pass from one end to the other of the rocks, and in the whole distance I could see nothing of the wreck, nor any place but one where it was possible for it to be. This was a large terrace in five fathoms of water, raised off the surface of the sand to a considerable height, and looking from above like a mere outgrowth of the rocks on which I walked. It was one mass of great sea-tangles like a grove, which prevented me judging of its nature, but in shape and size it bore some likeness to a vessel's hull. At least it was my best chance. If the *Espirito Santo* lay not there under the tangles, it lay nowhere at all in Sandag Bay; and I prepared to put the question to the proof, once for all, and either go back to Aros a rich man or cured for ever of my dreams of wealth.

I stripped to the skin, and stood on the extreme margin with my hands clasped, irresolute. The bay at that time was utterly quiet; there was no sound but from a school of porpoises somewhere out of sight behind the point; yet a certain fear withheld me on the threshold of my venture. Sad sea-feelings, scraps of my uncle's superstitions, thoughts of the dead, of the grave, of the old broken ships, drifted through my mind. But the strong sun upon my shoulders warmed me to the heart, and I stooped forward and plunged into the sea.

It was all that I could do to catch a trail of the sea-tangle that grew so thickly on the terrace; but once so far anchored I secured myself by grasping a whole armful of these thick and slimy stalks, and, planting my feet against the edge, I looked around me. On all sides the clear sand stretched forth unbroken; it came to the foot of the rocks, scoured into the likeness of an alley in a garden by the action of the tides; and before me, for as far as I could see, nothing was visible but the same many-folded sand upon the sun-bright bottom of the bay. Yet the terrace to which I was then holding was as thick with strong sea-growths as a tuft of heather, and the cliff from which it bulged hung draped below the water-line with brown lianas. In this complexity of forms, all swaying together in the current, things were hard to be distinguished; and I was still uncertain whether my feet were pressed upon the natural rock or upon the timbers of the Armada treasure-ship, when the whole tuft of tangle came away in my hand, and in an instant I was on the surface, and the shores of the bay and the bright water swam before my eyes in a glory of crimson.

I clambered back upon the rocks, and threw the plant of tangle at my feet. Something at the same moment rang sharply, like a falling coin. I stooped, and there, sure enough, crusted with the red rust, there lay an iron shoe-buckle. The sight of this poor human relic thrilled me to the heart, but not with hope nor fear, only with a desolate melancholy. I held it in my hand, and the thought of its owner appeared before me like the presence of an actual man. His weather-beaten face, his sailor's hands, his sea-voice hoarse with singing at the capstan, the very foot that had once worn that buckle and trod so much along the swerving decks – the whole human fact of him, as a creature like myself, with hair and blood and seeing eyes, haunted me in that sunny, solitary place, not like a spectre, but like some friend whom I had basely injured. Was the great treasure ship indeed below there, with her guns and chain and treasure, as she had sailed from Spain; her decks a garden for the seaweed, her cabin a breeding place for fish, soundless but for the dredging water, motionless but for the waving of the tangle upon her battlements – that old, populous, sea-riding castle, now a reef in Sandag Bay? Or, as I thought it likelier, was this a waif from the disaster of the foreign brig – was this shoe-buckle bought but the other day and worn by a man of my own period in the world's history, hearing the same news from day to day, thinking the same thoughts, praying, perhaps, in the same temple with myself? However it was, I was assailed with dreary thoughts; my uncle's words, 'the dead are down there,' echoed in my ears; and though I determined to dive once more, it was with a strong repugnance that I stepped forward to the margin of the rocks.

A great change passed at that moment over the appearance of the bay. It was no more that clear, visible interior, like a house roofed with glass, where the green, submarine sunshine slept so stilly. A breeze, I suppose, had flawed the surface, and a sort of trouble and blackness filled its bosom, where flashes of light and clouds of shadow tossed confusedly together. Even the terrace below obscurely rocked and quivered. It seemed a graver thing to venture on this place of ambushes; and when I leaped into the sea the second time it was with a quaking in my soul.

I secured myself as at first, and groped among the waving tangle. All that met my touch was cold and soft and gluey. The thicket was alive with crabs and lobsters, trundling to and fro lobsidedly, and I had to harden my heart against the horror of their carrion neighbourhood. On all sides I could feel the grain and the clefts of hard, living stone; no planks, no iron, not a sign of any wreck; the *Espirito Santo* was not there. I remember I had almost a sense of relief in my disappointment, and I was about ready to leave go, when something happened that sent me to the surface with my heart in my mouth. I had already stayed somewhat late over my explorations; the current was freshening with the change of the tide, and Sandag Bay was no longer a safe place for a single swimmer. Well, just at the last moment there came a sudden flush of current, dredging through the tangles like a wave. I lost one hold, was flung sprawling on my side, and, instinctively grasping for a fresh support, my fingers closed on something hard and cold. I think I knew at that moment what it was. At least I instantly left hold of the tangle, leaped for the surface, and clambered out next moment on the friendly rocks with the bone of a man's leg in my grasp.

Mankind is a material creature, slow to think and dull to perceive connections. The grave, the wreck of the brig, and the rusty shoe-buckle were surely plain advertisements. A child might have read their story, and yet it was not until I touched that actual piece of mankind that the full horror of the charnel ocean burst upon my spirit. I laid the bone beside the buckle, picked up my clothes, and ran as I was along the rocks towards the human shore. I could not be far enough from the spot; no fortune was vast enough to tempt me back again. The bones of the drowned dead should henceforth roll undisturbed by me, whether on tangle or minted gold. But as soon as I trod the good earth again, and had covered my nakedness against the sun, I knelt down over against the ruins of the brig, and out of the fulness of my heart prayed long and passionately for all poor souls upon the sea. A generous prayer is never presented in vain; the petition may be refused, but the petitioner is always, I believe, rewarded by some gracious visitation. The horror, at least, was lifted from my mind; I could look with calm of spirit on that great bright creature, God's ocean; and as I set off homeward up the rough sides of Aros, nothing remained of my concern beyond a deep determination to meddle no more with the spoils of wrecked vessels or the treasures of the dead.

I was already some way up the hill before I paused to breathe and look behind me. The sight that met my eyes was doubly strange.

For, first, the storm that I had foreseen was now advancing with almost tropical rapidity. The whole surface of the sea had been dulled from its conspicuous brightness to an ugly hue of corrugated lead; already in the distance the white waves, the 'skipper's daughters,' had begun to flee before a breeze that was still insensible on Aros; and already along the curve of Sandag Bay there was a splashing run of sea that I could hear from where I stood. The change upon the sky was even more remarkable. There had begun to arise out of the south-west a huge and solid continent of scowling cloud; here and there, through rents in its contexture, the sun still poured a sheaf of spreading rays; and here and there, from all its edges, vast inky streamers lay forth along the yet unclouded sky. The menace was express and imminent. Even as I gazed, the sun was blotted out. At any moment the tempest might fall upon Aros in its might.

The suddenness of this change of weather so fixed my eyes on heaven that it was some seconds before they alighted on the bay, mapped out below my feet, and robbed a moment later of the sun. The knoll which I had just surmounted overflanked a little amphitheatre of lower hillocks sloping towards the sea, and beyond that the yellow arc of beach and the whole extent of Sandag Bay. It was a scene on which I had often looked down, but where I had never before beheld a human figure. I had but just turned my back upon it and left it empty, and my wonder may be fancied when I saw a boat and several men in that deserted spot. The boat was lying by the rocks. A pair of fellows, bareheaded, with their sleeves rolled up, and one with a boathook, kept her with difficulty to her moorings, for the current was growing brisker every moment. A little way off upon the ledge two men in black clothes, whom I judged to be superior in rank, laid their heads together over some task which at first I did not understand, but a second after I had made it out – they were taking bearings with the compass; and just then I saw one of them unroll a sheet of paper and lay his finger down, as though identifying features in a map. Meanwhile a third was walking to and fro, poking among the rocks and peering over the edge into the water. While I was still watching them with the stupefaction of surprise, my mind hardly yet able to work on what my eyes reported, this third person suddenly stooped and summoned his companions with a cry so loud that it reached my ears upon the hill. The others ran to him, even dropping the compass in their hurry, and I could see the bone and the shoe-buckle going from hand to hand, causing the most unusual gesticulations of surprise and interest. Just then I could hear the seamen crying from the boat, and saw them point westward to that cloud continent which was ever the more rapidly unfurling its blackness over heaven. The others seemed to consult; but the danger was too pressing to be braved, and they bundled into the boat, carrying my relics with them, and set forth out of the bay with all speed of oars.

I made no more ado about the matter, but turned and ran for the house. Whoever these men were, it was fit my uncle should be instantly informed. It was not then altogether too late in the day for a descent of the Jacobites; and maybe Prince Charlie, whom I knew my uncle to detest, was one of the three superiors whom I had seen upon the rock. Yet as I ran, leaping from rock to rock, and turned the matter loosely in my mind, this theory grew ever the longer the less welcome to my reason. The compass, the map, the interest awakened by the buckle, and the conduct of that one among the strangers who had looked so often below him in the water, all seemed to point to a different explanation of their presence on that outlying, obscure islet of the western sea. The Madrid historian, the search instituted by Dr Robertson, the bearded stranger with the rings, my own fruitless search that very morning in the deep water of Sandag Bay, ran together, piece by piece, in my memory, and I made sure that these strangers must be Spaniards in quest of ancient treasure and the lost ship of the Armada. But the people living in outlying islands, such as Aros, are answerable for their own security; there is none near by to protect or even to help them; and the presence in such a spot of a crew of foreign adventurers – poor, greedy, and most likely lawless – filled me with apprehensions for my uncle's money, and even for the safety of his daughter. I was still wondering how we were to get rid of them when I came, all breathless, to the top of Aros. The whole world was shadowed over; only in the extreme east, on a hill of the mainland, one last gleam of sunshine lingered like a jewel; rain had begun to fall, not heavily, but in great drops; the sea was rising with each moment, and already a band of white encircled Aros and the nearer coasts of Grisapol. The boat was still pulling seaward, but I now became aware of what had been hidden from me lower down – a large, heavily sparred, handsome schooner lying to at the south end of Aros. Since I had not seen her in the morning when I had looked around so closely at the signs of the weather, and upon these lone waters where a sail was rarely visible, it was clear she must have lain last night behind the uninhabited Eilean Gour, and this proved conclusively that she was manned by strangers to our coast, for that anchorage, though good enough to look at, is little better than a trap for ships. With such ignorant sailors upon so wild a coast, the coming gale was not unlikely to bring death upon its wings.

CHAPTER IV

The Gale

I FOUND MY UNCLE at the gable end, watching the signs of the weather, with a pipe in his fingers.

'Uncle,' said I, 'there were men ashore at Sandag Bay –'

I had no time to go further; indeed, I not only forgot my words, but even my weariness, so strange was the effect on Uncle Gordon. He dropped his pipe and fell back against the end of the house with his jaw fallen, his eyes staring, and his long face as white as paper. We must have looked at one another silently for a quarter of a minute, before he made answer in this extraordinary fashion: 'Had he a hair kep on?'

I knew as well as if I had been there that the man who now lay buried at Sandag had worn a hairy cap, and that he had come ashore alive. For the first and only time I lost toleration for the man who was my benefactor and the father of the woman I hoped to call my wife.

'These were living men,' said I, 'perhaps Jacobites, perhaps the French, perhaps pirates, perhaps adventurers come here to seek the Spanish treasure ship; but, whatever they may be, dangerous at least to your daughter and my cousin. As for your own guilty terrors, man, the dead sleeps well where you have laid him. I stood this morning by his grave; he will not wake before the trump of doom.'

My kinsman looked upon me, blinking, while I spoke; then he fixed his eyes for a little on the ground, and pulled his fingers foolishly; but it was plain that he was past the power of speech.

'Come,' said I. 'You must think for others. You must come up the hill with me, and see this ship.'

He obeyed without a word or a look, following slowly after my impatient strides. The spring seemed to have gone out of his body, and he scrambled heavily up and down the rocks, instead of leaping, as he was wont, from one to another. Nor could I, for all my cries, induce him to make better haste. Only once he replied to me complainingly, and like one in bodily pain: 'Ay, ay, man, I'm coming.' Long before we had reached the top, I had no other thought for him but pity. If the crime had been monstrous, the punishment was in proportion.

At last we emerged above the sky-line of the hill, and could see around us. All was black and stormy to the eye; the last gleam of sun had vanished; a wind had sprung up, not yet high, but gusty and unsteady to the point; the rain, on the other hand, had ceased. Short as was the interval, the sea already ran vastly higher than when I had stood there last; already it had begun to break over some of the outward reefs, and already it moaned aloud in the sea-caves of Aros. I looked, at first, in vain for the schooner.

'There she is,' I said at last. But her new position, and the course she was now lying, puzzled me. 'They cannot mean to beat to sea,' I cried.

'That's what they mean,' said my uncle, with something like joy; and just then the schooner went about and stood upon another tack, which put the question beyond the reach of doubt. These strangers, seeing a gale on hand, had thought first of sea-room. With the wind that threatened, in these reef-sown waters and contending against so violent a stream of tide, their course was certain death.

'Good God!' said I, 'they are all lost.'

'Ay,' returned my uncle, 'a' – a' lost. They hadnae a chance but to rin for Kyle Dona. The gate they're gaun the noo, they couldnae win through an the muckle deil were there to pilot them. Eh, man,' he continued, touching me on the sleeve, 'it's a braw nicht for a ship-wreck! Twa in ae twalmonth! Eh, but the Merry Men'll dance bonny!'

I looked at him, and it was then that I began to fancy him no longer in his right mind. He was peering up to me, as if for sympathy, a timid joy in his eyes. All that had passed between us was already forgotten in the prospect of this fresh disaster.

'If it were not too late,' I cried with indignation, 'I would take the coble and go out to warn them.'

'Na, na,' he protested, 'ye maunnae interfere; ye maunnae meddle wi' the like o' that. It's His' – doffing his bonnet – 'His wull. And, eh, man! but it's a braw nicht for't!'

Something like fear began to creep into my soul; and, reminding him that I had not yet dined, I proposed we should return to the house. But no; nothing would tear him from his place of outlook.

'I maun see the hail thing, man, Charlie,' he explained; and then as the schooner went about a second time, 'Eh, but they han'le her bonny!' he cried. 'The *Christ-Anna* was naething to this.'

Already the men on board the schooner must have begun to realise some part, but not yet the twentieth, of the dangers that environed their doomed ship. At every lull of the capricious wind they must have seen how fast the current swept them back. Each tack was made shorter, as they saw how little it prevailed. Every moment the rising swell began to boom and foam upon another sunken reef; and ever and again a breaker would fall in sounding ruin under the very bows of her, and the brown reef and streaming tangle appear in the hollow of the wave. I tell you, they had to stand to their tackle: there was no idle man aboard that ship, God knows. It was upon the progress of a scene so horrible to any human-hearted man that my misguided uncle now pored and gloated like a connoisseur. As I turned to go down the hill, he was lying on his belly on the summit, with his hands stretched forth and clutching in the heather. He seemed rejuvenated, mind and body.

When I got back to the house already dismally affected, I was still more sadly downcast at the sight of Mary. She had her sleeves rolled up over her strong arms, and was quietly making bread. I got a bannock from the dresser and sat down to eat it in silence.

'Are ye wearied, lad?' she asked after a while.

'I am not so much wearied, Mary,' I replied, getting on my feet, 'as I am weary of delay, and perhaps of Aros too. You know me well enough to judge me fairly, say what I like. Well, Mary, you may be sure of this: you had better be anywhere but here.'

'I'll be sure of one thing,' she returned: 'I'll be where my duty is.'

'You forget, you have a duty to yourself,' I said.

'Ay, man?' she replied, pounding at the dough; 'will you have found that in the Bible, now?'

'Mary,' I said solemnly, 'you must not laugh at me just now. God knows I am in no heart for laughing. If we could get your father with us, it would be best; but with him or without him, I want you far away from here, my girl; for your own sake, and for mine, ay, and for your father's too, I want you far – far away from here. I came with other thoughts; I came here as a man comes home; now it is all changed, and I have no desire nor hope but to flee – for that's the word – flee, like a bird out of the fowler's snare, from this accursed island.'

She had stopped her work by this time.

'And do you think, now,' said she, 'do you think, now, I have neither eyes nor ears? Do ye think I havenae broken my heart to have these braws (as he calls them, God forgive him!) thrown into the sea? Do ye think I have lived with him, day in, day out, and not seen what you saw in an hour or two? No,' she said, 'I know there is wrong in it; what wrong, I neither know nor want to know. There was never an ill thing made better by meddling, that I could hear of. But, my lad, you must never ask me to leave my father. While the breath is in his body, I'll be with him. And he's not long for here, either: that I can tell you, Charlie – he's not long for here. The mark is on his brow; and better so – maybe better so.'

I was a while silent, not knowing what to say; and when I roused my head at last to speak, she got before me.

'Charlie,' she said, 'what's right for me, neednae be right for you. There's sin upon this house and trouble; you are a stranger; take your things upon your back and go your ways to better places and to better folk, and if you were ever minded to come back, though it were twenty years syne, you would find me aye waiting.'

'Mary Ellen,' I said, 'I asked you to be my wife, and you said as good as yes. That's done for good. Wherever you are, I am; as I shall answer to my God.'

As I said the words, the wind suddenly burst out raving, and then seemed to stand still and shudder round the house of Aros. It was the first squall, or prologue, of the coming tempest, and as we started and looked about us, we found that a gloom, like the approach of evening, had settled round the house.

'God pity all poor folks at sea!' she said. 'We'll see no more of my father till the morrow's morning.'

And then she told me, as we sat by the fire and hearkened to the rising gusts, of how this change had fallen upon my uncle. All last winter he had been dark and fitful in his mind. Whenever the Roost ran high, or, as Mary said, whenever the Merry Men were dancing, he would lie out for hours together on the Head, if it were at night, or on the top of Aros by day, watching the tumult of the sea, and sweeping the horizon for a sail. After February the tenth, when the wealth-bringing wreck was cast ashore at Sandag, he had been at first unnaturally gay, and his excitement had never fallen in degree, but only changed in kind from dark to darker. He neglected his work, and kept Rorie idle. They two would speak together by the hour at the gable end, in guarded tones and with an air of secrecy and almost of guilt; and if she questioned either, as at first she sometimes did, her inquiries were put aside with confusion. Since Rorie had first remarked the fish that hung about the ferry, his master had never set foot but once upon the mainland of the Ross. That once – it was in the height of the springs – he had passed dryshod while the tide was out; but, having lingered overlong on the far side, found himself cut off from Aros by the returning waters. It was with a shriek of agony that he had leaped across the gut, and he had reached home thereafter in a fever-fit of fear. A fear of the sea, a constant haunting thought of the sea, appeared in his talk and devotions, and even in his looks when he was silent.

Rorie alone came in to supper; but a little later my uncle appeared, took a bottle under his arm, put some bread in his pocket, and set forth again to his outlook, followed this time by Rorie. I heard that the schooner was losing ground, but the crew were still fighting every inch with hopeless ingenuity and courage; and the news filled my mind with blackness.

A little after sundown the full fury of the gale broke forth, such a gale as I have never seen in summer, nor, seeing how swiftly it had come, even in winter. Mary and I sat in silence, the house quaking overhead, the tempest howling without, the fire between us sputtering with raindrops. Our thoughts were far away with the poor fellows on the schooner, or my not less unhappy uncle, houseless on the promontory; and yet ever and again we were startled back to ourselves, when the wind would rise and strike the gable like a solid body, or suddenly fall and draw away, so that the fire leaped into flame and our hearts bounded in our sides. Now the storm in its might would seize and shake the four corners of the roof, roaring like Leviathan in anger. Anon, in a lull, cold eddies of tempest moved shudderingly in the room, lifting the hair upon our heads and passing between us as we sat. And again the wind would break forth in a chorus of melancholy sounds, hooting low in the chimney, wailing with flutelike softness round the house.

It was perhaps eight o'clock when Rorie came in and pulled me mysteriously to the door. My uncle, it appeared, had frightened even his constant comrade; and Rorie, uneasy at his extravagance, prayed me to come out and share the watch. I hastened to do as I was asked; the more readily as, with fear and horror, and the electrical tension of the night, I was myself restless and disposed for action. I told Mary to be under no alarm, for I should be a safeguard on her father; and wrapping myself warmly in a plaid, I followed Rorie into the open air.

The night, though we were so little past midsummer, was as dark as January. Intervals of a groping twilight alternated with spells of utter blackness; and it was impossible to trace the reason of these changes in the flying horror of the sky. The wind blew the breath out of a man's nostrils; all heaven seemed to thunder overhead like one huge sail; and when there fell a momentary lull on Aros, we could hear the gusts dismally sweeping in the distance. Over all the lowlands of the Ross, the wind must have blown as fierce as on the open sea; and God only knows the uproar that was raging round the head of Ben Kyaw. Sheets of mingled spray and rain were driven in our faces. All round the isle of Aros the surf, with an incessant, hammering thunder, beat upon the reefs and beaches. Now louder in one place, now lower in another, like the combinations of orchestral music, the constant mass of sound was hardly varied for a moment. And loud above all this hurly-burly I could hear the changeful voices of the Roost and the intermittent roaring of the Merry Men. At that hour, there flashed into my mind the reason of the name that they were called. For the noise of them seemed almost mirthful, as it out-topped the other noises of the night; or if not mirthful, yet instinct with a portentous joviality. Nay, and it seemed even human. As when savage men have drunk away their reason, and, discarding speech, bawl together in their madness by the hour; so, to my ears, these deadly breakers shouted by Aros in the night.

Arm in arm, and staggering against the wind, Rorie and I won every yard of ground with conscious effort. We slipped on the wet sod, we fell together sprawling on the rocks. Bruised, drenched, beaten, and breathless, it must have taken us near half an hour to get from the house down to the Head that overlooks the Roost. There, it seemed, was my uncle's favourite observatory. Right in the face of it, where the cliff is highest and most sheer, a hump of earth, like a parapet, makes a place of shelter from the common winds where a man may sit in quiet and see the tide and the mad billows contending at his feet. As he might look down from the window of a house upon some street disturbance, so, from this post, he looks down upon the tumbling of the Merry Men. On such a night, of course, he peers upon a world of blackness, where the waters wheel and boil, where the waves joust together with the noise of an explosion, and the foam towers and vanishes in the twinkling of an eye. Never before had I seen the Merry Men thus violent. The fury, height, and transiency of their spoutings was a thing to be seen and not recounted. High over our heads on the cliff rose their white columns in the darkness; and the same instant, like phantoms, they were gone. Sometimes three at a time would thus aspire and vanish; sometimes a gust took them, and the spray would fall about us, heavy as a wave. And yet the spectacle was rather maddening in its levity than impressive by its force. Thought was beaten down by the confounding uproar; a gleeful vacancy possessed the brains of men, a state akin to madness; and I found myself at times following the dance of the Merry Men as it were a tune upon a jigging instrument.

I first caught sight of my uncle when we were still some yards away in one of the flying glimpses of twilight that chequered the pitch darkness of the night. He was standing up behind the parapet, his head thrown back and the bottle to his mouth. As he put it down, he saw and recognised us with a toss of one hand fleeringly above his head.

'Has he been drinking?' shouted I to Rorie.

'He will aye be drunk when the wind blaws,' returned Rorie in the same high key, and it was all that I could do to hear him.

'Then – was he so – in February?' I inquired.

Rorie's 'Ay' was a cause of joy to me. The murder, then, had not sprung in cold blood from calculation; it was an act of madness no more to be condemned than to be pardoned. My uncle was a dangerous madman, if you will, but he was not cruel and base as I had feared. Yet what a scene for a carouse, what an incredible vice, was this that the poor man had chosen! I have always thought drunkenness a wild and almost fearful pleasure, rather demoniacal than human; but drunkenness, out here in the roaring blackness, on the edge of a cliff above that hell of waters, the man's head spinning like the Roost, his foot tottering on the edge of death, his ear watching for the signs of shipwreck, surely that, if it were credible in any one, was morally impossible in a man like my uncle, whose mind was set upon a damnatory creed and haunted by the darkest superstitions. Yet so it was; and, as we reached the bight of shelter and could breathe again, I saw the man's eyes shining in the night with an unholy glimmer.

'Eh, Charlie, man, it's grand!' he cried. 'See to them!' he continued, dragging me to the edge of the abyss from whence arose that deafening clamour and those clouds of spray; 'see to them dancin', man! Is that no wicked?'

He pronounced the word with gusto, and I thought it suited with the scene.

'They're yowlin' for thon schooner,' he went on, his thin, insane voice clearly audible in the shelter of the bank, 'an' she's comin' aye nearer, aye nearer, aye nearer an' nearer an' nearer; an' they ken't, the folk kens it, they ken weel it's by wi' them. Charlie, lad, they're a' drunk in yon schooner, a' dozened wi' drink. They were a' drunk in the *Christ-Anna*, at the hinder end. There's nane could droon at sea wantin' the brandy. Hoot awa, what do you ken?' with a sudden blast of anger. 'I tell ye, it cannae be; they daurnae droon withoot it. Ha'e,' holding out the bottle, 'tak' a sowp.'

I was about to refuse, but Rorie touched me as if in warning; and indeed I had already thought better of the movement. I took the bottle, therefore, and not only drank freely myself, but contrived to spill even more as I was doing so. It was pure spirit, and almost strangled me to swallow. My kinsman did not observe the loss, but, once more throwing back his head, drained the remainder to the dregs. Then, with a loud laugh, he cast the bottle forth among the Merry Men, who seemed to leap up, shouting to receive it.

'Ha'e, bairns!' he cried, 'there's your han'sel. Ye'll get bonnier nor that, or morning.'

Suddenly, out in the black night before us, and not two hundred yards away, we heard, at a moment when the wind was silent, the clear note of a human voice. Instantly the wind swept howling down upon the Head, and the Roost bellowed, and churned, and danced with a new fury. But we had heard the sound, and we knew, with agony, that this was the doomed ship now close on ruin, and that what we had heard was the voice of her master issuing his last command. Crouching together on the edge, we waited, straining every sense, for the inevitable end. It was long, however, and to us it seemed like ages, ere the schooner suddenly appeared for one brief instant, relieved against a tower of glimmering foam. I still see her reefed mainsail flapping loose, as the boom fell heavily across the deck; I still see the black outline of the hull, and still think I can distinguish the figure of a man stretched upon the tiller. Yet the whole sight we had of her passed swifter than lightning; the very wave that disclosed her fell burying her for ever; the mingled cry of many voices at the point of death rose and was quenched in the roaring of the Merry Men. And with that the tragedy was at an end. The strong ship with all her gear, and the lamp perhaps still burning in the cabin, the lives of so many men, precious surely to others, dear, at least, as heaven to themselves, had all, in that one moment, gone down into the surging waters. They were gone like a dream. And the wind still ran and shouted, and the senseless waters in the Roost still leaped and tumbled as before.

How long we lay there together, we three, speechless and motionless, is more than I can tell, but it must have been for long. At length, one by one, and almost mechanically, we crawled back into the shelter of the bank. As I lay against the parapet, wholly wretched and not entirely master of my mind, I could hear my kinsman maundering to himself in an altered and melancholy mood. Now he would repeat to himself with maudlin iteration, 'Sic a fecht as they had – sic a sair fecht as they had, puir lads, puir lads!' and anon he would bewail that 'a' the gear was as gude's tint,' because the ship had gone down among the Merry Men instead of stranding on the shore; and throughout, the name – the *Christ-Anna* – would come and go in his divagations, pronounced with shuddering awe. The storm all this time was rapidly abating. In half an hour the wind had fallen to a breeze, and the change was accompanied or caused by a heavy, cold, and plumping rain. I must then have fallen asleep, and when I came to myself, drenched, stiff, and unrefreshed, day had already broken, gray, wet, discomfortable day; the wind blew in faint and shifting capfuls, the tide was out, the Roost was at its lowest, and only the strong beating surf round all the coasts of Aros remained to witness of the furies of the night.

CHAPTER V

A Man out of the Sea

RORIE SET OUT FOR the house in search of warmth and breakfast; but my uncle was bent upon examining the shores of Aros, and I felt it a part of duty to accompany him throughout. He was now docile and quiet, but tremulous and weak in mind and body; and it was with the eagerness of a child that he pursued his exploration. He climbed down far upon the rocks; on the beaches he pursued the retreating breakers. The merest broken plank or rag of cordage was a treasure in his eyes to be secured at the peril of his life. To see him, with weak and stumbling footsteps, expose himself to the pursuit of the surf, or the snares and pitfalls of the weedy rock, kept me in a perpetual terror. My arm was ready to support him, my hand clutched him by the skirt, I helped him to draw his pitiful discoveries beyond the reach of the returning wave; a nurse accompanying a child of seven would have had no different experience.

Yet, weakened as he was by the reaction from his madness of the night before, the passions that smouldered in his nature were those of a strong man. His terror of the sea, although conquered for the moment, was still undiminished; had the sea been a lake of living flames, he could not have shrunk more panically from its touch; and once, when his foot slipped and he plunged to the mid-leg into a pool of water, the shriek that came up out of his soul was like the cry of death. He sat still for a while, panting like a dog, after that; but his desire for the spoils of shipwreck triumphed once more over his fears; once more he tottered among the curded foam; once more he crawled upon the rocks among the bursting bubbles; once more his whole heart seemed to be set on driftwood, fit, if it was fit for anything, to throw upon the fire. Pleased as he was with what he found, he still incessantly grumbled at his ill-fortune.

'Aros,' he said, 'is no a place for wrecks ava' – no ava'. A' the years I've dwalt here, this ane maks the second; and the best o' the gear clean tint!'

'Uncle,' said I, for we were now on a stretch of open sand, where there was nothing to divert his mind, 'I saw you last night as I never thought to see you – you were drunk.'

'Na, na,' he said, 'no as bad as that. I had been drinking, though. And to tell ye the God's truth, it's a thing I cannae mend. There's nae soberer man than me in my ordnar; but when I hear the wind blaw in my lug, it's my belief that I gang gyte.'

'You are a religious man,' I replied, 'and this is sin.'

'Ou,' he returned, 'if it wasnae sin, I dinnae ken that I would care for't. Ye see, man, it's defiance. There's a sair spang o' the auld sin o' the warld in yon sea; it's an unchristian business at the best o't; an' whiles when it gets up, an' the wind skreighs – the wind an' her are a kind of sib, I'm thinkin' – an' thae Merry Men, the daft callants, blawin' and lauchin', and puir souls in the deid thraws warstlin' the leelang nicht wi' their bit ships – weel, it comes ower me like a glamour. I'm a deil, I ken't. But I think naething o' the puir sailor lads; I'm wi' the sea, I'm just like ane o' her ain Merry Men.'

I thought I should touch him in a joint of his harness. I turned me towards the sea; the surf was running gaily, wave after wave, with their manes blowing behind them, riding one after another up the beach, towering, curving, falling one upon another on the trampled sand. Without, the salt air, the scared gulls, the widespread army of the sea-chargers, neighing to each other, as they gathered together to the assault of Aros; and close before us, that line on the flat sands that, with all their number and their fury, they might never pass.

'Thus far shalt thou go,' said I, 'and no farther.' And then I quoted as solemnly as I was able a verse that I had often before fitted to the chorus of the breakers:

> 'But yet the Lord that is on high
> Is more of might by far,
> Than noise of many waters is,
> As great sea billows are.'

'Ay,' said my kinsman, 'at the hinder end, the Lord will triumph; I dinnae misdoobt that. But here on earth, even silly men-folk daur Him to His face. It is nae wise; I am nae sayin' that it's wise; but it's the pride of the eye, and it's the lust o' life, an' it's the wale o' pleesures.'

I said no more, for we had now begun to cross a neck of land that lay between us and Sandag; and I withheld my last appeal to the man's better reason till we should stand upon the spot associated with his crime. Nor did he pursue the subject; but he walked beside me with a firmer step. The call that I had made upon his mind acted like a stimulant, and I could see that he had forgotten his search for worthless jetsam, in a profound, gloomy, and yet stirring train of thought. In three or four minutes we had topped the brae and begun to go down upon Sandag. The wreck had been roughly handled by the sea; the stem had been spun round and dragged a little lower down; and perhaps the stern had been forced a little higher, for the two parts now lay entirely separate on the beach. When we came to the grave I stopped, uncovered my head in the thick rain, and, looking my kinsman in the face, addressed him.

'A man,' said I, 'was in God's providence suffered to escape from mortal dangers; he was poor, he was naked, he was wet, he was weary, he was a stranger; he had every claim upon the bowels of your compassion; it may be that he was the salt of the earth, holy, helpful, and kind; it may be that he was a man laden with iniquities to whom death was the beginning of torment. I ask you in the sight of heaven: Gordon Darnaway, where is the man for whom Christ died?'

He started visibly at the last words; but there came no answer, and his face expressed no feeling but a vague alarm.

'You were my father's brother,' I continued; 'you have taught me to count your house as if it were my father's house; and we are both sinful men walking before the Lord among the sins and dangers of this life. It is by our evil that God leads us into good; we sin, I dare not say by His temptation, but I must say with His consent; and to any but the brutish man his sins are the beginning of wisdom. God has warned you by this crime; He warns you still by the bloody grave between our feet; and if there shall follow no repentance, no improvement, no return to Him, what can we look for but the following of some memorable judgment?'

Even as I spoke the words, the eyes of my uncle wandered from my face. A change fell upon his looks that cannot be described; his features seemed to dwindle in size, the colour faded from his cheeks, one hand rose waveringly and pointed over my shoulder into the distance, and the oft-repeated name fell once more from his lips: 'The *Christ-Anna*!'

I turned, and if I was not appalled to the same degree, as I return thanks to Heaven that I had not the cause, I was still startled by the sight that met my eyes. The form of a man stood upright on the cabin-hutch of the wrecked ship; his back was towards us; he appeared to be scanning the offing with shaded eyes, and his figure was relieved to its full height, which was plainly very great, against the sea and sky. I have said a thousand times that I am not superstitious; but at that moment, with my mind running upon death and sin, the unexplained appearance of a stranger on that sea-girt, solitary island filled me with a surprise that bordered close on terror. It seemed scarce possible that any human soul should have come ashore alive in such a sea as had raged last night along the coasts of Aros; and the only vessel within miles had gone down before our eyes among the Merry Men. I was assailed with doubts that made suspense unbearable, and, to put the matter to the touch at once, stepped forward and hailed the figure like a ship.

He turned about, and I thought he started to behold us. At this my courage instantly revived, and I called and signed to him to draw near, and he, on his part, dropped immediately to the sands, and began slowly to approach, with many stops and hesitations. At each repeated mark of the man's uneasiness I grew the more confident myself, and I advanced another step, encouraging him as I did so with my head and hand. It was plain the castaway had heard indifferent accounts of our island hospitality; and indeed, about this time, the people farther north had a sorry reputation.

'Why,' I said, 'the man is black!'

And just at that moment, in a voice that I could scarce have recognised, my kinsman began swearing and praying in a mingled stream. I looked at him; he had fallen on his knees, his face was agonised; at each step of the castaway's the pitch of his voice rose, the volubility of his utterance and the fervour of his language redoubled. I call it prayer, for it was addressed to God; but surely no such ranting incongruities were ever before addressed to the Creator by a creature; surely, if prayer can be a sin, this mad harangue was sinful. I ran to my kinsman, I seized him by the shoulders, I dragged him to his feet.

'Silence, man,' said I, 'respect your God in words, if not in action.

Here, on the very scene of your transgressions, He sends you an occasion of atonement. Forward and embrace it; welcome like a father yon creature who comes trembling to your mercy.'

With that, I tried to force him towards the black; but he felled me to the ground, burst from my grasp, leaving the shoulder of his jacket, and fled up the hillside towards the top of Aros like a deer. I staggered to my feet again, bruised and somewhat stunned; the negro had paused in surprise, perhaps in terror, some halfway between me and the wreck; my uncle was already far away, bounding from rock to rock; and I thus found myself torn for a time between two duties. But I judged, and I pray Heaven that I judged rightly, in favour of the poor wretch upon the sands; his misfortune was at least not plainly of his own creation; it was one, besides, that I could certainly relieve; and I had begun by that time to regard my uncle as an incurable and dismal lunatic. I advanced accordingly towards the black who now awaited my approach with folded arms, like one prepared for either destiny. As I came nearer, he reached forth his hand with a great gesture, such as I had seen from the pulpit, and spoke to me in something of a pulpit voice, but not a word was comprehensible. I tried him first in English, then in Gaelic, both in vain; so that it was clear we must rely upon the tongue of looks and gestures. Thereupon I signed to him to follow me, which he did readily and with a grave obeisance like a fallen king; all the while there had come no shade of alteration in his face, neither of anxiety while he was still waiting, nor of relief now that he was reassured; if he were a slave, as I supposed, I could not but judge he must have fallen from some high place in his own country, and fallen as he was, I could not but admire his bearing. As we passed the grave, I paused and raised my hands and eyes to heaven in token of respect and sorrow for the dead; and he, as if in answer, bowed low and spread his hands abroad; it was a strange motion, but done like a thing of common custom; and I supposed it was ceremonial in the land from which he came. At the same time he pointed to my uncle, whom we could just see perched upon a knoll, and touched his head to indicate that he was mad.

We took the long way round the shore, for I feared to excite my uncle if we struck across the island; and as we walked, I had time enough to mature the little dramatic exhibition by which I hoped to satisfy my doubts. Accordingly, pausing on a rock, I proceeded to imitate before the negro the action of the man whom I had seen the day before taking bearings with the compass at Sandag. He understood me at once, and, taking the imitation out of my hands, showed me where the boat was, pointed out seaward as if to indicate the position of the schooner, and then down along the edge of the rock with the words

'*Espirito Santo*,' strangely pronounced, but clear enough for recognition. I had thus been right in my conjecture; the pretended historical inquiry had been but a cloak for treasure-hunting; the man who had played on Dr Robertson was the same as the foreigner who visited Grisapol in spring, and now, with many others, lay dead under the Roost of Aros: there had their greed brought them, there should their bones be tossed for evermore. In the meantime the black continued his imitation of the scene, now looking up skyward as though watching the approach of the storm; now, in the character of a seaman, waving the rest to come aboard; now as an officer, running along the rock and entering the boat; and anon bending over imaginary oars with the air of a hurried boatman; but all with the same solemnity of manner, so that I was never even moved to smile. Lastly, he indicated to me, by a pantomime not to be described in words, how he himself had gone up to examine the stranded wreck, and, to his grief and indignation, had been deserted by his comrades; and thereupon folded his arms once more, and stooped his head, like one accepting fate.

The mystery of his presence being thus solved for me, I explained to him by means of a sketch the fate of the vessel and of all aboard her. He showed no surprise nor sorrow, and, with a sudden lifting of his open hand, seemed to dismiss his former friends or masters (whichever they had been) into God's pleasure. Respect came upon me and grew stronger, the more I observed him; I saw he had a powerful mind and a sober and severe character, such as I loved to commune with; and before we reached the house of Aros I had almost forgotten, and wholly forgiven him, his uncanny colour.

To Mary I told all that had passed without suppression, though I own my heart failed me; but I did wrong to doubt her sense of justice.

'You did the right,' she said. 'God's will be done.' And she set out meat for us at once.

As soon as I was satisfied, I bade Rorie keep an eye upon the castaway, who was still eating, and set forth again myself to find my uncle. I had not gone far before I saw him sitting in the same place, upon the very topmost knoll, and seemingly in the same attitude as when I had last observed him. From that point, as I have said, the most of Aros and the neighbouring Ross would be spread below him like a map; and it was plain that he kept a bright look-out in all directions, for my head had scarcely risen above the summit of the first ascent before he had leaped to his feet and turned as if to face me. I hailed him at once, as well as I was able, in the same tones and words as I had often used before, when I had come to summon him to dinner. He made not so much as a movement in reply. I passed on a little farther, and again tried parley, with the same result. But when I began a second time to advance, his insane fears blazed up again, and still in dead silence, but with incredible speed, he began to flee from before me along the rocky summit of the hill. An hour before, he had been dead weary, and I had been comparatively active. But now his strength was recruited by the fervour of insanity, and it would have been vain for me to dream of pursuit. Nay, the very attempt, I thought, might have inflamed his terrors, and thus increased the miseries of our position. And I had nothing left but to turn homeward and make my sad report to Mary.

She heard it, as she had heard the first, with a concerned composure, and, bidding me lie down and take that rest of which I stood so much in need, set forth herself in quest of her misguided father. At that age it would have been a strange thing that put me from either meat or sleep; I slept long and deep; and it was already long past noon before I awoke and came downstairs into the kitchen. Mary, Rorie, and the black castaway were seated about the fire in silence, and I could see that Mary had been weeping. There was cause enough, as I soon learned, for tears. First she, and then Rorie, had been forth to seek my uncle; each in turn had found him perched upon the hill-top, and from each in turn he had silently and swiftly fled. Rorie had tried to chase him, but in vain; madness lent a new vigour to his bounds; he sprang from rock to rock over the wildest gullies; he scoured like the wind along the hill-tops; he doubled and twisted like a hare before the dogs; and Rorie at length gave in; and the last that he saw, my uncle was seated as before upon the crest of Aros. Even during the hottest excitement of the chase, even when the fleet-footed servant had come, for a moment, very near to capture him, the poor lunatic had uttered not a sound. He fled, and he was silent like a beast, and this silence had terrified his pursuer.

There was something heart-breaking in the situation. How to capture the madman, how to feed him in the meanwhile, and what to do with him when he was captured, were the three difficulties that we had to solve.

'The black,' said I, 'is the cause of this attack. It may even be his presence in the house that keeps my uncle on the hill. We have done the fair thing; he has been fed and warmed under this roof; and now I propose that Rorie put him across the bay in the coble, and take him through the Ross as far as Grisapol.'

In this proposal Mary heartily concurred; and bidding the black follow us, we all three descended to the pier. Certainly, Heaven's will was declared against Gordon Darnaway; a thing had happened, never paralleled before in Aros; during the storm the coble had broken loose, and, striking on the rough splinters of the pier, now lay in four feet of water with one side stove in. Three days of work at least would be required to make her float. But I was not to be beaten. I led the whole party round to where the gut was narrowest, swam to the other side, and called to the black to follow me. He signed, with the same clearness and quiet as before, that he knew not the art; and there was truth apparent in his signals, it would have occurred to none of us to doubt his truth; and that hope being over, we must all go back even as we came to the house of Aros, the negro walking in our midst without embarrassment.

All we could do that day was to make one more attempt to communicate with the unhappy madman. Again he was visible on his perch; again he fled in silence. But food and a great cloak were at least left for his comfort; the rain, besides, had cleared away, and the night promised to be even warm. We might compose ourselves, we thought, until the morrow; rest was the chief requisite, that we might be strengthened for unusual exertions, and as none cared to talk, we separated at an early hour.

I lay long awake planning a campaign for the morrow. I was to place the black on the side of Sandag, whence he should head my uncle towards the house; Rorie on the west, I on the east, were to complete the cordon, as best we might. It seemed to me, the more I recalled the configuration of the island, that it should be possible, though hard, to force him down upon the low ground along Aros Bay; and once there, even with the strength of his madness, ultimate escape was hardly to be feared. It was on his terror of the black that I relied; for I made sure, however he might run, it would not be in the direction of the man whom he supposed to have returned from the dead, and thus one point of the compass at least would be secure.

When at length I fell asleep, it was to be awakened shortly after by a dream of wrecks, black men, and submarine adventure; and I found myself so shaken and fevered that I arose, descended the stair, and stepped out before the house. Within, Rorie and the black were asleep together in the kitchen; outside was a wonderful night clear of stars, with here and there a cloud still hanging, last stragglers of the tempest. It was near the top of the flood, and the Merry Men were roaring in the windless quiet of the night. Never, not even in the height of the tempest, had I heard their song with greater awe. Now, when the winds were gathered home, when the deep was dandling itself back into its summer slumber, and when the stars rained their gentle light over land and sea, the voice of these tide-breakers was still raised for havoc. They seemed, indeed, to be a part of the world's evil and the tragic side of life. Nor were their meaningless vociferations the only sounds that broke the silence of the night. For I could hear, now shrill and thrilling and now almost drowned, the note of a human voice that accompanied the uproar of the Roost. I knew it for my kinsman's, and a great fear fell upon me of God's judgments and the evil in the world. I went back again into the darkness of the house as into a place of shelter, and lay long upon my bed pondering these mysteries.

It was late when I again woke, and I leaped into my clothes and hurried to the kitchen. No one was there; Rorie and the black had both stealthily departed long before, and my heart stood still at the discovery. I could rely on Rorie's heart, but I placed no trust in his discretion. If he had thus set out without a word, he was plainly bent upon some service to my uncle. But what service could he hope to render even alone, far less in the company of the man in whom my uncle found his fears incarnated? Even if I were not already too late to prevent some deadly mischief, it was plain I must delay no longer. With the thought I was out of the house, and often as I have run on the rough sides of Aros, I never ran as I did that fatal morning. I do not believe I put twelve minutes to the whole ascent.

My uncle was gone from his perch. The basket had indeed been torn open and the meat scattered on the turf; but, as we found afterwards, no mouthful had been tasted, and there was not another trace of human existence in that wide field of view. Day had already filled the clear heavens; the sun already lighted in a rosy bloom upon the crest of Ben Kyaw; but all below me the rude knolls of Aros and the shield of sea lay steeped in the clear darkling twilight of the dawn.

'Rorie!' I cried; and again 'Rorie!' My voice died in the silence, but there came no answer back. If there were indeed an enterprise afoot to catch my uncle, it was plainly not in fleetness of foot, but in dexterity of stalking, that the hunters placed their trust. I ran on farther, keeping the higher spurs, and looking right and left, nor did I pause again till I was on the mount above Sandag. I could see the wreck, the uncovered belt of sand, the waves idly beating the long ledge of rocks, and on either hand the tumbled knolls, boulders, and gullies of the island. But still no human being.

At a stride the sunshine fell on Aros, and the shadows and colours leaped into being. Not half a moment later, below me to the west, sheep began to scatter as in a panic. There came a cry. I saw my uncle running. I saw the black jump up in hot pursuit; and before I had time to understand, Rorie also had appeared, calling directions in Gaelic as to a dog herding sheep.

I took to my heels to interfere, and perhaps I had done better to have waited where I was, for I was the means of cutting off the madman's last escape. There was nothing before him from that moment but the grave, the wreck, and the sea in Sandag Bay. And yet Heaven knows that what I did was for the best.

My uncle Gordon saw in what direction, horrible to him, the chase was driving him. He doubled, darting to the right and left; but high as the fever ran in his veins, the black was still the swifter. Turn where he would, he was still forestalled, still driven toward the scene of his crime. Suddenly he began to shriek aloud, so that the coast re-echoed; and now both I and Rorie were calling on the black to stop. But all was vain, for it was written otherwise. The pursuer still ran, the chase still sped before him screaming; they avoided the grave and skimmed close past the timbers of the wreck; in a breath they had cleared the sand, and still my kinsman did not pause, but dashed straight into the surf; and the black, now almost within reach, still followed swiftly behind him. Rorie and I both stopped, for the thing was now beyond the hands of men, and these were the decrees of God that came to pass before our eyes. There was never a sharper ending. On that steep beach they were beyond their depth at a bound; neither could swim; the black rose once for a moment with a throttling cry; but the current had them, racing seaward, and if ever they came up again, which God alone can tell, it would be ten minutes after, at the far end of Aros Roost, where the seabirds hover fishing.

WILL O' THE MILL

The Plain and the Stars

THE MILL WHERE Will lived with his adopted parents stood in a falling valley between pinewoods and great mountains. Above, hill after hill soared upwards until they soared out of the depth of the hardiest timber, and stood naked against the sky. Some way up, a long grey village lay like a seam or a rag of vapour on a wooded hillside; and when the wind was favourable, the sound of the church bells would drop down, thin and silvery, to Will. Below, the valley grew ever steeper and steeper, and at the same time widened out on either hand; and from an eminence beside the mill it was possible to see its whole length and away beyond it over a wide plain, where the river turned and shone, and moved on from city to city on its voyage towards the sea. It chanced that over this valley there lay a pass into a neighbouring kingdom, so that, quiet and rural as it was, the road that ran along beside the river was a high thoroughfare between two splendid and powerful societies. All through the summer, travelling-carriages came crawling up, or went plunging briskly downwards past the mill; and as it happened that the other side was very much easier of ascent, the path was not much frequented, except by people going in one direction; and of all the carriages that Will saw go by, five-sixths were plunging briskly downwards and only one-sixth crawling up. Much more was this the case with foot-passengers. All the light-footed tourists, all the pedlars laden with strange wares, were tending downward like the river that accompanied their path. Nor was this all; for when Will was yet a child a disastrous war arose over a great part of the world. The newspapers were full of defeats and victories, the earth rang with cavalry hoofs, and often for days together and for miles around, the coil of battle terrified good people from their labours in the field. Of all this, nothing was heard for a long time in the valley; but at last one of the commanders pushed an army over the pass by forced marches, and for three days horse and foot, cannon and tumbril, drum and standard, kept pouring downward past the mill. All day the child stood and watched them on their passage – the rhythmical stride, the pale, unshaven faces tanned about the eyes, the discoloured regimentals and the tattered flags, filled him with a sense of weariness, pity, and wonder; and all night long, after he was in bed, he could hear the cannon pounding and the feet trampling, and the great armament sweeping onward and downward past the mill. No one in the valley ever heard the fate of the expedition, for they lay out of the way of gossip in those troublous times; but Will saw one thing plainly, that not a man returned. Whither had they all gone? Whither went all the tourists and pedlars with strange wares? whither all the brisk barouches with servants in the dicky? whither the water of the stream, ever coursing downward and ever renewed from above? Even the wind blew oftener down the valley, and carried the dead leaves along with it in the fall. It seemed like a great conspiracy of things animate and inanimate; they all went downward, fleetly and gaily downward, and only he, it seemed, remained behind, like a stock upon the wayside. It sometimes made him glad when he noticed how the fishes kept their heads up stream. They, at least, stood faithfully by him, while all else were posting downward to the unknown world.

One evening he asked the miller where the river went.

'It goes down the valley,' answered he, 'and turns a power of mills – six score mills, they say, from here to Unterdeck – and it none the wearier after all. And then it goes out into the lowlands, and waters the great corn country, and runs through a sight of fine cities (so they say) where kings live all alone in great palaces, with a sentry walking up and down before the door. And it goes under bridges with stone men upon them, looking down and smiling so curious at the water, and living folks leaning their elbows on the wall and looking over too. And then it goes on and on, and down through marshes and sands, until at last it falls into the sea, where the ships are that bring parrots and tobacco from the Indies. Ay, it has a long trot before it as it goes singing over our weir, bless its heart!'

'And what is the sea?' asked Will.

'The sea!' cried the miller. 'Lord help us all, it is the greatest thing God made! That is where all the water in the world runs down into a great salt lake. There it lies, as flat as my hand and as innocent-like as a child; but they do say when the wind blows it gets up into water-mountains bigger than any of ours, and swallows down great ships bigger than our mill, and makes such a roaring that you can hear it miles away upon the land. There are great fish in it five times bigger than a bull, and one old serpent as long as our river and as old as all the world, with whiskers like a man, and a crown of silver on her head.'

Will thought he had never heard anything like this, and he kept on asking question after question about the world that lay away down the river, with all its perils and marvels, until the old miller became quite interested himself, and at last took him by the hand and led him to the hill-top that overlooks the valley and the plain. The sun was near setting, and hung low down in a cloudless sky. Everything was defined and glorified in golden light. Will had never seen so great an expanse of country in his life; he stood and gazed with all his eyes. He could see the cities, and the woods and fields, and the bright curves of the river, and far away to where the rim of the plain trenched along the shining heavens. An overmastering emotion seized upon the boy, soul and body; his heart beat so thickly that he could not breathe; the scene swam before his eyes; the sun seemed to wheel round and round, and throw off, as it turned, strange shapes which disappeared with the rapidity of thought, and were succeeded by others. Will covered his face with his hands, and burst into a violent fit of tears; and the poor miller, sadly disappointed and perplexed, saw nothing better for it than to take him up in his arms and carry him home in silence.

From that day forward Will was full of new hopes and longings. Something kept tugging at his heart-strings; the running water carried his desires along with it as he dreamed over its fleeting surface; the wind, as it ran over innumerable tree-tops, hailed him with encouraging words; branches beckoned downward; the open road, as it shouldered round the angles and went turning and vanishing fast and faster down the valley, tortured him with its solicitations. He spent long whiles on the eminence, looking down the river-shed and abroad on the fat lowlands, and watched the clouds that travelled forth upon the sluggish wind and trailed their purple shadows on the plain; or he would linger by the wayside, and follow the carriages with his eyes as they rattled downward by the river. It did not matter what it was; everything that went that way, were it cloud or carriage, bird or brown water in the stream, he felt his heart flow out after it in an ecstasy of longing.

We are told by men of science that all the ventures of mariners on the sea, all that counter-marching of tribes and races that confounds old history with its dust and rumour, sprang from nothing more abstruse than the laws of supply and demand, and a certain natural instinct for cheap rations. To any one thinking deeply, this will seem a dull and pitiful explanation. The tribes that came swarming out of the North and East, if they were indeed pressed onward from behind by others, were drawn at the same time by the magnetic influence of the South and West. The fame of other lands had reached them; the name of the Eternal City rang in their ears; they were not colonists, but pilgrims; they travelled towards wine and gold and sunshine, but their hearts were set on something higher. That divine unrest, that old stinging trouble of humanity that makes all high achievements and all miserable failure, the same that spread wings with Icarus, the same that sent Columbus into the desolate Atlantic, inspired and supported these barbarians on their perilous march. There is one legend which profoundly represents their spirit, of how a flying party of these wanderers encountered a very old man shod with iron. The old man asked them whither they were going, and they answered with one voice: 'To the Eternal City!' He looked upon them gravely. 'I have sought it,' he said, 'over the most part of the world. Three such pairs as I now carry on my feet have I worn out upon this pilgrimage, and now the fourth is growing slender underneath my steps. And all this while I have not found the city.' And he turned and went his own way alone, leaving them astonished.

And yet this would scarcely parallel the intensity of Will's feeling for the plain. If he could only go far enough out there, he felt as if his eyesight would be purged and clarified, as if his bearing would grow more delicate, and his very breath would come and go with luxury. He was transplanted and withering where he was; he lay in a strange country and was sick for home. Bit by bit, he pieced together broken notions of the world below: of the river, ever moving and growing until it sailed forth into the majestic ocean; of the cities, full of brisk and beautiful people, playing fountains, bands of music and marble palaces, and lighted up at night from end to end with artificial stars of gold; of the great churches, wise universities, brave armies, and untold money lying stored in vaults; of the high-flying vice that moved in the sunshine, and the stealth and swiftness of midnight murder. I have said he was sick as if for home: the figure halts. He was like someone lying in twilit, formless pre-existence, and stretching out his hands lovingly towards many-coloured, many-sounding life. It was no wonder he was unhappy, he would go and tell the fish: they were made for their life, wished for no more than worms and running water, and a hole below a falling bank; but he was differently designed, full of desires and aspirations, itching at the fingers, lusting with the eyes, whom the whole variegated world could not satisfy with aspects. The true life, the true bright sunshine, lay far out upon the plain. And oh! to see this sunlight once more before he died! to move with a jocund spirit in a golden land! to hear the trained singers and sweet church bells, and see the holiday gardens! 'And oh, fish!' he would cry, 'if you would only turn your noses down stream, you could swim so easily into the fabled waters and see the vast ships passing over your head like clouds, and hear the great water-hills making music over you all day long!' But the fish kept looking patiently in their own direction, until Will hardly knew whether to laugh or cry.

Hitherto the traffic on the road had passed by Will like something seen in a picture: he had perhaps exchanged salutations with a tourist, or caught sight of an old gentleman in a travelling cap at a carriage window; but for the most part it had been a mere symbol, which he contemplated from apart and with something of a superstitious feeling. A time came at last when this was to be changed. The miller, who was a greedy man in his way, and never forwent an opportunity of honest profit, turned the mill-house into a little wayside inn and, several pieces of good fortune falling in opportunely, built stables and got the position of postmaster on the road. It now became Will's duty to wait upon people, as they sat to break their fasts in the little arbour at the top of the mill-garden; and you may be sure that he kept his ears open, and learned many new things about the outside world as he brought the omelette or the wine. Nay, he would often get into conversation with single guests, and by adroit questions and polite attention, not only gratify his own curiosity, but win the goodwill of the travellers. Many complimented the old couple on their serving-boy; and a professor was eager to take him away with him, and have him properly educated in the plain. The miller and his wife were mightily astonished and even more pleased. They thought it a very good thing that they should have opened their inn. 'You see,' the old man would remark, 'he has the kind of talent for a publican; he never would have made anything else!' And so life wagged on in the valley, with high satisfaction to all concerned but Will. Every carriage that left the inn-door seemed to take a part of him away with it; and when people jestingly offered him a lift, he could with difficulty command his emotion. Night after night he would dream that he was awakened by flustered servants, and that a splendid equipage waited at the door to carry him down into the plain; night after night, until the dream, which had seemed all jollity to him at first, began to take on a colour of gravity, and the nocturnal summons and waiting equipage occupied a place in his mind as something to be both feared and hoped for.

One day, when Will was about sixteen, a fat young man arrived at sunset to pass the night. He was a contented-looking fellow, with a jolly eye, and carried a knapsack. While dinner was preparing, he sat in the arbour to read a book; but as soon as he had begun to observe Will, the book was laid aside; he was plainly one of those who prefer living people to people made of ink and paper. Will, on his part, although he had not been much interested in the stranger at first sight, soon began to take a great deal of pleasure in his talk, which was full of good nature and good sense, and at last conceived a great respect for his character and wisdom. They sat far into the night, and about two in the morning Will opened his heart to the young man, and told him how he longed to leave the valley and what bright hopes he had connected with the cities of the plain. The young man whistled, and then broke into a smile.

'My young friend,' he remarked, 'you are a very curious little fellow to be sure, and wish a great many things which you will never get. Why, you would feel quite ashamed if you knew how the little fellows in these fairy cities of yours are all after the same sort of nonsense, and keep breaking their hearts to get up into the mountains. And let me tell you, those who go down into the plains are a very short while there before they wish themselves heartily back again. The air is not so light nor so pure; nor is the sun any brighter. As for the beautiful men and women, you would see many of them in rags and many of them deformed with horrible disorders; and a city is so hard a place for people who are poor and sensitive that many choose to die by their own hand.'

'You must think me very simple,' answered Will. 'Although I have never been out of this valley, believe me, I have used my eyes. I know one thing lives on another; for instance, how the fish hangs in the eddy to catch his fellows; and the shepherd, who makes so pretty a picture carrying home a lamb, is only carrying it home for dinner. I do not expect to find all things right in your cites. That is not what troubles me; it might have been that once upon a time; but although I live here always, I have asked many questions and learned a great deal in these last years, and certainly enough to cure me of my old fancies. But you would not have me die like a dog and not see all that is to be seen, and do all that a man can do, let it be good or evil? you would not have me spend all my days between this road here and the river, and not so much as make a motion to be up and live my life? – I would rather die out of hand,' he cried, 'than linger on as I am doing.'

'Thousands of people,' said the young man, 'live and die like you, and are none the less happy.'

'Ah!' said Will, 'if there are thousands who would like, why should not one of them have my place?'

It was quite dark; there was a hanging lamp in the arbour which lit up the table and the faces of the speakers, and along the arch, the leaves upon the trellis stood out illuminated against the night sky, a pattern of transparent green upon a dusky purple. The fat young man rose and, taking Will by the arm, led him out under the open heavens.

'Did you ever look at the stars?' he asked, pointing upwards.

'Often and often,' answered Will.

'And do you know what they are?'

'I have fancied many things.'

'They are worlds like ours,' said the young man. 'Some of them less; many of them a million times greater; and some of the least sparkles that you see are not only worlds, but whole clusters of worlds turning about each other in the midst of space. We do not know what there may be in any of them; perhaps the answer to all our difficulties or the cure of all our sufferings: and yet we can never reach them; not all the skill of the craftiest of men can fit out a ship for the nearest of these our neighbours, nor would the life of the most aged suffice for such a journey. When a great battle has been lost or a dear friend is dead, when we are hipped or in high spirits, there they are unweariedly shining overhead. We may stand down here, a whole army of us together, and shout until we break our hearts, and not a whisper reaches them. We may climb the highest mountain, and we are no nearer them. All we can do is to stand down here in the garden and take off our hats; the starshine lights upon our heads, and where mine is a little bald, I dare say you can see it glisten in the darkness. The mountain and the mouse. That is like to be all we shall ever have to do with Arcturus or Aldebaran. Can you apply a parable?' he added, laying his hand upon Will's shoulder. 'It is not the same thing as a reason, but usually vastly more convincing.'

Will hung his head a little, and then raised it once more to heaven. The stars seemed to expand and emit a sharper brilliancy; and as he kept turning his eyes higher and higher, they seemed to increase in multitude under his gaze.

'I see,' he said, turning to the young man. 'We are in a rat-trap.'

'Something of that size. Did you ever see a squirrel turning in a cage? and another squirrel sitting philosophically over his nuts? I needn't ask you which of them looked more of a fool.'

The Parson's Marjory

AFTER SOME YEARS the old people died, both in one winter, very carefully tended by their adopted son, and very quietly mourned when they were gone. People who had heard of his roving fancies supposed he would hasten to sell the property, and go down the river to push his fortunes. But there was never any sign of such an intention on the part of Will. On the contrary, he had the inn set out on a better footing, and hired a couple of servants to assist him in carrying it on; and there he settled down, a kind, talkative, inscrutable young man, six feet three in his stockings, with an iron constitution and a friendly voice. He soon began to take rank in the district as a bit of an oddity: it was not much to be wondered at from the first, for he was always full of notions, and kept calling the plainest common-sense in question; but what most raised the report upon him was the odd circumstance of his courtship with the parson's Marjory.

The parson's Marjory was a lass about nineteen when Will would be about thirty; well enough looking, and much better educated than any other girl in that part of the country, as became her parentage. She held her head very high, and had already refused several offers of marriage with a grand air, which had got her hard names among the neighbours. For all that she was a good girl, and one that would have made any man well contented.

Will had never seen much of her; for although the church and parsonage were only two miles from his own door, he was never known to go there but on Sundays. It chanced, however, that the parsonage fell into disrepair, and had to be dismantled; and the parson and his daughter took lodgings for a month or so, on very much reduced terms, at Will's inn. Now, what with the inn, and the mill, and the old miller's savings, our friend was a man of substance; and besides that, he had a name for good temper and shrewdness, which make a capital portion in marriage; and so it was currently gossiped, among their ill-wishers, that the parson and his daughter had not chosen their temporary lodging with their eyes shut. Will was about the last man in the world to be cajoled or frightened into marriage. You had only to look into his eyes, limpid and still like pools of water, and yet with a sort of clear light that seemed to come from within, and you would understand at once that here was one who knew his own mind, and would stand to it immovably. Marjory herself was no weakling by her looks, with strong, steady eyes and a resolute and quiet bearing. It might be a question whether she was not Will's match in steadfastness, after all, or which of them would rule the roost in marriage. But Marjory had never given it a thought, and accompanied her father with the most unshaken innocence and unconcern.

The season was still so early that Will's customers were few and far between; but the lilacs were already flowering, and the weather was so mild that the party took dinner under the trellis, with the noise of the river in their ears and the woods ringing about them with the songs of birds. Will soon began to take a particular pleasure in these dinners. The parson was rather a dull companion, with the habit of dozing at table; but nothing rude or cruel ever fell from his lips. And as for the parson's daughter, she suited her surroundings with the best grace imaginable; and whatever she said seemed so pat and pretty that Will conceived a great idea of her talents. He could see her face, as she leaned forward, against a background of rising pinewoods; her eyes shone peaceably; the light lay around her hair like a kerchief; something that was hardly a smile rippled her pale cheeks, and Will could not contain himself from gazing on her in an agreeable dismay. She looked, even in her quietest moments, so complete in herself, and so quick with life down to her finger-tips and the very skirts of her dress, that the remainder of created things became no more than a blot by comparison, and if Will glanced away from her to her surroundings, the trees looked inanimate and senseless, the clouds hung in heaven like dead things, and even the mountain-tops were disenchanted. The whole valley could not compare in looks with this one girl.

Will was always observant in the society of his fellow-creatures; but his observations became almost painfully eager in the case of Marjory. He listened to all she uttered, and read her eyes, at the same time, for the unspoken commentary. Many kind, simple, and sincere speeches found an echo in his heart. He became conscious of a soul beautifully poised upon itself, nothing doubting, nothing desiring, clothed in peace. It was not possible to separate her thoughts from her appearance. The turn of her wrist, the still sound of her voice, the light in her eyes, the lines of her body, fell in tune with her grave and gentle words, like the accompaniment that sustains and harmonises the voice of the singer. Her influence was one thing not to be divided or discussed, only to be felt with gratitude and joy. To Will, her presence recalled something of his childhood, and the thought of her took its place in his mind beside that of dawn, of running water, and of the earliest violets and lilacs. It is the property of things seen for the first time, or for the first time after long, like the flowers in spring, to reawaken in us the sharp edge of sense and that impression of mystic strangeness which otherwise passes out of life with the coming of years; but the sight of a loved face is what renews a man's character from the fountain upwards.

One day after dinner Will took a stroll among the firs; a grave beatitude possessed him from top to toe, and he kept smiling to himself and the landscape as he went. The river ran between the stepping-stones with a pretty wimple; a bird sang loudly in the wood; the hill-tops looked immeasurably high, and as he glanced at them from time to time seemed to contemplate his movements with a beneficent but awful curiosity. His way took him to the eminence which over-looked the plain; and there he sat down upon a stone, and fell into deep and pleasant thought. The plain lay abroad with its cities and silver river; everything was asleep, except a great eddy of birds which kept rising and falling and going round and round in the blue air. He repeated Marjory's name aloud, and the sound of it gratified his ear.

He shut his eyes, and her image sprang up before him, quietly luminous and attended with good thoughts. The river might run for ever; the birds fly higher and higher till they touched the stars. He saw it was empty bustle after all; for here, without stirring a foot, waiting patiently in his own narrow valley, he also had attained the better sunlight.

The next day Will made a sort of declaration across the dinner-table, while the parson was filling his pipe.

'Miss Marjory,' he said, 'I never knew anyone I liked so well as you. I am mostly a cold, unkindly sort of man; not from want of heart, but out of strangeness in my way of thinking; and people seem far away from me. 'Tis as if there were a circle round me, which kept everyone out but you; I can hear the others talking and laughing; but you come quite close. Maybe, this is disagreeable to you?' he asked.

Marjory made no answer.

'Speak up, girl,' said the parson.

'Nay, now,' returned Will, 'I wouldn't press her, parson. I feel tongue-tied myself, who am not used to it; and she's a woman, and little more than a child, when all is said. But for my part, as far as I can understand what people mean by it, I fancy I must be what they call in love. I do not wish to be held as committing myself, for I may be wrong; but that is how I believe things are with me. And if Miss Marjory should feel any otherwise on her part, mayhap she would be so kind as shake her head.'

Marjory was silent, and gave no sign that she had heard.

'How is that, parson?' asked Will.

'The girl must speak,' replied the parson, laying down his pipe. 'Here's our neighbour who says he loves you, Madge. Do you love him, ay or no?'

'I think I do,' said Marjory faintly.

'Well then, that's all that could be wished!' cried Will heartily. And he took her hand across the table, and held it a moment in both of his with great satisfaction.

'You must marry,' observed the parson, replacing his pipe in his mouth.

'Is that the right thing to do, think you?' demanded Will.

'It is indispensable,' said the parson.

'Very well,' replied the wooer.

Two or three days passed by with great delight to Will, although a bystander might scarce have found it out. He continued to take his meals opposite Marjory, and to talk with her and gaze upon her in her father's presence; but he made no attempt to see her alone, nor in any other way changed his conduct towards her from what it had been since the beginning. Perhaps the girl was a little disappointed, and perhaps not unjustly; and yet if it had been enough to be always in the thoughts of another person, and so pervade and alter his whole life, she might have been thoroughly contented. For she was never out of Will's mind for an instant. He sat over the stream, and watched the dust of the eddy, and the poised fish and straining weeds; he wandered out alone into the purple even, with all the blackbirds piping round him in the wood; he rose early in the morning, and saw the sky turn from grey to gold, and the light leap upon the hill-tops; and all the while he kept wondering if he had never seen such things before, or how it was that they should look so different now. The sound of his own mill-wheel, or of the wind among the trees, confounded and charmed his heart. The most enchanting thoughts presented themselves unbidden in his mind. He was so happy that he could not sleep at night, and so restless that he could hardly sit still out of her company. And yet it seemed as if he avoided her rather than sought her out.

One day, as he was coming home from a ramble, Will found Marjory in the garden picking flowers, and as he came up with her, slackened his pace and continued walking by her side.

'You like flowers?' he said.

'Indeed I love them dearly,' she replied. 'Do you?'

'Why, no,' said he, 'not so much. They are a very small affair, when all is done. I can fancy people caring for them greatly, but not doing as you are just now.'

'How?' she asked, pausing and looking up at him.

'Plucking them,' said he. 'They are a deal better off where they are, and look a deal prettier, if you go to that.'

'I wish to have them for my own,' she answered, 'to carry them near my heart, and keep them in my room. They tempt me when they grow here; they seem to say, 'Come and do something with us'; but once I have cut them and put them by, the charm is laid, and I can look at them with quite an easy heart.'

'You wish to possess them,' replied Will, 'in order to think no more about them. It's a bit like killing the goose with the golden eggs. It's a bit like what I wished to do when I was a boy. Because I had a fancy for looking out over the plain, I wished to go down there – where I couldn't look out over it any longer. Was not that fine reasoning? Dear, dear, if they only thought of it, all the world would do like me; and you would let your flowers alone, just as I stay up here in the mountains.' Suddenly he broke off sharp. 'By the Lord!' he cried. And when she asked him what was wrong, he turned the question off, and walked away into the house with rather a humorous expression of face.

He was silent at table, and after the night had fallen and the stars had come out overhead, he walked up and down for hours in the courtyard and garden with an uneven pace. There was still a light in the window of Marjory's room: one little oblong patch of orange in a world of dark blue hills and silver starlight. Will's mind ran a great deal on the window; but his thoughts were not very lover-like. 'There she is in her room,' he thought, 'and there are the stars overhead: – a blessing upon both!' Both were good influences in his life; both soothed and braced him in his profound contentment with the world. And what more should he desire with either? The fat young man and his counsels were so present to his mind, that he threw back his head, and, putting his hands before his mouth, shouted aloud to the populous heavens. Whether from the position of his head or the sudden strain of the exertion, he seemed to see a momentary shock among the stars, and a diffusion of frosty light pass from one to another along the sky. At the same instant, a corner of the blind was lifted and lowered again at once. He laughed a loud ho-ho! 'One and another!' thought Will. 'The stars tremble, and the blind goes up. Why, before Heaven, what a great magician I must be! Now, if I were only a fool should not I be in a pretty way?' And he went off to bed, chuckling to himself: 'If I were only a fool!'

The next morning, pretty early, he saw her once more in the garden, and sought her out.

'I have been thinking about getting married,' he began abruptly; 'and after having turned it all over, I have made up my mind it's not worth while.'

She turned upon him for a single moment; but his radiant, kindly appearance would, under the circumstances, have disconcerted an angel, and she looked down again upon the ground in silence. He could see her tremble.

'I hope you don't mind,' he went on, a little taken aback. 'You ought not. I have turned it all over, and upon my soul there's nothing in it. We should never be one whit nearer than we are just now, and, if I am a wise man, nothing like so happy.'

'It is unnecessary to go round about with me,' she said. 'I very well remember that you refused to commit yourself; and now that I see you were mistaken, and in reality have never cared for me, I can only feel sad that I have been so far misled.'

'I ask your pardon,' said Will stoutly; 'you do not understand my meaning. As to whether I have ever loved you or not, I must leave that to others. But for one thing, my feeling is not changed; and for another, you may make it your boast that you have made my whole life and character something different from what they were. I mean what I say; no less. I do not think getting married is worth while. I would rather you went on living with your father, so that I could walk over and see you once, or maybe twice a week, as people go to church, and then we should both be all the happier between whiles. That's my notion. But I'll marry you if you will,' he added.

'Do you know that you are insulting me?' she broke out.

'Not I, Marjory,' said he; 'if there is anything in a clear conscience, not I. I offer all my heart's best affection; you can take it or want it, though I suspect it's beyond either your power or mine to change what has once been done, and set me fancy-free. I'll marry you, if you like; but I tell you again and again, it's not worth while, and we had best stay friends. Though I am a quiet man I have noticed a heap of things in my life. Trust in me, and take things as I propose; or, if you don't like that, say the word, and I'll marry you out of hand.'

There was a considerable pause, and Will, who began to feel uneasy, began to grow angry in consequence.

'It seems you are too proud to say your mind,' he said. 'Believe me that's a pity. A clean shrift makes simple living. Can a man be more downright or honourable to a woman than I have been? I have said my say, and given you your choice. Do you want me to marry you? or will you take my friendship, as I think best? or have you had enough of me for good? Speak out for the dear God's sake! You know your father told you a girl should speak her mind in these affairs.'

She seemed to recover herself at that, turned without a word, walked rapidly through the garden, and disappeared into the house, leaving Will in some confusion as to the result. He walked up and down the garden, whistling softly to himself. Sometimes he stopped and contemplated the sky and hill-tops; sometimes he went down to the tail of the weir and sat there, looking foolishly in the water. All this dubiety and perturbation was so foreign to his nature and the life which he had resolutely chosen for himself, that he began to regret Marjory's arrival. 'After all,' he thought, 'I was as happy as a man need be. I could come down here and watch my fishes all day long if I wanted; I was as settled and contented as my old mill.'

Marjory came down to dinner looking very trim and quiet; and no sooner were all three at table than she made her father a speech, with her eyes fixed upon her plate, but showing no other sign of embarrassment or distress.

'Father,' she began, 'Mr Will and I have been talking things over. We see that we have each made a mistake about our feelings, and he has agreed, at my request, to give up all idea of marriage, and be no more than my very good friend, as in the past. You see, there is no shadow of a quarrel, and indeed I hope we shall see a great deal of him in the future, for his visits will always be welcome in our house. Of course, father, you will know best, but perhaps we should do better to leave Mr Will's house for the present. I believe, after what has passed, we should hardly be agreeable inmates for some days.'

Will, who had commanded himself with difficulty from the first, broke out upon this into an inarticulate noise, and raised one hand with an appearance of real dismay, as if he were about to interfere and contradict. But she checked him at once, looking up at him with a swift glance and an angry flush upon her cheek.

'You will perhaps have the good grace,' she said, 'to let me explain these matters for myself.'

Will was put entirely out of countenance by her expression and the ring of her voice. He held his peace, concluding that there were some things about this girl beyond his comprehension, in which he was exactly right.

The poor parson was quite crestfallen. He tried to prove that this was no more than a true lovers' tiff, which would pass off before night; and when he was dislodged from that position, he went on to argue that where there was no quarrel there could be no call for a separation; for the good man liked both his entertainment and his host. It was curious to see how the girl managed them, saying little all the time, and that very quietly, and yet twisting them round her finger and insensibly leading them wherever she would by feminine tact and generalship. It scarcely seemed to have been her doing – it seemed as if things had merely so fallen out – that she and her father took their departure that same afternoon in a farm-cart, and went farther down the valley, to wait, until their own house was ready for them, in another hamlet. But Will had been observing closely, and was well aware of her dexterity and resolution. When he found himself alone he had a great many curious matters to turn over in his mind. He was very sad and solitary, to begin with. All the interest had gone out of his life, and he might look up at the stars as long as he pleased, he somehow failed to find support or consolation. And then he was in such a turmoil of spirit about Marjory. He had been puzzled and irritated at her behaviour, and yet he could not keep himself from admiring it. He thought he recognised a fine, perverse angel in that still soul which he had never hitherto suspected; and though he saw it was an influence that would fit but ill with his own life of artificial calm, he could not keep himself from ardently desiring to possess it. Like a man who has lived among shadows and now meets the sun, he was both pained and delighted.

As the days went forward he passed from one extreme to another; now pluming himself on the strength of his determination, now despising his timid and silly caution. The former was, perhaps, the true thought of his heart, and represented the regular tenor of the man's reflections; but the latter burst forth from time to time with an unruly violence, and then he would forget all consideration, and go up and down his house and garden, or walk among the firwoods like one who is beside himself with remorse. To equable, steady-minded Will this state of matters was intolerable; and he determined, at whatever cost, to bring it to an end. So, one warm summer afternoon he put on his best clothes, took a thorn switch in his hand, and set out down the valley by the river. As soon as he had taken his determination, he had regained at a bound his customary peace of heart, and he enjoyed the bright weather and the variety of the scene without any admixture of alarm or unpleasant eagerness. It was nearly the same to him how the matter turned out. If she accepted him he would have to marry her this time, which perhaps was all for the best. If she refused him, he would have done his utmost, and might follow his own way in the future with an untroubled conscience. He hoped, on the whole, she would refuse him; and then, again, as he saw the brown roof which sheltered her, peeping through some willows at an angle of the stream, he was half inclined to reverse the wish, and more than half ashamed of himself for this infirmity of purpose.

Marjory seemed glad to see him, and gave him her hand without affectation or delay.

'I have been thinking about this marriage,' he began.

'So have I,' she answered. 'And I respect you more and more for a very wise man. You understood me better than I understood myself; and I am now quite certain that things are all for the best as they are.'

'At the same time – ' ventured Will.

'You must be tired,' she interrupted. 'Take a seat and let me fetch you a glass of wine. The afternoon is so warm; and I wish you not to be displeased with your visit. You must come quite often; once a week, if you can spare the time; I am always so glad to see my friends.'

'Oh, very well,' thought Will to himself. 'It appears I was right after all.' And he paid a very agreeable visit, walked home again in capital spirits, and gave himself no further concern about the matter.

For nearly three years Will and Marjory continued on these terms, seeing each other once or twice a week without any word of love between them; and for all that time I believe Will was nearly as happy as a man can be. He rather stinted himself the pleasure of seeing her;

and he would often walk half-way over to the parsonage, and then back again, as if to whet his appetite. Indeed there was one corner of the road, whence he could see the church-spire wedged into a crevice of the valley between sloping firwoods, with a triangular snatch of plain by way of background, which he greatly affected as a place to sit and moralise in before returning homewards; and the peasants got so much into the habit of finding him there in the twilight that they gave it the name of 'Will o' the Mill's Corner.'

At the end of the three years Marjory played him a sad trick by suddenly marrying somebody else. Will kept his countenance bravely, and merely remarked that, for as little as he knew of women, he had acted very prudently in not marrying her himself three years before. She plainly knew very little of her own mind, and, in spite of a deceptive manner, was as fickle and flighty as the rest of them. He had to congratulate himself on an escape, he said, and would take a higher opinion of his own wisdom in consequence. But at heart, he was reasonably displeased, moped a good deal for a month or two, and fell away in flesh, to the astonishment of his serving-lads.

It was perhaps a year after this marriage that Will was awakened late one night by the sound of a horse galloping on the road, followed by precipitate knocking at the inn-door. He opened his window and saw a farm-servant, mounted and holding a led horse by the bridle, who told him to make what haste he could and go along with him, for Marjory was dying, and had sent urgently to fetch him to her bedside. Will was no horseman, and made so little speed upon the way that the poor young wife was very near her end before he arrived. But they had some minutes' talk in private, and he was present and wept very bitterly while she breathed her last.

Death

YEAR AFTER YEAR went away into nothing, with great explosions and outcries in the cities on the plain; red revolt springing up and being suppressed in blood, battle swaying hither and thither, patient astronomers in observatory towers picking out and christening new stars, plays being performed in lighted theatres, people being carried into hospital on stretchers, and all the usual turmoil and agitation of men's lives in crowded centres. Up in Will's valley only the winds and seasons made an epoch; the fish hung in the swift stream, the birds circled overhead, the pine-tops rustled underneath the stars, the tall hills stood over all; and Will went to and fro, minding his wayside inn, until the snow began to thicken on his head. His heart was young and vigorous; and if his pulses kept a sober time, they still beat strong and steady in his wrists. He carried a ruddy stain on either cheek, like a ripe apple; he stooped a little, but his step was still firm; and his sinewy hands were reached out to all men with a friendly pressure. His face was covered with those wrinkles which are got in open air, and which, rightly looked at, are no more than a sort of permanent sunburning; such wrinkles heighten the stupidity of stupid faces; but to a person like Will, with his clear eyes and smiling mouth, only give another charm by testifying to a simple and easy life. His talk was full of wise sayings. He had a taste for other people; and other people had a taste for him. When the valley was full of tourists in the season, there were merry nights in Will's arbour; and his views, which seemed whimsical to his neighbours, were often admired by learned people out of towns and colleges. Indeed, he had a very noble old age, and grew daily better known; so that his fame was heard of in the cities of the plain; and the young men who had been summer travellers spoke together in cafés of Will o' the Mill and his rough philosophy. Many and many an invitation, you may be sure, he had; but nothing could tempt him from his upland valley. He would shake his head and smile over his tobacco-pipe with a deal of meaning. 'You come too late,' he would answer. 'I am a dead man now: I have lived and died already. Fifty years ago you would have brought my heart into my mouth; and now you do not even tempt me. But that is the object of long living, that man should cease to care about life.' And again: 'There is only one difference between a long life and a good dinner: that, in the dinner, the sweets come last.' Or once more: 'When I was a boy, I was a bit puzzled, and hardly knew whether it was myself or the world that was curious and worth looking into. Now, I know it is myself, and stick to that.'

He never showed any symptom of frailty, but kept stalwart and firm to the last; but they say he grew less talkative towards the end, and would listen to other people by the hour in an amused and sympathetic silence. Only, when he did speak, it was more to the point and more charged with old experience. He drank a bottle of wine gladly; above all, at sunset on the hill-top or quite late at night under the stars in the arbour. The sight of something attractive and unattainable seasoned his enjoyment, he would say; and he professed he had lived long enough to admire a candle all the more when he could compare it to a planet.

One night, in his seventy-second year, he awoke in bed in such uneasiness of body and mind that he arose and dressed himself and went out to meditate in the arbour. It was pitch dark, without a star; the river was swollen, and the wet woods and meadows loaded the air with perfume. It had thundered during the day, and it promised more thunder for the morrow. A murky, stifling night for a man of seventy-two! Whether it was the weather or the wakefulness, or some little touch of fever in his old limbs, Will's mind was besieged by tumultuous and crying memories. His boyhood, the night with the fat young man, the death of his adopted parents, the summer days with Marjory, and many of those small circumstances, which seem nothing to another, and are yet the very gist of a man's own life to himself – things seen, words heard, looks misconstrued – arose from their forgotten corners and usurped his attention The dead themselves were with him, not merely taking part in this thin show of memory that defiled before his brain, but revisiting his bodily senses as they do in profound and vivid dreams. The fat young man leaned his elbows on the table opposite; Marjory came and went with an apronful of flowers between the garden and the arbour; he could hear the old parson knocking out his pipe or blowing his resonant nose. The tide of his consciousness ebbed and flowed: he was sometimes half-asleep and drowned in his recollections of the past; and sometimes he was broad awake, wondering at himself. But about the middle of the night he was startled by the voice of the dead miller calling to him out of the house as he used to do on the arrival of custom. The hallucination was so perfect that Will sprang from his seat and stood listening for the summons to be repeated; and as he listened he became conscious of another noise besides the brawling of the river and the ringing in his feverish ears. It was like the stir of horses and the creaking of harness, as though a carriage with an impatient team had been brought up upon the road before the courtyard gate. At such an hour, upon this rough and dangerous pass, the supposition was no better than absurd; and Will dismissed it from his mind, and resumed his seat upon the arbour chair; and sleep closed over him again like running water. He was once again awakened by the dead miller's call, thinner and more spectral than before; and once again he heard the noise of an equipage upon the road. And so thrice and four times, the same dream, or the same fancy, presented itself to his senses: until at length, smiling to himself as when one humours a nervous child, he proceeded towards the gate to set his uncertainty at rest.

From the arbour to the gate was no great distance, and yet it took Will some time; it seemed as if the dead thickened around him in the court, and crossed his path at every step. For, first, he was suddenly surprised by an overpowering sweetness of heliotropes; it was as if his garden had been planted with this flower from end to end, and the hot, damp night had drawn forth all their perfumes in a breath. Now the heliotrope had been Marjory's favourite flower, and since her death not one of them had ever been planted in Will's ground.

'I must be going crazy,' he thought. 'Poor Marjory and her heliotropes!'

And with that he raised his eyes towards the window that had once been hers. If he had been bewildered before, he was now almost terrified; for there was a light in the room; the window was an orange oblong as of yore; and the corner of the blind was lifted and let fall as on the night when he stood and shouted to the stars in his perplexity. The illusion only endured an instant; but it left him somewhat unmanned, rubbing his eyes and staring at the outline of the house and the black night behind it. While he thus stood, and it seemed as if he must have stood there quite a long time, there came a renewal of the noises on the road: and he turned in time to meet a stranger who was advancing to meet him across the court. There was something like the outline of a great carriage discernible on the road behind the stranger, and, above that, a few black pine-tops, like so many plumes.

'Master Will?' asked the new-comer, in brief military fashion. 'That same, sir,' answered Will. 'Can I do anything to serve you?'

'I have heard you much spoken of, Master Will,' returned the other; 'much spoken of, and well. And though I have both hands full of business, I wish to drink a bottle of wine with you in your arbour. Before I go, I shall introduce myself.'

Will led the way to the trellis, and got a lamp lighted and a bottle uncorked. He was not altogether unused to such complimentary interviews, and hoped little enough from this one, being schooled by many disappointments. A sort of cloud had settled on his wits and prevented him from remembering the strangeness of the hour. He moved like a person in his sleep; and it seemed as if the lamp caught fire and the bottle came uncorked with the facility of thought. Still, he had some curiosity about the appearance of his visitor, and tried in vain to turn the light into his face; either he handled the lamp clumsily, or there was a dimness over his eyes; but he could make out little more than a shadow at table with him. He stared and stared at this shadow, as he wiped out the glasses, and began to feel cold and strange about the heart. The silence weighed upon him, for he could hear nothing now, not even the river, but the drumming of his own arteries in his ears.

'Here's to you,' said the stranger roughly.

'Here is my service, sir,' replied Will, sipping his wine, which somehow tasted oddly.

'I understand you are a very positive fellow,' pursued the stranger.

Will made answer with a smile of some satisfaction and a little nod.

'So am I,' continued the other; 'and it is the delight of my heart to tramp on people's corns. I will have nobody positive but myself; not one. I have crossed the whims, in my time, of kings and generals and great artists. And what would you say,' he went on, 'if I had come up here on purpose to cross yours?'

Will had it on his tongue to make a sharp rejoinder; but the politeness of an old innkeeper prevailed; and he held his peace and made answer with a civil gesture of the hand.

'I have,' said the stranger. 'And if I did not hold you in a particular esteem, I should make no words about the matter. It appears you pride yourself on staying where you are. You mean to stick by your inn. Now I mean you shall come for a turn with me in my barouche; and before this bottle's empty, so you shall.'

'That would be an odd thing, to be sure,' replied Will, with a chuckle. 'Why, sir, I have grown here like an old oak-tree; the Devil himself could hardly root me up: and for all I perceive you are a very entertaining old gentleman, I would wager you another bottle you lose your pains with me.'

The dimness of Will's eyesight had been increasing all this while; but he was somehow conscious of a sharp and chilling scrutiny which irritated and yet overmastered him.

'You need not think,' he broke out suddenly, in an explosive, febrile manner, that startled and alarmed himself, 'that I am a stay-at-home, because I fear anything under God. God knows I am tired enough of it all; and when the time comes for a longer journey than ever you dream of, I reckon I shall find myself prepared.'

The stranger emptied the glass and pushed it away from him. He looked down for a little, and then, leaning over the table, tapped Will three times upon the forearm with a single finger. 'The time has come!' he said solemnly.

An ugly thrill spread from the spot he touched. The tones of his voice were dull and startling, and echoed strangely in Will's heart.

'I beg your pardon,' he said, with some discomposure. 'What do you mean?'

'Look at me, and you will find your eyesight swim. Raise your hand; it is dead-heavy. This is your last bottle of wine, Master Will, and your last night upon the earth.'

'You are a doctor?' quavered Will.

'The best that ever was,' replied the other; 'for I cure both mind and body with the same prescription. I take away all pain and I forgive all sins; and where my patients have gone wrong in life, I smooth out all complications and set them free again upon their feet.'

'I have no need of you,' said Will.

'A time comes for all men, Master Will,' replied the doctor, 'when the helm is taken out of their hands. For you, because you were prudent and quiet, it has been long of coming, and you have had long to discipline yourself for its reception. You have seen what is to be seen about your mill; you have sat close all your days like a hare in its form; but now that is at an end; and,' added the doctor, getting on his feet, 'you must arise and come with me.'

'You are a strange physician,' said Will, looking steadfastly upon his guest.

'I am a natural law,' he replied, 'and people call me Death.'

'Why did you not tell me so at first?' cried Will. 'I have been waiting for you these many years. Give me your hand, and welcome.'

'Lean upon my arm,' said the stranger, 'for already your strength abates. Lean on me as heavily as you need; for though I am old, I am very strong. It is but three steps to my carriage, and there all your trouble ends. Why, Will,' he added, 'I have been yearning for you as if you were my own son; and of all the men that ever I came for in my long days, I have come for you most gladly. I am caustic, and sometimes offend people at first sight; but I am a good friend at heart to such as you.'

'Since Marjory was taken,' returned Will, 'I declare before God you were the only friend I had to look for.'

So the pair went arm-in-arm across the courtyard.

One of the servants awoke about this time and heard the noise of horses pawing before he dropped asleep again; all down the valley that night there was a rushing as of a smooth and steady wind descending towards the plain; and when the world rose next morning, sure enough Will o' the Mill had gone at last upon his travels.

MARKHEIM

'YES,' SAID THE DEALER, 'our windfalls are of various kinds. Some customers are ignorant, and then I touch a dividend on my superior knowledge. Some are dishonest,' and here he held up the candle, so that the light fell strongly on his visitor, 'and in that case,' he continued, 'I profit by my virtue.'

Markheim had but just entered from the daylight streets, and his eyes had not yet grown familiar with the mingled shine and darkness in the shop. At these pointed words, and before the near presence of the flame, he blinked painfully and looked aside.

The dealer chuckled. 'You come to see me on Christmas Day,' he resumed, 'when you know that I am alone in my house, put up my shutters, and make a point of refusing business. Well, you will have to pay for that; you will have to pay for my loss of time, when I should be balancing my books; you will have to pay, besides, for a kind of manner that I remark in you today very strongly. I am the essence of discretion, and ask no awkward questions; but when a customer cannot look me in the eye, he has to pay for it.' The dealer once more chuckled; and then, changing to his usual business voice, though still with a note of irony, 'You can give, as usual, a clear account of how you came into the possession of the object?' he continued. 'Still your uncle's cabinet? A remarkable collector, sir!'

And the little pale, round-shouldered dealer stood almost on tip-toe, looking over the top of his gold spectacles, and nodding his head with every mark of disbelief. Markheim returned his gaze with one of infinite pity, and a touch of horror.

'This time,' said he, 'you are in error. I have not come to sell, but to buy. I have no curios to dispose of; my uncle's cabinet is bare to the wainscot; even were it still intact, I have done well on the Stock Exchange, and should more likely add to it than otherwise, and my errand today is simplicity itself. I seek a Christmas present for a lady,' he continued, waxing more fluent as he struck into the speech he had prepared; 'and certainly I owe you every excuse for thus disturbing you upon so small a matter. But the thing was neglected yesterday; I must produce my little compliment at dinner; and, as you very well know, a rich marriage is not a thing to be neglected.'

There followed a pause, during which the dealer seemed to weigh this statement incredulously. The ticking of many clocks among the curious lumber of the shop, and the faint rushing of the cabs in a near thoroughfare, filled up the interval of silence.

'Well, sir,' said the dealer, 'be it so. You are an old customer after all; and if, as you say, you have the chance of a good marriage, far be it from me to be an obstacle. Here is a nice thing for a lady now,' he went on, 'this hand-glass – fifteenth century, warranted; comes from a good collection, too; but I reserve the name, in the interests of my customer, who was just like yourself, my dear sir, the nephew and sole heir of a remarkable collector.'

The dealer, while he thus ran on in his dry and biting voice, had stooped to take the object from its place; and, as he had done so, a shock had passed through Markheim, a start both of hand and foot, a sudden leap of many tumultuous passions to the face. It passed as swiftly as it came, and left no trace beyond a certain trembling of the hand that now received the glass.

'A glass,' he said hoarsely, and then paused, and repeated it more clearly. 'A glass? For Christmas? Surely not?'

'And why not?' cried the dealer. 'Why not a glass?'

Markheim was looking upon him with an indefinable expression. 'You ask me why not?' he said. 'Why, look here – look in it – look at yourself! Do you like to see it? No! nor I – nor any man.'

The little man had jumped back when Markheim had so suddenly confronted him with the mirror; but now, perceiving there was nothing worse on hand, he chuckled. 'Your future lady, sir, must be pretty hard favoured,' said he.

'I ask you,' said Markheim, 'for a Christmas present, and you give me this – this damned reminder of years, and sins and follies – this hand-conscience! Did you mean it? Had you a thought in your mind? Tell me. It will be better for you if you do. Come, tell me about yourself. I hazard a guess now, that you are in secret a very charitable man?'

The dealer looked closely at his companion. It was very odd, Markheim did not appear to be laughing; there was something in his face like an eager sparkle of hope, but nothing of mirth.

'What are you driving at?' the dealer asked.

'Not charitable?' returned the other gloomily. 'Not charitable; not pious; not scrupulous; unloving, unbeloved; a hand to get money, a safe to keep it. Is that all? Dear God, man, is that all?'

'I will tell you what it is,' began the dealer, with some sharpness, and then broke off again into a chuckle. 'But I see this is a love-match of yours, and you have been drinking the lady's health.'

'Ah!' cried Markheim, with a strange curiosity. 'Ah, have you been in love? Tell me about that.'

'I,' cried the dealer. 'I in love! I never had the time, nor have I the time today for all this nonsense. Will you take the glass?'

'Where is the hurry?' returned Markheim. 'It is very pleasant to stand here talking; and life is so short and insecure that I would not hurry away from any pleasure – no, not even from so mild a one as this. We should rather cling, cling to what little we can get, like a man at a cliff's edge. Every second is a cliff, if you think upon it – a cliff a mile high – high enough, if we fall, to dash us out of every feature of humanity. Hence it is best to talk pleasantly. Let us talk of each other: why should we wear this mask? Let us be confidential. Who knows, we might become friends?'

'I have just one word to say to you,' said the dealer. 'Either make your purchase, or walk out of my shop!'

'True, true,' said Markheim. 'Enough fooling. To business. Show me something else.'

The dealer stooped once more, this time to replace the glass upon the shelf, his thin blonde hair falling over his eyes as he did so. Markheim moved a little nearer, with one hand in the pocket of his greatcoat; he drew himself up and filled his lungs; at the same time many different emotions were depicted together on his face – terror, horror, and resolve, fascination and a physical repulsion; and through a haggard lift of his upper lip, his teeth looked out.

'This, perhaps, may suit,' observed the dealer: and then, as he began to re-arise, Markheim bounded from behind upon his victim. The long, skewerlike dagger flashed and fell. The dealer struggled like a hen, striking his temple on the shelf, and then tumbled on the floor in a heap.

Time had some score of small voices in that shop, some stately and slow as was becoming to their great age; others garrulous and hurried. All these told out the seconds in an intricate chorus of tickings. Then the passage of a lad's feet, heavily running on the pavement, broke in upon these smaller voices and startled Markheim into the consciousness of his surroundings. He looked about him awfully. The candle stood on the counter, its flame solemnly wagging in a draught; and by that inconsiderable movement, the whole room was filled with noiseless bustle and kept heaving like a sea; the tall shadows nodding, the gross blots of darkness swelling and dwindling as with respiration, the faces of the portraits and the china gods changing and wavering like images in water. The inner door stood ajar, and peered into that leaguer of shadows with a long slit of daylight like a pointing finger.

From these fear-stricken rovings Markheim's eyes returned to the body of his victim, where it lay both humped and sprawling, incredibly small and strangely meaner than in life. In these poor, miserly clothes, in that ungainly attitude, the dealer lay like so much sawdust. Markheim had feared to see it, and lo! it was nothing. And yet, as he gazed, this bundle of old clothes and pool of blood began to find eloquent voices. There it must lie; there was none to work the cunning hinges or direct the miracle of locomotion – there it must lie till it was found. Found! ay, and then? Then would his dead flesh lift up a cry that would ring over England, and fill the world with the echoes of pursuit. Ay, dead or not, this was still the enemy. 'Time was that when the brains were out,' he thought; and the first word struck into his mind. Time, now that the deed was accomplished – time, which had closed for the victim, had become instant and momentous for the slayer.

The thought was yet in his mind, when, first one and then another, with every variety of pace and voice – one deep as the bell from a cathedral turret, another ringing on its treble notes the prelude of a waltz – the clocks began to strike the hour of three in the afternoon.

The sudden outbreak of so many tongues in that dumb chamber staggered him. He began to bestir himself, going to and fro with the candle, beleaguered by moving shadows, and startled to the soul by chance reflections. In many rich mirrors, some of home design, some from Venice or Amsterdam, he saw his face repeated and repeated, as it were an army of spies; his own eyes met and detected him; and the sound of his own steps, lightly as they fell, vexed the surrounding quiet. And still, as he continued to fill his pockets, his mind accused him with a sickening iteration of the thousand faults of his design. He should have chosen a more quiet hour; he should have prepared an alibi; he should not have used a knife; he should have been more cautious and only bound and gagged the dealer, and not killed him; he should have been more bold and killed the servant also; he should have done all things otherwise; poignant regrets, weary, incessant toiling of the mind to change what was unchangeable, to plan what was now useless, to be the architect of the irrevocable past. Meanwhile, and behind all this activity, brute terrors, like the scurrying of rats in a deserted attic, filled the more remote chambers of his brain with riot; the hand of the constable would fall heavy on his shoulder, and his nerves would jerk like a hooked fish; or he beheld, in galloping defile, the dock, the prison, the gallows, and the black coffin.

Terror of the people in the street sat down before his mind like a besieging army. It was impossible, he thought, but that some rumour of the struggle must have reached their ears and set on edge their curiosity; and now, in all the neighbouring houses, he divined them sitting motionless and with uplifted ear – solitary people, condemned to spend Christmas dwelling alone on memories of the past, and now startingly recalled from that tender exercise; happy family parties, struck into silence round the table, the mother still with raised finger: every degree and age and humour, but all, by their own hearths, prying and hearkening and weaving the rope that was to hang him. Sometimes it seemed to him he could not move too softly; the clink of the tall Bohemian goblets rang out loudly like a bell; and alarmed by the bigness of the ticking, he was tempted to stop the clocks. And then, again, with a swift transition of his terrors, the very silence of the place appeared a source of peril, and a thing to strike and freeze the passer-by; and he would step more boldly, and bustle aloud among the contents of the shop and imitate, with elaborate bravado, the movements of a busy man at ease in his own house.

But he was now so pulled about by different alarms that, while one portion of his mind was still alert and cunning, another trembled on the brink of lunacy. One hallucination in particular took a strong hold on his credulity. The neighbour hearkening with white face beside his window, the passer-by arrested by a horrible surmise on the pavement – these could at worst suspect, they could not know; through the brick walls and shuttered windows only sounds could penetrate. But here, within the house, was he alone? He knew he was; he had watched the servant set forth sweethearting, in her poor best, 'out for the day' written in every ribbon and smile. Yes, he was alone, of course; and yet, in the bulk of empty house above him, he could surely hear a stir of delicate footing – he was surely conscious, inexplicably conscious of some presence. Ay, surely; to every room and corner of the house his imagination followed it; and now it was a faceless thing, and yet had eyes to see with; and again it was a shadow of himself; and yet again behold the image of the dead dealer, re-inspired with cunning and hatred.

At times, with a strong effort, he would glance at the open door which still seemed to repel his eyes. The house was tall, the skylight small and dirty, the day blind with fog; and the light that filtered down to the ground storey was exceedingly faint, and showed dimly on the threshold of the shop. And yet, in that strip of doubtful brightness, did there not hang wavering a shadow?

Suddenly, from the street outside, a very jovial gentleman began to beat with a staff on the shop-door, accompanying his blows with shouts and railleries in which the dealer was continually called upon by name. Markheim, smitten into ice, glanced at the dead man. But no! he lay quite still; he was fled away far beyond earshot of these blows and shoutings; he was sunk beneath seas of silence; and his name, which would once have caught his notice above the howling of a storm, had become an empty sound. And presently the jovial gentleman desisted from his knocking and departed.

Here was a broad hint to hurry what remained to be done, to get forth from this accusing neighbourhood, to plunge into a bath of London multitudes, and to reach, on the other side of day, that haven of safety and apparent innocence – his bed. One visitor had come: at any moment another might follow and be more obstinate. To have done the deed, and yet not to reap the profit, would be too abhorrent a failure. The money, that was now Markheim's concern; and as a means to that, the keys.

He glanced over his shoulder at the open door, where the shadow was still lingering and shivering; and with no conscious repugnance of the mind, yet with a tremor of the belly, he drew near the body of his victim. The human character had quite departed. Like a suit half-stuffed with bran, the limbs lay scattered, the trunk doubled, on the floor; and yet the thing repelled him. Although so dingy and inconsiderable to the eye, he feared it might have more significance to the touch. He took the body by the shoulders and turned it on its back. It was strangely light and supple, and the limbs, as if they had been broken, fell into the oddest postures. The face was robbed of all expression; but it was as pale as wax, and shockingly smeared with blood about one temple. That was, for Markheim, the one displeasing circumstance. It carried him back, upon the instant, to a certain fair-day in a fishers' village: a grey day, a piping wind, a crowd upon the street, the blare of brasses, the booming of drums, the nasal voice of a ballad singer; and a boy going to and fro, buried over head in the crowd and divided between interest and fear, until, coming out on the chief place of concourse, he beheld a booth and a great screen with pictures, dismally designed, garishly coloured: Brownrigg with her apprentice; the Mannings with their murdered guest; Weare in the death-grip of Thurtell; and a score besides of famous crimes. The thing was as dear as an illusion; he was once again that little boy; he was looking once again, and with the same sense of physical revolt, at these vile pictures; he was still stunned by the thumping of the drums. A bar of that day's music returned upon his memory; and at that, for the first time, a qualm came over him, a breath of nausea, a sudden weakness of the joints, which he must instantly resist and conquer.

He judged it more prudent to confront than to flee from these considerations; looking the more hardily in the dead face, bending his mind to realise the nature and greatness of his crime. So little a while ago that face had moved with every change of sentiment, that pale mouth had spoken, that body had been all on fire with governable energies; and now, and by his act, that piece of life had been arrested, as the horologist, with interjected finger, arrests the beating of the clock. So he reasoned in vain; he could rise to no more remorseful consciousness; the same heart which had shuddered before the painted effigies of crime, looked on its reality unmoved. At best, he felt a gleam of pity for one who had been endowed in vain with all those faculties that can make the world a garden of enchantment, one who had never lived and who was now dead. But of penitence, no, not a tremor.

With that, shaking himself clear of these considerations, he found the keys and advanced towards the open door of the shop. Outside, it had begun to rain smartly; and the sound of the shower upon the roof had banished silence. Like some dripping cavern, the chambers of the house were haunted by an incessant echoing, which filled the ear and mingled with the ticking of the clocks. And, as Markheim approached the door, he seemed to hear, in answer to his own cautious tread, the steps of another foot withdrawing up the stair. The shadow still palpitated loosely on the threshold. He threw a ton's weight of resolve upon his muscles, and drew back the door.

The faint, foggy daylight glimmered dimly on the bare floor and stairs; on the bright suit of armour posted, halbert in hand, upon the landing; and on the dark wood-carvings and framed pictures that hung against the yellow panels of the wainscot. So loud was the beating of the rain through all the house, that, in Markheim's ears, It began to be distinguished into many different sounds. Footsteps and sighs, the tread of regiments marching in the distance, the chink of money in the counting, and the creaking of doors held stealthily ajar, appeared to mingle with the patter of the drops upon the cupola and the gushing of the water in the pipes. The sense that he was not alone grew upon him to the verge of madness. On every side he was haunted and begirt by presences. He heard them moving in the upper chambers; from the shop, he heard the dead man getting to his legs; and as he began with a great effort to mount the stairs, feet fled quietly before him and followed stealthily behind. If he were but deaf, he thought, how tranquilly he would possess his soul! And then again, and hearkening with ever fresh attention, he blessed himself for that unresting sense which held the outposts and stood a trusty sentinel upon his life. His head turned continually on his neck; his eyes, which seemed starting from their orbits, scouted on every side, and on every side were half-rewarded as with the tail of something nameless vanishing. The four-and-twenty steps to the first floor were four-and-twenty agonies.

On that first storey the doors stood ajar, three of them like three ambushes, shaking his nerves like the throats of cannon. He could never again, he felt, be sufficiently immured and fortified from men's observing eyes; he longed to be home, girt in by walls, buried among bed-clothes, and invisible to all but God. And at that thought he wondered a little, recollecting tales of other murderers and the fear they were said to entertain of heavenly avengers. It was not so, at least, with him. He feared the laws of nature, lest in their callous and immutable procedure they should preserve some damning evidence of his crime. He feared tenfold more, with a slavish, superstitious terror, some scission in the continuity of man's experience, some wilful illegality of nature. He played a game of skill, depending on the rules, calculating consequence from cause; and what if nature, as the defeated tyrant overthrew the chess-board, should break the mould of their succession? The like had befallen Napoleon (so writers said) when the winter changed the time of its appearance. The like might befall Markheim; the solid walls might become transparent and reveal his doings like those of bees in a glass hive; the stout planks might yield under his foot like quicksands and detain him in their clutch; ay, and there were soberer accidents that might destroy him; if, for instance, the house should fall and imprison him beside the body of his victim; or the house next door should fly on fire, and the firemen invade him from all sides. These things he feared; and, in a sense, these things might be called the hands of God reached forth against sin. But about God Himself he was at ease; his act was doubtless exceptional, but so were his excuses, which God knew; it was there, and not among men, that he felt sure of justice.

When he had got safe into the drawing-room and shut the door behind him, he was aware of a respite from alarms. The room was quite dismantled, uncarpeted besides, and strewn with packing-cases and incongruous furniture; several great pier-glasses, in which he beheld himself at various angles, like an actor on a stage; many pictures, framed and unframed, standing, with their faces to the wall; a fine Sheraton sideboard, a cabinet of marquetry, and a great old bed, with tapestry hangings. The windows opened to the floor; but by great good fortune the lower part of the shutters had been closed, and this concealed him from the neighbours. Here, then, Markheim drew in a packing-case before the cabinet and began to search among the keys. It was a long business, for there were many, and it was irksome, besides; for, after all, there might be nothing in the cabinet, and time was on the wing. But the closeness of the occupation sobered him. With the tail of his eye he saw the door – even glanced at it from time to time directly, like a besieged commander pleased to verify the good estate of his defences. But in truth he was at peace. The rain falling in the street

sounded natural and pleasant. Presently, on the other side, the notes of
a piano were wakened to the music of a hymn, and the voices of many
children took up the air and words. How stately, how comfortable was
the melody! How fresh the youthful voices! Markheim gave ear to it
smilingly, as he sorted out the keys; and his mind was thronged with
answerable ideas and images; church-going children and the pealing of
the high organ; children afield, bathers by the brookside, ramblers on
the brambly common, kite-flyers in the windy and cloud-navigated sky;
and then, at another cadence of the hymn, back again to church, and
the somnolence of summer Sundays, and the high genteel voice of the
parson (which he smiled a little to recall), and the painted Jacobean
tombs, and the dim lettering of the Ten Commandments in the
chancel.

And as he sat thus, at once busy and absent, he was startled to his
feet. A flash of ice, a flash of fire, a bursting gush of blood, went over
him, and then he stood transfixed and thrilling. A step mounted the
stair slowly and steadily, and presently a hand was laid upon the knob,
and the lock clicked, and the door opened.

Fear held Markheim in a vice. What to expect he knew not, whether
the dead man walking, or the official ministers of human justice, or
some chance witness blindly stumbling in to consign him to the
gallows. But when a face was thrust into the aperture, glanced round
the room, looked at him, nodded and smiled as if in friendly recognition, and then withdrew again, and the door closed behind it, his fear
broke loose from his control in a hoarse cry. At the sound of this the
visitant returned.

'Did you call me?' he asked pleasantly, and with that he entered the
room and closed the door behind him.

Markheim stood and gazed at him with all his eyes. Perhaps there
was a film upon his sight, but the outlines of the newcomer seemed to
change and waver like those of the idols in the wavering candlelight of
the shop; and at times he thought he knew him; and at times he
thought he bore a likeness to himself; and always, like a lump of living
terror, there lay in his bosom the conviction that this thing was not of
the earth and not of God.

And yet the creature had a strange air of the commonplace, as he
stood looking on Markheim with a smile; and when he added: 'You are
looking for the money, I believe?' it was in the tones of everyday
politeness.

Markheim made no answer.

'I should warn you,' resumed the other, 'that the maid has left her
sweetheart earlier than usual and will soon be here. If Mr Markheim be

found in this house, I need not describe to him the consequences.'

'You know me?' cried the murderer.

The visitor smiled. 'You have long been a favourite of mine,' he said; 'and I have long observed and often sought to help you.'

'What are you?' cried Markheim: 'the Devil?'

'What I may be,' returned the other, 'cannot affect the service I propose to render you.'

'It can,' cried Markheim; 'it does! Be helped by you? No, never; not by you! You do not know me yet; thank God, you do not know me!'

'I know you,' replied the visitant, with a sort of kind severity or rather firmness. 'I know you to the soul.'

'Know me!' cried Markheim. 'Who can do so? My life is but a travesty and slander on myself. I have lived to belie my nature. All men do; all men are better than this disguise that grows about and stifles them. You see each dragged away by life, like one whom bravos have seized and muffled in a cloak. If they had their own control – if you could see their faces, they would be altogether different, they would shine out for heroes and saints! I am worse than most; myself is more overlaid; my excuse is known to me and God. But, had I the time, I could disclose myself.'

'To me?' inquired the visitant.

'To you before all,' returned the murderer. 'I supposed you were intelligent. I thought – since you exist – you would prove a reader of the heart. And yet you would propose to judge me by my acts! Think of it; my acts! I was born and I have lived in a land of giants; giants have dragged me by the wrists since I was born out of my mother – the giants of circumstance. And you would judge me by my acts! But can you not look within? Can you not understand that evil is hateful to me? Can you not see within me the clear writing of conscience, never blurred by any wilful sophistry, although too often disregarded? Can you not read me for a thing that surely must be common as humanity – the unwilling sinner?'

'All this is very feelingly expressed,' was the reply, 'but it regards me not. These points of consistency are beyond my province, and I care not in the least by what compulsion you may have been dragged away, so as you are but carried in the right direction. But time flies; the servant delays, looking in the faces of the crowd and at the pictures on the hoardings, but still she keeps moving nearer; and remember, it is as if the gallows itself was striding towards you through the Christmas streets! Shall I help you; I, who know all? Shall I tell you where to find the money?'

'For what price?' asked Markheim.

'I offer you the service for a Christmas gift,' returned the other.

Markheim could not refrain from smiling with a kind of bitter triumph. 'No,' said he, 'I will take nothing at your hands; if I were dying of thirst, and it was your hand that put the pitcher to my lips, I should find the courage to refuse. It may be credulous, but I will do nothing to commit myself to evil.'

'I have no objection to a death-bed repentance,' observed the visitant.

'Because you disbelieve their efficacy!' Markheim cried.

'I do not say so,' returned the other; 'but I look on these things from a different side, and when the life is done my interest falls. The man has lived to serve me, to spread black looks under colour of religion, or to sow tares in the wheat-field, as you do, in a course of weak compliance with desire. Now that he draws so near to his deliverance, he can add but one act of service to repent, to die smiling, and thus to build up in confidence and hope the more timorous of my surviving followers. I am not so hard a master. Try me. Accept my help. Please yourself in life as you have done hitherto; please yourself more amply, spread your elbows at the board; and when the night begins to fall and the curtains to be drawn, I tell you, for your greater comfort, that you will find it even easy to compound your quarrel with your conscience, and to make a truckling peace with God. I came but now from such a death-bed, and the room was full of sincere mourners, listening to the man's last words: and when I looked into that face, which had been set as a flint against mercy, I found it smiling with hope.'

'And do you, then, suppose me such a creature?' asked Markheim. 'Do you think I have no more generous aspirations than to sin, and sin, and sin, and, at the last, sneak into heaven? My heart rises at the thought. Is this, then, your experience of mankind? or is it because you find me with red hands that you presume such baseness? and is this crime of murder indeed so impious as to dry up the very springs of good?'

'Murder is to me no special category,' replied the other. 'All sins are murder, even as all life is war. I behold your race, like starving mariners on a raft, plucking crusts out of the hands of famine and feeding on each other's lives. I follow sins beyond the moment of their acting; I find in all that the last consequence is death; and to my eyes, the pretty maid who thwarts her mother with such taking graces on a question of a ball, drips no less visibly with human gore than such a murderer as yourself. Do I say that I follow sins? I follow virtues also; they differ not by the thickness of a nail, they are both scythes for the reaping angel of Death. Evil, for which I live, consists not in action but in character.

The bad man is dear to me; not the bad act, whose fruits, if we could
follow them far enough down the hurtling cataract of the ages, might
yet be found more blessed than those of the rarest virtues. And it is not
because you have killed a dealer, but because you are Markheim, that I
offer to forward your escape.'

'I will lay my heart open to you,' answered Markheim. 'This crime
on which you find me is my last. On my way to it I have learned many
lessons; itself is a lesson, a momentous lesson. Hitherto I have been
driven with revolt to what I would not; I was a bond-slave to poverty,
driven and scourged. There are robust virtues that can stand in these
temptations; mine was not so: I had a thirst of pleasure. But today, and
out of this deed, I pluck both warning and riches – both the power and
a fresh resolve to be myself. I become in all things a free actor in the
world; I begin to see myself all changed, these hands the agents of
good, this heart at peace. Something comes over me out of the past;
something of what I have dreamed on Sabbath evenings to the sound of
the church organ, of what I forecast when I shed tears over noble
books, or talked, an innocent child, with my mother. There lies my life;
I have wandered a few years, but now I see once more my city of
destination.'

'You are to use this money on the Stock Exchange, I think?'
remarked the visitor; 'and there, if I mistake not, you have already lost
some thousands?'

'Ah,' said Markheim, 'but this time I have a sure thing.'

'This time, again, you will lose,' replied the visitor quietly.

'Ah, but I keep back the half!' cried Markheim.

'That also you will lose,' said the other.

The sweat started upon Markheim's brow. 'Well, then, what matter?' he exclaimed. 'Say it be lost, say I am plunged again in poverty,
shall one part of me, and that the worse, continue until the end to
override the better? Evil and good run strong in me, haling me both
ways. I do not love the one thing, I love all. I can conceive great deeds,
renunciations, martyrdoms; and though I be fallen to such a crime as
murder, pity is no stranger to my thoughts. I pity the poor; who knows
their trials better than myself? I pity and help them; I prize love, I love
honest laughter; there is no good thing nor true thing on earth but I
love it from my heart. And are my vices only to direct my life, and my
virtues to lie without effect, like some passive lumber of the mind? Not
so; good, also, is a spring of acts.'

But the visitant raised his finger. 'For six-and-thirty years that you
have been in this world,' said he, 'through many changes of fortune and
varieties of humour, I have watched you steadily fall. Fifteen years ago

you would have started at a theft. Three years back you would have blenched at the name of murder. Is there any crime, is there any cruelty or meanness, from which you still recoil? – five years from now I shall detect you in the fact! Downward, downward, lies your way; nor can anything but death avail to stop you.'

'It is true,' Markheim said huskily, 'I have in some degree complied with evil. But it is so with all; the very saints, in the mere exercise of living, grow less dainty, and take on the tone of their surroundings.'

'I will propound to you one simple question,' said the other; 'and as you answer, I shall read to you your moral horoscope. You have grown in many things more lax; possibly you do right to be so; and at any account, it is the same with all men. But granting that, are you in any one particular, however trifling, more difficult to please with your own conduct, or do you go in all things with a looser rein?'

'In any one?' repeated Markheim, with an anguish of consideration. 'No,' he added, with despair, 'in none! I have gone down in all.'

'Then,' said the visitor, 'content yourself with what you are, for you will never change; and the words of your part on this stage are irrevocably written down.'

Markheim stood for a long while silent, and indeed it was the visitor who first broke the silence. 'That being so,' he said, 'shall I show you the money?'

'And grace?' cried Markheim.

'Have you not tried it?' returned the other. 'Two or three years ago, did I not see you on the platform of revival meetings, and was not your voice the loudest in the hymn?'

'It is true,' said Markheim; 'and I see clearly what remains for me by way of duty. I thank you for these lessons from my soul; my eyes are opened, and I behold myself at last for what I am.'

At this moment the sharp note of the door-bell rang through the house; and the visitant, as though this were some concerted signal for which he had been waiting, changed at once in his demeanour.

'The maid!' he cried. 'She has returned, as I forewarned you, and there is now before you one more difficult passage. Her master, you must say, is ill; you must let her in, with an assured but rather serious countenance – no smiles, no overacting, and I promise you success! Once the girl within, and the door closed, the same dexterity that has already rid you of the dealer will relieve you of this last danger in your path. Thenceforward you have the whole evening – the whole night, if needful – to ransack the treasures of the house and to make good your safety. This is help that comes to you with the mask of danger. Up!' he cried; 'up, friend; your life hangs trembling in the scales: up, and act!'

Markheim steadily regarded his counsellor. 'If I be condemned to evil acts,' he said, 'there is still one door of freedom open – I can cease from action. If my life be an ill thing, I can lay it down. Though I be, as you say truly, at the beck of every small temptation, I can yet, by one decisive gesture, place myself beyond the reach of all. My love of good is damned to barrenness; it may, and let it be! But I have still my hatred of evil; and from that, to your galling disappointment, you shall see that I can draw both energy and courage.'

The features of the visitor began to undergo a wonderful and lovely change: they brightened and softened with a tender triumph, and, even as they brightened, faded and dislimned. But Markheim did not pause to watch or understand the transformation. He opened the door and went downstairs very slowly, thinking to himself. His past went soberly before him; he beheld it as it was, ugly and strenuous like a dream, random as chancemedley – a scene of defeat. Life, as he thus reviewed it, tempted him no longer; but on the farther side he perceived a quiet haven for his bark. He paused in the passage and looked into the shop, where the candle still burned by the dead body. It was strangely silent. Thoughts of the dealer swarmed into his mind as he stood gazing. And then the bell once more broke out into impatient clamour.

He confronted the maid upon the threshold with something like a smile.

'You had better go for the police,' said he: 'I have killed your master.'

THRAWN JANET

THE REVEREND MURDOCH SOULIS was long minister of the moorland parish of Balweary, in the vale of Dule. A severe, bleak-faced old man, dreadful to his hearers, he dwelt in the last years of his life, without relative or servant or any human company, in the small and lonely manse under the Hanging Shaw. In spite of the iron composure of his features, his eye was wild, scared, and uncertain; and when he dwelt, in private admonitions, on the future of the impenitent, it seemed as if his eye pierced through the storms of time to the terrors of eternity. Many young persons coming to prepare themselves against the season of the Holy Communion were dreadfully affected by his talk. He had a sermon on 1 Peter v. 8, 'The devil as a roaring lion,' on the Sunday after every seventeenth of August, and he was accustomed to surpass himself upon that text both by the appalling nature of the matter and the terror of his bearing in the pulpit. The children were frightened into fits, and the old looked more than usually oracular, and were, all that day, full of those hints that Hamlet deprecated. The manse itself, where it stood by the water of Dule among some thick trees, with the Shaw overhanging it on the one side, and on the other many cold, moorish hill-tops rising towards the sky, had begun, at a very early period of Mr Soulis's ministry, to be avoided in the dusk hours by all who valued themselves upon their prudence; and guidmen sitting at the clachan alehouse shook their heads together at the thought of passing late by that uncanny neighbourhood. There was one spot, to be more particular, which was regarded with especial awe. The manse stood between the high-road and the water of Dule, with a gable to each; its back was towards the kirk-town of Balweary, nearly half a mile away; in front of it, a bare garden, hedged with thorn, occupied the land between the river and the road. The house was two storeys high, with two large rooms on each. It opened not directly on the garden, but on a causewayed path or passage, giving on the road on the one hand, and closed on the other by the tall willows and elders that bordered on the stream. And it was this strip of causeway that enjoyed among the young parishioners of Balweary so infamous a reputation. The minister walked there often after dark, sometimes groaning aloud in the instancy of his unspoken prayers; and when he was from home, and the manse door was locked, the more daring schoolboys ventured, with beating hearts, to 'follow my leader' across that legendary spot.

This atmosphere of terror, surrounding, as it did, a man of God of spotless character and orthodoxy, was a common cause of wonder and subject of inquiry among the few strangers who were led by chance or business into that unknown, outlying country. But many even of the people of the parish were ignorant of the strange events which had marked the first year of Mr Soulis's ministrations; and among those who were better informed, some were naturally reticent, and others shy of that particular topic. Now and again, only, one of the older folk would warm into courage over his third tumbler, and recount the cause of the minister's strange looks and solitary life.

Fifty years syne, when Mr Soulis cam' first into Ba'weary, he was still a young man – a callant, the folk said – fu' o' book learnin' and grand at the exposition, but, as was natural in sae young a man, wi' nae leevin' experience in religion. The younger sort were greatly taken wi' his gifts and his gab; but auld, concerned, serious men and women were moved even to prayer for the young man, whom they took to be a self-deceiver, and the parish that was like to be sae ill-supplied. It was before the days o' the Moderates – weary fa' them; but ill things are like guid – they baith come bit by bit, a pickle at a time; and there were folk even then that said the Lord had left the college professors to their ain devices, an' the lads that went to study wi' them wad hae done mair and better sittin' in a peat-bog, like their forebears of the persecution, wi' a Bible under their oxter and a speerit o' prayer in their heart. There was nae doubt, onyway, but that Mr Soulis had been ower lang at the college. He was careful and troubled for mony things besides the ae thing needful. He had a feck o' books wi' him – mair than had ever been seen before in a' that presbytery; and a sair wark the carrier had wi' them, for they were a' like to have smoored in the Deil's Hag between this and Kilmackerlie. They were books o' divinity, to be sure, or so they ca'd them; but the serious were o' opinion there was little service for sae mony, when the hail o' God's Word would gang in the neuk o' a plaid. Then he wad sit half the day and half the nicht forbye, which was scant decent – writin', nae less; and first, they were feared he wad read his sermons; and syne it was proved he was writin' a book himsel', which was surely no fittin' for ane of his years an' sma' experience.

Onyway it behoved him to get an auld, decent wife to keep the manse for him an' see to his bit denners; and he was recommended to an auld limmer – Janet M'Clour, they ca'd her – and sae far left to himsel' as to be ower persuaded. There was mony advised him to the contrar, for Janet was mair than suspeckit by the best folk in Ba'weary.

Lang or that, she had had a wean to a dragoon; she hadnae come forrit* for maybe thretty year; and bairns had seen her mumblin' to hersel' up on Key's Loan in the gloamin', whilk was an unco time an' place for a God-fearin' woman. Howsoever, it was the laird himsel' that had first tauld the minister o' Janet; and in thae days he wad have gane a far gate to pleesure the laird. When folk tauld him that Janet was sib to the deil, it was a' superstition by his way of it; an' when they cast up the Bible to him an' the witch of Endor, he wad threep it doun their thrapples that thir days were a' gane by, and the deil was mercifully restrained.

Weel, when it got about the clachan that Janet M'Clour was to be servant at the manse, the folk were fair mad wi' her an' him thegether; and some of the guidwives had nae better to dae than get round her door cheeks and chairge her wi' a' that was ken't again her, frae the sodger's bairn to John Tamson's twa kye. She was nae great speaker; folk usually let her gang her ain gate, an' she let them gang theirs, wi' neither Fair-guid-een nor Fair-guid-day; but when she buckled to, she had a tongue to deave the miller. Up she got, an' there wasnae an auld story in Ba'weary but she gart somebody lowp for it that day; they couldnae say ae thing but she could say twa to it; till, at the hinder end, the guidwives up and claught haud of her, and clawed the coats aff her back, and pu'd her doun the clachan to the water o' Dule, to see if she were a witch or no, soum or droun. The carline skirled till ye could hear her at the Hangin' Shaw, and she focht like ten; there was mony a guidwife bure the mark of her neist day an' mony a lang day after; and just in the hettest o' the collieshangie, wha suld come up (for his sins) but the new minister.

'Women,' said he (and he had a grand voice), 'I charge you in the Lord's name to let her go.'

Janet ran to him – she was fair wud wi' terror – an' clang to him, an' prayed him, for Christ's sake, save her frae the cummers; an' they, for their pairt, tauld him a' that was ken't, and maybe mair.

'Woman,' says he to Janet, 'is this true?'

'As the Lord sees me,' says she, 'as the Lord made me, no a word o't. Forbye the bairn,' says she, 'I've been a decent woman a' my days.'

'Will you,' says Mr Soulis, 'in the name of God, and before me, His unworthy minister, renounce the devil and his works?'

Weel, it wad appear that when he askit that, she gave a girn that fairly frichtit them that saw her, an' they could hear her teeth play dirl thegether in her chafts; but there was naething for it but the ae way or

* To come forrit – to offer oneself as a communicant.

the ither; an' Janet lifted up her hand and renounced the deil before them a'.

'And now,' says Mr Soulis to the guidwives, 'home with ye, one and all, and pray to God for His forgiveness.'

And he gied Janet his arm, though she had little on her but a sark, and took her up the clachan to her ain door like a leddy of the land; an' her screighin' and laughin' as was a scandal to be heard.

There were mony grave folk lang ower their prayers that nicht; but when the morn cam' there was sic a fear fell upon a' Ba'weary that the bairns hid theirsels, and even the men folk stood and keekit frae their doors. For there was Janet comin' doun the clachan – her or her likeness, nane could tell – wi' her neck thrawn, and her heid on ae side, like a body that has been hangit, and a girn on her face like an unstreakit corp. By-an'-by they got used wi' it, and even speered at her to ken what was wrang; but frae that day forth she couldnae speak like a Christian woman, but slavered and played click wi' her teeth like a pair o' shears; and frae that day forth the name o' God cam' never on her lips. Whiles she would try to say it, but it michtnae be. Them that kenned best said least; but they never gied that Thing the name o' Janet M'Clour; for the auld Janet, by their way o't, was in muckle hell that day. But the minister was neither to haud nor to bind; he preached about naething but the folk's cruelty that had gi'en her a stroke of the palsy; he skelpt the bairns that meddled her; and he had her up to the manse that same nicht, and dwalled there a' his lane wi' her under the Hangin' Shaw.

Weel, time gaed by; and the idler sort commenced to think mair lichtly o' that black business. The minister was weel thocht o'; he was aye late at the writing, folk wad see his can'le doun by the Dule water after twal' at e'en; and he seemed pleased wi' himsel' and upsitten as at first, though a' body could see that he was dwining. As for Janet she cam' an' she gaed; if she didnae speak muckle afore, it was reason she should speak less then; she meddled naebody; but she was an eldritch thing to see, an' nane wad hae mistrysted wi' her for Ba'weary glebe.

About the end o' July there cam' a spell o' weather, the like o't never was in that countryside; it was lown an' het an' heartless; the herds couldnae win up the Black Hill, the bairns were ower weariet to play; an' yet it was gousty too, wi' claps o' het wund that rumm'led in the glens, and bits o' shouers that slockened naething. We aye thocht it but to thun'er on the morn; but the morn cam', an' the morn's morning, and it was aye the same uncanny weather, sair on folks and bestial. Of a' that were the waur, nane suffered like Mr Soulis; he could neither sleep, nor eat, he tauld his elders; an' when he wasnae writin' at his

weary book, he wad be stravaguin' ower a' the countryside like a man
possessed, when a' body else was blythe to keep caller ben the house.

Abune Hangin' Shaw, in the bield o' the Black Hill, there's a bit
enclosed grund wi' an iron yett; and it seems, in the auld days, that was
the kirkyaird o' Ba'weary, and consecrated by the Papists before the
blessed licht shone upon the kingdom. It was a great howff o' Mr
Soulis's onyway; there he would sit an' consider his sermons; and
indeed it's a bieldy bit. Weel, as he cam' ower the wast end o' the Black
Hill, ae day, he saw first twa, an' syne fower, an' syne seeven corbie
craws fleein' round an' round abune the auld kirkyaird. They flew laigh
and heavy, an' squawked to ither as they gaed; and it was clear to Mr
Soulis that something had put them frae their ordinar. He wasnae easy
fleyed, an' gaed straucht up to the wa's; an' what suld he find there but
a man, or the appearance of a man, sittin' in the inside upon a grave.
He was of a great stature, an' black as hell, and his e'en were singular to
see.* Mr Soulis had heard tell o' black men, mony's the time; but there
was something unco about this black man that daunted him. Het as he
was, he took a kind o' cauld grue in the marrow o' his banes; but up he
spak for a' that; an' says he: 'My friend, are you a stranger in this place?'
The black man answered never a word; he got upon his feet, an'
begude to hirsle to the wa' on the far side; but he aye lookit at the
minister; an' the minister stood an' lookit back; till a' in a meenute the
black man was ower the wa' an' rinnin' for the bield o' the trees. Mr
Soulis, he hardly kenned why, ran after him; but he was sair forjaskit
wi' his walk an' the het, unhalesome weather; and rin as he likit, he got
nae mair than a glisk o' the black man amang the birks, till he won
doun to the foot o' the hill-side, an' there he saw him ance mair, gaun,
hap, step, an' lowp, ower Dule water to the manse.

Mr Soulis wasnae weel pleased that this fearsome gangrel suld mak'
sae free wi' Ba'weary manse; an' he ran the harder, an', wet shoon, ower
the burn, an' up the walk; but the deil a black man was there to see. He
stepped out upon the road, but there was naebody there; he gaed a'
ower the gairden, but na, nae black man. At the hinder end, and a bit
feared as was but natural, he lifted the hasp and into the manse; and
there was Janet M'Clour before his een, wi' her thrawn craig, and nane
sae pleased to see him. And he aye minded sinsyne, when first he set his
een upon her, he had the same cauld and deidly grue.

'Janet,' says he, 'have you seen a black man?'

---

* It was a common belief in Scotland that the devil appeared as a black man.
This appears in several witch trials and I think in Law's *Memorials*, that
delightful storehouse of the quaint and grisly.

'A black man?' quo' she. 'Save us a'! Ye're no wise, minister. There's nae black man in a' Ba'weary.'

But she didnae speak plain, ye maun understand; hut yammered, like a powney wi' the bit in its moo.

'Weel,' says he, 'Janet, if there was nae black man, I have spoken with the Accuser of the Brethren.'

And he sat down like ane wi' a fever, an' his teeth chittered in his heid.

'Hoots,' says she, 'think shame to yoursel', minister'; an' gied him a drap brandy that she keept aye by her.

Syne Mr Soulis gaed into his study amang a' his books. It's a lang, laigh, mirk chalmer, perishin' cauld in winter, an' no very dry even in the tap o' the simmer, for the manse stands near the burn. Sae doun he sat, and thocht of a' that had come an' gane since he was in Ba'weary, an' his hame, an' the days when he was a bairn an' ran daffin' on the braes; and that black man aye ran in his heid like the owercome of a sang. Aye the mair he thocht, the mair he thocht o' the black man. He tried the prayer, an' the words wouldnae come to him; an' he tried, they say, to write at his book, but he could nae mak' nae mair o' that. There was whiles he thocht the black man was at his oxter, an' the swat stood upon him cauld as well-water; and there was other whiles, when he cam' to himsel' like a christened bairn and minded naething.

The upshot was that he gaed to the window an' stood glowrin' at Dule Water. The trees are unco thick, an' the water lies deep an' black under the manse; an' there was Janet washin' the cla'es wi' her coats kilted. She had her back to the minister, an' he, for his pairt, hardly kenned what he was lookin' at. Syne she turned round, an' shawed her face; Mr Soulis had the same cauld grue as twice that day afore, an' it was borne in upon him what folk said, that Janet was deid lang syne, an' this was a bogle in her clay-cauld flesh. He drew back a pickle and he scanned her narrowly. She was tramp-trampin' in the cla'es, croonin' to hersel'; and eh! Gude guide us, but it was a fearsome face. Whiles she sang louder, but there was nae man born o' woman that could tell the words o' her sang; an' whiles she lookit side-lang doun, but there was naething there for her to look at. There gaed a scunner through the flesh upon his banes; and that was Heeven's advertisement. But Mr Soulis just blamed himsel', he said, to think sae ill of a puir auld afflicted wife that hadnae a freend forbye himsel'; an' he put up a bit prayer for him and her, an' drank a little caller water – for his heart rose again the meat – an' gaed up to his naked bed in the gloaming.

That was a nicht that has never been forgotten in Ba'weary, the nicht o' the seventeenth of August, seventeen hun'er' an' twal'. It had been het afore, as I hae said, but that nicht it was hetter than ever. The sun gaed doun among unco-lookin' clouds; it fell as mirk as the pit; no a star, no a breath o' wund; ye couldnae see your han' afore your face, and even the auld folk cuist the covers frae their beds and lay pechin' for their breath. Wi' a' that he had upon his mind, it was gey and unlikely Mr Soulis wad get muckle sleep. He lay an' he tummled; the gude, caller bed that he got into brunt his very banes; whiles he slept, and whiles he waukened; whiles he heard the time o' nicht, and whiles a tyke yowlin' up the muir, as if somebody was deid; whiles he thocht he heard bogles claverin' in his lug, an' whiles he saw spunkies in the room. He behoved, he judged, to be sick; an' sick he was – little he jaloosed the sickness.

At the hinder end, he got a clearness in his mind, sat up in his sark on the bedside, and fell thinkin' ance mair o' the black man an' Janet. He couldnae weel tell how – maybe it was the cauld to his feet – but it cam' in upon him wi' a spate that there was some connection between thir twa, an' that either or baith o' them were bogles. And just at that moment, in Janet's room, which was neist to his, there cam' a stramp o' feet as if men were wars'lin', an' then a loud bang; an' then a wund gaed reishling round the fower quarters of the house; an' then a' was aince mair as seelent as the grave.

Mr Soulis was feared for neither man nor deevil. He got his tinder-box, an' lit a can'le, an' made three steps o't ower to Janet's door. It was on the hasp, an' he pushed it open, an' keeked bauldly in. It was a big room, as big as the minister's ain, an' plenished wi' grand, auld solid gear, for he had naething else. There was a fower-posted bed wi' auld tapestry; and a braw cabinet of aik, that was fu' o' the minister's divinity books, an' put there to be out o' the gate; an' a wheen duds o' Janet's lying here and there about the floor. But nae Janet could Mr Soulis see; nor ony sign of a contention. In he gaed (an' there's few that wad ha'e followed him) an' lookit a' round, an' listened. But there was naethin' to be heard, neither inside the manse nor in a' Ba'weary parish, an' naethin' to be seen but the muckle shadows turnin' round the can'le. An' then a' at aince, the minister's heart played dunt an' stood stock-still; an' a cauld wund blew amang the hairs o' his heid. Whaten a weary sicht was that for the puir man's een! For there was Janet hangin' frae a nail beside the auld aik cabinet: her heid aye lay on her shoother, her een were steeked, the tongue projekit frae her mouth, and her heels were twa feet clear abune the floor.

'God forgive us all!' thocht Mr Soulis; 'poor Janet's dead.'

He cam' a step nearer to the corp; an' then his heart fair whammled in his inside. For by what cantrip it wad ill-beseem a man to judge, she was hingin' frae a single nail an' by a single wursted thread for darnin' hose.

It's an awfu' thing to be your lane at nicht wi' siccan prodigies o' darkness; but Mr Soulis was strong in the Lord. He turned an' gaed his ways oot o' that room, and lockit the door ahint him; and step by step, down the stairs, as heavy as leed; and set doon the can'le on the table at the stairfoot. He couldnae pray, he couldnae think, he was dreepin' wi' caul' swat, an' naething could he hear but the dunt-dunt-duntin' o' his ain heart. He micht maybe have stood there an hour, or maybe twa, he minded sae little; when a' o' a sudden, he heard a laigh, uncanny steer upstairs; a foot gaed to an' fro in the cha'mer whaur the corp was hingin'; syne the door was opened, though he minded weel that he had lockit it; an' syne there was a step upon the landin', an' it seemed to him as if the corp was lookin' ower the rail and doun upon him whaur he stood.

He took up the can'le again (for he couldnae want the licht), and as saftly as ever he could, gaed straucht out o' the manse an' to the far end o' the causeway. It was aye pit-mirk; the flame o' the can'le, when he set it on the grund, brunt steedy and clear as in a room; naething moved, but the Dule water seepin' and sabbin' doon the glen, an' yon unhaly footstep that cam' ploddin' doun the stairs inside the manse. He kenned the foot over weel, for it was Janet's; and at ilka step that cam' a wee thing nearer, the cauld got deeper in his vitals. He commended his soul to Him that made an' keepit him; 'and O Lord,' said he, 'give me strength this night to war against the powers of evil.'

By this time the foot was comin' through the passage for the door; he could hear a hand skirt alang the wa', as if the fearsome thing was feelin' for its way. The saughs tossed an' maned thegether, a lang sigh cam' ower the hills, the flame o' the can'le was blawn aboot; an' there stood the corp of Thrawn Janet, wi' her grogram goun an' her black mutch, wi' the heid aye upon the shouther, an' the girn still upon the face o't – leevin', ye wad hae said – deid, as Mr Soulis weel kenned – upon the threshold o' the manse.

It's a strange thing that the saul of man should be that thirled into his perishable body; but the minister saw that, an' his heart didnae break.

She didnae stand there lang; she began to move again an' cam' slowly towards Mr Soulis whaur he stood under the saughs. A' the life o' his body, a' the strength o' his speerit, were glowerin' frae his een. It seemed she was gaun to speak, but wanted words, an' made a sign wi' the left hand. There cam' a clap o' wund, like a cat's fuff; oot gaed the can'le, the saughs skreighed like folk; an' Mr Soulis kenned that, live or die, this was the end o't.

'Witch, beldame, devil!' he cried, 'I charge you, by the power of God, begone – if you be dead, to the grave – if you be damned, to hell.'

An' at that moment the Lord's ain hand out o' the Heevens struck the Horror whaur it stood; the auld, deid, desecrated corp o' the witch-wife, sae lang keepit frae the grave and hirsled round by deils, lowed up like a brunstane spunk and fell in ashes to the grund; the thunder followed, peal on dirling peal, the rairing rain upon the back o' that; and Mr Soulis lowped through the garden hedge, and ran, wi' skelloch upon skelloch, for the clachan.

That same mornin', John Christie saw the Black Man pass the Muckle Cairn as it was chappin' six; before eicht, he gaed by the change-house at Knockdow; an' no lang after, Sandy M'Lellan saw him gaun linkin' doun the braes frae Kilmackerlie. There's little doubt but it was him that dwalled sae lang in Janet's body; but he was awa' at last; and sinsyne the deil has never fashed us in Ba'weary.

But it was a sair dispensation for the minister; lang, lang he lay ravin' in his bed; and frae that hour to this, he was the man ye ken the day.

OLALLA

'Now,' SAID THE DOCTOR, 'my part is done, and, I may say, with some vanity, well done. It remains only to get you out of this cold and poisonous city, and to give you two months of a pure air and an easy conscience. The last is your affair. To the first I think I can help you. It falls indeed rather oddly; it was but the other day the Padre came in from the country; and as he and I are old friends, although of contrary professions, he applied to me in a matter of distress among some of his parishioners. This was a family – but you are ignorant of Spain, and even the names of our grandees are hardly known to you; suffice it, then, that they were once great people, and are now fallen to the brink of destitution. Nothing now belongs to them but the residencia, and certain leagues of desert mountain, in the greater part of which not even a goat could support life. But the house is a fine old place, and stands at a great height among the hills, and most salubriously; and I had no sooner heard my friend's tale than I remembered you. I told him I had a wounded officer, wounded in the good cause, who was now able to make a change; and I proposed that his friends should take you for a lodger. Instantly the Padre's face grew dark, as I had maliciously foreseen it would. It was out of the question, he said. Then let them starve, said I, for I have no sympathy with tatterdemalion pride. Thereupon we separated, not very content with one another; but yesterday, to my wonder, the Padre returned and made a submission: the difficulty, he said, he had found upon enquiry to be less than he had feared; or, in other words, these proud people had put their pride in their pocket. I closed with the offer; and, subject to your approval, I have taken rooms for you in the residencia. The air of these mountains will renew your blood; and the quiet in which you will there live is worth all the medicines in the world.'

'Doctor,' said I, 'you have been throughout my good angel, and your advice is a command. But tell me, if you please, something of the family with which I am to reside.'

'I am coming to that,' replied my friend; 'and, indeed, there is a difficulty in the way. These beggars are, as I have said, of very high descent and swollen with the most baseless vanity; they have lived for some generations in a growing isolation, drawing away, on either hand, from the rich who had now become too high for them, and from the poor, whom they still regarded as too low; and even today, when poverty forces them to unfasten their door to a guest, they cannot do so without a most ungracious stipulation. You are to remain, they say, a stranger; they will give you attendance, but they refuse from the first the idea of the smallest intimacy.'

I will not deny that I was piqued, and perhaps the feeling strengthened my desire to go, for I was confident that I could break down that barrier if I desired. 'There is nothing offensive in such a stipulation,' said I; 'and I even sympathise with the feeling that inspired it.'

'It is true they have never seen you,' returned the doctor politely; 'and if they knew you were the handsomest and the most pleasant man that ever came from England (where I am told that handsome men are common, but pleasant ones not so much so), they would doubtless make you welcome with a better grace. But since you take the thing so well, it matters not. To me, indeed, it seems discourteous. But you will find yourself the gainer. The family will not much tempt you. A mother, a son, and a daughter; an old woman said to be half-witted, a country lout, and a country girl, who stands very high with her confessor, and is, therefore,' chuckled the physician, 'most likely plain; there is not much in that to attract the fancy of a dashing officer.'

'And yet you say they are high-born,' I objected.

'Well, as to that, I should distinguish,' returned the doctor. 'The mother is; not so the children. The mother was the last representative of a princely stock, degenerate both in parts and fortune. Her father was not only poor, he was mad: and the girl ran wild about the residencia till his death. Then, much of the fortune having died with him, and the family being quite extinct, the girl ran wilder than ever, until at last she married, Heaven knows whom; a muleteer some say, others a smuggler; while there are some who uphold there was no marriage at all, and that Felipe and Olalla are bastards. The union, such as it was, was tragically dissolved some years ago; but they live in such seclusion, and the country at that time was in so much disorder, that the precise manner of the man's end is known only to the priest – if even to him.'

'I begin to think I shall have strange experiences,' said I.

'I would not romance, if I were you,' replied the doctor; 'you will find, I fear, a very grovelling and commonplace reality. Felipe, for instance, I have seen. And what am I to say? He is very rustic, very cunning, very loutish, and, I should say, an innocent; the others are probably to match. No, no, señor commandante, you must seek congenial society among the great sights of our mountains; and in these at least, if you are at all a lover of the works of nature, I promise you will not be disappointed.'

The next day Felipe came for me in a rough country cart, drawn by a mule; and a little before the stroke of noon, after I had said farewell to the doctor, the innkeeper, and different good souls who had befriended me during my sickness, we set forth out of the city by the eastern gate, and began to ascend into the sierra. I had been so long a prisoner, since I was left behind for dying after the loss of the convoy, that the mere smell of the earth set me smiling. The country through which we went was wild and rocky, partially covered with rough woods, now of the cork-tree, and now of the great Spanish chestnut, and frequently intersected by the beds of mountain torrents. The sun shone, the wind rustled joyously, and we had advanced some miles, and the city had already shrunk into an inconsiderable knoll upon the plain behind us, before my attention began to be diverted to the companion of my drive. To the eye, he seemed but a diminutive, loutish, well-made country lad, such as the doctor had described, mighty quick and active, but devoid of any culture; and this first impression was with most observers final. What began to strike me was his familiar, chattering talk; so strangely inconsistent with the terms on which I was to be received; and partly from his imperfect enunciation, partly from the sprightly incoherence of the matter, so very difficult to follow clearly without an effort of the mind. It is true I had before talked with persons of a similar mental constitution; persons who seemed to live (as he did) by the senses, taken and possessed by the visual object of the moment and unable to discharge their minds of that impression. His seemed to me (as I sat, distantly giving ear) a kind of conversation proper to drivers, who pass much of their time in a great vacancy of the intellect and threading the sights of a familiar country. But this was not the case of Felipe; by his own account, he was a home-keeper; 'I wish I was there now,' he said; and then, spying a tree by the wayside, he broke off to tell me that he had once seen a crow among its branches.

'A crow?' I repeated, struck by the ineptitude of the remark, and thinking I had heard imperfectly.

But by this time he was already filled with a new idea; hearkening with a rapt intentness, his head on one side, his face puckered; and he struck me rudely, to make me hold my peace. Then he smiled and shook his head.

'What did you hear?' I asked.

'Oh, it is all right,' he said; and began encouraging his mule with cries that echoed unhumanly up the mountain walls.

I looked at him more closely. He was superlatively well-built, light, and lithe and strong; he was well-featured; his yellow eyes were very large, though, perhaps, not very expressive; take him altogether, he was a pleasant-looking lad, and I had no fault to find with him, beyond that he was of a dusky hue, and inclined to hairiness; two characteristics that I disliked. It was his mind that puzzled and yet attracted me. The doctor's phrase – an innocent – came back to me; and I was wondering if that were, after all, the true description, when the road began to go down into the narrow and naked chasm of a torrent. The waters thundered tumultuously in the bottom; and the ravine was filled full of the sound, the thin spray, and the claps of wind, that accompanied their descent. The scene was certainly impressive; but the road was in that part very securely walled in; the mule went steadily forward; and I was astonished to perceive the paleness of terror in the face of my companion. The voice of that wild river was inconstant, now sinking lower as if in weariness, now doubling its hoarse tones; momentary freshets seemed to swell its volume, sweeping down the gorge, raving and booming against the barrier walls; and I observed it was at each of these accessions to the clamour that my driver more particularly winced and blanched. Some thoughts of Scottish superstition and the river Kelpie passed across my mind; I wondered if perchance the like were prevalent in that part of Spain; and turning to Felipe, sought to draw him out.

'What is the matter?' I asked.

'Oh, I am afraid,' he replied.

'Of what are you afraid?' I returned. 'This seems one of the safest places on this very dangerous road.'

'It makes a noise,' he said, with a simplicity of awe that set my doubts at rest.

The lad was but a child in intellect; his mind was like his body, active and swift, but stunted in development; and I began from that time forth to regard him with a measure of pity, and to listen at first with indulgence, and at last even with pleasure, to his disjointed babble.

By about four in the afternoon we had crossed the summit of the mountain line, said farewell to the western sunshine, and began to go down upon the other side, skirting the edge of many ravines and moving through the shadow of dusky woods. There rose upon all sides the voice of falling water, not condensed and formidable as in the gorge of the river, but scattered and sounding gaily and musically from glen to glen. Here, too, the spirits of my driver mended, and he began to sing aloud in a falsetto voice, and with a singular bluntness of musical perception, never true either to melody or key, but wandering at will, and yet somehow with an effect that was natural and pleasing, like that of the song of birds. As the dusk increased, I fell more and more under the spell of this artless warbling, listening and waiting for some articulate air, and still disappointed; and when at last I asked him what

it was he sang – 'Oh,' cried he, 'I am just singing!' Above all, I was taken
with a trick he had of unweariedly repeating the same note at little
intervals; it was not so monotonous as you would think, or, at least, not
disagreeable; and it seemed to breathe a wonderful contentment with
what is, such as we love to fancy in the attitude of trees, or the
quiescence of a pool.

Night had fallen dark before we came out upon a plateau, and drew
up a little after, before a certain lump of superior blackness which I
could only conjecture to be the residencia. Here, my guide, getting
down from the cart, hooted and whistled for a long time in vain; until
at last an old peasant man came towards us from somewhere in the
surrounding dark, carrying a candle in his hand. By the light of this I
was able to perceive a great arched doorway of a Moorish character: it
was closed by iron-studded gates, in one of the leaves of which Felipe
opened a wicket. The peasant carried off the cart to some out-building;
but my guide and I passed through the wicket, which was closed again
behind us; and by the glimmer of the candle, passed through a court,
up a stone stair, along a section of an open gallery, and up more stairs
again, until we came at last to the door of a great and somewhat bare
apartment. This room, which I understood was to be mine, was pierced
by three windows, lined with some lustrous wood disposed in panels,
and carpeted with the skins of many savage animals. A bright fire
burned in the chimney, and shed abroad a changeful flicker; close up to
the blaze there was drawn a table, laid for supper; and in the far end a
bed stood ready. I was pleased by these preparations, and said so to
Felipe; and he, with the same simplicity of disposition that I had
already remarked in him, warmly re-echoed my praises. 'A fine room,'
he said; 'a very fine room. And fire, too; fire is good; it melts out the
pleasure in your bones. And the bed,' he continued, carrying over the
candle in that direction – 'see what fine sheets – how soft, how smooth,
smooth'; and he passed his hand again and again over their texture, and
then laid down his head and rubbed his cheeks among them with a
grossness of content that somehow offended me. I took the candle
from his hand (for I feared he would set the bed on fire) and walked
back to the supper-table, where, perceiving a measure of wine, I poured
out a cup and called to him to come and drink of it. He started to his
feet at once and ran to me with a strong expression of hope; but when
he saw the wine, he visibly shuddered.

'Oh, no,' he said, 'not that; that is for you. I hate it.'

'Very well, señor,' said I; 'then I will drink to your good health, and
to the prosperity of your house and family. Speaking of which,' I added,
after I had drunk, 'shall I not have the pleasure of laying my salutations

in person at the feet of the señora, your mother?'

But at these words all the childishness passed out of his face and was succeeded by a look of indescribable cunning and secrecy. He backed away from me at the same time, as though I were an animal about to leap or some dangerous fellow with a weapon, and when he had got near the door, glowered at me sullenly with contracted pupils. 'No,' he said at last, and the next moment was gone noiselessly out of the room; and I heard his footing die away downstairs as light as rainfall, and silence closed over the house.

After I had supped I drew up the table nearer to the bed and began to prepare for rest; but in the new position of the light, I was struck by a picture on the wall. It represented a woman, still young. To judge by her costume and the mellow unity which reigned over the canvas, she had long been dead; to judge by the vivacity of the attitude, the eyes and the features, I might have been beholding in a mirror the image of life. Her figure was very slim and strong, and of a just proportion; red tresses lay like a crown over her brow; her eyes, of a very golden brown, held mine with a look; and her face, which was perfectly shaped, was yet marred by a cruel, sullen, and sensual expression. Something in both face and figure, something exquisitely intangible, like the echo of an echo, suggested the features and bearing of my guide; and I stood awhile, unpleasantly attracted and wondering at the oddity of the resemblance. The common carnal stock of that race, which had been originally designed for such high dames as the one now looking on me from the canvas, had fallen to baser uses, wearing country clothes, sitting on the shaft and holding the reins of a mule cart, to bring home a lodger. Perhaps an actual link subsisted; perhaps some scruple of the delicate flesh that was once clothed upon with the satin and brocade of the dead lady, now winced at the rude contact of Felipe's frieze.

The first light of the morning shone full upon the portrait, and, as I lay awake, my eyes continued to dwell upon it with growing complacency; its beauty crept about my heart insidiously, silencing my scruples one after another; and while I knew that to love such a woman were to sign and seal one's own sentence of degeneration, I still knew that, if she were alive, I should love her. Day after day the double knowledge of her wickedness and of my weakness grew clearer. She came to be the heroine of many day-dreams, in which her eyes led on to, and sufficiently rewarded, crimes. She cast a dark shadow on my fancy; and when I was out in the free air of heaven, taking vigorous exercise and healthily renewing the current of my blood, it was often a glad thought to me that my enchantress was safe in the grave, her wand of beauty broken, her lips closed in silence, her philtre spilt. And yet I had a half-lingering terror that she might not be dead after all, but re-arisen in the body of some descendant.

Felipe served my meals in my own apartment; and his resemblance to the portrait haunted me. At times it was not; at times, upon some change of attitude or flash of expression, it would leap out upon me like a ghost. It was above all in his ill-tempers that the likeness triumphed. He certainly liked me; he was proud of my notice, which he sought to engage by many simple and childlike devices; he loved to sit close before my fire, talking his broken talk or singing his odd, endless, wordless songs, and sometimes drawing his hand over my clothes with an affectionate manner of caressing that never failed to cause in me an embarrassment of which I was ashamed. But for all that, he was capable of flashes of causeless anger and fits of sturdy sullenness. At a word of reproof, I have seen him upset the dish of which I was about to eat, and this not surreptitiously, but with defiance; and similarly at a hint of inquisition. I was not unnaturally curious, being in a strange place and surrounded by strange people; but at the shadow of a question, he shrank back, lowering and dangerous. Then it was that, for a fraction of a second, this rough lad might have been the brother of the lady in the frame. But these humours were swift to pass; and the resemblance died along with them.

In these first days I saw nothing of any one but Felipe, unless the portrait is to be counted; and since the lad was plainly of weak mind, and had moments of passion, it may be wondered that I bore his dangerous neighbourhood with equanimity. As a matter of fact, it was for some time irksome; but it happened before long that I obtained over him so complete a mastery as set my disquietude at rest.

It fell in this way. He was by nature slothful, and much of a vagabond, and yet he kept by the house, and not only waited upon my wants, but laboured every day in the garden or small farm to the south of the residencia. Here he would be joined by the peasant whom I had seen on the night of my arrival, and who dwelt at the far end of the enclosure, about half a mile away, in a rude out-house; but it was plain to me that, of these two, it was Felipe who did most; and though I would sometimes see him throw down his spade and go to sleep among the very plants he had been digging, his constancy and energy were admirable in themselves, and still more so since I was well assured they were foreign to his disposition and the fruit of an ungrateful effort. But while I admired, I wondered what had called forth in a lad so shuttle-witted this enduring sense of duty. How was it sustained? I asked myself, and to what length did it prevail over his instincts? The priest was possibly his inspirer. But the priest came one day to the residencia;

I saw him both come and go after an interval of close upon an hour, from a knoll where I was sketching, and all that time Felipe continued to labour undisturbed in the garden.

At last, in a very unworthy spirit, I determined to debauch the lad from his good resolutions and, waylaying him at the gate, easily persuaded him to join me in a ramble. It was a fine day, and the woods to which I led him were green and pleasant and sweet-smelling and alive with the hum of insects. Here he discovered himself in a fresh character, mounting up to heights of gaiety that abashed me, and displaying an energy and grace of movement that delighted the eye. He leaped, he ran round me in mere glee; he would stop, and look and listen, and seem to drink in the world like a cordial; and then he would suddenly spring into a tree with one bound, and hang and gambol there like one at home. Little as he said to me, and that of not much import, I have rarely enjoyed more stirring company; the sight of his delight was a continual feast; the speed and accuracy of his movements pleased me to the heart; and I might have been so thoughtlessly unkind as to make a habit of these walks, had not chance prepared a very rude conclusion to my pleasure. By some swiftness or dexterity the lad captured a squirrel in a tree-top. He was then some way ahead of me, but I saw him drop to the ground and crouch there, crying aloud for pleasure like a child. The sound stirred my sympathies, it was so fresh and innocent; but as I bettered my pace to draw near, the cry of the squirrel knocked upon my heart. I have heard and seen much of the cruelty of lads, and above all of peasants; but what I now beheld struck me into a passion of anger. I thrust the fellow aside, plucked the poor brute out of his hands, and with swift mercy killed it. Then I turned upon the torturer, spoke to him long out of the heat of my indignation, calling him names at which he seemed to wither; and at length, pointing toward the residencia, bade him begone and leave me, for I chose to walk with men, not with vermin. He fell upon his knees and, the words coming to him with more clearness than usual, poured out a stream of the most touching supplications, begging me in mercy to forgive him, to forget what he had done, to look to the future. 'Oh, I try so hard,' he said. 'O, commandante, bear with Felipe this once; he will never be a brute again!' Thereupon, much more affected than I cared to show, I suffered myself to be persuaded, and at last shook hands with him and made it up. But the squirrel, by way of penance, I made him bury; speaking of the poor thing's beauty, telling him what pains it had suffered, and how base a thing was the abuse of strength. 'See, Felipe,' said I, 'you are strong indeed; but in my hands you are as helpless as that poor thing of the trees. Give me your hand in mine.

You cannot remove it. Now suppose that I were cruel like you, and took a pleasure in pain. I only tighten my hold, and see how you suffer.' He screamed aloud, his face stricken ashy and dotted with needle points of sweat; and when I set him free he fell to the earth and nursed his hand and moaned over it like a baby. But he took the lesson in good part; and whether from that, or from what I had said to him, or the higher notion he now had of my bodily strength, his original affection was changed into a dog-like, adoring fidelity.

Meanwhile I gained rapidly in health. The residencia stood on the crown of a stony plateau; on every side the mountains hemmed it about; only from the roof, where was a bartizan, there might be seen between two peaks, a small segment of plain, blue with extreme distance. The air in these altitudes moved freely and largely; great clouds congregated there, and were broken up by the wind and left in tatters on the hill-tops; a hoarse, and yet faint rumbling of torrents rose from all round; and one could there study all the ruder and more ancient characters of nature in something of their pristine force. I delighted from the first in the vigorous scenery and changeful weather; nor less in the antique and dilapidated mansion where I dwelt. This was a large oblong, flanked at two opposite corners by bastion-like projections, one of which commanded the door, while both were loopholed for musketry. The lower storey was, besides, naked of windows, so that the building, if garrisoned, could not be carried without artillery. It enclosed an open court planted with pomegranate trees. From this a broad flight of marble stairs ascended to an open gallery, running all round and resting, towards the court, on slender pillars. Thence again, several enclosed stairs led to the upper storeys of the house, which were thus broken up into distinct divisions. The windows, both within and without, were closely shuttered; some of the stonework in the upper parts had fallen; the roof in one place had been wrecked in one of the flurries of wind which were common in these mountains; and the whole house, in the strong, beating sunlight, and standing out above a grove of stunted cork-trees, thickly laden and discoloured with dust, looked like the sleeping palace of the legend. The court, in particular, seemed the very home of slumber. A hoarse cooing of doves haunted about the eaves; the winds were excluded, but when they blew outside, the mountain dust fell here as thick as rain, and veiled the red bloom of the pomegranates; shuttered windows and the closed doors of numerous cellars, and the vacant arches of the gallery, enclosed it; and all day long the sun made broken profiles on the four sides, and paraded the shadow of the pillars on the gallery floor. At the ground level there was, however, a certain pillared recess, which bore the marks of human habitation. Though it was open in front upon the court, it was yet provided with a chimney, where a wood fire would be always prettily blazing; and the tile floor was littered with the skins of animals.

It was in this place that I first saw my hostess. She had drawn one of the skins forward and sat in the sun, leaning against a pillar. It was her dress that struck me first of all, for it was rich and brightly coloured, and shone out in that dusty court-yard with something of the same relief as the flowers of the pomegranates. At a second look it was her beauty of person that took hold of me. As she sat back – watching me, I thought, though with invisible eyes – and wearing at the same time an expression of almost imbecile good-humour and contentment, she showed a perfectness of feature and a quiet nobility of attitude that were beyond a statue's. I took off my hat to her in passing, and her face puckered with suspicion as swiftly and lightly as a pool ruffles in the breeze; but she paid no heed to my courtesy. I went forth on my customary walk a trifle daunted, her idol-like impassivity haunting me; and when I returned, although she was still in much the same posture, I was half surprised to see that she had moved as far as the next pillar, following the sunshine. This time, however, she addressed me with some trivial salutation, civilly enough conceived, and uttered in the same deep-chested, and yet indistinct and lisping tones, that had already baffled the utmost niceness of my hearing from her son. I answered rather at a venture; for not only did I fail to take her meaning with precision, but the sudden disclosure of her eyes disturbed me. They were unusually large, the iris golden like Felipe's, but the pupil at that moment so distended that they seemed almost black; and what affected me was not so much their size as (what was perhaps its consequence) the singular insignificance of their regard. A look more blankly stupid I have never met. My eyes dropped before it even as I spoke, and I went on my way upstairs to my own room, at once baffled and embarrassed. Yet, when I came there and saw the face of the portrait, I was again reminded of the miracle of family descent. My hostess was, indeed, both older and fuller in person; her eyes were of a different colour; her face, besides, was not only free from the ill-significance that offended and attracted me in the painting; it was devoid of either good or bad – a moral blank expressing literally naught. And yet there was a likeness, not so much speaking as immanent, not so much in any particular feature as upon the whole. It should seem, I thought, as if when the master set his signature to that grave canvas, he had not only caught the image of one smiling and false-eyed woman, but stamped the essential quality of a race.

From that day forth, whether I came or went, I was sure to find the señora seated in the sun against a pillar, or stretched on a rug before the fire; only at times she would shift her station to the top round of the stone staircase, where she lay with the same nonchalance right across my path. In all these days, I never knew her to display the least spark of energy beyond what she expended in brushing and re-brushing her copious copper-coloured hair, or in lisping out, in the rich and broken hoarseness of her voice, her customary idle salutations to myself. These, I think, were her two chief pleasures, beyond that of mere quiescence. She seemed always proud of her remarks, as though they had been witticisms; and, indeed, though they were empty enough, like the conversation of many respectable persons, and turned on a very narrow range of subjects, they were never meaningless or incoherent; nay, they had a certain beauty of their own, breathing, as they did, of her entire contentment. Now she would speak of the warmth, in which (like her son) she greatly delighted; now of the flowers of the pomegranate trees, and now of the white doves and long-winged swallows that fanned the air of the court. The birds excited her. As they raked the eaves in their swift flight, or skimmed sidelong past her with a rush of wind, she would sometimes stir and sit a little up, and seem to awaken from her doze of satisfaction. But for the rest of her days she lay luxuriously folded on herself and sunk in sloth and pleasure. Her invincible content at first annoyed me, but I came gradually to find repose in the spectacle, until at last it grew to be my habit to sit down beside her four times in the day both coming and going, and to talk with her sleepily, I scarce knew of what. I had come to like her dull, almost animal neighbourhood; her beauty and her stupidity soothed and amused me. I began to find a kind of transcendental good sense in her remarks, and her unfathomable good nature moved me to admiration and envy. The liking was returned; she enjoyed my presence half-unconsciously, as a man in deep meditation may enjoy the babbling of a brook. I can scarce say she brightened when I came, for satisfaction was written on her face eternally, as on some foolish statue's; but I was made conscious of her pleasure by some more intimate communication than the sight. And one day, as I sat within reach of her on the marble step, she suddenly shot forth one of her hands and patted mine. The thing was done, and she was back in her accustomed attitude, before my mind had received intelligence of the caress; and when I turned to look her in the face I could perceive no answerable sentiment. It was plain she attached no moment to the act, and I blamed myself for my own more uneasy consciousness.

The sight and (if I may so call it) the acquaintance of the mother confirmed the view I had already taken of the son. The family blood had been impoverished, perhaps by long inbreeding, which I knew to be a common error among the proud and the exclusive. No decline, indeed, was to be traced in the body, which had been handed down unimpaired in shapeliness and strength; and the faces of today were struck as sharply from the mint as the face of two centuries ago that smiled upon me from the portrait. But the intelligence (that more precious heirloom) was degenerate; the treasure of ancestral memory ran low; and it had required the potent, plebeian crossing of a muleteer or mountain contrabandista to raise, what approached hebetude in the mother, into the active oddity of the son. Yet of the two, it was the mother I preferred. Of Felipe, vengeful and placable, full of starts and shyings, inconstant as a hare, I could even conceive as a creature possibly noxious. Of the mother I had no thoughts but those of kindness. And indeed, as spectators are apt ignorantly to take sides, I grew something of a partisan in the enmity which I perceived to smoulder between them. True, it seemed mostly on the mother's part. She would sometimes draw in her breath as he came near, and the pupils of her vacant eyes would contract as if with horror or fear. Her emotions, such as they were, were much upon the surface and readily shared; and this latent repulsion occupied my mind, and kept me wondering on what grounds it rested, and whether the son was certainly in fault.

I had been about ten days in the residencia, when there sprang up a high and harsh wind, carrying clouds of dust. It came out of malarious lowlands, and over several snowy sierras. The nerves of those on whom it blew were strung and jangled; their eyes smarted with the dust; their legs ached under the burthen of their body; and the touch of one hand upon another grew to be odious. The wind, besides, came down the gullies of the hills and stormed about the house with a great, hollow buzzing and whistling that was wearisome to the ear and dismally depressing to the mind. It did not so much blow in gusts as with the steady sweep of a waterfall, so that there was no remission of discomfort while it blew. But higher upon the mountain it was probably of a more variable strength, with accesses of fury; for there came down at times a far-off wailing, infinitely grievous to hear; and at times, on one of the high shelves or terraces, there would start up and then disperse a tower of dust, like the smoke of an explosion.

I no sooner awoke in bed than I was conscious of the nervous tension and depression of the weather, and the effect grew stronger as the day proceeded. It was in vain that I resisted; in vain that I set forth upon my customary morning's walk; the irrational, unchanging fury of the storm had soon beat down my strength and wrecked my temper; and I returned to the residencia, glowing with dry heat and foul and gritty with dust. The court had a forlorn appearance; now and then a glimmer of sun fled over it; now and then the wind swooped down upon the pomegranàtes and scattered the blossoms, and set the window-shutters clapping on the wall. In the recess the señora was pacing to and fro with a flushed countenance and bright eyes; I thought, too, she was speaking to herself, like one in anger. But when I addressed her with my customary salutation she only replied by a sharp gesture and continued her walk. The weather had distempered even this impassive creature; and as I went on upstairs I was the less ashamed of my own discomposure.

All day the wind continued; and I sat in my room and made a feint of reading, or walked up and down and listened to the riot overhead. Night fell and I had not so much as a candle. I began to long for some society and stole down to the court. It was now plunged in the blue of the first darkness, but the recess was redly lighted by the fire. The wood had been piled high and was crowned by a shock of flames, which the draught of the chimney brandished to and fro. In this strong and shaken brightness the señora continued pacing from wall to wall with disconnected gestures, clasping her hands, stretching forth her arms, throwing back her head as in appeal to Heaven. In these disordered movements the beauty and grace of the woman showed more clearly; but there was a light in her eye that struck on me unpleasantly; and when I had looked on awhile in silence, and seemingly unobserved, I turned tail as I had come, and groped my way back again to my own chamber.

By the time Felipe brought my supper and lights, my nerve was utterly gone; and, had the lad been such as I was used to seeing him, I should have kept him (even by force had that been necessary) to take off the edge from my distasteful solitude. But on Felipe, also, the wind had exercised its influence. He had been feverish all day; now that the night had come he was fallen into a low and tremulous humour that reacted on my own. The sight of his scared face, his starts and pallors and sudden hearkenings, unstrung me; and when he dropped and broke a dish, I fairly leaped out of my seat.

'I think we are all mad today,' said I affecting to laugh.

'It is the black wind,' he replied dolefully. 'You feel as if you must do something, and you don't know what it is.'

I noted the aptness of the description; but, indeed, Felipe had sometimes a strange felicity in rendering into words the sensations of the body. 'And your mother, too,' said I; 'she seems to feel this weather much. Do you not fear she may be unwell?'

He stared at me a little, and then said, 'No,' almost defiantly and the next moment, carrying his hand to his brow, cried out lamentably on the wind and the noise that made his head go round like a mill-wheel. 'Who can be well?' he cried; and, indeed, I could only echo his question, for I was disturbed enough myself.

I went to bed early, wearied with day-long restlessness, but the poisonous nature of the wind, and its ungodly and unintermittent uproar, would not suffer me to sleep. I lay there and tossed, my nerves and senses on the stretch. At times I would doze, dream horribly, and wake again; and these snatches of oblivion confused me as to time. But it must have been late on in the night, when I was suddenly startled by an outbreak of pitiable and hateful cries. I leaped from my bed, supposing I had dreamed; but the cries still continued to fill the house, cries of pain, I thought, but certainly of rage also, and so savage and discordant that they shocked the heart. It was no illusion; some living thing, some lunatic or some wild animal, was being foully tortured. The thought of Felipe and the squirrel flashed into my mind, and I ran to the door, but it had been locked from the outside; and I might shake it as I pleased, I was a fast prisoner. Still the cries continued. Now they would dwindle down into a moaning that seemed to be articulate, and at these times I made sure they were to be human; and again they would break forth and fill the house with ravings worthy of hell. I stood at the door and gave ear to them, till at last they died away. Long after that I still lingered and still continued to hear them mingle in fancy with the storming of the wind; and when at last I crept to my bed, it was with a deadly sickness and a blackness of horror on my heart.

It was little wonder if I slept no more. Why had I been locked in? What had passed? Who was the author of these indescribable and shocking cries? A human being? It was unconceivable. A beast? The cries were scarce quite bestial; and what animal, short of a lion or a tiger, could thus shake the solid walls of the residencia? And while I was thus turning over the elements of the mystery, it came into my mind that I had not yet set eyes upon the daughter of the house. What was more probable than that the daughter of the señora, and the sister of Felipe, should be herself insane? Or, what more likely than that these ignorant and half-witted people should seek to manage an afflicted kinswoman by violence? Here was a solution; and yet when I called to mind the cries (which I never did without a shuddering chill) it seemed altogether insufficient: not even cruelty could wring such cries from madness. But of one thing I was sure: I could not live in a house where such a thing was half conceivable and not probe the matter home and, if necessary, interfere.

The next day came, the wind had blown itself out, and there was nothing to remind me of the business of the night. Felipe came to my bedside with obvious cheerfulness; as I passed through the court, the señora was sunning herself with her accustomed immobility; and when I issued from the gateway, I found the whole face of nature austerely smiling, the heavens of a cold blue, and sown with great cloud islands, and the mountain-sides mapped forth into provinces of light and shadow. A short walk restored me to myself, and renewed within me the resolve to plumb this mystery; and when, from the vantage of my knoll, I had seen Felipe pass forth to his labours in the garden, I returned at once to the residencia to put my design in practice. The señora appeared plunged in slumber; I stood awhile and marked her, but she did not stir; even if my design were indiscreet, I had little to fear from such a guardian; and turning away, I mounted to the gallery and began my exploration of the house.

All morning I went from one door to another, and entered spacious and faded chambers, some rudely shuttered, some receiving their full charge of daylight, all empty and unhomely. It was a rich house, on which Time had breathed his tarnish and dust had scattered disillusion. The spider swung there; the bloated tarantula scampered on the cornices; ants had their crowded highways on the floor of halls of audience; the big and foul fly, that lives on carrion and is often the messenger of death, had set up his nest in the rotten woodwork, and buzzed heavily about the rooms. Here and there a stool or two, a couch, a bed, or a great carved chair remained behind, like islets on the bare floors, to testify of man's bygone habitation; and everywhere the walls were set with the portraits of the dead. I could judge, by these decaying effigies, in the house of what a great and what a handsome race I was then wandering. Many of the men wore orders on their breasts and had the port of noble offices; the women were all richly attired; the canvases most of them by famous hands. But it was not so much these evidences of greatness that took hold upon my mind, even contrasted, as they were, with the present depopulation and decay of that great house. It was rather the parable of family life that I read in this succession of fair faces and shapely bodies. Never before had I so realised the miracle of the continued race, the creation and re-creation, the weaving and changing and handing down of fleshly elements. That a child should be born of its mother, that it should grow and clothe itself (we know not how) with humanity, and put on inherited looks, and turn its head with the manner of one ascendant, and offer its hand with the gesture of another, are wonders dulled for us by repetition. But in the singular unity of look, in the common features and common bearing, of all these painted generations on the walls of the residencia, the miracle started out and looked me in the face. And an ancient mirror falling opportunely in my way, I stood and read my own features a long while, tracing out on either hand the filaments of descent and the bonds that knit me with my family.

At last, in the course of these investigations, I opened the door of a chamber that bore the marks of habitation. It was of large proportions and faced to the north, where the mountains were most wildly figured. The embers of a fire smouldered and smoked upon the hearth, to which a chair had been drawn close. And yet the aspect of the chamber was ascetic to the degree of sternness; the chair was uncushioned; the floor and walls were naked; and beyond the books which lay here and there in some confusion, there was no instrument of either work or pleasure. The sight of books in the house of such a family exceedingly amazed me; and I began with a great hurry, and in momentary fear of interruption, to go from one to another and hastily inspect their character. They were of all sorts, devotional, historical, and scientific, but mostly of a great age and in the Latin tongue. Some I could see to bear the marks of constant study; others had been torn across and tossed aside as if in petulance or disapproval. Lastly, as I cruised about that empty chamber, I espied some papers written upon with pencil on a table near the window. An unthinking curiosity led me to take one up. It bore a copy of verses, very roughly metred in the original Spanish, and which I may render somewhat thus:

> Pleasure approached with pain and shame,
> Grief with a wreath of lilies came.
> Pleasure showed the lovely sun;
> Jesu dear, how sweet it shone!
> Grief with her worn hand pointed on,
> Jesu dear, to thee!

Shame and confusion at once fell on me; and, laying down the paper, I beat an immediate retreat from the apartment. Neither Felipe nor his mother could have read the books nor written these rough but feeling verses. It was plain I had stumbled with sacrilegious feet into the room of the daughter of the house. God knows, my own heart most sharply punished me for my indiscretion. The thought that I had thus secretly pushed my way into the confidence of a girl so strangely situated, and the fear that she might somehow come to hear of it, oppressed me like guilt. I blamed myself besides for my suspicions of the night before; wondered that I should ever have attributed those shocking cries to one of whom I now conceived as of a saint, spectral of mien, wasted with maceration, bound up in the practices of a mechanical devotion, and dwelling in a great isolation of soul with her incongruous relatives; and as I leaned on the balustrade of the gallery and looked down into the bright close of pomegranates and at the gaily dressed and somnolent woman, who just then stretched herself and delicately licked her lips as in the very sensuality of sloth, my mind swiftly compared the scene with the cold chamber looking northward on the mountains, where the daughter dwelt.

That same afternoon, as I sat upon my knoll, I saw the Padre enter the gates of the residencia. The revelation of the daughter's character had struck home to my fancy, and almost blotted out the horrors of the night before; but at sight of this worthy man the memory revived. I descended, then, from the knoll, and making a circuit among the woods, posted myself by the wayside to await his passage. As soon as he appeared I stepped forth and introduced myself as the lodger of the residencia. He had a very strong, honest countenance, on which it was easy to read the mingled emotions with which he regarded me, as a foreigner, a heretic, and yet one who had been wounded for the good cause. Of the family at the residencia he spoke with reserve, and yet with respect. I mentioned that I had not yet seen the daughter, whereupon he remarked that that was as it should be, and looked at me a little askance. Lastly, I plucked up courage to refer to the cries that had disturbed me in the night. He heard me out in silence, and then stopped and partly turned about, as though to mark beyond doubt that he was dismissing me.

'Do you take tobacco powder?' said he, offering his snuff-box; and then, when I had refused, 'I am an old man,' he added, 'and I may be allowed to remind you that you are a guest.'

'I have, then, your authority,' I returned, firmly enough, although I flushed at the implied reproof, 'to let things take their course, and not to interfere?'

He said 'Yes,' and with a somewhat uneasy salute turned and left me where I was. But he had done two things: he had set my conscience at rest, and he had awakened my delicacy. I made a great effort, once more dismissed the recollections of the night, and fell once more to brooding on my saintly poetess. At the same time, I could not quite forget that I had been locked in, and that night when Felipe brought me my supper I attacked him warily on both points of interest.

'I never see your sister,' said I casually.

'Oh, no,' said he; 'she is a good, good girl,' and his mind instantly veered to something else.

'Your sister is pious, I suppose?' I asked in the next pause.

'Oh!' he cried, joining his hands with extreme fervour, 'a saint; it is she that keeps me up.'

'You are very fortunate,' said I, 'for the most of us, I am afraid, and myself among the number, are better at going down.'

'Señor,' said Felipe earnestly, 'I would not say that. You should not tempt your angel. If one goes down, where is he to stop?'

'Why, Felipe,' said I, 'I had no guess you were a preacher, and I may say a good one; but I suppose that is your sister's doing?'

He nodded at me with round eyes.

'Well, then,' I continued, 'she has doubtless reproved you for your sin of cruelty?'

'Twelve times!' he cried; for this was the phrase by which the odd creature expressed the sense of frequency. 'And I told her you had done so – I remembered that,' he added proudly – 'and she was pleased.'

'Then, Felipe,' said I, 'what were those cries that I heard last night? for surely they were cries of some creature in suffering.'

'The wind,' returned Felipe, looking in the fire.

I took his hand in mine, at which, thinking it to be a caress, he smiled with a brightness of pleasure that came near disarming my resolve. But I trod the weakness down. 'The wind,' I repeated; 'and yet I think it was this hand,' holding it up, 'that had first locked me in.' The lad shook visibly, but answered never a word. 'Well,' said I, 'I am a stranger and a guest. It is not my part either to meddle or to judge in your affairs; in these you shall take your sister's counsel, which I cannot doubt to be excellent. But in so far as concerns my own, I will be no man's prisoner, and I demand that key.' Half an hour later my door was suddenly thrown open, and the key tossed ringing on the floor.

A day or two after I came in from a walk a little before the point of noon. The señora was lying lapped in slumber on the threshold of the recess; the pigeons dozed below the eaves like snowdrifts; the house was under a deep spell of noontide quiet; and only a wandering and gentle wind from the mountain stole round the galleries, rustled among the pomegranates, and pleasantly stirred the shadows. Something in the stillness moved me to imitation, and I went very lightly across the court and up the marble staircase. My foot was on the topmost round, when a door opened, and I found myself face to face with Olalla. Surprise transfixed me; her loveliness struck to my heart; she glowed in the deep shadow of the gallery a gem of colour; her eyes took hold upon mine and clung there, and bound us together like the joining of hands; and the moments we thus stood face to face, drinking each other in, were sacramental and the wedding of souls. I know not how long it was before I awoke out of a deep trance, and, hastily bowing, passed on into the upper stair. She did not move, but followed me with her great, thirsting eyes; and as I passed out of sight it seemed to me as if she paled and faded.

In my own room, I opened the window and looked out, and could not think what change had come upon that austere field of mountains that it should thus sing and shine under the lofty heaven. I had seen her – Olalla! And the stone crags answered Olalla! and the dumb, unfathomable azure answered, Olalla! The pale saint of my dreams had vanished for ever; and in her place I beheld this maiden on whom God had lavished the richest colours and the most exuberant energies of life, whom He had made active as a deer, slender as a reed, and in whose great eyes He had lighted the torches of the soul. The thrill of her young life, strung like a wild animal's, had entered into me; the force of soul that had looked out from her eyes and conquered mine, mantled about my heart and sprang to my lips in singing. She passed through my veins: she was one with me.

I will not say that this enthusiasm declined; rather my soul held out in its ecstasy as in a strong castle, and was there besieged by cold and sorrowful considerations. I could not doubt but that I loved her at first sight, and already with a quivering ardour that was strange to my experience. What then was to follow? She was the child of an afflicted house, the señora's daughter, the sister of Felipe; she bore it even in her beauty. She had the lightness and swiftness of the one, swift as an arrow, light as dew; like the other, she shone on the pale background of the world with the brilliancy of flowers. I could not call by the name of brother that half-witted lad, nor by the name of mother that immovable and lovely thing of flesh, whose silly eyes and perpetual simper now recurred to my mind like something hateful. And if I could not marry, what then? She was helplessly unprotected; her eyes, in that single and long glance which had been all our intercourse, had confessed a weakness equal to my own; but in my heart I knew her for the student of the cold northern chamber, and the writer of the sorrowful lines; and this was a knowledge to disarm a brute. To flee was more than I could find courage for; but I registered a vow of unsleeping circumspection.

As I turned from the window, my eyes alighted on the portrait. It had fallen dead, like a candle after sunrise; it followed me with eyes of paint. I knew it to be like, and marvelled at the tenacity of type in that declining race; but the likeness was swallowed up in difference. I remembered how it had seemed to me a thing unapproachable in the life, a creature rather of the painter's craft than of the modesty of nature, and I marvelled at the thought, and exulted in the image of Olalla. Beauty I had seen before, and not been charmed, and I had been often drawn to women who were not beautiful except to me; but in Olalla all that I desired and had not dared to imagine was united.

I did not see her the next day, and my heart ached and my eyes longed for her, as men long for morning. But the day after, when I returned, about my usual hour, she was once more on the gallery, and our looks once more met and embraced. I would have spoken, I would have drawn near to her; but strongly as she plucked at my heart, drawing me like a magnet, something yet more imperious withheld me; and I could only bow and pass by; and she, leaving my salutation unanswered, only followed me with her noble eyes.

I had now her image by rote, and as I conned the traits in memory it seemed as if I read her very heart. She was dressed with something of her mother's coquetry, and love of positive colour. Her robe, which I knew she must have made with her own hands, clung about her with a cunning grace. After the fashion of that country, besides, her bodice stood open in the middle, in a long slit, and here, in spite of the poverty of the house, a gold coin, hanging by a ribbon, lay on her brown bosom. These were proofs, had any been needed, of her inborn delight in life and her own loveliness. On the other hand, in her eyes that hung upon mine, I could read depth beyond depth of passion and sadness, lights of poetry and hope, blacknesses of despair, and thoughts that were above the earth. It was a lovely body, but the inmate, the soul, was more than worthy of that lodging. Should I leave this incomparable flower to wither unseen on these rough mountains? Should I despise the great gift offered me in the eloquent silence of her eyes? Here was a soul immured; should I not burst its prison? All side considerations fell off from me; were she the child of Herod I swore I should make her mine; and that very evening I set myself, with a mingled sense of treachery and disgrace, to captivate the brother. Perhaps I read him with more favourable eyes, perhaps the thought of his sister always summoned up the better qualities of that imperfect soul; but he had never seemed to be so amiable, and his very likeness to Olalla, while it annoyed, yet softened me.

A third day passed in vain – an empty desert of hours. I would not lose a chance, and loitered all afternoon in the court where (to give myself a countenance) I spoke more than usual with the señora. God knows it was with a most tender and sincere interest that I now studied her; and even as for Felipe, so now for the mother, I was conscious of a growing warmth of toleration. And yet I wondered. Even while I spoke with her, she would doze off into a little sleep, and presently awake again without embarrassment; and this composure staggered me. And again, as I marked her make infinitesimal changes in her posture, savouring and lingering on the bodily pleasure of the movement, I was driven to wonder at this depth of passive sensuality. She lived in her body; and her consciousness was all sunk into and disseminated through her members, where it luxuriously dwelt. Lastly, I could not grow accustomed to her eyes. Each time she turned on me these great beautiful and meaningless orbs, wide open to the day, but closed against human inquiry – each time I had occasion to observe the lively changes of her pupils which expanded and contracted in a breath – I know not what it was came over me, I can find no name for the mingled feeling of disappointment, annoyance, and distaste that jarred along my nerves. I tried her on a variety of subjects, equally in vain; and at last led the talk to her daughter. But even there she proved indifferent; said she was pretty, which (as with children) was her highest word of commendation, but was plainly incapable of any higher thought; and when I remarked that Olalla seemed silent, merely yawned in my face and replied that speech was of no great use when you had nothing to say. 'People speak much, very much,' she added, looking at me with expanded pupils; and then again yawned, and again showed me a mouth that was as dainty as a toy. This time I took the hint, and, leaving her to her repose, went up into my own chamber to sit by the open window, looking on the hills and not beholding them, sunk in lustrous and deep dreams, and hearkening in fancy to the note of a voice that I had never heard.

I awoke on the fifth morning with a brightness of anticipation that seemed to challenge fate. I was sure of myself, light of heart and foot, and resolved to put my love incontinently to the touch of knowledge. It should lie no longer under the bonds of silence, a dumb thing, living by the eye only, like the love of beasts; but should now put on the spirit, and enter upon the joys of the complete human intimacy. I thought of it with wild hopes, like a voyager to El Dorado; into that unknown and lovely country of her soul, I no longer trembled to adventure. Yet when I did encounter her, the same force of passion descended on me and at once submerged my mind; speech seemed to drop away from me like a childish habit; and I but drew near to her as the giddy man draws near to the margin of a gulf. She drew back from me a little as I came; but her eyes did not waver from mine, and these lured me forward. At last, when I was already within reach of her, I stopped. Words were denied me; if I advanced I could but clasp her to my heart in silence; and all that was sane in me, all that was still unconquered, revolted against the thought of such an accost. So we stood for a second, all our life in our eyes, exchanging salvos of attraction and yet each resisting; and then, with a great effort of the will, and conscious at the same time of a sudden bitterness of disppointment, I turned and went away in the same silence.

What power lay upon me that I could not speak? And she, why was she also silent? Why did she draw away before me dumbly, with fascinated eyes? Was this love? or was it a mere brute attraction, mindless and inevitable, like that of the magnet for the steel? We had never spoken, we were wholly strangers; and yet an influence, strong as the grasp of a giant, swept us silently together. On my side it filled me with impatience; and yet I was sure that she was worthy; I had seen her books, read her verses, and thus, in a sense, divined the soul of my mistress. But on her side it struck me almost cold. Of me she knew nothing but my bodily favour; she was drawn to me as stones fall to the earth; the laws that rule the earth conducted her, unconsenting, to my arms; and I drew back at the thought of such a bridal, and began to be jealous for myself. It was not thus that I desired to be loved. And then I began to fall into a great pity for the girl herself. I thought how sharp must be her mortification, that she, the student, the recluse, Felipe's saintly monitress, should have thus confessed an overweening weakness for a man with whom she had never exchanged a word. And at the coming of pity, all other thoughts were swallowed up; and I longed only to find and console and reassure her; to tell her how wholly her love was returned on my side, and how her choice, even if blindly made, was not unworthy.

The next day it was glorious weather; depth upon depth of blue over-canopied the mountains; the sun shone wide; and the wind in the trees and the many falling torrents in the mountains filled the air with delicate and haunting music. Yet I was prostrated with sadness. My heart wept for the sight of Olalla, as a child weeps for its mother. I sat down on a boulder on the verge of the low cliffs that bound the plateau to the north. Thence I looked down into the wooded valley of a stream, where no foot came. In the mood I was in, it was even touching to behold the place untenanted; it lacked Olalla; and I thought of the delight and glory of a life passed wholly with her in that strong air, and among these rugged and lovely surroundings, at first with a whimper-ing sentiment, and then again with such a fiery joy that I seemed to grow in strength and stature, like a Samson.

And then suddenly I was aware of Olalla drawing near. She appeared out of a grove of cork-trees, and came straight towards me; and I stood up and waited. She seemed in her walking a creature of such life and fire and lightness as amazed me; yet she came quietly and slowly. Her energy was in the slowness; but for inimitable strength, I felt she would have run, she would have flown to me. Still, as she approached, she kept her eyes lowered to the ground; and when she had drawn quite near, it was without one glance that she addressed me. At the first note of her voice I started. It was for this I had been waiting; this was the last test of my love. And lo, her enunciation was precise and clear, not lisping and incomplete like that of her family; and the voice, though deeper than usual with women, was still both youthful and womanly. She spoke in a rich chord; golden contralto strains mingled with hoarseness, as the red threads were mingled with the brown among her tresses. It was not only a voice that spoke to my heart directly; but it spoke to me of her. And yet her words immediately plunged me back upon despair.

'You will go away,' she said, 'today.'

Her example broke the bonds of my speech; I felt as lightened of a weight, or as if a spell had been dissolved. I know not in what words I answered; but, standing before her on the cliffs, I poured out the whole ardour of my love, telling her I lived upon the thought of her, slept only to dream of her loveliness, and would gladly forswear my country, my language, and my friends, to live for ever by her side. And then, strongly commanding myself, I changed the note; I reassured, I comforted her; I told her I had divined in her a pious and heroic spirit, with which I was worthy to sympathise, and which I longed to share and lighten. 'Nature,' I told her, 'was the voice of God, which men disobey at peril; and if we were thus dumbly drawn together, ay, even as by a miracle of love, it must imply a divine fitness in our souls; we must be made,' I said – 'made for one another. We should be mad rebels,' I cried out – 'mad rebels against God, not to obey this instinct.'

She shook her head. 'You will go today,' she repeated, and then with a gesture, and in a sudden, sharp note – 'no, not today,' she cried, 'tomorrow!'

But at this sign of relenting, power came in upon me in a tide. I stretched out my arms and called upon her name; and she leaped to me and clung to me. The hills rocked about us, the earth quailed; a shock as of a blow went through me and left me blind and dizzy. And the next moment she had thrust me back, broken rudely from my arms, and fled with the speed of a deer among the cork-trees.

I stood and shouted to the mountains; I turned and went back towards the residencia, walking upon air. She sent me away, and yet I had but to call upon her name and she came to me. These were but the weaknesses of girls, from which even she, the strangest of her sex, was not exempted. Go? not I, Olalla – oh, not I, Olalla, my Olalla! A bird sang near by; and in that season birds were rare. It bade me be of good cheer. And once more the whole countenance of nature, from the ponderous and stable mountains down to the lightest leaf and the smallest darting fly in the shadow of the groves, began to stir before me and to put on the lineaments of life and wear a face of awful joy. The sunshine struck upon the hills, strong as a hammer on the anvil, and the hills shook; the earth, under that vigorous insolation, yielded up heady scents; the woods smouldered in the blaze. I felt the thrill of travail and delight run through the earth. Something elemental, something rude, violent, and savage, in the love that sang in my heart, was like a key to nature's secrets; and the very stones that rattled under my feet appeared alive and friendly. Olalla! Her touch had quickened, and renewed, and strung me up to the old pitch of concert with the rugged earth, to a swelling of the soul that men learned to forget in their polite assemblies. Love burned in me like rage; tenderness waxed fierce; I hated, I adored, I pitied, I revered her with ecstasy. She seemed the link that bound me in with dead things on the one hand, and with our pure and pitying God upon the other: a thing brutal and divine, and akin at once to the innocence and to the unbridled forces of the earth.

My head thus reeling, I came into the courtyard of the residencia, and the sight of the mother struck me like a revelation. She sat there, all sloth and contentment, blinking under the strong sunshine, branded with a passive enjoyment, a creature set quite apart, before whom my ardour fell away like a thing ashamed. I stopped a moment, and, commanding such shaken tones as I was able, said a word or two. She looked at me with her unfathomable kindness; her voice in reply sounded vaguely out of the realm of peace in which she slumbered, and there fell on my mind, for the first time, a sense of respect for one so uniformly innocent and happy, and I passed on in a kind of wonder at myself, that I should be so much disquieted.

On my table there lay a piece of the same yellow paper I had seen in the north room; it was written on with pencil in the same hand, Olalla's hand, and I picked it up with a sudden sinking of alarm, and read: 'If you have any kindness for Olalla, if you have any chivalry for a creature sorely wrought, go from here today; in pity, in honour, for the sake of Him who died, I supplicate that you shall go.' I looked at this awhile in mere stupidity, then I began to awaken to a weariness and horror of life; the sunshine darkened outside on the bare hills, and I began to shake like a man in terror. The vacancy thus suddenly opened in my life unmanned me like a physical void. It was not my heart, it was not my happiness, it was life itself that was involved. I could not lose her. I said so, and stood repeating it. And then, like one in a dream, I moved to the window, put forth my hand to open the casement, and thrust it through the pane. The blood spurted from my wrist; and with an instantaneous quietude and command of myself, I pressed my thumb on the little leaping fountain and reflected what to do. In that empty room there was nothing to my purpose; I felt, besides, that I required assistance. There shot into my mind a hope that Olalla herself might be my helper, and I turned and went downstairs, still keeping my thumb upon the wound.

There was no sign of either Olalla or Felipe, and I addressed myself to the recess, whither the señora had now drawn quite back and sat dozing close before the fire, for no degree of heat appeared too much for her.

'Pardon me,' said I, 'if I disturb you, but I must apply to you for help.'

She looked up sleepily and asked me what it was, and with the very words I thought she drew in her breath with a widening of the nostrils and seemed to come suddenly and fully alive.

'I have cut myself,' I said, 'and rather badly. See!' And I held out my two hands from which the blood was oozing and dripping.

Her great eyes opened wide, the pupils shrank into points; a veil seemed to fall from her face, and leave it sharply expressive and yet inscrutable. And as I still stood, marvelling a little at her disturbance, she came swiftly up to me, and stooped and caught me by the hand; and the next moment my hand was at her mouth, and she had bitten me to the bone. The pang of the bite, the sudden spurting of blood, and the monstrous horror of the act, flashed through me all in one, and I beat her back; and she sprang at me again and again, with bestial cries, cries that I recognised, such cries as had awakened me on the night of the high wind. Her strength was like that of madness; mine was rapidly ebbing with the loss of blood; my mind besides was whirling with the abhorrent strangeness of the onslaught, and I was already forced against the wall, when Olalla ran betwixt us, and Felipe, following at a bound, pinned down his mother on the floor.

A trance-like weakness fell upon me; I saw, heard, and felt, but I was incapable of movement. I heard the struggle roll to and fro upon the floor, the yells of that catamount ringing up to Heaven as she strove to reach me. I felt Olalla clasp me in her arms, her hair falling on my face, and, with the strength of a man, raise and half drag, half carry me upstairs into my own room, where she cast me down upon the bed. Then I saw her hasten to the door and lock it, and stand an instant listening to the savage cries that shook the residencia. And then, swift and light as a thought, she was again beside me, binding up my hand, laying it in her bosom, moaning and mourning over it with dove-like sounds. They were not words that came to her, they were sounds more beautiful than speech, infinitely touching, infinitely tender; and yet as I lay there, a thought stung to my heart, a thought wounded me like a sword, a thought, like a worm in a flower, profaned the holiness of my love. Yes, they were beautiful sounds, and they were inspired by human tenderness; but was their beauty human?

All day I lay there. For a long time the cries of that nameless female thing, as she struggled with her half-witted whelp, resounded through the house, and pierced me with despairing sorrow and disgust. They were the death-cry of my love; my love was murdered; it was not only dead, but an offence to me; and yet, think as I pleased, feel as I must, it still swelled within me like a storm of sweetness, and my heart melted at her looks and touch. This horror that had sprung out, this doubt upon Olalla, this savage and bestial strain that ran not only through the whole behaviour of her family, but found a place in the very foundations and story of our love – though it appalled, though it shocked and sickened me, was yet not of power to break the knot of my infatuation.

When the cries had ceased, there came a scraping at the door, by which I knew Felipe was without; and Olalla went and spoke to him – I know not what. With that exception, she stayed close beside me, now kneeling by my bed and fervently praying, now sitting with her eyes upon mine. So then, for these six hours I drank in her beauty, and silently perused the story in her face. I saw the golden coin hover on her breasts; I saw her eyes darken and brighten, and still speak no language but that of an unfathomable kindness; I saw the faultless face, and, through the robe, the lines of the faultless body. Night came at last, and in the growing darkness of the chamber, the sight of her slowly melted; but even then the touch of her smooth hand lingered in mine and talked with me. To lie thus in deadly weakness and drink in the traits of the beloved, is to reawake to love from whatever shock of disillusion. I reasoned with myself, and I shut my eyes on horrors, and again I was very bold to accept the worst. What mattered it, if that imperious sentiment survived; if her eyes still beckoned and attached me; if now, even as before, every fibre of my dull body yearned and turned to her? Late on in the night some strength revived in me, and I spoke:

'Olalla,' I said, 'nothing matters; I ask nothing; I am content; I love you.'

She knelt down awhile and prayed, and I devoutly respected her devotions. The moon had begun to shine in upon one side of each of the three windows, and make a misty clearness in the room, by which I saw her indistinctly. When she re-arose she made the sign of the cross.

'It is for me to speak,' she said, 'and for you to listen. I know; you can but guess. I prayed, how I prayed for you to leave this place. I begged it of you, and I know you would have granted me even this; or if not, oh, let me think so!'

'I love you,' I said.

'And yet you have lived in the world,' she said; after a pause, 'you are a man and wise; and I am but a child. Forgive me, if I seem to teach, who am as ignorant as the trees of the mountain; but those who learn much do but skim the face of knowledge; they seize the laws, they conceive the dignity of the design – the horror of the living fact fades from their memory. It is we who sit at home with evil who remember, I think, and are warned and pity. Go, rather, go now, and keep me in mind. So I shall have a life in the cherished places of your memory: a life as much my own as that which I lead in this body.'

'I love you,' I said once more; and reaching out my weak hand, took hers, and carried it to my lips and kissed it. Nor did she resist, but winced a little; and I could see her look upon me with a frown that was not unkindly, only sad and baffled. And then it seemed she made a call upon her resolution; plucked my hand towards her, herself at the same time leaning somewhat forward, and laid it on the beating of her heart. 'There,' she cried, 'you feel the very footfall of my life. It only moves for you; it is yours. But is it even mine? It is mine indeed to offer you, as I might take the coin from my neck, as I might break a live branch from a tree and give it you. And yet not mine! I dwell, or I think I dwell (if I exist at all), somewhere apart, an impotent prisoner, and carried about and deafened by a mob that I disown. This capsule, such as throbs against the sides of animals, knows you at a touch for its master; ay, it loves you! But my soul, does my soul? I think not; I know not, fearing to ask. Yet when you spoke to me, your words were of the soul; it is of the soul that you ask – it is only from the soul that you would take me.'

'Olalla,' I said, 'the soul and the body are one, and mostly so in love. What the body chooses, the soul loves; where the body clings, the soul cleaves; body for body, soul to soul, they come together at God's signal; and the lower part (if we can call aught low) is only the footstool and foundation of the highest.'

'Have you,' she said, 'seen the portraits in the house of my fathers? Have you looked at my mother or at Felipe? Have your eyes never rested on that picture that hangs by your bed? She who sat for it died ages ago; and she did evil in her life. But, look again: there is my hand to the least line, there are my eyes and my hair. What is mine, then, and what am I? If not a curve in this poor body of mine (which you love, and for the sake of which you dotingly dream that you love me), not a gesture that I can frame, not a tone of my voice, not any look from my eyes, no, not even now when I speak to him I love, but has belonged to others? Others, ages dead, have wooed other men with my eyes; other men have heard the pleading of the same voice that now sounds in your ears. The hands of the dead are in my bosom; they move me, they pluck me, they guide me; I am a puppet at their command; and I but reinform features and attributes that have long been laid aside from evil in the quiet of the grave. Is it me you love, friend? or the race that made me? The girl who does not know and cannot answer for the least portion of herself? or the stream of which she is a transitory eddy, the tree of which she is the passing fruit? The race exists; it is old, it is ever young, it carries its eternal destiny in its bosom; upon it, like waves upon the sea, individual succeeds to individual, mocked with a semblance of self-control, but they are nothing. We speak of the soul, but the soul is in the race.'

'You fret against the common law,' I said. 'You rebel against the voice of God, which He has made so winning to convince, so imperious to command. Hear it, and how it speaks between us! Your hand clings to mine, your heart leaps at my touch, the unknown elements of which we are compounded awake and run together at a look; the clay of the earth remembers its independent life and yearns to join us; we are drawn together as the stars are turned about in space, or as the tides ebb and flow, by things older and greater than we ourselves.'

'Alas!' she said, 'what can I say to you? My fathers, eight hundred years ago, ruled all this province: they were wise, great, cunning, and cruel; they were a picked race of the Spanish; their flags led in war; the king called them his cousin; the people, when the rope was slung for them or when they returned and found their hovels smoking, blasphemed their name. Presently a change began. Man has risen; if he has sprung from the brutes, he can descend again to the same level. The breath of weariness blew on their humanity and the cords relaxed; they began to go down; their minds fell on sleep, their passions awoke in gusts, heady and senseless like the wind in the gutters of the mountains; beauty was still handed down, but no longer the guiding wit nor the human heart; the seed passed on, it was wrapped in flesh, the flesh covered the bones, but they were the bones and the flesh of brutes, and their mind was as the mind of flies. I speak to you as I dare; but you have seen for yourself how the wheel has gone backward with my doomed race. I stand, as it were, upon a little rising ground in this desperate descent, and see both before and behind, both what we have lost and to what we are condemned, to go farther downward. And shall

I – I that dwell apart in the house of the dead, my body, loathing its ways – shall I repeat the spell? Shall I bind another spirit, reluctant as my own, into this bewitched and tempest-broken tenement that I now suffer in? Shall I hand down this cursed vessel of humanity, charge it with fresh life as with fresh poison, and dash it, like a fire, in the faces of posterity? But my vow has been given; the race shall cease from off the earth. At this hour my brother is making ready; his foot will soon be on the stair; and you will go with him and pass out of my sight for ever. Think of me sometimes as one to whom the lesson of life was very harshly told, but who heard it with courage; as one who loved you indeed, but who hated herself so deeply that her love was hateful to her; as one who sent you away and yet would have longed to keep you for ever; who had no dearer hope than to forget you, and no greater fear than to be forgotten.'

She had drawn towards the door as she spoke, her rich voice sounding softer and farther away; and with the last word she was gone, and I lay alone in the moonlit chamber. What I might have done had not I lain bound by my extreme weakness, I know not; but as it was there fell upon me a great and blank despair. It was not long before there shone in at the door the ruddy glimmer of a lantern, and Felipe coming, charged me without a word upon his shoulders, and carried me down to the great gate, where the cart was waiting. In the moonlight the hills stood out sharply, as if they were of cardboard; on the glimmering surface of the plateau, and from among the low trees which swung together and sparkled in the wind, the great black cube of the residencia stood out bulkily, its mass only broken by three dimly lighted windows in the northern front above the gate. They were Olalla's windows, and as the cart jolted onwards I kept my eyes fixed upon them till, where the road dipped into a valley, they were lost to my view for ever. Felipe walked in silence beside the shafts, but from time to time he would check the mule and seem to look back upon me; and at length drew quite near and laid his hand upon my head. There was such kindness in the touch, and such a simplicity, as of the brutes, that tears broke from me like the bursting of an artery.

'Felipe,' I said, 'take me where they will ask no questions.'

He said never a word, but he turned his mule about, end for end, retraced some part of the way we had gone, and, striking into another path, led me to the mountain village, which was, as we say in Scotland, the kirkton of that thinly peopled district. Some broken memories dwell in my mind of the day breaking over the plain, of the cart stopping, of arms that helped me down, of a bare room into which I was carried, and of a swoon that fell upon me like sleep.

The next day and the days following the old priest was often at my side with his snuff-box and prayer-book, and after a while, when I began to pick up strength, he told me that I was now on a fair way to recovery, and must as soon as possible hurry my departure; whereupon, without naming any reason, he took snuff and looked at me sideways. I did not affect ignorance; I knew he must have seen Olalla. 'Sir,' said I, 'you know that I do not ask in wantonness. What of that family?'

He said they were very unfortunate; that it seemed a declining race, and that they were very poor and had been much neglected.

'But she has not,' I said. 'Thanks, doubtless, to yourself, she is instructed and wise beyond the use of women.'

'Yes,' he said; 'the señorita is well-informed. But the family has been neglected.'

'The mother?' I queried.

'Yes, the mother too,' said the Padre, taking snuff. 'But Felipe is a well-intentioned lad.'

'The mother is odd?' I asked.

'Very odd,' replied the priest.

'I think, sir, we beat about the bush,' said I. 'You must know more of my affairs than you allow. You must know my curiosity to be justified on many grounds. Will you not be frank with me?'

'My son,' said the old gentleman, 'I will be very frank with you on matters within my competence; on those of which I know nothing it does not require much discretion to be silent. I will not fence with you, I take your meaning perfectly; and what can I say, but that we are all in God's hands, and that His ways are not as our ways? I have even advised with my superiors in the Church, but they, too, were dumb. It is a great mystery.'

'Is she mad?' I asked.

'I will answer you according to my belief. She is not,' returned the Padre, 'or she was not. When she was young – God help me, I fear I neglected that wild lamb – she was surely sane; and yet, although it did not run to such heights, the same strain was already notable; it had been so before her in her father, ay, and before him, and this inclined me, perhaps, to think too lightly of it. But these things go on growing, not only in the individual but in the race.'

'When she was young,' I began, and my voice failed me for a moment, and it was only with a great effort that I was able to add, 'was she like Olalla?'

'Now God forbid!' exclaimed the Padre. 'God forbid that any man should think so slightingly of my favourite penitent. No, no; the señorita (but for her beauty, which I wish most honestly she had less of) has not a hair's resemblance to what her mother was at the same age. I could not bear to have you think so; though, Heaven knows, it were, perhaps, better that you should.'

At this, I raised myself in bed and opened my heart to the old man; telling him of our love and of her decision, owning my own horrors, my own passing fancies, but telling him that these were at an end, and with something more than a purely formal submission, appealing to his judgment.

He heard me very patiently and without surprise; and when I had done, he sat for some time silent. Then he began: 'The Church,' and instantly broke off again to apologise. 'I had forgotten, my child, that you were not a Christian,' said he. 'And indeed, upon a point so highly unusual, even the Church can scarce be said to have decided. But would you have my opinion? The señorita is, in a matter of this kind, the best judge; I would accept her judgment.'

On the back of that he went away, nor was he thenceforward so assiduous in his visits; indeed, even when I began to get about again, he plainly feared and deprecated my society, not as in distaste but much as a man might be disposed to flee from the riddling sphynx. The villagers, too, avoided me; they were unwilling to be my guides upon the mountain. I thought they looked at me askance, and I made sure that the more superstitious crossed themselves on my approach. At first I set this down to my heretical opinions; but it began at length to dawn upon me that if I was thus redoubted it was because I had stayed at the residencia. All men despise the savage notions of such peasantry; and yet I was conscious of a chill shadow that seemed to fall and dwell upon my love. It did not conquer, but I may not deny that it restrained my ardour.

Some miles westward of the village there was a gap in the sierra, from which the eye plunged direct upon the residencia, and thither it became my daily habit to repair. A wood crowned the summit, and just where the pathway issued from its fringes, it was overhung by a considerable shelf of rock, and that, in its turn, was surmounted by a crucifix of the size of life and more than usually painful in design. This was my perch; thence, day after day, I looked down upon the plateau and the great old house, and could see Felipe, no bigger than a fly, going to and fro about the garden. Sometimes mists would draw across the view, and be broken up again by mountain winds; sometimes the plain slumbered below me in unbroken sunshine; it would sometimes be all blotted out by rain. This distant post, these interrupted sights of the place where my life had been so strangely changed, suited the indecision of my humour. I passed whole days there, debating with myself the various elements of our position; now leaning to the suggestions of love, now giving an ear to prudence, and in the end halting irresolute between the two.

One day, as I was sitting on my rock, there came by that way a somewhat gaunt peasant wrapped in a mantle. He was a stranger, and plainly did not know me even by repute; for, instead of keeping the other side, he drew near and sat down beside me, and we had soon fallen in talk. Among other things he told me he had been a muleteer, and in former years had much frequented these mountains; later on, he had followed the army with his mules, had realised a competence, and was now living retired with his family.

'Do you know that house?' I inquired at last, pointing to the residencia, for I readily wearied of any talk that kept me from the thought of Olalla.

He looked at me darkly and crossed himself.

'Too well,' he said, 'it was there that one of my comrades sold himself to Satan; the Virgin shield us from temptations! He has paid the price; he is now burning in the reddest place in Hell!'

A fear came upon me; I could answer nothing; and presently the man resumed, as if to himself: 'Yes,' he said, 'oh yes, I know it. I have passed its doors. There was snow upon the pass, the wind was driving it; sure enough there was death that night upon the mountains, but there was worse beside the hearth. I took him by the arm, señor, and dragged him to the gate; I conjured him, by all he loved and respected, to go forth with me; I went on my knees before him in the snow, and I could see he was moved by my entreaty. And just then she came out on the gallery and called him by his name; and he turned, and there was she standing with a lamp in her hand and smiling on him to come back. I cried out aloud to God, and threw my arms about him, but he put me by and left me alone. He had made his choice; God help us. I would pray for him, but to what end? there are sins that not even the Pope can loose.'

'And your friend,' I asked, 'what became of him?'

'Nay, God knows,' said the muleteer. 'If all be true that we hear, his end was like his sin, a thing to raise the hair.'

'Do you mean that he was killed?' I asked.

'Sure enough, he was killed,' returned the man. 'But how? Ay, how? But these are things that it is sin to speak of.'

'The people of that house . . . ' I began.

But he interrupted me with a savage outburst. 'The people?' he cried. 'What people? There are neither men nor women in that house of Satan's! What? have you lived here so long and never heard?' And here he put his mouth to my ear and whispered, as if even the fowls of the mountain might have overheard and been stricken with horror.

What he told me was not true, nor was it even original; being, indeed, but a new edition, vamped up again by village ignorance and superstition, of stories nearly as ancient as the race of man. It was rather the application that appalled me. In the old days, he said, the Church would have burned out that nest of basilisks; but the arm of the Church was now shortened; his friend Miguel had been unpunished by the hands of men, and left to the more awful judgment of an offended God. This was wrong; but it should be so no more. The Padre was sunk in age; he was even bewitched himself; but the eyes of his flock were now awake to their own danger; and some day – ay, and before long – the smoke of that house should go up to Heaven.

He left me filled with horror and fear. Which way to turn I knew not; whether first to warn the Padre, or to carry my ill-news direct to the threatened inhabitants of the residencia. Fate was to decide for me, for, while I was still hesitating, I beheld the veiled figure of a woman drawing near to me up the pathway. No veil could deceive my penetration; by every line and every movement I recognised Olalla; and keeping hidden behind a corner of the rock, I suffered her to gain the summit. Then I came forward. She knew me and paused, but did not speak; I, too, remained silent, and we continued for some time to gaze upon each other with a passionate sadness.

'I thought you had gone,' she said at length. 'It is all that you can do for me – to go. It is all I ever asked of you. And you still stay. But do you know that every day heaps up the peril of death, not only on your head, but on ours? A report has gone about the mountain; it is thought you love me, and the people will not suffer it.'

I saw she was already informed of her danger, and I rejoiced at it. 'Olalla,' I said, 'I am ready to go this day, this very hour, but not alone.'

She stepped aside and knelt down before the crucifix to pray, and I stood by and looked now at her and now at the object of her adoration, now at the living figure of the penitent, and now at the ghastly daubed countenance, the painted wounds, and the projected ribs of the image. The silence was only broken by the wailing of some large birds that circled sidelong, as if in surprise or alarm, about the summit of the hills. Presently Olalla rose again, turned towards me, raised her veil, and, still leaning with one hand on the shaft of the crucifix, looked upon me with a pale and sorrowful countenance.

'I have laid my hand upon the cross,' she said. 'The Padre says you are no Christian; but look up for a moment with my eyes, and behold the face of the Man of Sorrows. We are all such as He was – the inheritors of sin; we must all bear and expiate a past which was not ours; there is in all of us – ay, even in me – a sparkle of the divine. Like Him, we must endure for a little while, until morning returns bringing peace. Suffer me to pass on upon my way alone; it is thus that I shall be least lonely, counting for my friend Him who is the friend of all the distressed; it is thus that I shall be the most happy, having taken my farewell of earthly happiness, and willingly accepted sorrow for my portion.'

I looked at the face of the crucifix, and, though I was no friend to images, and despised that imitative and grimacing art of which it was a rude example, some sense of what the thing implied was carried home to my intelligence. The face looked down upon me with a painful and deadly contraction; but the rays of a glory encircled it, and reminded me that the sacrifice was voluntary. It stood there, crowning the rock, as it still stands on so many highway sides, vainly preaching to passers-by, an emblem of sad and noble truths; that pleasure is not an end, but an accident; that pain is the choice of the magnanimous; that it is best to suffer all things and do well. I turned and went down the mountain in silence; and when I looked back for the last time before the wood closed about my path, I saw Olalla still leaning on the crucifix.

THE TREASURE OF FRANCHARD

CHAPTER I

By the Dying Mountebank

THEY HAD SENT FOR the doctor from Bourron before six. About eight some villagers came round for the performance, and were told how matters stood. It seemed a liberty for a mountebank to fall ill like real people, and they made off again in dudgeon. By ten Madame Tentaillon was gravely alarmed, and had sent down the street for Doctor Desprez.

The Doctor was at work over his manuscripts in one corner of the little dining-room, and his wife was asleep over the fire in another, when the messenger arrived.

'Sapristi!' said the Doctor, 'you should have sent for me before. It was a case for hurry.' And he followed the messenger as he was, in his slippers and skull-cap.

The inn was not thirty yards away, but the messenger did not stop there; he went in at one door and out by another into the court, and then led the way by a flight of steps beside the stable to the loft where the mountebank lay sick. If Doctor Desprez were to live a thousand years, he would never forget his arrival in that room; for not only was the scene picturesque, but the moment made a date in his existence. We reckon our lives, I hardly know why, from the date of our first sorry appearance in society, as if from a first humiliation; for no actor can come upon the stage with a worse grace. Not to go farther back, which would be judged too curious, there are subsequently many moving and decisive accidents in the lives of all, which would make as logical a period as this of birth. And here, for instance, Doctor Desprez, a man past forty, who had made what is called a failure in life, and was moreover married, found himself at a new point of departure when he opened the door of the loft above Tentaillon's stable.

It was a large place, lighted only by a single candle set upon the floor. The mountebank lay on his back upon a pallet; a large man, with a Quixotic nose inflamed with drinking. Madame Tentaillon stooped over him, applying a hot water and mustard embrocation to his feet; and on a chair close by sat a little fellow of eleven or twelve, with his feet dangling. These three were the only occupants, except the shadows. But the shadows were a company in themselves; the extent of the room exaggerated them to a gigantic size, and from the low position of the candle the light struck upwards and produced deformed foreshortenings. The mountebank's profile was enlarged upon the wall in caricature, and it was strange to see his nose shorten and lengthen as the flame was blown about by draughts. As for Madame Tentaillon, her shadow was no more than a gross hump of shoulders, with now and again a hemisphere of head. The chair legs were spindled out as long as stilts, and the boy sat perched atop of them, like a cloud, in the corner of the roof.

It was the boy who took the Doctor's fancy. He had a great arched skull, the forehead and the hands of a musician, and a pair of haunting eyes. It was not merely that these eyes were large, or steady, or the softest ruddy brown. There was a look in them, besides, which thrilled the Doctor and made him half uneasy. He was sure he had seen such a look before, and yet he could not remember how or where. It was as if this boy, who was quite a stranger to him, had the eyes of an old friend or an old enemy. And the boy would give him no peace; he seemed profoundly indifferent to what was going on, or rather abstracted from it in a superior contemplation, beating gently with his feet against the bars of the chair, and holding his hands folded on his lap. But, for all that, his eyes kept following the Doctor about the room with a thoughtful fixity of gaze. Desprez could not tell whether he was fascinating the boy, or the boy was fascinating him. He busied himself over the sick man: he put questions, he felt the pulse, he jested, he grew a little hot and swore: and still, whenever he looked round, there were the brown eyes waiting for his with the same inquiring, melancholy gaze.

At last the Doctor hit on the solution at a leap. He remembered the look now. The little fellow, although he was as straight as a dart, had the eyes that go usually with a crooked back; he was not at all deformed, and yet a deformed person seemed to be looking at you from below his brows. The Doctor drew a long breath, he was so much relieved to find a theory (for he loved theories) and to explain away his interest.

For all that, he despatched the invalid with unusual haste, and, still kneeling with one knee on the floor, turned a little round and looked the boy over at his leisure. The boy was not in the least put out, but looked placidly back at the Doctor.

'Is this your father?' asked Desprez.

'Oh, no,' returned the boy; 'my master.'

'Are you fond of him?' continued the Doctor.

'No, sir,' said the boy.

Madame Tentaillon and Desprez exchanged expressive glances.

'That is bad, my man,' resumed the latter, with a shade of sternness. 'Everyone should be fond of the dying, or conceal their sentiments; and your master here is dying. If I have watched a bird a little while stealing my cherries, I have a thought of disappointment when he flies away over my garden wall, and I see him steer for the forest and vanish. How much more a creature such as this, so strong, so astute, so richly endowed with faculties! When I think that, in a few hours, the speech will be silenced, the breath extinct, and even the shadow vanished from the wall, I who never saw him, this lady who knew him only as a guest, are touched with some affection.'

The boy was silent for a little, and appeared to be reflecting.

'You did not know him,' he replied at last. 'He was a bad man.'

'He is a little pagan,' said the landlady. 'For that matter, they are all the same, these mountebanks, tumblers, artists, and what not. They have no interior.'

But the Doctor was still scrutinising the little pagan, his eyebrows knotted and uplifted.

'What is your name?' he asked.

'Jean-Marie,' said the lad.

Desprez leaped upon him with one of his sudden flashes of excitement, and felt his head all over from an ethnological point of view.

'Celtic, Celtic!' he said.

'Celtic!' cried Madame Tentaillon, who had perhaps confounded the word with hydrocephalous. 'Poor lad! is it dangerous?'

'That depends,' returned the Doctor grimly. And then once more addressing the boy: 'And what do you do for your living, Jean-Marie?' he inquired.

'I tumble,' was the answer.

'So! Tumble?' repeated Desprez. 'Probably healthful. I hazard the guess, Madame Tentaillon, that tumbling is a healthful way of life. And have you never done anything else but tumble?'

'Before I learned that, I used to steal,' answered Jean-Marie gravely.

'Upon my word!' cried the Doctor. 'You are a nice little man for your age. Madame, when my *confrère* comes from Bourron, you will communicate my unfavourable opinion. I leave the case in his hands; but of course, on any alarming symptom, above all if there should be a sign of rally, do not hesitate to knock me up. I am a doctor no longer, I thank God; but I have been one. Good-night, madame. Good sleep to you, Jean-Marie.'

CHAPTER II

Morning Talk

DOCTOR DESPREZ always rose early. Before the smoke arose, before the first cart rattled over the bridge to the day's labour in the fields, he was to be found wandering in his garden. Now he would pick a bunch of grapes; now he would eat a big pear under the trellis; now he would draw all sorts of fancies on the path with the end of his cane; now he would go down and watch the river running endlessly past the timber landing-place at which he moored his boat. There was no time, he used to say, for making theories like the early morning. 'I rise earlier than anyone else in the village,' he once boasted. 'It is a fair consequence that I know more and wish to do less with my knowledge.'

The Doctor was a connoisseur of sunrises, and loved a good theatrical effect to usher in the day. He had a theory of dew, by which he could predict the weather. Indeed, most things served him to that end: the sound of the bells from all the neighbouring villages, the smell of the forest, the visits and the behaviour of both birds and fishes, the look of the plants in his garden, the disposition of cloud, the colour of the light, and last, although not least, the arsenal of meteorological instruments in a louvre-boarded hutch upon the lawn. Ever since he had settled at Gretz, he had been growing more and more into the local meteorologist, the unpaid champion of the local climate. He thought at first there was no place so healthful in the arrondissement. By the end of the second year he protested there was none so wholesome in the whole department. And for some time before he met Jean-Marie he had been prepared to challenge all France and the better part of Europe for a rival to his chosen spot.

'Doctor,' he would say – 'doctor is a foul word. It should not be used to ladies. It implies disease. I remark it, as a flaw in our civilisation, that we have not the proper horror of disease. Now I, for my part, have washed my hands of it; I have renounced my laureation; I am no doctor; I am only a worshipper of the true goddess Hygieia. Ah, believe me, it is she who has the cestus! And here, in this exiguous hamlet, has she placed her shrine: here she dwells and lavishes her gifts; here I walk with her in the early morning, and she shows me how strong she has made the peasants, how fruitful she has made the fields, how the trees grow up tall and comely under her eyes, and the fishes in the river become clean and agile at her presence. – Rheumatism!' he would cry, on some malapert interruption, 'oh, yes, I believe we do have a little rheumatism. That could hardly be avoided, you know, on a river. And of course the place stands a little low; and the meadows are marshy, there's no doubt. But, my dear sir, look at Bourron! Bourron stands high. Bourron is close to the forest; plenty of ozone there, you would say. Well, compared with Gretz, Bourron is a perfect shambles.'

The morning after he had been summoned to the dying mountebank, the Doctor visited the wharf at the tail of his garden, and had a long look at the running water. This he called prayer; but whether his adorations were addressed to the goddess Hygieia or some more orthodox deity, never plainly appeared. For he had uttered doubtful oracles, sometimes declaring that a river was the type of bodily health, sometimes extolling it as the great moral preacher, continually preaching peace, continuity, and diligence to man's tormented spirits. After he had watched a mile or so of the clear water running by before his eyes, seen a fish or two come to the surface with a gleam of silver, and sufficiently admired the long shadows of the trees falling half across the river from the opposite bank, with patches of moving sunlight in between, he strolled once more up the garden and through his house into the street, feeling cool and renovated.

The sound of his feet upon the causeway began the business of the day; for the village was still sound asleep. The church tower looked very airy in the sunlight; a few birds that turned about it seemed to swim in an atmosphere of more than usual rarity; and the Doctor, walking in long transparent shadows, filled his lungs amply, and proclaimed himself well contented with the morning.

On one of the posts before Tentaillon's carriage entry he espied a little dark figure perched in a meditative attitude, and immediately recognised Jean-Marie.

'Aha!' he said, stopping before him humorously, with a hand on either knee. 'So we rise early in the morning, do we? It appears to me that we have all the vices of a philosopher.'

The boy got to his feet and made a grave salutation.

'And how is our patient?' asked Desprez.

It appeared the patient was about the same.

'And why do you rise early in the morning?' he pursued.

Jean-Marie, after a long silence, professed that he hardly knew.

'You hardly know?' repeated Desprez. 'We hardly know anything, my man, until we try to learn. Interrogate your consciousness. Come, push me this inquiry home. Do you like it?'

'Yes,' said the boy slowly; 'yes, I like it.'

'And why do you like it?' continued the Doctor. '(We are now pursuing the Socratic method.) Why do you like it?'

'It is quiet,' answered Jean-Marie; 'and I have nothing to do; and then I feel as if I were good.'

Doctor Desprez took a seat on the post at the opposite side. He was beginning to take an interest in the talk, for the boy plainly thought before he spoke, and tried to answer truly. 'It appears you have a taste for feeling good,' said the Doctor. 'Now, there you puzzle me extremely; for I thought you said you were a thief; and the two are incompatible.'

'Is it very bad to steal?' asked Jean-Marie.

'Such is the general opinion, little boy,' replied the Doctor.

'No; but I mean as I stole,' explained the other. 'For I had no choice. I think it is surely right to have bread; it must be right to have bread, there comes so plain a want of it. And then they beat me cruelly if I returned with nothing,' he added. 'I was not ignorant of right and wrong; for before that I had been well taught by a priest, who was very kind to me.' (The Doctor made a horrible grimace at the word 'priest.') 'But it seemed to me, when one had nothing to eat and was beaten, it was a different affair. I would not have stolen for tartlets, I believe; but anyone would steal for baker's bread.'

'And so I suppose,' said the Doctor, with a rising sneer, 'you prayed God to forgive you, and explained the case to Him at length.'

'Why, sir?' asked Jean-Marie. 'I do not see.'

'Your priest would see, however,' retorted Desprez.

'Would he?' asked the boy, troubled for the first time. 'I should have thought God would have known.'

'Eh?' snarled the Doctor.

'I should have thought God would have understood me,' replied the other. 'You do not, I see; but then it was God that made me think so, was it not?'

'Little boy, little boy,' said Doctor Desprez, 'I told you already you had the vices of philosophy; if you display the virtues also, I must go. I am a student of the blessed laws of health, an observer of plain and temperate nature in her common walks; and I cannot preserve my equanimity in presence of a monster. Do you understand?'

'No, sir,' said the boy.

'I will make my meaning clear to you,' replied the Doctor. 'Look there at the sky – behind the belfry first, where it is so light, and then up and up, turning your chin back, right to the top of the dome, where it is already as blue as at noon. Is not that a beautiful colour? Does it not please the heart? We have seen it all our lives, until it has grown in with our familiar thoughts. Now,' changing his tone, 'suppose that sky to become suddenly of a live and fiery amber, like the colour of clear coals, and growing scarlet towards the top – I do not say it would be any the less beautiful; but would you like it as well?'

'I suppose not,' answered Jean-Marie.

'Neither do I like you,' returned the Doctor roughly. 'I hate all odd people, and you are the most curious little boy in all the world.'

Jean-Marie seemed to ponder for a while, and then he raised his head again and looked over at the Doctor with an air of candid inquiry. 'But are not you a very curious gentleman?' he asked.

The Doctor threw away his stick, bounded on the boy, clasped him to his bosom, and kissed him on both cheeks. 'Admirable, admirable imp!' he cried. 'What a morning, what an hour for a theorist of forty-two! No,' he continued, apostrophising Heaven. 'I did not know such boys existed; I was ignorant they made them so; I had doubted my race; and now! It is like,' he added, picking up his stick, 'like a lovers' meeting. I have bruised my favourite staff in that moment of enthusiasm. The injury, however, is not grave.' He caught the boy looking at him in obvious wonder, embarrassment, and alarm. 'Hullo!' said he, 'why do you look at me like that? Egad, I believe the boy despises me. Do you despise me, boy?'

'Oh, no,' replied Jean-Marie seriously; 'only I do not understand.'

'You must excuse me, sir,' returned the Doctor, with gravity; 'I am still so young. Oh, hang him!' he added to himself. And he took his seat again and observed the boy sardonically. 'He has spoiled the quiet of my morning,' thought he. 'I shall be nervous all day, and have a febricule when I digest. Let me compose myself.' And so he dismissed his preoccupations by an effort of the will which he had long practised, and let his soul roam abroad in the contemplation of the morning. He inhaled the air, tasting it critically as a connoisseur tastes a vintage, and prolonging the expiration with hygienic gusto. He counted the little flecks of cloud along the sky. He followed the movements of the birds round the church tower – making long sweeps, hanging poised, or turning airy somersaults in fancy, and beating the wind with imaginary pinions. And in this way he regained peace of mind and animal composure, conscious of his limbs, conscious of the sight of his eyes, conscious that the air had a cool taste, like a fruit, at the top of his throat; and at last, in complete abstraction, he began to sing. The Doctor had but one air – 'Malbrouck s'en va-t-en guerre'; even with that he was on terms of mere politeness; and his musical exploits were always reserved for moments when he was alone and entirely happy.

He was recalled to earth rudely by a pained expression on the boy's face. 'What do you think of my singing?' he inquired, stopping in the middle of a note; and then, after he had waited some little while and received no answer: 'What do you think of my singing?' he repeated imperiously.

'I do not like it,' faltered Jean-Marie.

'Oh, come!' cried the Doctor. 'Possibly you are a performer yourself?'

'I sing better than that,' replied the boy.

The Doctor eyed him for some seconds in stupefaction. He was aware that he was angry, and blushed for himself in consequence, which made him angrier. 'If this is how you address your master!' he said at last, with a shrug and a flourish of his arms.

'I do not speak to him at all,' returned the boy. 'I do not like him.'

'Then you like me?' snapped Doctor Desprez, with unusual eagerness.

'I do not know,' answered Jean-Marie.

The Doctor rose. 'I shall wish you a good morning,' he said. 'You are too much for me. Perhaps you have blood in your veins, perhaps celestial ichor, or perhaps you circulate nothing more gross than respirable air; but of one thing I am inexpugnably assured – that you are no human being. No, boy' – shaking his stick at him – 'you are not a human being. Write, write it in your memory – "I am not a human being – I have no pretension to be a human being – I am a dive, a dream, an angel, an acrostic, an illusion – what you please, but not a human being." And so accept my humble salutations and farewell!'

And with that the Doctor made off along the street in some emotion, and the boy stood, mentally gaping, where he left him.

CHAPTER III

The Adoption

MADAME DESPREZ, who answered to the Christian name of Anastasie, presented an agreeable type of her sex; exceedingly wholesome to look upon, a stout *brune*, with cool smooth cheeks, steady, dark eyes, and hands that neither art nor nature could improve. She was like the sort of person over whom adversity passes like a summer cloud; she might in the worst of conjunctions knit her brows into one vertical furrow for a moment, but the next it would be gone. She had much of the placidity of a contented nun; with little of her piety, however; for Anastasie was of a very mundane nature, fond of oysters and old wine, and somewhat bold pleasantries, and devoted to her husband for her own sake rather than for his. She was imperturbably good-natured, but had no idea of self-sacrifice. To live in that pleasant old house, with a green garden behind and bright flowers about the window, to eat and drink of the best, to gossip with a neighbour for a quarter of an hour, never to wear stays or a dress except when she went to Fontainebleau shopping, to be kept in a continual supply of racy novels, and to be married to Doctor Desprez and have no ground of jealousy, filled the cup of her nature to the brim. Those who had known the Doctor in bachelor days, when he had aired quite as many theories, but of a different order, attributed his present philosophy to the study of Anastasie. It was her brute enjoyment that he rationalised and perhaps vainly imitated.

Madame Desprez was an artist in the kitchen, and made coffee to a nicety. She had a knack of tidiness, with which she had infected the Doctor; everything was in its place; everything capable of polish shone gloriously; and dust was a thing banished from her empire. Aline, their single servant, had no other business in the world but to scour and burnish. So Doctor Desprez lived in his house like a fatted calf, warmed and cosseted to his heart's content.

The midday meal was excellent. There was a ripe melon, a fish from the river in a memorable Béarnaise sauce, a fat fowl in a fricassee, and a dish of asparagus, followed by some fruit. The Doctor drank half a bottle *plus* one glass, the wife half a bottle *minus* the same quantity, which was a marital privilege, of an excellent Côte-Rôtie, seven years old. Then the coffee was brought, and a flask of Chartreuse for madam, for the Doctor despised and distrusted such decoctions; and then Aline left the wedded pair to the pleasures of memory and digestion.

'It is a very fortunate circumstance, my cherished one,' observed the Doctor – 'this coffee is adorable – a very fortunate circumstance upon the whole – Anastasie, I beseech you, go without that poison for today; only one day, and you will feel the benefit, I pledge my reputation.'

'What is this fortunate circumstance, my friend?' inquired Anastasie, not heeding his protest, which was of daily recurrence.

'That we have no children, my beautiful,' replied the Doctor. 'I think of it more and more as the years go on, and with more and more gratitude towards the Power that dispenses such afflictions. Your health, my darling, my studious quiet, our little kitchen delicacies, how they would all have suffered, how they would all have been sacrificed! And for what? Children are the last word of human imperfection. Health flees before their face. They cry, my dear; they put vexatious questions; they demand to be fed, to be washed, to be educated, to have their noses blown; and then, when the time comes, they break our hearts, as I break this piece of sugar. A pair of professed egoists, like you and me, should avoid offspring, like an infidelity.'

'Indeed!' said she; and she laughed. 'Now, that is like you – to take credit for the thing you could not help.'

'My dear,' returned the Doctor solemnly, 'we might have adopted.'

'Never!' cried madame. 'Never, Doctor, with my consent. If the child were my own flesh and blood, I would not say no. But to take another person's indiscretions on my shoulders – my dear friend, I have too much sense.'

'Precisely,' replied the Doctor. 'We both had. And I am all the better pleased with our wisdom, because – because –'

He looked at her sharply.

'Because what?' she asked, with a faint premonition of danger.

'Because I have found the right person,' said the Doctor firmly, 'and shall adopt him this afternoon.'

Anastasie looked at him out of a mist. 'You have lost your reason,' she said; and there was a clang in her voice that seemed to threaten trouble.

'Not so, my dear,' he replied; 'I retain its complete exercise. To the proof: instead of attempting to cloak my inconsistency, I have, by way of preparing you, thrown it into strong relief. You will there, I think, recognise the philosopher who has the ecstasy to call you wife. The fact is, I have been reckoning all this while without an accident. I never thought to find a son of my own. Now, last night, I found one. Do not unnecessarily alarm yourself, my dear; he is not a drop of blood to me that I know. It is his mind, darling, his mind that calls me father.'

'His mind!' she repeated with a titter between scorn and hysterics. 'His mind, indeed! Henri, is this an idiotic pleasantry, or are you mad? His mind! And what of my mind?'

'Truly,' replied the Doctor with a shrug, 'you have your finger on the hitch. He will be strikingly antipathetic to my ever beautiful Anastasie. She will never understand him; he will never understand her. You married the animal side of my nature, dear; and it is on the spiritual side that I find my affinity for Jean-Marie. So much so, that, to be perfectly frank, I stand in some awe of him myself. You will easily perceive that I am announcing a calamity for you. Do not,' he broke out in tones of real solicitude – 'do not give way to tears after a meal, Anastasie. You will certainly give yourself a false digestion.'

Anastasie controlled herself. 'You know how willing I am to humour you,' she said, 'in all reasonable matters. But on this point –'

'My dear love,' interrupted the Doctor, eager to prevent refusal, 'who wished to leave Paris? Who made me give up cards, and the opera, and the boulevard, and my social relations, and all that was my life before I knew you? Have I been faithful? Have I been obedient? Have I not borne my doom with cheerfulness? In all honesty, Anastasie, have I not a right to a stipulation on my side? I have, and you know it. I stipulate my son.'

Anastasie was aware of defeat; she struck her colours instantly. 'You will break my heart,' she sighed.

'Not in the least,' said he. 'You will feel a trifling inconvenience for a month, just as I did when I was first brought to this vile hamlet; then your admirable sense and temper will prevail, and I see you already as content as ever, and making your husband the happiest of men.'

'You know I can refuse you nothing,' she said, with a last flicker of resistance; 'nothing that will make you truly happier. But will this? Are you sure, my husband? Last night, you say, you found him! He may be the worst of humbugs.'

'I think not,' replied the Doctor. 'But do not suppose me so unwary as to adopt him out of hand. I am, I flatter myself, a finished man of the world; I have had all possibilities in view; my plan is contrived to meet them all. I take the lad as stable-boy. If he pilfer, if he grumble, if he desire to change, I shall see I was mistaken; I shall recognise him for no son of mine, and send him tramping.'

'You will never do so when the time comes,' said his wife; 'I know your good heart.'

She reached out her hand to him, with a sigh; the Doctor smiled as he took it and carried it to his lips; he had gained his point with greater ease than he had dared to hope; for perhaps the twentieth time he had proved the efficacy of his trusty argument, his Excalibur, the hint of a return to Paris. Six months in the capital, for a man of the Doctor's antecedents and relations, implied no less calamity than total ruin. Anastasie had saved the remainder of his fortune by keeping him strictly in the country. The very name of Paris put her in a blue fear; and she would have allowed her husband to keep a menagerie in the back garden, let alone adopting a stable-boy, rather than permit the question of return to be discussed.

About four of the afternoon, the mountebank rendered up his ghost; he had never been conscious since his seizure. Doctor Desprez was present at his last passage, and declared the farce over. Then he took Jean-Marie by the shoulder and led him out into the inn garden where there was a convenient bench beside the river. Here he sat him down and made the boy place himself on his left.

'Jean-Marie,' he said very gravely, 'this world is exceedingly vast; and even France, which is only a small corner of it, is a great place for a little lad like you. Unfortunately it is full of eager, shouldering people moving on; and there are very few bakers' shops for so many eaters. Your master is dead; you are not fit to gain a living by yourself; you do not wish to steal? No. Your situation then is undesirable; it is for the moment critical. On the other hand, you behold in me a man not old, though elderly, still enjoying the youth of the heart and the intelligence; a man of instruction; easily situated in this world's affairs; keeping a good table – a man, neither as friend nor host, to be despised. I offer you your food and clothes, and to teach you lessons in the evening, which will be infinitely more to the purpose for a lad of your stamp than those of all the priests in Europe. I propose no wages, but if ever you take a thought to leave me, the door shall be open, and I will give you a hundred francs to start the world upon. In return, I have an old horse and chaise, which you would very speedily learn to clean and keep in order. Do not hurry yourself to answer, and take it or leave it as you judge aright. Only remember this, that I am no sentimentalist or charitable person, but a man who lives rigorously to himself; and that if I make the proposal, it is for my own ends – it is because I perceive clearly an advantage to myself. And now, reflect.'

'I shall be very glad. I do not see what else I can do. I thank you, sir, most kindly, and I will try to be useful,' said the boy.

'Thank you,' said the Doctor warmly, rising at the same time and wiping his brow, for he had suffered agonies while the thing hung in the wind. A refusal, after the scene at noon, would have placed him in a ridiculous light before Anastasie. 'How hot and heavy is the evening, to be sure! I have always had a fancy to be a fish in summer, Jean-Marie, here in the Loing beside Gretz. I should lie under a water-lily and listen to the bells, which must sound most delicately down below. That would be a life – do you not think so too?'

'Yes,' said Jean-Marie.

'Thank God you have imagination!' cried the Doctor, embracing the boy with his usual effusive warmth, though it was a proceeding that seemed to disconcert the sufferer almost as much as if he had been an English schoolboy of the same age. 'And now,' he added, 'I will take you to my wife.'

Madame Desprez sat in the dining-room in a cool wrapper. All the blinds were down, and the tile floor had been recently sprinkled with water; her eyes were half shut, but she affected to be reading a novel as they entered. Though she was a bustling woman, she enjoyed repose between whiles and had a remarkable appetite for sleep.

The Doctor went through a solemn form of introduction, adding, for the benefit of both parties, 'You must try to like each other for my sake.'

'He is very pretty,' said Anastasie. 'Will you kiss me, my pretty little fellow?'

The Doctor was furious, and dragged her into the passage. 'Are you a fool, Anastasie?' he said. 'What is all this I hear about the tact of women? Heaven knows, I have not met with it in my experience. You address my little philosopher as if he were an infant. He must be spoken to with more respect, I tell you; he must not be kissed and Georgy-porgy'd like an ordinary child.'

'I only did it to please you, I am sure,' replied Anastasie; 'but I will try to do better.'

The doctor apologised for his warmth. 'But I do wish him,' he continued, 'to feel at home among us. And really your conduct was so idiotic, my cherished one, and so utterly and distantly out of place, that a saint might have been pardoned a little vehemence in disapproval. Do, do try – if it is possible for a woman to understand young people – but of course it is not, and I waste my breath. Hold your tongue as much as possible at least, and observe my conduct narrowly; it will serve you for a model.'

Anastasie did as she was bidden, and considered the Doctor's behaviour. She observed that he embraced the boy three times in the course of the evening, and managed generally to confound and abash the little fellow out of speech and appetite. But she had the true womanly heroism in little affairs. Not only did she refrain from the cheap revenge of exposing the Doctor's errors to himself, but she did her best to remove their ill-effect on Jean-Marie. When Desprez went out for his last breath of air before retiring for the night, she came over to the boy's side and took his hand.

'You must not be surprised nor frightened by my husband's manners,' she said. 'He is the kindest of men, but so clever that he is sometimes difficult to understand. You will soon grow used to him, and then you will love him, for that nobody can help. As for me, you may be sure, I shall try to make you happy, and will not bother you at all. I think we should be excellent friends, you and I. I am not clever, but I am very good-natured. Will you give me a kiss?'

He held up his face, and she took him in her arms and then began to cry. The woman had spoken in complaisance; but she had warmed to her own words, and tenderness followed. The Doctor, entering, found them enlaced: he concluded that his wife was in fault; and he was just beginning, in an awful voice, 'Anastasie – ,' when she looked up at him, smiling, with an upraised finger; and he held his peace, wondering, while she led the boy to his attic.

CHAPTER IV

The Education of a Philosopher

THE INSTALLATION OF the adopted stable-boy was thus happily effected, and the wheels of life continued to run smoothly in the Doctor's house. Jean-Marie did his horse and carriage duty in the morning; sometimes helped in the housework; sometimes walked abroad with the Doctor, to drink wisdom from the fountain-head; and was introduced at night to the sciences and the dead tongues. He retained his singular placidity of mind and manner; he was rarely in fault; but he made only a very partial progress in his studies, and remained much of a stranger in the family.

The Doctor was a pattern of regularity. All forenoon he worked on his great book, the 'Comparative Pharmacopœia, or Historical Dictionary of all Medicines,' which as yet consisted principally of slips of paper and pins. When finished, it was to fill many personable volumes, and to combine antiquarian interest with professional utility. But the Doctor was studious of literary graces and the picturesque; an anecdote, a touch of manners, a moral qualification, or a sounding epithet was sure to be preferred before a piece of science; a little more, and he would have written the 'Comparative Pharmacopœia' in verse! The article 'Mummia,' for instance, was already complete, though the remainder of the work had not progressed beyond the letter A. It was exceedingly copious and entertaining, written with quaintness and colour, exact, erudite, a literary article; but it would hardly have afforded guidance to a practising physician of today. The feminine good sense of his wife had led her to point this out with uncompromising sincerity; for the Dictionary was duly read aloud to her, betwixt sleep and waking, as it proceeded towards an infinitely distant completion; and the Doctor was a little sore on the subject of mummies, and sometimes resented an allusion with asperity.

After the midday meal and a proper period of digestion, he walked, sometimes alone, sometimes accompanied by Jean-Marie; for madame would have preferred any hardship rather than walk.

She was, as I have said, a very busy person, continually occupied about material comforts, and ready to drop asleep over a novel the instant she was disengaged. This was the less objectionable as she never snored or grew distempered in complexion when she slept. On the contrary, she looked the very picture of luxurious and appetising ease, and woke without a start to the perfect possession of her faculties. I am afraid she was greatly an animal, but she was a very nice animal to have about. In this way she had little to do with Jean-Marie; but the sympathy which had been established between them on the first night remained unbroken; they held occasional conversations, mostly on household matters; to the extreme disappointment of the Doctor, they occasionally sallied off together to that temple of debasing superstition, the village church; madame and he, both in their Sunday best, drove twice a month to Fontainebleau and returned laden with purchases; and in short, although the Doctor still continued to regard them as irreconcilably antipathetic, their relation was as intimate, friendly, and confidential as their natures suffered.

I fear, however, that in her heart of hearts madame kindly despised and pitied the boy. She had no admiration for his class of virtues; she liked a smart, polite, forward, roguish sort of boy, cap in hand, light of foot, meeting the eye; she liked volubility, charm, a little vice – the promise of a second Doctor Desprez. And it was her indefeasible belief that Jean-Marie was dull. 'Poor dear boy,' she had said once, 'how sad it is that he should be so stupid!' She had never repeated that remark, for the Doctor had raged like a wild bull, denouncing the brutal bluntness of her mind, bemoaning his own fate to be so unequally mated with an ass, and, what touched Anastasie more nearly, menacing the table china by the fury of his gesticulations. But she adhered silently to her opinion; and when Jean-Marie was sitting, stolid, blank, but not unhappy, over his unfinished tasks, she would snatch her opportunity in the Doctor's absence, go over to him, put her arms about his neck, lay her cheek to his, and communicate her sympathy with his distress. 'Do not mind,' she would say; 'I, too, am not at all clever, and I can assure you that it makes no difference in life.'

The Doctor's view was naturally different. That gentleman never wearied of the sound of his own voice, which was, to say the truth, agreeable enough to hear. He now had a listener, who was not cynically indifferent as Anastasie, and who sometimes put him on his mettle by the most relevant objections. Besides, was he not educating the boy? And education, philosophers are agreed, is the most philosophical of duties. What can be more heavenly to poor mankind than to have one's hobby grow into a duty to the State? Then, indeed, do the ways of life become ways of pleasantness. Never had the doctor seen reason to be more content with his endowments. Philosophy flowed smoothly from his lips. He was so agile a dialectician that he could trace his nonsense, when challenged, back to some root in sense, and prove it to be a sort of flower upon his system. He slipped out of antinomies like a fish, and left his disciple marvelling at the rabbi's depth.

Moreover, deep down in his heart the Doctor was disappointed with the ill-success of his more formal education. A boy, chosen by so acute an observer for his aptitude, and guided along the path of learning by so philosophic an instructor, was bound, by the nature of the universe, to make a more obvious and lasting advance. Now Jean-Marie was slow in all things, impenetrable in others; and his power of forgetting was fully on a level with his power to learn. Therefore the Doctor cherished his peripatetic lectures, to which the boy attended, and which he generally appeared to enjoy, and by which he often profited.

Many and many were the talks they had together; and health and moderation proved the subject of the Doctor's divagations. To these he lovingly returned.

'I lead you,' he would say, 'by the green pastures. My system, my beliefs, my medicines, are resumed in one phrase – to avoid excess. Blessed nature, healthy, temperate nature, abhors and exterminates excess. Human law, in this matter, imitates at a great distance her provisions; and we must strive to supplement the efforts of the law. Yes, boy, we must be a law to ourselves and for our neighbours – *lex armata* – armed, emphatic, tyrannous law. If you see a crapulous human ruin snuffing, dash from him his box! The judge, though in a way an admission of disease, is less offensive to me than either the doctor or the priest. Above all the doctor – the doctor and the purulent trash and garbage of his pharmacopœia! Pure air – from the neighbourhood of a pinetum for the sake of the turpentine – unadulterated wine, and the reflections of an unsophisticated spirit in the presence of the works of nature – these, my boy, are the best medical appliances and the best religious comforts. Devote yourself to these. Hark! there are the bells of Bourron (the wind is in the north, it will be fair). How clear and airy is the sound! The nerves are harmonised and quieted; the mind attuned to silence; and observe how easily and regularly beats the heart! Your enlightened doctor would see nothing in these sensations; and yet you yourself perceive they are a part of health. – Did you remember your cinchona this morning? Good. Cinchona also is a work of nature; it is, after all, only the bark of a tree which we might gather for ourselves if we lived in the locality. – What a world is this! Though a professed atheist, I delight to bear my testimony to the world. Look at the gratuitous remedies and pleasures that surround our path! The river runs by the garden end, our bath, our fishpond, our natural system of drainage. There is a well in the court which sends up sparkling water from the earth's very heart, clean, cool, and, with a little wine, most wholesome. The district is notorious for its salubrity;

rheumatism is the only prevalent complaint, and I myself have never had a touch of it. I tell you – and my opinion is based upon the coldest, clearest processes of reason – if I, if you, desired to leave this home of pleasures, it would be the duty, it would be the privilege, of our best friend to prevent us with a pistol bullet.'

One beautiful June day they sat upon the hill outside the village. The river, as blue as heaven, shone here and there among the foliage. The indefatigable birds turned and flickered about Gretz church tower. A healthy wind blew from over the forest, and the sound of innumerable thousands of tree-tops and innumerable millions on millions of green leaves was abroad in the air, and filled the ear with something between whispered speech and singing. It seemed as if every blade of grass must hide a cigale; and the fields rang merrily with their music, jingling far and near as with the sleigh-bells of the fairy queen. From their station on the slope the eye embraced a large space of poplar'd plain upon the one hand, the waving hill-tops of the forest on the other, and Gretz itself in the middle, a handful of roofs. Under the bestriding arch of the blue heavens, the place seemed dwindled to a toy. It seemed incredible that people dwelt, and could find room to turn or air to breathe, in such a corner of the world. The thought came home to the boy, perhaps for the first time, and he gave it words.

'How small it looks!' he sighed.

'Ay,' replied the Doctor, 'small enough now. Yet it was once a walled city; thriving, full of furred burgesses and men in armour, humming with affairs – with tall spires, for aught that I know, and portly towers along the battlements. A thousand chimneys ceased smoking at the curfew bell. There were gibbets at the gate as thick as scarecrows. In time of war, the assault swarmed against it with ladders, the arrows fell like leaves, the defenders sallied hotly over the drawbridge, each side uttered its cry as they plied their weapons. Do you know that the walls extended as far as the Commanderie? Tradition so reports. Alas, what a long way off is all this confusion – nothing left of it but my quiet words spoken in your ear – and the town itself shrunk to the hamlet underneath us! By-and-by came the English wars – you shall hear more of the English, a stupid people, who sometimes blundered into good – and Gretz was taken, sacked, and burned. It is the history of many towns; but Gretz never rose again; it was never rebuilt; its ruins were a quarry to serve the growth of rivals; and the stones of Gretz are now erect along the streets of Nemours. It gratifies me that our old house was the first to rise after the calamity; when the town had come to an end, it inaugurated the hamlet.'

'I, too, am glad of that,' said Jean-Marie.

'It should be the temple of the humbler virtues,' responded the Doctor with a savoury gusto. 'Perhaps one of the reasons why I love my little hamlet as I do, is that we have a similar history, she and I. Have I told you that I was once rich?'

'I do not think so,' answered Jean-Marie. 'I do not think I should have forgotten. I am sorry you should have lost your fortune.'

'Sorry?' cried the Doctor. 'Why, I find I have scarce begun your education after all. Listen to me! Would you rather live in the old Gretz or in the new, free from the alarms of war, with the green country at the door, without noise, passports, the exactions of the soldiery, or the jangle of the curfew-bell to send us off to bed by sundown?'

'I suppose I should prefer the new,' replied the boy.

'Precisely,' returned the Doctor; 'so do I. And in the same way, I prefer my present moderate fortune to my former wealth. Golden mediocrity! cried the adorable ancients; and I subscribe to their enthusiasm. Have I not got good wine, good food, good air, the fields and the forest for my walk, a house, an admirable wife, a boy whom I protest I cherish like a son? Now, if I were still rich, I should indubitably make my residence in Paris – you know Paris – Paris and Paradise are not convertible terms. This pleasant noise of the wind streaming among leaves changed into the grinding Babel of the street, the stupid glare of plaster substituted for this quiet pattern of greens and greys, the nerves shattered, the digestion falsified – picture the fall! Already you perceive the consequences; the mind is stimulated, the heart steps to a different measure, and the man is himself no longer. I have passionately studied myself – the true business of philosophy. I know my character as the musician knows the ventages of his flute. Should I return to Paris, I should ruin myself gambling; nay, I go further – I should break the heart of my Anastasie with infidelities.'

This was too much for Jean-Marie. That a place should so transform the most excellent of men transcended his belief. Paris, he protested, was even an agreeable place of residence. 'Nor when I lived in that city did I feel much difference,' he pleaded.

'What!' cried the Doctor. 'Did you not steal when you were there?'

But the boy could never be brought to see that he had done anything wrong when he stole. Nor, indeed, did the Doctor think he had; but that gentleman was never very scrupulous when in want of a retort.

'And now,' he concluded, 'do you begin to understand? My only friends were those who ruined me. Gretz has been my academy, my sanatorium, my heaven of innocent pleasures. If millions are offered me, I wave them back: *Retro, Sathanas!* – Evil one, begone! Fix your mind on my example; despise riches, avoid the debasing influence of cities. Hygiene – hygiene and mediocrity of fortune – these be your watchwords during life!'

The Doctor's system of hygiene strikingly coincided with his tastes; and his picture of the perfect life was a faithful description of the one he was leading at the time. But it is easy to convince a boy, whom you supply with all the facts for the discussion. And besides, there was one thing admirable in the philosophy, and that was the enthusiasm of the philosopher. There was never any one more vigorously determined to be pleased; and if he was not a great logician, and so had no right to convince the intellect, he was certainly something of a poet, and had a fascination to seduce the heart. What he could not achieve in his customary humour of a radiant admiration of himself and his circumstances, he sometimes effected in his fits of gloom.

'Boy,' he would say, 'avoid me today. If I were superstitious, I should even beg for an interest in your prayers. I am in the black fit; the evil spirit of King Saul, the hag of the merchant Abudah, the personal devil of the mediæval monk, is with me – is in me,' tapping on his breast. 'The vices of my nature are now uppermost; innocent pleasures woo me in vain; I long for Paris, for my wallowings in the mire. See,' he would continue, producing a handful of silver, 'I denude myself, I am not to be trusted with the price of a fare. Take it, keep it for me, squander it on deleterious candy, throw it in the deepest of the river – I will homologate your action. Save me from that part of myself which I disown. If you see me falter, do not hesitate; if necessary, wreck the train! I speak, of course, by a parable. Any extremity were better than for me to reach Paris alive.'

Doubtless the Doctor enjoyed these little scenes, as a variation in his part; they represented the Byronic element in the somewhat artificial poetry of his existence; but to the boy, though he was dimly aware of their theatricality, they represented more. The Doctor made perhaps too little, the boy possibly too much, of the reality and gravity of these temptations.

One day a great light shone for Jean-Marie. 'Could not riches be used well?' he asked.

'In theory, yes,' replied the Doctor. 'But it is found in experience that no one does so. All the world imagine they will be exceptional when they grow wealthy; but possession is debasing, new desires spring up; and the silly taste for ostentation eats out the heart of pleasure.'

'Then you might be better if you had less,' said the boy.

'Certainly not,' replied the Doctor; but his voice quavered as he spoke.

'Why?' demanded pitiless innocence.

Doctor Desprez saw all the colours of the rainbow in a moment; the stable universe appeared to be about capsizing with him. 'Because,' said he – affecting deliberation after an obvious pause – 'because I have formed my life for my present income. It is not good for men of my years to be violently disseevered from their habits.'

That was a sharp brush. The Doctor breathed hard, and fell into taciturnity for the afternoon. As for the boy, he was delighted with the resolution of his doubts; even wondered that he had not foreseen the obvious and conclusive answer. His faith in the Doctor was a stout piece of goods. Desprez was inclined to be a sheet in the wind's eye after dinner, especially after Rhone wine, his favourite weakness. He would then remark on the warmth of his feeling for Anastasie, and with inflamed cheeks and a loose, flustered smile, debate upon all sorts of topics and be feebly and indiscreetly witty. But the adopted stable-boy would not permit himself to entertain a doubt that savoured of ingratitude. It is quite true that a man may be a second father to you, and yet take too much drink; but the best natures are ever slow to accept such truths.

The Doctor thoroughly possessed his heart, but perhaps he exaggerated his influence over his mind. Certainly Jean-Marie adopted some of his master's opinions, but I have yet to learn that he ever surrendered one of his own. Convictions existed in him by divine right; they were virgin, unwrought, the brute metal of decision. He could add others indeed, but he could not put away; neither did he care if they were perfectly agreed among themselves; and his spiritual pleasures had nothing to do with turning them over or justifying them in words. Words were with him a mere accomplishment, like dancing. When he was by himself, his pleasures were almost vegetable. He would slip into the woods towards Achères, and sit in the mouth of a cave among grey birches. His soul stared straight out of his eyes; he did not move or think; sunlight, thin shadows moving in the wind, the edge of firs against the sky, occupied and bound his faculties. He was pure unity, a spirit wholly abstracted. A single mood filled him, to which all the objects of sense contributed, as the colours of the spectrum merge and disappear in white light.

So while the Doctor made himself drunk with words, the adopted stable-boy bemused himself with silence.

CHAPTER V

Treasure Trove

THE DOCTOR'S CARRIAGE was a two-wheeled gig with a hood; a kind of vehicle in much favour among country doctors. On how many roads has one not seen it, a great way off between the poplars! – in how many village streets, tied to a gate-post! This sort of chariot is affected – particularly at the trot – by a kind of pitching movement to and fro across the axle, which well entitles it to the style of a noddy. The hood describes a considerable arc against the landscape, with a solemnly absurd effect on the contemplative pedestrian. To ride in such carriage cannot be numbered among the things that appertain to glory; but I have no doubt it may be useful in liver complaint. Thence, perhaps, its wide popularity among physicians.

One morning early, Jean-Marie led forth the Doctor's noddy, opened the gate, and mounted to the driving-seat. The Doctor followed, arrayed from top to toe in spotless linen, armed with an immense flesh-coloured umbrella, and girt with a botanical case on a baldric; and the equipage drove off smartly in a breeze of its own provocation. They were bound for Franchard, to collect plants, with an eye to the 'Comparative Pharmacopœia.'

A little rattling on the open roads, and they came to the borders of the forest and struck into an unfrequented track; the noddy yawed softly over the sand, with an accompaniment of snapping twigs. There was a great, green, softly murmuring cloud of congregated foliage overhead. In the arcades of the forest the air retained the freshness of the night. The athletic bearing of the trees, each carrying its leafy mountain, pleased the mind like so many statues; and the lines of the trunk led the eye admiringly upward to where the extreme leaves sparkled in a patch of azure. Squirrels leaped in mid-air. It was a proper spot for a devotee of the goddess Hygieia.

'Have you been to Franchard, Jean-Marie?' inquired the Doctor. 'I fancy not.'

'Never,' replied the boy.

'It is ruin in a gorge,' continued Desprez, adopting his expository voice; 'the ruin of a hermitage and chapel. History tells us much of Franchard; how the recluse was often slain by robbers; how he lived on a most insufficient diet; how he was expected to pass his days in prayer. A letter is preserved, addressed to one of these solitaries by the superior

of his order, full of admirable hygienic advice; bidding him go from his
book to praying, and so back again, for variety's sake, and when he was
weary of both, to stroll about his garden and observe the honey-bees. It
is to this day my own system. You must often have remarked me leaving
the 'Pharmacopœia' – often even in the middle of a phrase – to come
forth into the sun and air. I admire the writer of that letter from my
heart; he was a man of thought on the most important subjects. But,
indeed, had I lived in the Middle Ages (I am heartily glad that I did not)
I should have been an eremite myself – if I had not been a professed
buffoon, that is. These were the only philosophical lives yet open:
laughter or prayer; sneers, we might say, and tears. Until the sun of the
Positive arose, the wise man had to make his choice between these two.'

'I have been a buffoon, of course,' observed Jean-Marie.

'I cannot imagine you to have excelled in your profession,' said the
Doctor, admiring the boy's gravity. 'Do you ever laugh?'

'Oh, yes,' replied the other. 'I laugh often. I am very fond of jokes.'

'Singular being!' said Desprez. 'But I divagate (I perceive in a
thousand ways that I grow old). Franchard was at length destroyed in
the English wars, the same that levelled Gretz. But – here is the point –
the hermits (for there were already more than one) had foreseen the
danger and carefully concealed the sacrificial vessels. These vessels
were of monstrous value, Jean-Marie – monstrous value – priceless, we
may say, exquisitely worked, of exquisite material. And now, mark me,
they have never been found. In the reign of Louis Quatorze some
fellows were digging hard by the ruins. Suddenly – tock! – the spade hit
upon an obstacle. Imagine the men looking one to another; imagine
how their hearts bounded, how their colour came and went. It was a
coffer, and in Franchard, the place of buried treasure! They tore it
open like famished beasts. Alas! it was not the treasure; only some
priestly robes, which, at the touch of the eating air, fell upon themselves and instantly wasted into dust. The perspiration of these good
fellows turned cold upon them, Jean-Marie. I will pledge my reputation, if there was anything like a cutting wind, one or other had a
pneumonia for his trouble.'

'I should like to have seen them turning into dust,' said Jean-Marie.
'Otherwise, I should not have cared so greatly.'

'You have no imagination,' cried the Doctor. 'Picture to yourself the
scene. Dwell on the idea – a great treasure lying in the earth for
centuries: the material for a giddy, copious, opulent existence not
employed; dresses and exquisite pictures unseen; the swiftest galloping
horses not stirring a hoof, arrested by a spell; women with the beautiful
faculty of smiles, not smiling; cards, dice, opera, singing, orchestras,

castles, beautiful parks and gardens, big ships with a tower of sailcloth, all lying unborn in a coffin – and the stupid trees growing overhead in the sunlight, year after year. The thought drives one frantic.'

'It is only money,' replied Jean-Marie. 'It would do harm.'

'Oh, come!' cried Desprez, 'that is philosophy; it is all very fine, but not to the point just now. And besides, it is not 'only money,' as you call it; there are works of art in the question; the vessels were carved. You speak like a child. You weary me exceedingly, quoting my words out of all logical connection, like a parroquet.'

'And at any rate, we have nothing to do with it,' returned the boy submissively.

They struck the Route Ronde at that moment; and the sudden change to the rattling causeway combined, with the Doctor's irritation, to keep him silent. The noddy jigged along; the trees went by, looking on silently, as if they had something on their minds. The Quadrilateral was passed; then came Franchard. They put up the horse at the little solitary inn, and went forth strolling. The gorge was dyed deeply with heather; the rocks and birches standing luminous in the sun. A great humming of bees about the flowers disposed Jean-Marie to sleep, and he sat down against a clump of heather, while the Doctor went briskly to and fro, with quick turns, culling his simples.

The boy's head had fallen a little forward, his eyes were closed, his fingers had fallen lax about his knees, when a sudden cry called him to his feet. It was a strange sound, thin and brief; it fell dead, and silence returned as though it had never been interrupted. He had not recognised the Doctor's voice; but, as there was no one else in all the valley, it was plainly the Doctor who had given utterance to the sound. He looked right and left, and there was Desprez, standing in a niche between two boulders, and looking round on his adopted son with a countenance as white as paper.

'A viper!' cried Jean-Marie, running towards him. 'A viper! You are bitten!'

The Doctor came down heavily out of the cleft, and advanced in silence to meet the boy, whom he took roughly by the shoulder.

'I have found it,' he said, with a gasp.

'A plant?' asked Jean-Marie.

Desprez had a fit of unnatural gaiety, which the rocks took up and mimicked. 'A plant!' he repeated scornfully. 'Well – yes – a plant. And here,' he added suddenly, showing his right hand, which he had hitherto concealed behind his back – 'here is one of the bulbs.'

Jean-Marie saw a dirty platter, coated with earth.

'That?' said he. 'It is a plate!'

'It is a coach and horses,' cried the Doctor. 'Boy,' he continued, growing warmer, 'I plucked away a great pad of moss from between these boulders, and disclosed a crevice; and when I looked in, what do you suppose I saw? I saw a house in Paris with a court and garden, I saw my wife shining with diamonds, I saw myself a deputy, I saw you – well, I – I saw your future,' he concluded, rather feebly. 'I have just discovered America,' he added.

'But what is it?' asked the boy.

'The Treasure of Franchard,' cried the Doctor; and, throwing his brown straw hat upon the ground, he whooped like an Indian and sprang upon Jean-Marie, whom he suffocated with embraces and bedewed with tears. Then he flung himself down among the heather and once more laughed until the valley rang.

But the boy had now an interest of his own, a boy's interest. No sooner was he released from the Doctor's accolade than he ran to the boulders, sprang into the niche, and, thrusting his hand into the crevice, drew forth one after another, encrusted with the earth of ages, the flagons, candlesticks, and patens of the hermitage of Franchard. A casket came last, tightly shut and very heavy.

'Oh, what fun!' he cried.

But when he looked back at the Doctor, who had followed close behind and was silently observing, the words died from his lips. Desprez was once more the colour of ashes; his lip worked and trembled; a sort of bestial greed possessed him.

'This is childish,' he said. 'We lose precious time. Back to the inn, harness the trap, and bring it to yon bank. Run for your life, and remember – not one whisper. I stay here to watch.'

Jean-Marie did as he was bid, though not without surprise. The noddy was brought round to the spot indicated; and the two gradually transported the treasure from its place of concealment to the boot below the driving-seat. Once it was all stored the Doctor recovered his gaiety.

'I pay my grateful duties to the genius of this dell,' he said. 'Oh, for a live coal, a heifer, and a jar of country wine! I am in the vein for sacrifice, for a superb libation. Well, and why not? We are at Franchard. English pale ale is to be had – not classical, indeed, but excellent. Boy, we shall drink ale.'

'But I thought it was so unwholesome,' said Jean-Marie, 'and very dear besides.'

'Fiddle-de-dee!' exclaimed the Doctor gaily. 'To the inn!'

And he stepped into the noddy, tossing his head, with an elastic, youthful air. The horse was turned, and in a few seconds they drew up beside the pailings of the inn garden.

'Here,' said Desprez – 'here, near the table, so that we may keep an eye upon things.'

They tied the horse and entered the garden, the Doctor singing, now in fantastic high notes, now producing deep reverberations from his chest. He took a seat, rapped loudly on the table, assailed the waiter with witticisms; and when the bottle of Bass was at length produced, far more charged with gas than the most delirious champagne, he filled out a long glassful of froth and pushed it over to Jean-Marie. 'Drink,' he said; 'drink deep.'

'I would rather not,' faltered the boy, true to his training.

'What?' thundered Desprez.

'I am afraid of it,' said Jean-Marie: 'my stomach – '

'Take it or leave it,' interrupted Desprez fiercely, 'but understand it once for all – there is nothing so contemptible as a precisian.'

Here was a new lesson! The boy sat bemused, looking at the glass but not tasting it, while the Doctor emptied and refilled his own, at first with clouded brow, but gradually yielding to the sun, the heady, prickling beverage, and his own predisposition to be happy.

'Once in a way,' he said at last, by way of a concession to the boy's more rigorous attitude, 'once in a way, and at so critical a moment, this ale is a nectar for the gods. The habit, indeed, is debasing; wine, the juice of the grape, is the true drink of the Frenchman, as I have often had occasion to point out; and I do not know that I can blame you for refusing this outlandish stimulant. You can have some wine and cakes. Is the bottle empty? Well, we will not be proud; we will have pity on your glass.'

The beer being done, the Doctor chafed bitterly while JeanMarie finished his cakes. 'I burn to be gone,' he said, looking at his watch. 'Good God, how slow you eat!' And yet to eat slowly was his own particular prescription, the main secret of longevity!

His martyrdom, however, reached an end at last; the pair resumed their places in the buggy, and Desprez, leaning luxuriously back, announced his intention of proceeding to Fontainebleau.

'To Fontainebleau?' repeated Jean-Marie.

'My words are always measured,' said the Doctor. 'On!'

The Doctor was driven through the glades of Paradise; the air, the light, the shining leaves, the very movements of the vehicle, seemed to fall in tune with his golden meditations; with his head thrown back, he dreamed a series of sunny visions, ale and pleasure dancing in his veins. At last he spoke.

'I shall telegraph for Casimir,' he said. 'Good Casimir! a fellow of the lower order of intelligence, Jean-Marie, distinctly not creative, not poetic; and yet he will repay your study; his fortune is vast, and is entirely due to his own exertions. He is the very fellow to help us to dispose of our trinkets, find us a suitable house in Paris, and manage the details of our installation. Admirable Casimir, one of my oldest comrades! It was on his advice, I may add, that I invested my little fortune in Turkish bonds; when we have added these spoils of the Mediæval Church to our stake in the Mohametan empire, little boy, we shall positively roll among doubloons, positively roll! Beautiful forest,' he cried, 'farewell! Though called to other scenes, I will not forget thee. Thy name is graven in my heart. Under the influence of prosperity I become dithyrambic, Jean-Marie. Such is the impulse of the natural soul; such was the constitution of primaeval man. And I – well, I will not refuse the credit – I have preserved my youth like a virginity; another, who should have led the same snoozing, countrified existence for these years, another had become rusted, become stereotype; but I, I praise my happy constitution, retain the spring unbroken. Fresh opulence and a new sphere of duties find me unabated in ardour and only more mature by knowledge. For this prospective change, Jean-Marie – it may probably have shocked you. Tell me now, did it not strike you as an inconsistency? Confess – it is useless to dissemble – it pained you?'

'Yes,' said the boy.

'You see,' returned the Doctor, with sublime fatuity, 'I read your thoughts! Nor am I surprised – your education is not yet complete; the higher duties of men have not been yet presented to you fully. A hint – till we have leisure – must suffice. Now that I am once more in possession of a modest competence; now that I have so long prepared myself in silent meditation, it becomes my superior duty to proceed to Paris. My scientific training, my undoubted command of language, mark me out for the service of my country. Modesty in such a case would be a snare. If sin were a philosophical expression, I should call it sinful. A man must not deny his manifest abilities, for that is to evade his obligations. I must be up and doing; I must be no skulker in life's battle.'

So he rattled on, copiously greasing the joint of his inconsistency with words; while the boy listened silently, his eyes fixed on the horse, his mind seething. It was all lost eloquence; no array of words could unsettle a belief of Jean-Marie's; and he drove into Fontainebleau filled with pity, horror, indignation, and despair.

In the town Jean-Marie was kept a fixture on the driving-seat, to guard the treasure; while the Doctor, with a singular, slightly tipsy airiness of manner, fluttered in and out of cafés, where he shook hands with garrison officers, and mixed an absinthe with the nicety of old experience; in and out of shops, from which he returned laden with costly fruits, real turtle, a magnificent piece of silk for his wife, a preposterous cane for himself, and a képi of the newest fashion for the boy; in and out of the telegraph office, whence he despatched his telegram, and where three hours later he received an answer promising a visit on the morrow; and generally pervaded Fontainebleau with the first fine aroma of his divine good humour.

The sun was very low when they set forth again; the shadows of the forest trees extended across the broad white road that led them home; the penetrating odour of the evening wood had already arisen, like a cloud of incense, from that broad field of tree-tops; and even in the streets of the town, where the air had been baked all day between white walls, it came in whiffs and pulses, like a distant music. Half-way home, the last gold flicker vanished from a great oak upon the left; and when they came forth beyond the borders of the wood, the plain was already sunken in pearly greyness, and a great, pale moon came swinging skyward through the filmy poplars.

The Doctor sang, the Doctor whistled, the Doctor talked. He spoke of the woods, and the wars, and the deposition of dew; he brightened and babbled of Paris; he soared into cloudy bombast on the glories of the political arena. All was to be changed; as the day departed, it took with it the vestiges of an outworn existence, and tomorrow's sun was to inaugurate the new. 'Enough,' he cried, 'of this life of maceration!' His wife (still beautiful, or he was sadly partial) was to be no longer buried; she should now shine before society. Jean-Marie would find the world at his feet; the roads open to success, wealth, honour, and posthumous renown. 'And oh, by the way,' said he, 'for God's sake keep your tongue quiet! You are, of course, a very silent fellow; it is a quality I gladly recognise in you – silence, golden silence! But this is a matter of gravity. No word must get abroad; none but the good Casimir is to be trusted; we shall probably dispose of the vessels in England.'

'But are they not even ours?' the boy said, almost with a sob – it was the only time he had spoken.

'Ours in this sense, that they are nobody else's,' replied the Doctor. 'But the State would have some claim. If they were stolen, for instance, we should be unable to demand their restitution; we should have no title; we should be unable even to communicate with the police. Such is the monstrous condition of the law.* It is a mere instance of what remains to be done, of the injustices that may yet be righted by an ardent, active, and philosophical deputy.'

* Let it be so, for my tale!

Jean-Marie put his faith in Madame Desprez; and as they drove forward down the road from Bourron, between the rustling poplars, he prayed in his teeth, and whipped up the horse to an unusual speed. Surely, as soon as they arrived, madame would assert her character, and bring this waking nightmare to an end.

Their entrance into Gretz was heralded and accompanied by a most furious barking; all the dogs in the village seemed to smell the treasure in the noddy. But there was no one in the street, save three lounging landscape painters at Tentaillon's door. Jean-Marie opened the green gate and led in the horse and carriage; and almost at the same moment Madame Desprez came to the kitchen threshold with a lighted lantern; for the moon was not yet high enough to clear the garden walls.

'Close the gates, Jean-Marie!' cried the Doctor, somewhat unsteadily alighting. 'Anastasie, where is Aline?'

'She has gone to Montereau to see her parents,' said madame.

'All is for the best!' exclaimed the Doctor fervently. 'Here, quick, come near to me; I do not wish to speak too loud,' he continued. 'Darling, we are wealthy!'

'Wealthy!' repeated the wife.

'I have found the Treasure of Franchard,' replied her husband. 'See, here are the first fruits; a pineapple, a dress for my ever-beautiful – it will suit her – trust a husband's, trust a lover's taste! Embrace me, darling! This grimy episode is over; the butterfly unfolds its painted wings. Tomorrow Casimir will come; in a week we may be in Paris – happy at last! You shall have diamonds. Jean-Marie, take it out of the boot, with religious care, and bring it piece by piece into the dining-room. We shall have plate at table! Darling, hasten and prepare this turtle; it will be a whet – it will be an addition to our meagre ordinary. I myself will proceed to the cellar. We shall have a bottle of that little Beaujolais you like, and finish with the Hermitage; there are still three bottles left. Worthy wine for a worthy occasion.'

'But, my husband; you put me in a whirl,' she cried. 'I do not comprehend.'

'The turtle, my adored, the turtle!' cried the Doctor; and he pushed her towards the kitchen, lantern and all.

Jean-Marie stood dumbfounded. He had pictured to himself a different scene – a more immediate protest, and his hope began to dwindle on the spot.

The Doctor was everywhere, a little doubtful on his legs, perhaps, and now and then taking the wall with his shoulder; for it was long since he had tasted absinthe, and he was even then reflecting that the absinthe had been a misconception. Not that he regretted excess on such a glorious day, but he made a mental memorandum to beware; he must not, a second time, become the victim of a deleterious habit. He had his wine out of the cellar in a twinkling; he arranged the sacrificial vessels, some on the white table-cloth, some on the sideboard, still crusted with historic earth. He was in and out of the kitchen, plying Anastasie with vermouth, heating her with glimpses of the future, estimating their new wealth at ever larger figures; and before they sat down to supper, the lady's virtue had melted in the fire of his enthusiasm, her timidity had disappeared; she, too, had begun to speak disparagingly of the life at Gretz; and as she took her place and helped the soup, her eyes shone with the glitter of prospective diamonds.

All through the meal, she and the Doctor made and unmade fairy plans. They bobbed and bowed and pledged each other. Their faces ran over with smiles; their eyes scattered sparkles, as they projected the Doctor's political honours and the lady's drawing-room ovations.

'But you will not be a Red!' cried Anastasie.

'I am Left Centre to the core,' replied the Doctor.

'Madame Gastein will present us – we shall find ourselves forgotten,' said the lady.

'Never,' protested the Doctor. 'Beauty and talent leave a mark.'

'I have positively forgotten how to dress,' she sighed.

'Darling, you make me blush,' cried he. 'Yours has been a tragic marriage!'

'But your success – to see you appreciated, honoured, your name in all the papers, that will be more than pleasure – it will be heaven!' she cried.

'And once a week,' said the Doctor, archly scanning the syllables, 'once a week – one good little game of baccarat?'

'Only once a week?' she questioned, threatening him with a finger.

'I swear it by my political honour,' cried he.

'I spoil you,' she said, and gave him her hand.

He covered it with kisses.

Jean-Marie escaped into the night. The moon swung high over Gretz. He went down to the garden end and sat on the jetty. The river ran by with eddies of oily silver, and a low, monotonous song. Faint veils of mist moved among the poplars on the farther side. The reeds were quietly nodding. A hundred times already had the boy sat, on such a night, and watched the streaming river with untroubled fancy. And this perhaps was to be the last. He was to leave this familiar hamlet, this green, rustling country, this bright and quiet stream; he was to pass into the great city; his dear lady mistress was to move bedizened in saloons; his good, garrulous, kind-hearted master to become a brawling deputy; and both be lost for ever to Jean-Marie and their better selves. He knew his own defects; he knew he must sink into less and less consideration in the turmoil of a city life, sink more and more from the child into the servant. And he began dimly to believe the Doctor's prophecies of evil. He could see a change in both. His generous incredulity failed him for this once; a child must have perceived that the Hermitage had completed what the absinthe had begun. If this were the first day, what would be the last? 'If necessary, wreck the train,' thought he, remembering the Doctor's parable. He looked round on the delightful scene; he drank deep of the charmed night air, laden with the scent of hay. 'If necessary, wreck the train,' he repeated. And he rose and returned to the house.

CHAPTER VI

A Criminal Investigation, in Two Parts

THE NEXT MORNING there was a most unusual outcry in the Doctor's house. The last thing before going to bed, the Doctor had locked up some valuables in the dining-room cupboard; and behold, when he rose again, as he did about four o'clock, the cupboard had been broken open, and the valuables in question had disappeared. Madame and Jean-Marie were summoned from their rooms, and appeared in hasty toilets; they found the Doctor raving, calling the heavens to witness and avenge his injury, pacing the room barefooted, with the tails of his nightshirt flirting as he turned.

'Gone!' he said; 'the things are gone, the fortune gone! We are paupers once more. Boy! what do you know of this? Speak up, sir, speak up. Do you know of it? Where are they?' He had him by the arm, shaking him like a bag, and the boy's words, if he had any, were jolted forth in inarticulate murmurs. The Doctor, with a revulsion from his own violence, set him down again. He observed Anastasie in tears. 'Anastasie,' he said, in quite an altered voice, 'compose yourself, command your feelings. I would not have you give way to passion like the vulgar. This – this trifling accident must be lived down. Jean-Marie, bring me my smaller medicine-chest. A gentle laxative is indicated.'

And he dosed the family all round, leading the way himself with a double quantity. The wretched Anastasie, who had never been ill in the whole course of her existence, and whose soul recoiled from remedies, wept floods of tears as she sipped, and shuddered, and protested, and then was bullied and shouted at until she sipped again. As for Jean-Marie, he took his portion down with stoicism.

'I have given him a less amount,' observed the Doctor, 'his youth protecting him against emotion. And now that we have thus parried any morbid consequences, let us reason.'

'I am so cold,' wailed Anastasie.

'Cold!' cried the Doctor. 'I give thanks to God that I am made of fierier material. Why, madame, a blow like this would set a frog into a transpiration. If you are cold, you can retire; and, by the way, you might throw me down my trousers. It is chilly for the legs.'

'Oh, no!' protested Anastasie; 'I will stay with you.'

'Nay, madam, you shall not suffer for your devotion,' said the Doctor. 'I will myself fetch you a shawl.' And he went upstairs and returned more fully clad and with an armful of wraps for the shivering Anastasie. 'And now,' he resumed, 'to investigate this crime. Let us proceed by induction. Anastasie, do you know anything that can help us?' Anastasie knew nothing. 'Or you, Jean-Marie?'

'Not I,' replied the boy steadily.

'Good,' returned the Doctor. 'We shall now turn our attention to the material evidences. (I was born to be a detective; I have the eye and the systematic spirit.) First, violence has been employed. The door was broken open; and it may be observed, in passing, that the lock was dear indeed at what I paid for it: a crow to pluck with Master Goguelat. Second, here is the instrument employed, one of our own table-knives, one of our best, my dear; which seems to indicate no preparation on the part of the gang – if gang it was. Thirdly, I observe that nothing has been removed except the Franchard dishes and the casket; our own silver has been minutely respected. This is wily; it shows intelligence, a knowledge of the code, a desire to avoid legal consequences. I argue from this fact that the gang numbers persons of respectability – outward, of course, and merely outward, as the robbery proves. But I argue, second, that we must have been observed at Franchard itself by some occult observer, and dogged throughout the day with a skill and patience that I venture to qualify as consummate. No ordinary man, no occasional criminal, would have shown himself capable of this combination. We have in our neighbourhood, it is far from improbable, a retired bandit of the highest order of intelligence.'

'Good heaven!' cried the horrified Anastasie. 'Henri, how can you?'

'My cherished one, this is a process of induction,' said the Doctor. 'If any of my steps are unsound, correct me. You are silent? Then do not, I beseech you, be so vulgarly illogical as to revolt from my conclusion. We have now arrived,' he resumed, 'at some idea of the composition of the gang – for I incline to the hypothesis of more than one – and we now leave this room, which can disclose no more, and turn our attention to the court and garden. (Jean-Marie, I trust you are observantly following my various steps; this is an excellent piece of education for you.) Come with me to the door. No steps on the court; it is unfortunate our court should be paved. On what small matters hang the destiny of these delicate investigations! Hey! What have we here? I have led you to the very spot,' he said, standing grandly backward and indicating the green gate. 'An escalade, as you can now see for yourselves, has taken place.'

Sure enough, the green paint was in several places scratched and broken; and one of the panels preserved the print of a nailed shoe. The foot had slipped, however, and it was difficult to estimate the size of the shoe, and impossible to distinguish the pattern of the nails.

'The whole robbery,' concluded the Doctor, 'step by step, has been reconstituted. Inductive science can no further go.'

'It is wonderful,' said his wife. 'You should indeed have been a detective, Henri. I had no idea of your talents.'

'My dear,' replied Desprez condescendingly, 'a man of scientific imagination combines the lesser faculties; he is a detective just as he is a publicist or a general; these are but local applications of his special talent. But now,' he continued, 'would you have me go further? Would you have me lay my finger on the culprits – or rather, for I cannot promise quite so much, point out to you the very house where they consort? It may be a satisfaction, at least it is all we are likely to get, since we are denied the remedy of law. I reach the further stage in this way. In order to fill my outline of the robbery, I require a man likely to be in the forest idling, I require a man of education, I require a man superior to considerations of morality. The three requisites all centre in Tentaillon's boarders. They are painters, therefore they are continually lounging in the forest. They are painters, therefore they are not unlikely to have some smattering of education. Lastly, because they are painters, they are probably immoral. And this I prove in two ways. First, painting is an art which merely addresses the eye; it does not in any particular exercise the moral sense. And second, painting, in common with all the other arts, implies the dangerous quality of imagination. A man of imagination is never moral; he outsoars literal demarcations and reviews life under too many shifting lights to rest content with the invidious distinctions of the law!'

'But you always say – at least, so I understood you' – said madame, 'that these lads display no imagination whatever.'

'My dear, they displayed imagination, and of a very fantastic order, too,' returned the Doctor, 'when they embraced their beggarly profession. Besides – and this is an argument exactly suited to your intellectual level – many of them are English and American. Where else should we expect to find a thief? – And now you had better get your coffee. Because we have lost a treasure, there is no reason for starving. For my part, I shall break my fast with white wine. I feel unaccountably heated and thirsty today. I can only attribute it to the shock of the discovery. And yet, you will bear me out, I supported the emotion nobly.'

The Doctor had now talked himself back into an admirable humour; and as he sat in the arbour and slowly imbibed a large allowance of white wine and picked a little bread and cheese with no very impetuous appetite, if a third of his meditations ran upon the missing treasure, the other two-thirds were more pleasingly busied in the retrospect of his detective skill.

About eleven Casimir arrived; he had caught an early train to Fontainebleau, and driven over to save time; and now his cab was stabled at Tentaillon's, and he remarked, studying his watch, that he could spare an hour and a half. He was much the man of business, decisively spoken, given to frowning in an intellectual manner. Anastasie's born brother, he did not waste much sentiment on the lady, gave her an English family kiss, and demanded a meal without delay.

'You can tell me your story while we eat,' he observed. 'Anything good today, Stasie?'

He was promised something good. The trio sat down to table in the arbour, Jean-Marie waiting as well as eating, and the Doctor recounted what had happened in his richest narrative manner. Casimir heard it with explosions of laughter.

'What a streak of luck for you, my good brother,' he observed, when the tale was over. 'If you had gone to Paris, you would have played dick-duck-drake with the whole consignment in three months. Your own would have followed; and you would have come to me in a procession like the last time. But I give you warning – Stasie may weep and Henri ratiocinate – it will not serve you twice. Your next collapse will be fatal. I thought I had told you so, Stasie? Hey? No sense?'

The Doctor winced and looked furtively at Jean-Marie; but the boy seemed apathetic.

'And then again,' broke out Casimir, 'what children you are – vicious children, my faith! How could you tell the value of this trash? It might have been worth nothing, or next door.'

'Pardon me,' said the Doctor. 'You have your usual flow of spirits, I perceive, but even less than your usual deliberation. I am not entirely ignorant of these matters.'

'Not entirely ignorant of anything ever I heard of,' interrupted Casimir, bowing, and raising his glass with a sort of pert politeness.

'At least,' resumed the Doctor, 'I gave my mind to the subject – that you may be willing to believe – and I estimate that our capital would be doubled.' And he described the nature of the find.

'My word of honour!' said Casimir, 'I half believe you! But much would depend on the quality of the gold.'

'The quality, my dear Casimir, was – ' And the Doctor, in default of language, kissed his finger-tips.

'I would not take your word for it, my good friend,' retorted the man of business. 'You are a man of very rosy views. But this robbery,' he continued – 'this robbery is an odd thing. Of course I pass over your nonsense about gangs and landscape painters. For me, that is a dream. Who was in the house last night?'

'None but ourselves,' replied the Doctor.

'And this young gentleman?' asked Casimir, jerking a nod in the direction of Jean-Marie.

'He too ' – the Doctor bowed.

'Well; and, if it is a fair question, who is he?' pursued the brother-in-law.

'Jean-Marie,' answered the Doctor, 'combines the functions of a son and a stable-boy. He began as the latter, but he rose rapidly to the more honourable rank in our affections. He is, I may say, the greatest comfort in our lives.'

'Ha!' said Casimir. 'And previous to becoming one of you?'

'Jean-Marie has lived a remarkable existence; his experience has been eminently formative,' replied Desprez. 'If I had had to choose an education for my son, I should have chosen such another. Beginning life with mountebanks and thieves, passing onward to the society and friendship of philosophers, he may be said to have skimmed the volume of human life.'

'Thieves?' repeated the brother-in-law, with a meditative air.

The Doctor could have bitten his tongue out. He foresaw what was coming, and prepared his mind for a vigorous defence.

'Did you ever steal yourself?' asked Casimir, turning suddenly on Jean-Marie, and for the first time employing a single eyeglass which hung round his neck.

'Yes, sir,' replied the boy, with a deep blush.

Casimir turned to the others with pursed lips, and nodded to them meaningly. 'Hey?' said he; 'how is that?'

'Jean-Marie is a teller of the truth,' returned the Doctor, throwing out his bust.

'He has never told a lie,' added madame. 'He is the best of boys.'

'Never told a lie, has he not?' reflected Casimir. 'Strange, very strange. Give me your attention, my young friend,' he continued. 'You knew about this treasure?'

'He helped to bring it home,' interposed the Doctor.

'Desprez, I ask you nothing but to hold your tongue,' returned Casimir. 'I mean to question this stable-boy of yours; and if you are so certain of his innocence, you can afford to let him answer for himself. Now, sir,' he resumed, pointing his eyeglass straight at Jean-Marie. 'You knew it could be stolen with impunity? You knew you could not be prosecuted? Come! Did you, or did you not?'

'I did,' answered Jean-Marie, in a miserable whisper. He sat there changing colour like a revolving pharos, twisting his fingers hysterically, swallowing air, the picture of guilt.

'You knew where it was put?' resumed the inquisitor.

'Yes,' from Jean-Marie.

'You say you have been a thief before,' continued Casimir. 'Now how am I to know that you are not one still? I suppose you could climb the green gate?'

'Yes,' still lower, from the culprit.

'Well, then, it was you who stole these things. You know it, and you dare not deny it. Look me in the face! Raise your sneak's eyes, and answer!'

But in place of anything of that sort Jean-Marie broke into a dismal howl and fled from the arbour. Anastasie, as she pursued to capture and reassure the victim, found time to send one Parthian arrow – 'Casimir, you are a brute!'

'My brother,' said Desprez, with the greatest dignity, 'you take upon yourself a licence – '

'Desprez,' interrupted Casimir, 'for Heaven's sake be a man of the world. You telegraph me to leave my business and come down here on yours. I come, I ask the business, you say "Find me this thief!" Well, I find him; I say "There he is!" You need not like it, but you have no manner of right to take offence.'

'Well,' returned the Doctor, 'I grant that; I will even thank you for your mistaken zeal. But your hypothesis was so extravagantly monstrous – '

'Look here,' interrupted Casimir; 'was it you or Stasie?'

'Certainly not,' answered the Doctor.

'Very well; then it was the boy. Say no more about it,' said the brother-in-law, and he produced his cigar-case.

'I will say this much more,' returned Desprez: 'if that boy came and told me so himself, I should not believe him; and if I did believe him, so implicit is my trust, I should conclude that he had acted for the best.'

'Well, well,' said Casimir indulgently. 'Have you a light? I must be going. And by the way, I wish you would let me sell your Turks for you. I always told you it meant smash. I tell you so again. Indeed, it was partly that that brought me down. You never acknowledge my letters – a most unpardonable habit.'

'My good brother,' replied the Doctor blandly, 'I have never denied your ability in business; but I can perceive your limitations.'

'Egad, my friend, I can return the compliment,' observed the man of business. 'Your limitation is to be downright irrational.'

'Observe the relative position,' returned the Doctor with a smile. 'It is your attitude to believe through thick and thin in one man's judgment – your own. I follow the same opinion, but critically and with open eyes. Which is the more irrational? – I leave it to yourself.'

'Oh, my dear fellow!' cried Casimir, 'stick to your Turks, stick to your stable-boy, go to the devil in general in your own way and be done with it. But don't ratiocinate with me – I cannot bear it. And so, ta-ta. I might as well have stayed away for any good I've done. Say good-bye from me to Stasie, and to the sullen hang-dog of a stable-boy, if you insist on it; I'm off.'

And Casimir departed. The Doctor that night dissected his character before Anastasie. 'One thing, my beautiful,' he said, 'he has learned one thing from his lifelong acquaintance with your husband: the word *ratiocinate*. It shines in his vocabulary, like a jewel in a muck-heap. And, even so, he continually misapplies it. For you must have observed he uses it as a sort of taunt, in the sense of *to ergotise*, implying, as it were – the poor, dear fellow! – a vein of sophistry. As for his cruelty to Jean-Marie, it must be forgiven him – it is not his nature, it is the nature of his life. A man who deals with money, my dear, is a man lost.'

With Jean-Marie the process of reconciliation had been somewhat slow. At first he was inconsolable, insisted on leaving the family, went from paroxysm to paroxysm of tears; and it was only after Anastasie had been closeted for an hour with him, alone, that she came forth, sought out the Doctor, and, with tears in her eyes, acquainted that gentleman with what had passed.

'At first, my husband, he would hear of nothing,' she said. 'Imagine! if he had left us! what would the treasure be to that! Horrible treasure, it has brought all this about! At last, after he had sobbed his very heart out, he agrees to stay on a condition – we are not to mention this matter, this infamous suspicion, not even to mention the robbery. On that agreement only, the poor, cruel boy will consent to remain among his friends.'

'But this inhibition,' said the Doctor, 'this embargo – it cannot possibly apply to me?'

'To all of us,' Anastasie assured him.

'My cherished one,' Desprez protested, 'you must have misunderstood. It cannot apply to me. He would naturally come to me.'

'Henri,' she said, 'it does; I swear to you it does.'

'This is a painful, a very painful circumstance,' the Doctor said, looking a little black. 'I cannot affect, Anastasie, to be anything but justly wounded. I feel this, I feel it, my wife, acutely.'

'I knew you would,' she said. 'But if you had seen his distress! We must make allowances, we must sacrifice our feelings.'

'I trust, my dear, you have never found me averse to sacrifices,' returned the Doctor very stiffly.

'And you will let me go and tell him that you have agreed? It will be like your noble nature,' she cried.

So it would, he perceived – it would be like his noble nature! Up jumped his spirits, triumphant at the thought. 'Go, darling,' he said nobly, 'reassure him. The subject is buried; more – I make an effort, I have accustomed my will to these exertions – and it is forgotten.'

A little after, but still with swollen eyes and looking mortally sheepish, Jean-Marie reappeared and went ostentatiously about his business. He was the only unhappy member of the party that sat down that night to supper. As for the Doctor, he was radiant. He thus sang the requiem of the treasure:

'This has been, on the whole, a most amusing episode,' he said. 'We are not a penny the worse – nay, we are immensely gainers. Our philosophy has been exercised; some of the turtle is still left – the most wholesome of delicacies; I have my staff, Anastasie has her new dress, Jean-Marie is the proud possessor of a fashionable képi. Besides, we had a glass of Hermitage last night; the glow still suffuses my memory. I was growing positively niggardly with that Hermitage, positively niggardly. Let me take the hint: we had one bottle to celebrate the appearance of our visionary fortune; let us have a second to console us for its occultation. The third I hereby dedicate to Jean-Marie's wedding breakfast.'

CHAPTER VII

The Fall of the House of Desprez

THE DOCTOR'S HOUSE has not yet received the compliment of a description, and it is now high time that the omission were supplied, for the house is itself an actor in the story, and one whose part is nearly at an end. Two storeys in height, walls of a warm yellow, tiles of an ancient ruddy brown diversified with moss and lichen, it stood with one wall to the street in the angle of the Doctor's property. It was roomy, draughty, and inconvenient. The large rafters were here and there engraven with rude marks and patterns; the hand-rail of the stair was carved in countrified arabesque; a stout timber pillar, which did duty to support the dining-room roof, bore mysterious characters on its darker sides, runes, according to the Doctor; nor did he fail, when he ran over the legendary history of the house and its possessors, to dwell upon the Scandinavian scholar who had left them. Floors, doors, and rafters made a great variety of angles; every room had a particular inclination; the gable had tilted towards the garden, after the manner of a leaning tower, and one of the former proprietors had buttressed the building from that side with a great strut of wood, like the derrick of a crane. Altogether, it had many marks of ruin; it was a house for the rats to desert; and nothing but its excellent brightness – the window-glass polished and shining, the paint well scoured, the brasses radiant, the very prop all wreathed about with climbing flowers – nothing but its air of a well-tended, smiling veteran, sitting, crutch and all, in the sunny corner of a garden, marked it as a house for comfortable people to inhabit. In poor or idle management it would soon have hurried into the blackguard stages of decay. As it was, the whole family loved it, and the Doctor was never better inspired than when he narrated its imaginary story and drew the character of its successive masters, from the Hebrew merchant who had re-edified its walls after the sack of the town, and past the mysterious engraver of the runes, down to the long-headed, dirty-handed boor from whom he had himself acquired it at a ruinous expense. As for any alarm about its security, the idea had never presented itself. What had stood four centuries might well endure a little longer.

Indeed, in this particular winter, after the finding and losing of the treasure, the Desprez had an anxiety of a very different order, and one which lay nearer their hearts. Jean-Marie was plainly not himself. He had fits of hectic activity, when he made unusual exertions to please, spoke more and faster, and redoubled in attention to his lessons. But these were interrupted by spells of melancholia and brooding silence, when the boy was little better than unbearable.

'Silence,' the Doctor moralised – 'you see, Anastasie, what comes of silence. Had the boy properly unbosomed himself, the little disappointment about the treasure, the little annoyance about Casimir's incivility would long ago have been forgotten. As it is, they prey upon him like a disease. He loses flesh, his appetite is variable and, on the whole, impaired. I keep him on the strictest regimen, I exhibit the most powerful tonics; both in vain.'

'Don't you think you drug him too much?' asked madame, with an irrepressible shudder.

'Drug?' cried the Doctor; 'I drug? Anastasie, you are mad!'

Time went on, and the boy's health still slowly declined. The Doctor blamed the weather, which was cold and boisterous. He called in his *confrère* from Bourron, took a fancy for him, magnified his capacity, and was pretty soon under treatment himself – it scarcely appeared for what complaint. He and Jean-Marie had each medicine to take at different periods of the day. The Doctor used to lie in wait for the exact moment, watch in hand. 'There is nothing like regularity,' he would say, fill out the doses, and dilate on the virtues of the draught; and if the boy seemed none the better, the Doctor was not at all the worse.

Gunpowder Day, the boy was particularly low. It was scowling, squally weather. Huge broken companies of cloud sailed swiftly overhead; raking gleams of sunlight swept the village, and were followed by intervals of darkness and white, flying rain. At times the wind lifted up its voice and bellowed. The trees were all scourging themselves along the meadows, the last leaves flying like dust.

The Doctor, between the boy and the weather, was in his element; he had a theory to prove. He sat with his watch out and a barometer in front of him, waiting for the squalls and noting their effect upon the human pulse. 'For the true philosopher,' he remarked delightedly, 'every fact in nature is a toy.' A letter came to him; but, as its arrival coincided with the approach of another gust, he merely crammed it into his pocket, gave the time to Jean-Marie, and the next moment they were both counting their pulses as if for a wager.

At nightfall the wind rose into a tempest. It besieged the hamlet, apparently from every side, as if with batteries of cannon; the houses shook and groaned; live coals were blown upon the floor. The uproar and terror of the night kept people long awake, sitting with pallid faces giving ear.

It was twelve before the Desprez family retired. By half-past one, when the storm was already somewhat past its height, the Doctor was awakened from a troubled slumber, and sat up. A noise still rang in his ears, but whether of this world or of the world of dreams he was not certain. Another clap of wind followed. It was accompanied by a sickening movement of the whole house, and in the subsequent lull Desprez could hear the tiles pouring like a cataract into the loft above his head. He plucked Anastasie bodily out of bed.

'Run!' he cried, thrusting some wearing apparel into her hands; 'the house is falling! To the garden!'

She did not pause to be twice bidden; she was down the stair in an instant. She had never before suspected herself of such activity. The Doctor meanwhile, with the speed of a piece of pantomime business, and undeterred by broken shins, proceeded to rout out Jean-Marie, tore Aline from her virgin slumbers, seized her by the hand, and tumbled downstairs and into the garden, with the girl tumbling behind him, still not half awake.

The fugitives rendezvoused in the arbour by some common instinct. Then came a bull's-eye flash of straggling moonshine, which disclosed their four figures standing huddled from the wind in a raffle of flying drapery, and not without a considerable need for more. At the humiliating spectacle Anastasie clutched her night-dress desperately about her and burst loudly into tears. The Doctor flew to console her; but she elbowed him away. She suspected everybody of being the general public, and thought the darkness was alive with eyes.

Another gleam and another violent gust arrived together; the house was seen to rock on its foundation, and, just as the light was once more eclipsed, a crash which triumphed over the shouting of the wind announced its fall, and for a moment the whole garden was alive with skipping tiles and brickbats. One such missile grazed the Doctor's ear; another descended on the bare foot of Aline, who instantly made night hideous with her shrieks.

By this time the hamlet was alarmed, lights flashed from the windows, hails reached the party, and the Doctor answered, nobly contending against Aline and the tempest. But this prospect of help only awakened Anastasie to a more active stage of terror.

'Henri, people will be coming,' she screamed in her husband's ear.

'I trust so,' he replied.

'They cannot. I would rather die,' she wailed.

'My dear,' said the Doctor reprovingly, 'you are excited. I gave you some clothes. What have you done with them?'

'Oh, I don't know – I must have thrown them away! Where are

they?' she sobbed.

Desprez groped about in the darkness. 'Admirable!' he remarked; 'my grey velveteen trousers! This will exactly meet your necessities.'

'Give them to me!' she cried fiercely; but as soon as she had them in her hands her mood appeared to alter – she stood silent for a moment, and then pressed the garment back upon the Doctor. 'Give it to Aline,' she said – 'poor girl.'

'Nonsense!' said the Doctor. 'Aline does not know what she is about. Aline is beside herself with terror; and at any rate, she is a peasant. Now I am really concerned at this exposure for a person of your house-keeping habits; my solicitude and your fantastic modesty both point to the same remedy – the pantaloons.' He held them ready.

'It is impossible. You do not understand,' she said with dignity.

By this time rescue was at hand. It had been found impracticable to enter by the street, for the gate was blocked with masonry, and the nodding ruin still threatened further avalanches. But between the Doctor's garden and the one on the right hand there was that very picturesque contrivance – a common well; the door on the Desprez' side had chanced to be unbolted, and now, through the arched aperture a man's bearded face and an arm supporting a lantern were introduced into the world of windy darkness where Anastasie concealed her woes. The light struck here and there among the tossing apple boughs, it glinted on the grass; but the lantern and the glowing face became the centre of the world. Anastasie crouched back from the intrusion.

'This way!' shouted the man. 'Are you all safe?'

Aline, still screaming, ran to the new-comer, and was presently hauled head-foremost through the wall.

'Now, Anastasie, come on; it is your turn,' said the husband.

'I cannot,' she replied.

'Are we all to die of exposure, madame?' thundered Doctor Desprez.

'You can go!' she cried. 'Oh, go, go away! I can stay here: I am quite warm.'

The Doctor took her by the shoulders with an oath.

'Stop!' she screamed. 'I will put them on.'

She took the detested lendings in her hand once more; but her repulsion was stronger than shame. 'Never!' she cried, shuddering, and flung them far away into the night.

Next moment the Doctor had whirled her to the well. The man was there and the lantern; Anastasie closed her eyes and appeared to herself to be about to die. How she was transported through the arch she knew not; but once on the other side she was received by the neighbour's wife, and enveloped in a friendly blanket.

Beds were made ready for the two women, clothes of very various sizes for the Doctor and Jean-Marie; and for the remainder of the night, while madame dozed in and out on the borderland of hysterics, her husband sat beside the fire and held forth to the admiring neighbours. He showed them, at length, the causes of the accident: for years, he explained, the fall had been impending; one sign had followed another, the joints had opened, the plaster had cracked, the old walls bowed inward; last, not three weeks ago, the cellar door had begun to work with difficulty in its grooves. 'The cellar!' he said, gravely shaking his head over a glass of mulled wine. 'That reminds me of my poor vintages. By a manifest providence the Hermitage was nearly at an end. One bottle – I lose but one bottle of that incomparable wine. It had been set apart against Jean-Marie's wedding. Well, I must lay down some more; it will be an interest in life. I am, however, a man somewhat advanced in years. My great work is now buried in the fall of my humble roof; it will never be completed – my name will have been writ in water. And yet you find me calm – I would say cheerful. Can your priest do more?'

By the first glimpse of day the party sallied forth from the fireside into the street. The wind had fallen, but still charioted a world of troubled clouds; the air bit like frost; and the party, as they stood about the ruins in the rainy twilight of the morning, beat upon their breasts and blew into their hands for warmth. The house had entirely fallen, the walls outward, the roof in; it was a mere heap of rubbish, with here and there a forlorn spear of broken rafter. A sentinel was placed over the ruins to protect the property, and the party adjourned to Tentaillon's to break their fast at the Doctor's expense. The bottle circulated somewhat freely; and before they left the table it had begun to snow.

For three days the snow continued to fall, and the ruins, covered with tarpaulin and watched by sentries, were left undisturbed. The Desprez meanwhile had taken up their abode at Tentaillon's. Madame spent her time in the kitchen, concocting little delicacies, with the admiring aid of Madame Tentaillon, or sitting by the fire in thoughtful abstraction. The fall of the house affected her wonderfully little; the blow had been parried by another; and in her mind she was continually fighting over again the battle of the trousers. Had she done right? Had she done wrong? And now she would applaud her determination; and anon, with a horrid flush of unavailing penitence, she would regret the trousers. No juncture in her life had so much exercised her judgment. In the meantime the Doctor had become vastly pleased with his situation. Two of the summer boarders still lingered behind the rest, prisoners for lack of a remittance; they were both English, but one of them spoke French pretty fluently, and was, besides, a humorous, agile-minded fellow, with whom the Doctor could reason by the hour, secure of comprehension. Many were the glasses they emptied, many the topics they discussed.

'Anastasie,' the Doctor said on the third morning, 'take an example from your husband, from Jean-Marie! The excitement has done more for the boy than all my tonics, he takes his turn as sentry with positive gusto. As for me, you behold me. I have made friends with the Egyptians; and my Pharaoh is, I swear it, a most agreeable companion. You alone are hipped. About a house – a few dresses? What are they in comparison to the 'Pharmacopœia' – the labour of years lying buried below stones and sticks in this depressing hamlet? The snow falls; I shake it from my cloak! Imitate me. Our income will be impaired, I grant it, since we must rebuild; but moderation, patience, and philosophy will gather about the hearth. In the meanwhile, the Tentaillons are obliging; the table, with your additions, will pass; only the wine is execrable – well, I shall send for some today. My Pharaoh will be gratified to drink a decent glass; aha! and I shall see if he possesses that acme of organisation – a palate. If he has a palate, he is perfect.'

'Henri,' she said, shaking her head; 'you are a man; you cannot understand my feelings; no woman could shake off the memory of so public a humiliation.'

The Doctor could not restrain a titter. 'Pardon me, darling,' he said; 'but really, to the philosophical intelligence, the incident appears so small a trifle. You looked extremely well – '

'Henri!' she cried.

'Well, well, I will say no more,' he replied. 'Though, to be sure, if you had consented to indue – À propos,' he broke off, 'and my trousers! They are lying in the snow – my favourite trousers!' And he dashed in quest of Jean-Marie.

Two hours afterwards the boy returned to the inn with a spade under one arm and a curious sop of clothing under the other.

The Doctor ruefully took it in his hands. 'They have been!' he said. 'Their tense is past. Excellent pantaloons, you are no more! Stay, something in the pocket,' and he produced a piece of paper. 'A letter! ay, now I mind me; it was received on the morning of the gale, when I was absorbed in delicate investigations. It is still legible. From poor, dear Casimir! It is as well,' he chuckled, 'that I have educated him to patience. Poor Casimir and his correspondence – his infinitesimal, timorous, idiotic correspondence!'

He had by this time cautiously unfolded the wet letter; but, as he bent himself to decipher the writing, a cloud descended on his brow.

'*Bigre!*' he cried, with a galvanic start.

And then the letter was whipped into the fire, and the Doctor's cap was on his head in the turn of a hand.

'Ten minutes! I can catch it, if I run,' he cried. 'It is always late. I go to Paris. I shall telegraph.'

'Henri! what is wrong?' cried his wife.

'Ottoman Bonds!' came from the disappearing Doctor; and Anastasie and Jean-Marie were left face to face with the wet trousers. Desprez had gone to Paris for the second time in seven years; he had gone to Paris with a pair of wooden shoes, a knitted spencer, a black blouse, a country night-cap, and twenty francs in his pocket. The fall of the house was but a secondary marvel; the whole world might have fallen and scarce left his family more petrified.

CHAPTER VIII

The Wages of Philosophy

ON THE MORNING of the next day, the Doctor, a mere spectre of himself, was brought back in the custody of Casimir. They found Anastasie and the boy sitting together by the fire; and Desprez, who had exchanged his toilette for a ready-made rig-out of poor materials, waved his hand as he entered, and sank speechless on the nearest chair. Madame turned direct to Casimir.

'What is wrong?' she cried.

'Well,' replied Casimir, 'what have I told you all along? It has come. It is a clean shave, this time; so you may as well bear up and make the best of it. House down, too, eh? Bad luck, upon my soul.'

'Are we – are we – ruined?' she gasped.

The Doctor stretched out his arms to her. 'Ruined,' he replied, 'you are ruined by your sinister husband.'

Casimir observed the consequent embrace through his eyeglass; then he turned to Jean-Marie. 'You hear?' he said. 'They are ruined; no more pickings, no more house, no more fat cutlets. It strikes me, my friend, that you had best be packing; the present speculation is about worked out.' And he nodded to him meaningly.

'Never!' cried Desprez, springing up. 'Jean-Marie, if you prefer to leave me, now that I am poor, you can go; you shall receive your hundred francs, if so much remains to me. But if you will consent to stay' – the Doctor wept a little – 'Casimir offers me a place – as clerk,' he resumed. 'The emoluments are slender, but they will be enough for three. It is too much already to have lost my fortune; must I lose my son?'

Jean-Marie sobbed bitterly, but without a word.

'I don't like boys who cry,' observed Casimir. 'This one is always crying. Here! you clear out of this for a little; I have business with your master and mistress, and these domestic feelings may be settled after I am gone. March!' and he held the door open.

Jean-Marie slunk out like a detected thief.

By twelve they were all at table but Jean-Marie.

'Hey?' said Casimir. 'Gone, you see. Took the hint at once.'

'I do not, I confess,' said Desprez – 'I do not seek to excuse his absence. It speaks a want of heart that disappoints me sorely.'

'Want of manners,' corrected Casimir. 'Heart, he never had. Why, Desprez, for a clever fellow, you are the most gullible mortal in creation. Your ignorance of human nature and human business is beyond belief. You are swindled by heathen Turks, swindled by vagabond children, swindled right and left, upstairs and downstairs. I think it must be your imagination. I thank my stars I have none.'

'Pardon me,' replied Desprez, still humbly, but with a return of spirit at sight of a distinction to be drawn; 'pardon me, Casimir. You possess, even to an eminent degree, the commercial imagination. It was the lack of that in me – it appears it is my weak point – that has led to these repeated shocks. By the commercial imagination the financier forecasts the destiny of his investments, marks the falling house – '

'Egad,' interrupted Casimir: 'our friend the stable-boy appears to have his share of it.'

The Doctor was silenced; and the meal was continued and finished principally to the tune of the brother-in-law's not very consolatory conversation. He entirely ignored the two young English painters, turning a blind eyeglass to their salutations, and continuing his remarks as if he were alone in the bosom of his family; and with every second word he ripped another stitch out of the air balloon of Desprez's vanity. By the time coffee was over the poor Doctor was as limp as a napkin.

'Let us go and see the ruins,' said Casimir.

They strolled forth into the street. The fall of the house, like the loss of a front tooth, had quite transformed the village. Through the gap the eye commanded a great stretch of open snowy country, and the place shrank in comparison. It was like a room with an open door. The sentinel stood by the green gate, looking very red and cold, but he had a pleasant word for the Doctor and his wealthy kinsman.

Casimir looked at the mound of ruins, he tried the quality of the tarpaulin. 'H'm,' he said, 'I hope the cellar arch has stood. If it has, my good brother, I will give you a good price for the wines.'

'We shall start digging tomorrow,' said the sentry. 'There is no more fear of snow.'

'My friend,' returned Casimir sententiously, 'you had better wait till you get paid.'

The Doctor winced, and began dragging his offensive brother-in-law towards Tentaillon's. In the house there would be fewer auditors and these already in the secret of his fall.

'Hullo!' cried Casimir, 'there goes the stable-boy with his luggage; no, egad, he is taking it into the inn.'

And sure enough, Jean-Marie was seen to cross the snowy street and enter Tentaillon's, staggering under a large hamper.

The Doctor stopped with a sudden, wild hope.

'What can he have?' he said. 'Let us go and see.' And he hurried on.

'His luggage, to be sure,' answered Casimir. 'He is on the move – thanks to the commercial imagination.'

'I have not seen that hamper for – for ever so long,' remarked the Doctor.

'Nor will you see it much longer,' chuckled Casimir; 'unless, indeed, we interfere. And by the way, I insist on an examination.'

'You will not require,' said Desprez, positively with a sob; and, casting a moist, triumphant glance at Casimir, he began to run.

'What the devil is up with him, I wonder?' Casimir reflected; and then, curiosity taking the upper hand, he followed the Doctor's example and took to his heels.

The hamper was so heavy and large, and Jean-Marie himself so little and so weary, that it had taken him a great while to bundle it upstairs to the Desprez' private room; and he had just set it down on the floor in front of Anastasie, when the Doctor arrived, and was closely followed by the man of business. Boy and hamper were both in a most sorry plight; for the one had passed four months underground in a certain cave on the way to Achères, and the other had run about five miles as hard as his legs would carry him, half that distance under a staggering weight.

'Jean-Marie,' cried the Doctor, in a voice that was only too seraphic to be called hysterical, 'is it – ? It is!' he cried. 'Oh, my son, my son!' And he sat down upon the hamper and sobbed like a little child.

'You will not go to Paris now,' said Jean-Marie sheepishly.

'Casimir,' said Desprez, raising his wet face, 'do you see that boy, that angel boy? He is the thief; he took the treasure from a man unfit to be entrusted with its use; he brings it back to me when I am sobered and humbled. These, Casimir, are the Fruits of my Teaching, and this moment is the Reward of my Life.'

'*Tiens*,' said Casimir.

WORDSWORTH CLASSICS

General Editors: Marcus Clapham & Clive Reynard

JANE AUSTEN
Emma
Mansfield Park
Northanger Abbey
Persuasion
Pride and Prejudice
Sense and Sensibility

ARNOLD BENNETT
Anna of the Five Towns

R. D. BLACKMORE
Lorna Doone

ANNE BRONTË
Agnes Grey
*The Tenant of
Wildfell Hall*

CHARLOTTE BRONTË
Jane Eyre
The Professor
Shirley
Villette

EMILY BRONTË
Wuthering Heights

JOHN BUCHAN
Greenmantle
Mr Standfast
The Thirty-Nine Steps

SAMUEL BUTLER
The Way of All Flesh

LEWIS CARROLL
Alice in Wonderland

CERVANTES
Don Quixote

G. K. CHESTERTON
*Father Brown:
Selected Stories*
*The Man who was
Thursday*

ERSKINE CHILDERS
The Riddle of the Sands

JOHN CLELAND
*Memoirs of a Woman of
Pleasure: Fanny Hill*

WILKIE COLLINS
The Moonstone
The Woman in White

JOSEPH CONRAD
Heart of Darkness
Lord Jim
The Secret Agent

J. FENIMORE COOPER
*The Last of the
Mohicans*

STEPHEN CRANE
*The Red Badge of
Courage*

THOMAS DE QUINCEY
*Confessions of an English
Opium Eater*

DANIEL DEFOE
Moll Flanders
Robinson Crusoe

CHARLES DICKENS
Bleak House
David Copperfield
Great Expectations
Hard Times
Little Dorrit
Martin Chuzzlewit
Oliver Twist
Pickwick Papers
A Tale of Two Cities

BENJAMIN DISRAELI
Sybil

THEODOR DOSTOEVSKY
Crime and Punishment

**SIR ARTHUR CONAN
DOYLE**
*The Adventures of
Sherlock Holmes*
*The Case-Book of
Sherlock Holmes*
*The Lost World &
Other Stories*
*The Return of
Sherlock Holmes*
Sir Nigel

GEORGE DU MAURIER
Trilby

ALEXANDRE DUMAS
The Three Musketeers

MARIA EDGEWORTH
Castle Rackrent

GEORGE ELIOT
The Mill on the Floss
Middlemarch
Silas Marner

HENRY FIELDING
Tom Jones

F. SCOTT FITZGERALD
*A Diamond as Big as the
Ritz & Other Stories*
The Great Gatsby
Tender is the Night

GUSTAVE FLAUBERT
Madame Bovary

JOHN GALSWORTHY
In Chancery
The Man of Property
To Let

ELIZABETH GASKELL
Cranford
North and South

KENNETH GRAHAME
*The Wind in the
Willows*

**GEORGE & WEEDON
GROSSMITH**
Diary of a Nobody

RIDER HAGGARD
She

THOMAS HARDY
*Far from the
Madding Crowd*
The Mayor of Casterbridge
*The Return of the
Native*
Tess of the d'Urbervilles
The Trumpet Major
*Under the Greenwood
Tree*

DISTRIBUTION

**AUSTRALIA
& PAPUA NEW GUINEA
Peribo Pty Ltd**
58 Beaumont Road, Mount Kuring-Gai
NSW 2080, Australia
Tel: (02) 457 0011 Fax: (02) 457 0022

**CYPRUS
Huckleberry Trading**
3 Othos Avvey, Tala Paphos
Tel: 06 653585

**CZECH REPUBLIC
Bohemian Ventures spol s r o**
Delnicka 13, 170 00 Prague 7
Tel: 02 877837 Fax: 02 801498

**FRANCE
Copernicus Diffusion**
23 Rue Saint Dominique, Paris 75007
Tel: 1 44 11 33 20 Fax: 1 44 11 33 21

**GERMANY
GLBmbH (Bargain, Promotional
& Remainder Shops)**
Schönhauser Strasse 25
D-50968 Köln
Tel: 0221 34 20 92 Fax: 0221 38 40 40

**Tradis Verlag und Vertrieb GmbH
(Bookshops)**
Postfach 90 03 69
D-51113 Köln
Tel: 022 03 31059
Fax: 022 03 3 93 40

**GREAT BRITAIN & IRELAND
Wordsworth Editions Ltd**
Cumberland House, Crib Street
Ware, Hertfordshire SG12 9ET

**INDIA
OM Book Service**
1690 First Floor
Nai Sarak, Delhi – 110006
Tel: 3279823-3265303 Fax: 3278091

**ISRAEL
Timmy Marketing Limited**
Israel Ben Zeev 12
Ramont Gimmel, Jerusalem
Tel: 02-865266 Fax: 02-880035

**ITALY
Magis Books SRL**
Via Raffaello 31/C
Zona Ind Mancasale
42100 Reggio Emilia
Tel: 1522 920999 Fax: 0522 920666

**NEW ZEALAND & FIJI
Allphy Book Distributors Ltd**
4-6 Charles Street, Eden Terrace
Auckland,
Tel: (09) 3773096 Fax: (09) 3022770

**NORTH AMERICA
Universal Sales & Marketing**
230 Fifth Avenue, Suite 1212
New York, NY 10001, USA
Tel: 212 481 3500 Fax: 212 481 3534

**PHILIPPINES
I J Sagun Enterprises**
P O Box 4322 CPO Manila
2 Topaz Road, Greenheights Village
Taytay, Rizal
Tel: 631 80 61 TO 66

**PORTUGAL
International Publishing Services Ltd**
Rua da Cruz da Carreira, 4B,
1100 Lisbon
Tel: 01 570051 Fax: 01 3522066

**SOUTHERN, CENTRAL
& EAST AFRICA
P.M.C.International Importers &
Exporters CC**
Unit 6, Ben-Sarah Place, 52-56 Columbine
Place, Glen Anil, Kwa-Zulu Natal 4051
P.O.Box 201520
 Durban North, Kwa-Zulu Natal 4016
 Tel: (031) 844441 Fax: (031) 844466

**SCOTLAND
Lomond Books**
36 West Shore Road, Granton
Edinburgh EH5 1QD

**SINGAPORE,
MALASIA & BRUNEI
Paul & Elizabeth Book Services Pte Ltd**
163 Tanglin Road No 03-15/16
Tanglin Mall, Singapore 1024
Tel: (65) 735 7308 Fax: (65) 735 9747

**SLOVAK REPUBLIC
Slovak Ventures spol s r o**
Stefanikova 128, 94901 Nitra
Tel/Fax: 087 25105

**SPAIN
Ribera Libros, S.L.**
Poligono Martiartu, Calle 1 - no 6
48480 Arrigorriaga, Vizcaya
Tel: 34 4 6713607 (Almacen)
       34 4 4418787 (Libreria)
Fax: 34 4 6713608 (Almacen)
       34 4 4418029 (Libreria)